NO MORE QUESTIONS

"Who do you think you are?" Clark asked, putting his boots up on the desk and lighting a Lucky Strike. "Why do you think you can come in here and start asking questions about people?"

The smoke rolled from his nostrils.

"Maybe because it's my Constitutional right?"

He sprang forward like a rattlesnake and pointed the Lucky Strike in my face.

"I'm sick of hearing about fucking Constitutional rights," Clark said. I could feel the heat from the tip of the cigarette, and the smoke burned my eyes. "I've been hearing that shit for forty years and look at the shape we're in. Hell, this country used to be a decent place to live, and now it's just a goddamned Sodom and Gomorrah."

The Bulldog came out of the holster.

"I should just splatter your brains all over that wall," he said. The stubby barrel wavered in front of my face. He hadn't thumbed the hammer back, but that didn't matter; the gun was double-action and his finger was on the trigger.

"You're going to murder me?"

"It wouldn't be murder," he said.

"What about the law?"

"I answer to a higher law...."

HINTERLAND

MAX McCOY

LEISURE BOOKS NEW YORK CITY

For Allen Jones, 1945–2004.

A LEISURE BOOK®

February 2005

Published by

Dorchester Publishing Co., Inc.
200 Madison Avenue
New York, NY 10016

ISBN 0-8439-5514-7

Printed in the United States of America.

Visit us on the web at www.dorchesterpub.com.

HINTERLAND

But the day of the Lord will come as a thief in the night; in which the heavens shall pass away with a great noise, and the elements shall melt with fervent heat, and the earth also and the works that are therein shall be burned up.

—2 Peter 3:10

Prologue
Falling Star

Raton Pass
Colorado—New Mexico Border
14 March 2004

Karl Larsen was standing on the roadbed between the rails, hidden in the darkness a few yards inside the lip of the tunnel. The 7,700-foot pass was dusted with snow, and the midnight air burned his lungs.

He stamped his feet to keep warm. He first felt the power of the triple GE 944 CW locomotives as a throbbing sensation in the soles of his combat boots.

As the 4,400-horsepower diesel-electric engines struggled to pull the mile-long mixed freight up the New Mexico side of the pass, Larsen unzipped his black field jacket and took a pack of Marlboros from an inside pocket. He rapped the pack against the back of one hand, put his lips to a filter, and pulled a cigarette from the pack. He produced a battered Zippo, thumbed the striker, and cupped his hands around the flame as the fire was reflected in a pair of pale blue eyes. For perhaps the thousandth time, he glanced at the inscription on the Zippo, still illuminated by the flame: *Yea, though I walk through the shadow of the Valley of Death I shall fear no evil, because I am the meanest sonuvabitch in the valley.*

He snapped the Zippo shut and returned it to his pocket.

Then he took a Waffen SS officer's hat from inside his jacket and placed it carefully on his head, getting just the right angle. The cap was an original prewar version, black, with the silver Totenkopf death's-head above the visor.

Larsen could now see the headlights mounted in the nose of the lead locomotive, an orange Burlington Northern and Santa Fe, number 1000. The grade had reduced the train's velocity to a crawl. By the time it entered the tunnel the freight would be making only about three miles an hour, approximately walking speed. While in the tunnel it would also be out of radio—and therefore satellite—contact.

The BNSF was experimenting with broadband communications over fiber-optics networks to keep train crews in communication with central dispatch, but so far the only tunnel to be so equipped was at an experimental site in Wyoming. At this tunnel not only would the train be out of contact with the outside, but because of the curvature of the tunnel, one end of the train would be out of touch with the other.

Larsen shot his right cuff, exposing his watch, and started its stopwatch function. The digital numbers began to count down from seven minutes. Larsen had prepared for months, and now he had 420 seconds to make good on that preparation. Larsen liked the number. *April twentieth,* he thought, and smiled.

The locomotive's dual headlights were cutting the darkness while the alternating ditch lights strobed the sides of the tunnel. Larsen stepped behind a pillar, turned his face to the wall, and placed his hands over his ears. The tunnel was wide enough for only a single track through the tunnel, and Larsen was close enough that, by taking a single step, he could have touched it. He felt the power of the engines thumping against his diaphragm.

Then Larsen began counting cars.

The twentieth behind the last engine was a green sixty-foot BNSF boxcar, and Larsen fell into a trot beside it. Glancing beneath it, he saw only darkness. There were only three possibilities: the order of the cars had been switched, he had miscounted, or the operation was compromised and they all were hopelessly fucked.

"Bloody hell," Larsen muttered.

Withdrawing an LED flashlight from the pocket of his field jacket, he switched it on only long enough to check the number on the side of the car: 357609.

It was the wrong car.

He crouched, looking beneath the line of cars ahead. Nothing, not even a glint of light from the polished tops of the rails.

Then he glanced behind him. Rippling on the roadbed between the rails, three boxcars behind, was a white rectangle of light. Larsen flicked the cigarette away, pulled a pair of leather gloves from his pocket, and quickly put them on, using his teeth to snug them over his wrists.

He went prone beside the rail, held his hat with one hand, and watched as the light approached. He had done the math, and at this speed the train was traveling at only 4.4 feet per second, which meant he would have less than eleven seconds to slip behind between the last wheels of the forward trucks and the first wheels of the rear trucks of the boxcar ahead of the one he wanted. It had seemed much longer than needed during planning, but now that he was actually about to climb over the cold rail, it hardly seemed enough. He could feel the mass of the boxcar above him, and saw the air-brake hoses and cylinders and other hardware that hung threateningly low. One mistake and he would be sliced in two, have his skull caved in, or both, all in less time than it takes to describe it.

He banished the image from his mind and, as the first set of wheels scraped by, began to count as he carefully pushed himself over the rail. He was on the other side before he reached "one thousand five."

He rolled onto his back, looking past the toes of his boots as the patch of light rippled toward him. After making sure he was not in the center of the roadbed, he flattened himself. In four seconds he felt the two sets of heavy axles pass overhead, followed by the massive couplers, which hung dangerously low over the center of the tracks. Then another pair of axles passed in the darkness.

He could now see the source of the light: a hole had been neatly cut in the floor of the boxcar between the frame members and clear of any of the brake hardware or other obstructions.

The brilliant opening passed overhead like a door to heaven. Larsen reached up and grasped the trailing edge and was glad he had remembered to put on the gloves: the edges were still hot. He was swept along for a moment beneath the boxcar, stones skittering and rolling beneath him. Then an arm grasped his wrist and pulled him up through the twenty-four-by-forty-eight-inch opening into the glaring interior of the boxcar.

He repositioned his hands on the sides and lifted himself up, as one would exit a swimming pool, then moved his left hand to the butt of the .50-caliber Desert Eagle pistol in a ballistic nylon holster strapped to his thigh.

"Stop."

An air force technical sergeant stood in the darkened doorway, a 9mm pistol in one hand.

"Three words," the airman said.

"Sic semper tyrannis," Larsen replied.

While the sergeant holstered his weapon, Larsen got to his feet and checked his hat. The angle was slightly off, and he adjusted it.

He had never met the sergeant before, and for the first time he knew the man's name, from the black plastic name badge on the right breast of his uniform: Baker.

"Python," Larsen said. "Pleased to finally meet you. I see the magnesium paste worked well. You did breathe from the air cylinder?"

"I'm here, aren't I?"

"Quite," Larsen said. "They switched cars, Sergeant Baker?"

"It was last-minute," Baker said defensively.

"All's well that ends well," Larsen said as he gazed at the body of a twenty-something lieutenant sprawled on the floor, his face in a widening puddle of blood. His throat had been cut, and it all seemed unnaturally red beneath the brilliant fluorescent lighting.

"Sorry about the cloak-and-dagger," Larsen said as he holstered the Desert Eagle and secured the thumb snap. "Had to make sure you were indeed our Python. For all I knew, Python was dead on the floor. Too bad about the leftenant."

"Forget him. He was a prick."

"No longer," Larsen said.

The interior of the car was stainless steel and reminded Larsen of an operating room. Ten nuclear bombs were secured in a rack made for a dozen along the far side. They were small bombs, less than four feet in length, and weighing 350 pounds. Each had a needlelike nose cone in high-visibility orange. Behind the nose cone were a couple of widening yellow bands, where the case broadened to thirteen inches. The rest of the device was painted in aircraft green. There were no fins at the end, but there were slots from which a trio of stabilizers would sprout once the bomb was released, allowing it to maintain a nose-down attitude during the drop.

The two weapons missing from the rack had been moved to a cart in the middle of the boxcar, not far from the opening.

Larsen knew more about the devices than anyone who had not actually designed or worked on them should have known, and he had paid well for the information.

The bombs were B67 Robust Nuclear Earth Penetrators, or RNEPs, as they were identified in the 2003 Federal Defense Budget. The budget had authorized only a study to determine the feasibility of such a weapon, but actual production of the weapon had proceeded as a national security imperative and a secret of the highest order. Whether it violated several international treaties prohibiting the development of a new nuclear weapon was open to lawyerly debate; even though the bombs were new, the grapefruit-sized plutonium "pits" used as the bomb's primary fission ignition had been harvested from a few of the twelve thousand pits stored in underground bunkers at the Pantex Plant in Albuquerque, New Mexico—the only site in the United States where nuclear weapons were dismantled, either through obsolescence or according to the terms of a handful arms-control treaties, most of which were agreed upon during the Cold War. But since the United States had agreed to these treaties, and had also closed down nuclear testing and the making of additional pits, a hot war had engulfed the Middle East. The thinking turned again to the development of new weapons, especially ones that would do the maximum amount of damage to underground complexes.

The Manhattan Project, which had begun after 2,400 American lives had been lost during a surprise attack on Pearl Harbor, had developed the first atomic weapons in secret—and had used two of them after test-firing only one prototype. It was not such a leap to believe, after three thousand were lost in the September 11 attacks, that secret programs were part and parcel of wartime America. After all, no new research was needed, no prototype would have to be tested, and it all required a simple adjustment of existing technology.

For those few who knew of it, the B67 series was seldom referred to as an RNEP—the acronym did not come trippingly off the tongue—but instead was called by its code name, Falling Star. The name was apt, since it was a gravity bomb, meaning it could simply be dropped from an aircraft.

Many of Larsen's sources believed the pits that made the heart of the bomb came from the B57 series of antisubmarine nuclear depth charges, which had been decommissioned at the Pantex Plant in the 1990s. Python, however, had doubted that, thinking the diameter of the weapon suggested the pits were borrowed from the B61 series. These nukes came in a variety of configurations, but all B61s had a casing diameter of thirteen inches.

Besides the warheads carried aboard U.S. ballistic missile submarines, the B61 series was officially the only nuclear weapon deployed outside the boundaries of the United States, and about 1,200 were believed to be operational. Although classified, the yield for the bombs in the class varied between .3 kilotons to 350 kilotons, the equivalent from a tactical "neighborhood" bomb to the thirty or so Hiroshimas.

The series also included the rather unsuccessful and untried "bunker buster" called the B61-11. Critics had said it would prove less effective than bunker bombs made of conventional explosives. The B61-11 was nearly twelve feet long from nose cone to tail fin, weighed nearly twelve hundred pounds, and, interestingly enough, could operate in "lay-down mode"—meaning it could be dropped from a height of several hundred feet by parachute, hit the ground, and still be operational once it stopped bouncing.

The Falling Star, in contrast, was smaller but used something the B61-11 did not—a physics package that included a forward-mounted canister that contained a few ounces of tritium gas and a plutonium wire that, once impact was made, would provide a secondary directed-fusion explosion to melt a hole in whatever it contacted—and create, for a blinding moment, a small star spewing forth heat, radiation, and blast that would consume whatever was beneath it.

Like other weapons in the nuclear arsenal, Falling Star was prevented from unauthorized firing by a sophisticated system that included Permissive Action Links (PALs), which prohibited arming unless the correct six-digit category-C code was entered. After a few wrong tries, the electrical system would automatically self-destruct. The bomb also incorporated an Aircraft Monitoring and Control System (AMACS), which operated from the aircraft's electrical system, and was the avenue of transmission for the six-digit category-C PAL codes.

Both systems were required for the safing, arming, fusing, and firing of the weapon. All of this would seem to make the B61 invulnerable to any attempt to use a stolen one for terrorist purposes, except for one detail: B61 or B57 pits were not fire resistant. While a Fire-resistant Pit (FRP) weapon could withstand temperatures of a thousand degrees Celsius, or 1,832 degrees Fahrenheit, the casing of a non-FRP could be breached at a temperature of less than half of that, which was about what a hot jet-fuel fire produced. Dousing the non-FRP in jet fuel, under the right conditions to promote combustion, would result in a "dirty" explosion, spewing fallout over a wide area, a catastrophe several times larger than had the bomb simply been detonated in tactical mode.

No fuss, no muss, Larsen had reasoned: no PALs or AMACS.

These twelve Falling Star bombs had been crafted at the Sandia National Laboratories in New Mexico and were on their way to Whiteman Air Force Base, sixty-five miles south of Kansas City. Since 1993, the base had been the operational home to the 509th Bomb Wing—the direct descendant of the U.S. Army Air Corps 509th Composite Group, which in August 1945 dropped the atomic bombs on Hiroshima and Nagasaki. Now, from the base in Missouri, the wing's B2 Stealth Bombers could be over Iraq or Afghanistan in a matter of hours.

What patriotic American would object if it required a redesigned tactical nuke to kill Osama bin Laden while he slept in a bunker in Afghanistan?

The Department of Defense had officially abandoned rail transport in favor of highway convoys. These nuclear couriers used special Marmon-Herrington tractors and heavily armored Safe Secure Trailers, and they stayed in constant satellite contact with courier headquarters in Albuquerque, New Mexico. The semis and their included heavily armed van escorts were as readily identifiable as the nuclear "white trains" that had drawn so much protest in the eighties. The greatest weapon in wartime, of course, had always been stealth—and the rail shipments, which were timed to mimic routine freight movements, were nearly indistinguishable, at least from the outside, to the thousands of other trains seen every day by the public.

"Never imagined you as a Nazi," Baker said. "Or English."

"I'm sure there is quite a lot about me you could not possibly imagine," Larsen said. He glanced at his watch. "Five minutes and counting. Let's get on with it."

"Keep your fucking voice down," Baker said, while using a cloth to wipe clean the smooth black handle of a Buck hunting knife with a bloody six-inch blade. "The soldiers in the other cars will hear us, and then we'll both be deader than Hitler."

"Afraid?" Larsen asked.

Baker tossed the knife onto the body of the lieutenant.

"Shouldn't I be?" he asked in a voice that threatened to break. "What about the rest of the money?"

"Already in your offshore account," Larsen said. "What will you do with five million dollars?"

The tech sergeant smiled.

"In a few years, when it's safe? Anything I want."

Larsen moved to the cart.

"The physics packages?"

"Intact," Baker said.

"Everything?" Larsen asked. "For both of them?"

"Pits and all."

There was a jolt, and Larsen nearly lost his footing.

"What the hell was that?"

"Nothing," Baker said. "Slack. Long train, you know."

Larsen looked at his watch. Three minutes.

Larsen took a heavy sheet of canvas and spread it on the floor next to the opening. Together they wrestled the bomb to the canvas, which Larsen wrapped around the bomb and secured with straps.

"Ready?" Larsen asked.

Baker nodded.

Each man grasped the end of a strap, fore and aft, and braced himself. Then they gently lowered the bomb through the opening. Baker was at the rear, and he lowered his end slightly more than did Larsen. When they could hear the canvas whispering against the roadbed,

Larsen said: "On three, you release your end and then I will follow a moment later. Ready?"

"Wait," Baker said. His face was bathed in sweat.

"We don't have time to wait," Larsen said. "One, two . . ."

On "three" Baker released his end, and as Larsen felt himself being jerked toward the opening, he let go as well. There was the sound of the canvas sliding for a moment, and then nothing.

"Jesus," Baker said.

Larsen spread out the next canvas.

"You know they can't go off that way."

"The physics package won't go off," Baker said. "But if we drop it crooked and it goes under a wheel, it will trigger enough high explosives that they will be scraping us off the tunnel walls with a spoon."

Larsen glanced at his watch.

"A minute ten," he said. "Let's go."

They repeated the process as before, but when Larsen got to "two," the strap slipped through Baker's sweaty palms. The bomb hit with a thud beneath them. Larsen was jerked off his feet and caught the edges of the opening before he fell through, but he had a good view of the underside of the train before he pulled himself up. He heard two gut-tightening, muffled metallic thuds as the bomb bounced off one rail and then the other.

"Oh, shit," Larsen said.

"We're safe, or you wouldn't have time to utter expletives. We'd, you know, be part of the tunnel walls."

"Right. I hope the grunts in the car behind us didn't hear that."

Most of the train was still behind them, on the downside of the grade, so it had not yet begun to pick up speed.

"Anything to worry about in terms of damage?"

"No worries," Baker said. "These things are made to survive a drop of several hundred feet."

Larsen looked at his watch. Thirty seconds.

"Time to go," he said. "Be sure to smash your face into something hard, to make it look convincing. Or would you rather I do it for you?"

"I'll handle it myself," Baker said.

"As you wish."

Baker removed the 9mm pistol, placed it on the deck, and kicked it away. Then he withdrew a pair of handcuffs from his back pocket and cuffed himself to the weapons rack to make a convincing scene. Albuquerque would resume satellite tracking once the car exited the tunnel, and when he didn't answer the call to check in, the soldiers would come looking. Of course, Baker would blame the hole cut from the inside on the dead lieutenant, say that he had blacked out from lack of oxygen caused by the burning magnesium, and add that once the terrorists had what they wanted, they had dispatched their accomplice.

"Nice doing business with you," Baker said, snugging the bracelet around his wrist. "And I don't ever want to hear from you again."

"I can assure you that you won't," Larsen promised. He was sitting on the edge of the opening, ready to ease himself down, his back to the tech sergeant. He rested his left hand on the butt of the Desert Eagle. "But you know what I hate?"

"What's that?"

Larsen looked at his watch.

"Traitors," he said.

The lead locomotive blew two blasts on its air horn as it emerged from the tunnel. On the second blast, Larsen turned and fired a single round from the Eagle.

The .50-caliber slug passed through Baker's chest and embedded itself with a thud in the stainless-steel wall behind. Baker was slammed against the bomb rack as if he had been kicked by a mule. The wall and the two B67s nearest Baker were misted with blood.

Baker looked over in disbelief, then slid to the floor. His body hung from the handcuff around his right wrist.

Larsen holstered the Eagle and lowered himself down. The SS cap fell from his head, but he snatched it up before it hit the ground. The air stank of diesel fumes, and Larsen fought an urge to cough. He waited until the first wheels of the next car screeched by, then rolled over the rail.

He stood, brushing himself off.

Then he pressed himself against the wall while waiting for the rest of the train to clear the tunnel. After the last car had passed, Larsen watched the flashing red caution light recede.

He lit a Marlboro.

In less than a minute, Larsen heard automobile engines coming down the tracks from the Colorado side. An old blue Jeep CJ-7 was followed by a new black Wrangler Rubicon, which was backing down the tracks. The tires of both Jeeps had been deflated to ten pounds, and since the wheelbase of both vehicles were a close match for the standard railway gauge of four feet, eight and one-half inches, the tires readily cupped the rails.

The CJ-7 was driven by a slim, dark-haired woman dressed in black. The other Jeep, the one pointed toward Colorado, was driven by a large and muscular man, also dressed in black combat fatigues.

The woman got out of the old Jeep, retrieving a Bushmaster assault rifle from the passenger's seat and slinging it over her shoulder.

Larsen went to the first device, and, without having to be directed to, the big man picked up the other end and they carried it to the open tailgate of the Rubicon. Then they went back for the second one.

Larsen pulled his red LED light from his pocket, loosened the straps, and examined the casing for damage. He could not find so much as a dent.

"Excellent," he said.

They carried the second device to the Rubicon and placed it inside.

"Otto?"

"Yes, sir."

"Launch the CJ."

With the engine of the old Jeep still running, he placed the automatic transmission in drive and watched as the old car began to roll toward New Mexico.

"Move out," Larsen said. The woman was in the driver's seat, a pair of night-vision goggles over her head, and she put the manual transmission in neutral as the men began to push. As the Jeep picked up speed, the men hopped up onto the rear bumper, then over the tailgate. They spread some blankets over the devices, then sat over the wheel wells of the Jeep, keeping one hand on the roll bar, Heckler & Koch MP5 assault rifles cradled across their laps.

"Time?" the woman asked.

"Zero plus ninety seconds," Larsen said.

A few yards outside the tunnel, the Rubicon glided past the white pylon with black lettering that marked the New Mexico–Colorado border.

"Welcome to colorful Colorado," the woman said, and they all laughed nervously. The woman took a Sony Discman from her pocket, slipped the headphones over her ears, and turned up the volume (with megabass setting number two) on a CD called *Power of the Blood* by the race metal band Dresden. The current track was "To Robert Mathews in Valhalla."

The Rubicon began to pick up more speed as it whispered down the curving rails.

"Do watch this turn, love," Larsen said.

The woman couldn't hear him.

Larsen leaned forward and touched her shoulder.

She removed one earphone and looked back.

"Watch this curve. Turn the music off."

"It relaxes me," she said.

"Then turn it down enough so that you can hear me."

The woman began to gently pump the brakes. The Jeep slowed somewhat, but when she pressed the brakes too hard, she could hear the tires slipping on the snow-glazed rails.

It was freezing in the soft-top Jeep, so the woman reached over and flipped on the vehicle's heater. Larsen asked her to turn it off.

"Heat is our enemy," he said. "It makes us a better infrared target—that's why we're coasting down this hill. Besides, I'm sure the heater core is as cold as the rest of the engine by now, and you're only blowing the cold air around. Still, let's not chance it."

It was going to be a cold two-mile ride to the first interesting road, where they would reinflate the tires, start the engine, and head out across a little-used mountain trail to an abandoned mining town near Trinity.

The big man behind Larsen leaned forward.

"Is this going to work, sir?" he shouted over the wind noise.

Before Larsen could reassure him, her heard a whispering noise in the distance.

"Shit," Larsen said. "It hasn't been two minutes and we already have interdiction. Okay, countermeasures," he said, taking off the SS cap and placing it in the passenger's seat. He put on a black ski mask. "Gloves on. Keep those gun barrels down, make sure there aren't any gaps in the top, and please do not look up."

The Apache helicopter roared overhead, and Larsen hoped the woman had not warmed the brakes enough to give them away. Even if she had, Larsen thought, it might resemble the signature of rails that had been heated by the friction of a heavy mixed-freight.

"Thank God for moonless nights," the man behind him said.

"Yes, all praises to Him," Larsen said. "The chopper is hauling ass. As soon as he gets on the other side of the pass, he'll spot the decoy. They won't think yet to look for us following a train we've just stolen two nuclear devices from."

"They can't be very far ahead of us," the other soldier said. "I'll bet all hell's broken loose."

"I would not bet against you," Larsen said.

He glanced in the rearview mirror, but could see nothing except blackness.

The decoy was undoubtedly gaining speed, and the cargo tub was loaded with a hundred pounds of black powder and a fifty-five-gallon drum of fuel oil and fertilizer, coupled to a 13.8-volt igniter in line with a mercury switch. It shouldn't be long before the CJ jumped the rails at the first sharp curve, or simply swayed enough to complete the ignition circuit.

An orange flash illuminated the western horizon, followed by a fireball that rose several hundred feet over the pass. Larsen began counting, and when he got to twenty, he heard the blast and the following rumble.

The CJ had exploded about four miles away.

"Too close for comfort," the woman said.

"But far enough for our needs," Larsen said. "Remember, the authorities will think the devices were on that Jeep, and they will be shitting bricks. It's Sunday morning. It will take them hours to scramble the right people, and by the time they realize the devices were not on board, we'll be back home."

The Jeep was doing nearly seventy now.

"Use the transmission," Larsen said.

The woman slipped the transmission into high, then began to downshift through the gears. It was time to get off the rails, because they did not want to run up on the weapons train, which was certainly stopped by now and swarming with heavily armed soldiers.

Jockeying the brakes and the transmission, the driver

slowed the Rubicon to ten miles per hour, and then to a stop. Larsen and the big soldier jumped out with bottles of compressed air connected to fill hoses, and quickly inflated the thirty-one-inch tires. Then they crawled back over the tailgate, the woman started the engine, and she eased the Jeep off the tracks.

"Got a fix?"

"Exactly," Larsen said, checking the backlit handheld GPS unit. "The trail is quarter of a mile down this slope. Even driving without lights, in a few minutes we will be on the trail. Then we will have an adventurous drive through the mountains and watch the dawn from the ghost town of Ludlow."

Larsen shook a cigarette from the pack and jammed his hand into his jeans pocket for his lighter.

"Bloody hell," he said.

The Zippo was gone.

He must have lost it when he found himself facedown beneath the rail car.

11:28 A.M. EDT 15 March, 2004

WASHINGTON (AP)—Citing unspecified but credible threats, federal officials today raised the nation's color-coded terror-alert status from yellow to orange, indicating a high risk of attack.

The joint announcement was made by Attorney General John Ashcroft and Homeland Security Secretary Tom Ridge, after representatives from the CIA and FBI had briefed members of the House and Senate this morning.

"This is sobering data about those who wish to do us and our way of life harm," Ridge said. "But every day the security of our nation grows stronger."

Ridge said he had no specific knowledge about where, when or how an attack might take place, but that intelligence sources were certain the threat was "credible and that authorities were actively working" to gain such knowledge.

Note:

The Polaroid is tacked up on the bulletin board over my writing desk. It shows the four of us (five, counting the prostitute named Maria) sitting at a too-small table bristling with empty Tecate and Dos Equis bottles.

The photograph is overexposed, so our faces—with the exception of Maria's—are ghastly white, while the background fades into oblivion. Skorzeny is sitting on the extreme right, his massive shoulders bulging beneath a khaki T-shirt, and he's clowning and holding a beer bottle to his ear, as if it were a field telephone. Next to him is Karl, sunglasses perched on the crown of his head, his blond hair short, and wearing all black, as usual. In his hand is the ever-present cigarette. He looks more than a little worried, as if he senses what is to come.

Beside Karl is Maria, a seventeen-year-old Yaqui who was sent by her family to work with her older sister in the brothel at Acuña. Her skin is gleaming bronze, her hair is spun copper, and her eyes are newly minted coins. Beneath the table her legs are gracefully crossed. She is wearing a turquoise blouse that is so low-cut that it seems to go all the way to her navel, and her Sphinx-like smile betrays nothing. One of her hands is on the table, but the other is beneath it, stroking my thigh.

The outside of my left knee is pressed against Maria, while Eva is sitting on my right leg. She had been sitting on her own chair, but when the old man came up and wanted to take our picture for five bucks (Karl gave him ten), he couldn't get us all in the frame. So Eva jumped over to my lap. Her face is pressed against mine, her black bangs threatening to hide her ice-blue eyes, and a cheroot is dangling from the corner of her mouth. The cigar is lit and her right eye is squinting against the smoke curling up from the tip. Her skin is so pale it appears powdered. She's dressed in a gray tank top with black suspenders that squeeze her breasts together, a pair of baggy camouflage fatigue pants, and combat boots.

She is very drunk.

Because I'm sitting at the edge of the table, you can see my faded jeans and the cowboy boots. I'm wearing a blue work shirt, and around my neck is a red bandanna that I had been soaking all day in water to fight the heat. My sleeves are rolled up, the muscles in my forearms are in relief, and my cheeks are ruddy.

I was thinner than I am now, my hair was much longer, and I have a three-day growth of beard. There is an air of menace. Some people who have seen the photograph don't recognize the person in the photograph as me.

I'm looking at the photograph now as I write, and it occurs to me that it might someday land me in prison. Even writing about it will draw questions that will be difficult to answer. Do I miss these people? If I'm a hostage, I'm certainly not acting like it. No guns are being pointed at me, either above or below the table. Eva is sitting on my lap, and neither Karl nor Skorzeny appears too concerned about me. And I'm smiling, which is not something I've ever been noted for.

At that moment I was happy just to be alive.

What follows is the story of how I came to be photographed in the company of terrorists in a brothel in Mexico and the events behind November 9, 2004.

But here's the thing: Stories are puzzles, and memory provides the pieces, but the memories don't always fit in chronological order. Even—or especially—when you're writing in the first person, and you have nobody else to blame, the memories might not make sense when you lay them out in linear fashion, even if you pound the edges together like a kid would cheat on a jigsaw puzzle.

That's what I did when I first tried to write this book. I've been a professional journalist for, what, twenty years? No problem. The story begins in April and ends on November 9, right?

I came up with a three-hundred-page mess.

I had pounded the edges together to make a chronology, even though the pieces didn't really fit. There were bits of information that didn't seem to belong anywhere, from press releases to news bulletins to my memories of being a kid and being terrified when my foot went through the rotten floor of an abandoned house where I used to play. Then there were things I knew from my research that were needed to make sense of things, such as Karl Larsen's activities at Raton Pass, which you will read about shortly.

And finally there are things I still know very little about, and probably never will, despite being personally involved. I have filed dozens of FOIA requests to determine the location and jurisdiction of detention camp Yankee Zulu, for example, but all I really know is what one of the cells looks like. And the Nuclear Security Administration, which oversees the nation's nuclear arsenal, will neither confirm nor deny that the B67 series of nuclear bunk busters, code-named Falling Star, even exists.

A journalistic approach simply wasn't working. How could I write a first draft of history when, in some instances, I didn't even know what had happened? Instead of reporting a story, I was trapped in the story.

So I tore what I had written apart and separated the pages by theme instead of chronology. I allowed the pieces to choose their own logic. Patterns began to emerge. For the first time I could see a broader outline, not only in the events that unfolded in 2004, but in the rest of my life as well. What once had seemed as random as a car wreck finally took on the shape of a story.

And I choose to start with the Polaroid.

It is the decisive moment, to borrow a phrase from Henri Cartier-Bresson, that split second that irrevocably determines the course of events. I was about to ask a question that would either end my life—or save it.

It will take the rest of the story to explain why.

Note 2:

Terry Nichols wore a cheap gray sport coat and white shirt. No tie. I remember that he sat wearily at the defense table, listening as his lead attorney delivered the opening statement to the jury.

It was March 22, and Nichols was on trial for his life.

His coconspirator, Timothy McVeigh, was dead, executed three years before at a federal death chamber in Indiana.

Nichols was already serving a life sentence for the killing of eight federal law officers in the 1995 bombing of the Alfred P. Murrah Federal Building in Oklahoma City. Now, nearly a decade later, the State of Oklahoma had charged the forty-nine-year-old federal prisoner with the murder of the other 160 people and an unborn child who had perished in the blast.

The prosecution had spent the morning telling the jury that Nichols was not only involved in the bombing, but was "a willing participant in terror." The defense countered that Nichols, a former army buddy of McVeigh, was duped. Some of the jurors leaned slightly forward in their seats as the defense portrayed the trial as being "about friendship, manipulation, and betrayal."

McVeigh was bingeing on methamphetamine and becoming increasingly paranoid about Russian tanks and black helicopters in America, the defense said. He believed a demonic "New World Order" was imminent. And the evidence would show that others were involved, the defense claimed.

These "others" were a group of neo-Nazi bank robbers that waged a shadow war against the federal government in the mid-1990s, hitting at least twenty-two banks across the country in an attempt to finance an all-out race war—and helping McVeigh bomb the Murrah building.

The FBI called them the Midwestern Bank Bandits, but they called themselves the Aryan Republican Army. Later, the group became the Aryan Resistance Movement.

I had never heard of them.

In all the hundreds of hours of television coverage and millions of words printed about the bombing, I didn't remember a single reference to a group of racist bank robbers. Yes, there were some reports that McVeigh might have been spotted with men other than Nichols, and there was an intense but brief search for somebody named "John Doe number two" in the weeks after the bombing, but these had been portrayed as dead ends.

There was a lull as the judge asked counsel to approach the bench. The courtroom artist was putting some finishing touches on a very good pastel portrait of Nichols that would be broadcast that night on the national news.

One of the suit-and-tie network reporters in front of me leaned across the back of a bench and smiled wickedly at me.

"I'm about to fall asleep," he said. "Got any meth?"

I just smiled and shook my head.

The paper had sent me to McAlester to cover the opening of the Nichols trial because of the connection between the bombing and the robbery of a northwest Arkansas gun dealer. If I had known that Larsen had just stolen two nuclear weapons, I would have been asking why the hell the terror alert hadn't been raised to red instead of orange.

The answer, I know now, was that a red alert would have

invited too many questions about the nature of the threat. Besides, I hated the Orwellian alert system. The War on Terror had no identifiable objective. When could we claim victory? At what point would the government stop reminding us that there was always *some* risk of attack?

In the Nichols trial, federal prosecutors had claimed the robbery provided the money to buy the materials for the fuel-oil-and-fertilizer bomb. The state trial had been moved to McAlester, in southeastern Oklahoma, because an impartial jury could not be impaneled in Oklahoma City.

It was unseasonably warm, and the crowded courtroom on the second floor of the courthouse in downtown McAlester was quickly becoming uncomfortable. The judge explained apologetically to the jury that it would take courthouse maintenance workers a couple of days to change over from the boiler system to the chiller, and he ordered a large industrial fan to be placed just outside the courtroom's open door.

The whirring of the big blades contributed just a touch of white noise to an atmosphere that was already veering deep into the surreal—or at least one of the better John Grisham novels. *White Noise,* I thought, wouldn't be a bad title for this one.

Wait. Hadn't Don DeLillo used that for a literary novel in the eighties? I had to remind myself that was twenty years ago. Funny, but I didn't feel that old.

Nichols was forty-nine.

I wondered how old *he* felt.

In his cheap shirt and open collar, Nichols looked more like a harried insurance salesman after a hard day at work than the only accomplice to the single worst act of domestic terrorism in American history.

Then I went back to Little Rock, filed my story, and forgot about the Aryan Republican Army, at least for a little while. The trial was expected to last months. In the end, the jury never heard about the racist bank robbers; the judge ruled that the defense could not explore the "others unknown" argument. I wonder now if it would have made any difference had the jury learned that when the leader of the gang was finally caught, he had in his possession a box of blasting caps wrapped in Christmas paper—a gift from Timothy McVeigh.

5:32 A.M. CDT 4 August, 2004

DAVENPORT, IOWA (AP)—Nearly every police officer in town is expected to be on the job today when President George W. Bush and Democratic challenger John Kerry make campaign appearances just a quarter of a mile away in this historic city on the banks of the Mississippi.

1:01 P.M. CDT 4 August, 2004

DAVENPORT, IOWA (AP)—A local television station is reporting that three bank robberies took place at approximately the same time today that President George W. Bush and Democratic nominee John Kerry were speaking at separate but nearby venues. Davenport police refused to offer immediate confirmation for the robberies, but said they were busy providing added security for the motorcades of the candidates.

10:23 A.M. CDT 9 August, 2004

MCALESTER, OKLA. (CNN)—Terry Nichols, who escaped the death penalty when jurors could not agree during the punishment phase of his state trial, was sentenced today to 161 consecutive life terms for the Oklahoma City bombing.

Nichols, already serving a life sentence after being convicted in 1998 on federal charges, broke a long-standing silence and asked survivors for forgiveness. He also asked "everyone to acknowledge God."

Book One:
The Threshing Floor

Deliver me, I pray thee, from the hand of my brother, from the hand of Esau: for I fear him, lest he will come and smite me, and the mother with the children.

—Genesis 32:11

One

There's a sign at the entrance to Texas Death Row: NO HOSTAGES BEYOND THIS POINT. It means that if you're stupid enough to voluntarily pass through that door, like some journalists are, the State of Texas won't bargain for your release even if you have the bad luck to be caught up in a riot or some other prison drama you've probably seen only on cable.

Of course, to get as far as the sign you've already driven past the protesters at the entrance to the Polunsky Unit, near Livingston. They have hung from your car and shouted anti–death penalty slogans or pleaded for you to check on the welfare of their loved ones. As you're driving away, they demand to know why you're afraid of the truth.

You've already turned left at the Exxon station onto FM 3126, per the instructions faxed by the Texas Department of Criminal Justice, turned left again at the stop sign onto FM 350, and followed the winding country road to the Polunsky Unit, which again is on the left.

You've already given your credentials and driver's license to the guard behind the one-inch glass, and received in return a big plastic badge that says VISITOR. You've already faxed the Texas Department of Corrections a copy of that driver's license and your Social Security number so they plug the data into their computers and the machines of God knows who else.

"No tobacco products, briefcases, cellular phones, pagers, magazines, packages, or similar items may be brought into the unit," the public relations hack recited in a monotone as he swung open the door to the unit. He was graying, probably fifty, and he had a Catfish Hunter mustache and was wearing a baseball cap with TDCJ on the front.

His name was Bo.

"Individuals under the influence of drugs or alcohol will not be admitted to the facility," Bo said as he opened the door. "All individuals are subject to search."

He held the door open while Elaine and I walked past, and then stepped through and closed the door behind him. He tested the door with his weight to make sure it was securely latched before fixing his gaze on me.

"You aren't under the influence, are you, Mr. Kelsey?" Bo asked in his lazy Texas drawl. "Your eyes are awfully red."

"Long drive," I said. "Just tired."

"How far was it?"

"Twelve, thirteen hours."

"You didn't stay in a motel last night?"

"Nope," I said. "The paper wouldn't spring for it. So we just drove straight through."

"Geesh," Bo said, with a tinge of awe and disgust. "Make sure you get some sleep before you head back to Arkansas, okay? And also, Miss . . ."

"Schaeffer," Elaine said sweetly. She had a digital Nikon slung over one shoulder, borrowed from the photo department, along with a camera bag full of lenses. The VISITOR badge had naturally settled between the cleavage revealed by the baby-blue blouse she was wearing.

"Right," Bo said, and gave Elaine his best smile. "Would you mind buttoning that blouse a couple of notches?"

"Sorry," she said.

"How long have you been a photojournalist, Miss Schaeffer?"

"It's Mrs. Schaeffer," she said. "I've been working with Andy for about six months now. Isn't that right?"

"Something like that," I said.

"You look rather . . . grown-up to be a recent grad," Bo said.

"I got a late start," Elaine said, and frowned.

"She went the art-school route," I explained.

Elaine glanced at me and smiled.

We were walking slowly through a fifty-yard tunnel made of chain-link fence. It was about nine o'clock in the morning, and the sun was just high enough over the walls to illuminate the little courtyard the chain-link tunnel bisected. A few yards beyond the links, a couple of black inmates were kneeling at the edge of a flower garden, digging with trowels in the dirt.

"Look at that," Elaine said, and in a moment she had swung the Nikon from her shoulder to eye level.

"Sorry," Bo said, moving toward her. I thought he was going to place his hand over the lens. "We don't allow photos in this area."

"Why not?" Elaine said, lowering the camera. "It's poignant."

"Security, for one," he said. "This isn't a public area. For another, those inmates have not consented to have their pictures taken. The purpose of your visit is to interview and photograph Randall Duane Slaughter, and that is all."

"I understand," Elaine said.

"Thanks," Bo said, but there was no gratitude in his voice. Then, to change the subject, he asked me: "Been to any other death rows?"

"Arkansas," I said. "Tennessee."

"How do we compare?"

"Compare how?" I asked.

"I don't know," he said. "Appearance, I guess."

"You have the others states beat hands down," I said. "This is the cleanest facility I've visited."

"That's what we like to hear."

"You've also killed more inmates than any other state since the Supreme Court lifted the ban in 1976," I said. "What is it now? Three hundred?"

"Three hundred and twenty-two," Bo said. When I didn't reply, he continued: "These folks have done some pretty grim things, Mr. Kelsey. Every time I start to feel sorry for them, I remind myself what they did to land here, and I end up feeling more sorry for their victims and their families than for them."

"So that's why the protesters don't bother you?"

"Not in the least."

"And Patterson didn't bother you?"

"Nope."

The tunnel ended at a door to a big concrete-block building that vaguely reminded me of something from my old high school. We waited at another heavy steel door while Bo talked into a handy-talkie, and in a moment there was an electromechanical *shnick* as the door unlocked. We stepped inside and passed through what appeared to be part of the canteen.

Bo cleared his throat and turned to Elaine as he walked.

"Slaughter can be pretty rough, Mrs. Schaeffer," he said. "The last interview he had was a couple of years ago, and we had to stop it because he became agitated."

"Agitated?" she asked.

"He started shouting threats and obscenities," Bo said, then paused. "He also exposed himself."

"Are you trying to scare me?" Elaine asked, and gave him a smile that said she'd never been scared in her life.

"Because if you are, it's going to take more than some wacko talking dirty and waving his dick at me."

"No, ma'am," Bo said, then coughed into his hand. "Just wanted to make sure you knew what you were getting into here. Actually, I was a little surprised that Slaughter granted the interview. He's never talked before about what happened." Then Bo lowered his voice. "Then I saw your picture on the credentials you faxed to us."

"Are you suggesting I'm bait?" Elaine asked. "I find that offensive. Just because I'm a woman should not prevent me from following my chosen career."

"No, no, of course not."

We skirted the edge of the canteen and passed into another portion of the building. We were facing a line of thirty or so visitation cages. The inmate entered the cage on the opposite side, and the visitor, protected by another thick pane of glass, sat at a little visitation booth and talked to the inmate by phone. The booths reminded me of the kind of study cubicles that were once common in university libraries. The visitation booths at the end of the line were occupied, apparently by lawyers or family members of the men in the orange jumpsuits.

Bo indicated a nearby booth.

"Get comfortable," Bo said.

I took the microcassette recorder out of my suit pocket and put it on the little table in front of me, along with my narrow Portage reporter's notebook and a black Pilot gel pen. An old-fashioned telephone handset hung from a heavy metal cable at the side of the booth. The handset was green, like the rest of the place.

"You said you had a phone patch?"

"Oh, yeah," Bo said. "I forgot." From the pocket of his jacket he took a cord that had an eighth-inch phone plug on one end and a pair of alligator clips on the other. He took the phone, unscrewed the mouthpiece, exposing the diaphragm and wires, and clipped the alligator clips into the guts of the thing.

"How am I supposed to talk through it now?" I asked.

"Use the other one," he said, indicating an identical handset on the other side of the booth.

"You guys listen in on these conversations?" I asked.

He paused.

"I don't know," he said.

"I'll take that for a yes," I said.

"No, really," he said. "It's a case-by-case basis. We can't listen to attorney-client conversations. But others . . ."

Bo shrugged and left the booth.

"Great."

"Is that a problem?" Elaine asked.

"Baby, we have no problems," I said. "When this is over, we get to leave. Need some help?"

Under the pretense of needing both hands to retrieve something from the camera bag at her side, she handed me the camera. Trying not to be obvious, I took a quick glance through the viewfinder and took a meter reading, set the shutter and aperture, and handed it back to her.

"Don't we need a flash?"

"The ambient light is good enough," I said. "Don't forget that you have to focus manually. The autofocus won't work through the glass."

She nodded.

"What the hell am I doing in here?" she asked.

"You're the bait, remember?"

"It seemed fun at the time," she said.

"Just pretend you know what you're doing."

"Oh, you mean like in the rest of my life?" she asked cheerfully. "We all know how well that has worked out for me. When does this guy fry, anyway?"

"They don't electrocute them anymore," I said. "Lethal injection. Day after tomorrow, six in the evening."

"Isn't there a chance the governor will call or something?"

"This is Texas, baby," I said. "The last bastard to get the needle was a paranoid schizophrenic named Patterson. For no discernible reason, Patterson shot and killed a businessman and his secretary, ran to a friend's house, then took off everything but his socks and was found screaming in the middle of the street when the police arrived. The Supreme Court has declared it unconstitutional to execute the mentally retarded, but Texas Governor Perry believes that doesn't extend to the mentally ill."

"How do you know all this stuff?" Elaine asked.

This has been Texas Death Row since 1999, and all of the 447 men housed here are awaiting death from an $86.08 injection of sodium thiopental, pancuronium bromide, and potassium chloride.

The words began unwinding in my mind, like the narration to my own private documentary, and I had to stop myself from reciting. At the same time, a stabbing pain sliced through my left temple.

This triple cocktail provides sedation, collapses the diaphragm and lungs, and stops the heart. Once the inmate was strapped with arms outstretched, Christlike, to a gurney in the death chamber, and calls had been received from the governor and the state attorney general giving the go-ahead, the warden would ask the inmate for any last words, and a boom mike would be lowered from the ceiling. Some prepared statements, others ranted, some cursed, and a few sang. Many remained silent. Once the statement was completed, the warden removed his glasses to signal the executioner. This anonymous prison worker, who was watching from behind a mirrored window, depressed the plunger on a syringe to send the drugs into the IV lines that tapped each of the prisoner's arms. The prisoner could taste the drugs, it was said, and he (or rarely, she) had about forty-five seconds of consciousness left. During this time, any comments the inmate had were private. Many confessed fear. One asked the warden what he should say to God. This was normally followed by a cough, a gasp, and a final exhale.

In three minutes, they were dead.

"Andy?" Elaine asked. "Are you okay?"

"Sorry," I said, rubbing my closed eyes. "I'm fine. Just have a headache. Did you bring any Tylenol?"

"It's in my purse, back in the van," she said. "Don't rub your eyes like that. It makes a creepy sound."

There was a rattle and a door opened on the other side of the cage. Randall Duane Slaughter stepped into the area. He was six-two, 240 pounds, his head was shaved, and he sported a neatly groomed Vandyke beard. He had a puckered circular scar in the middle of his right cheek and, on the other side of his face, a jagged scar that went up to his cheekbone, which was lumpy and did not quite match the other one. His hands were shackled behind his back. The door closed and a guard reached through the bars and freed his hands. The sleeves of his prison coveralls were rolled up, and as he stood rubbing his wrists, the muscles in his arms writhed like snakes. In the webbing between his left thumb and forefinger was a spiderweb tattoo. Another prison tattoo, on the back of his other hand, said, #25:6.

Slaughter was standing and looking down at me. He would have been looking down at me even if I had been standing as well. He gave me a cold stare and then glanced over my shoulder at Elaine.

Elaine smiled.

I placed my right hand on the glass, palm facing him. He hesitated a moment, then pressed his hand against mine in the universal prison-interview handshake. Then he sat down.

I pressed the record and play buttons on the microcassette recorder, then lifted the telephone handset. Slaughter already had his to his ear.

"Hey, man," he rasped. It sounded like he hadn't spoken much recently. "You must be the reporter."

"Call me Andy," I said.

"I want to talk to her," Slaughter said.

"Let's chat first," I suggested.

"Tell your Jew masters to go fuck themselves," Slaughter said. "I won't help you sell papers. It's all lies, anyway. All I want to do is talk to a good-looking woman one last time."

"You'll get your chance," I said. "Come on, you know we have to talk first. That was the deal. She does look like her photo, doesn't she?"

"She looks better than her picture," Slaughter said greedily. Then he smiled. "Okay, what is it you want? You going to ask me how I feel about dying? I ain't scared. You think I'm sorry for what I did? No fucking way. I feel *good* about it."

"We'll get to that," I said.

"Then what do you wanna know?"

"Tell me about the Aryan Republican Army."

"We robbed banks," Slaughter said. "We got caught."

"You did more than that," I said. "You were trying to overthrow the government, and you were all members of the Phineas Priesthood. To join you had to kill someone considered a traitor to the white race. Most hunted interracial couples in city parks and other public places."

"You'd have to ask the others about that," he said.

"You know Langan won't talk," I said. "And Guthrie hanged himself in his jail cell. He was a thrill killer. He hunted mixed-race couples for sport. But you . . . now, you were different."

Slaughter shrugged.

"Ten years ago you shot your way through a pair of sheriff's deputies on the steps of the Bowie County Plaza at New Boston to kill a nineteen-year-old punk who was about to become the grand jury's star witness about a series of bank robberies in eastern Texas."

"Duane was a sack of shit," Slaughter said. "Ever hear of Robert Ford? Duane Snyder was our Robert Ford. We took him in and he was going to betray us to get out of a fucking traffic ticket. I just got to him before he could fuck us over."

"It was his third DWI," I said.

"It was still a traffic ticket," Slaughter said. "He got what he deserved. He was a traitor."

"How about Robert Brown?" I asked. "Did he get what he deserved? You dropped him at twenty yards with one shot from your Dan Wesson forty-four Magnum revolver. The hollow-point slug hit him here and took most of his face off." I pointed to the bridge of my nose. "He'd been a deputy for five years. He had a wife and two kids. A boy named Bobby and a girl, Susan. They're teenagers now. They don't remember their father."

"I told him to get out of the way."

"Then you fired two shots at Deputy Hector Gonzales, narrowly missing. Gonzales managed to draw his service revolver and fire, and about the same time you hit him three times in the upper body, boom, boom, boom. He was down on the ground, the wind knocked out of him, his ribs and an upper arm broken, and losing consciousness fast. But he managed another shot as you advanced. It hit you in the left check, broke your jaw, and exited the opposite cheekbone."

Slaughter rubbed his cheek.

"Standing over him, your blood splattering down on his uniform, you pinned his gun hand with your foot while you opened the cylinder and sprinkled your spent cartridges onto the ground. Then you took a speed loader from your belt and placed six fresh rounds in the cylinder of the Wesson. I think you would have killed Gonzales then, except Snyder was already stumbling up the steps toward the courthouse, and you were afraid he would get away. He might have, except his hands and feet were shackled, and he kept falling."

"How the hell do you know all this? It's not in the transcripts. I didn't say anything during my trial. And I fired my lawyer."

"I do my research," I said. "I read the autopsies, the police reports, the witness statements. I interviewed Gonzales. He's a Texas Ranger now, you know. You made his career."

"Fuck that greaser," Slaughter said.

"You were nearly crawling up those steps yourself by this time," I said. "I can't imagine how much pain you were in. I have a hard time when I have a toothache, and you took a thirty-eight-caliber slug in the jaw that bounced out the other side of your face. You were spitting teeth and bone out. Snyder was on his back, trying to get his belt-shackled hands high enough to protect his face, and you emptied the second clip into his head. Am I still getting this right? You know, they had to replace that section of step where his head had been, because the pock marks were too deep to repair."

"His head pretty much caved in like a rotten melon."

"Then you sat down next to Snyder's body, placed your gun carefully on the steps, shoved your jaw back in place with your hands, and waited."

"Didn't figure there was any point in running," Slaughter said. "You kill a cop in Texas and run, you're pretty much toast. You don't make it to jail. Actually, I was surprised they didn't off me where I sat. Most days I wish they had. Just get it over with, you know?"

I was scribbling in the notebook, acting like I was trying to catch up, just so I wouldn't have to respond immediately. I had succeeded in engaging Slaughter in a conversation because he was curious about how much I really knew, but I had played him about as far as I could with my knowledge. Now it was time to be quiet. Since we were already talking, the urge for him to continue the conversation would be growing.

Behind me, I could hear the click of the Nikon.

Slaughter glanced from me to Elaine, then back.

"Why are you so interested in me?"

There it was.

I put down my pen and leaned forward. It was important to tell the truth, because psychopaths have a superhuman ability to detect bullshit.

"I think your story is significant."

"What do you mean?"

"Whatever people may think about you," I said slowly, "and whatever the state of Texas does to you, cannot change the fact that you were involved in one of the most important and least understood causes of our times. And even though I think what you did was horrendous, you obviously believed enough in that cause to sacrifice yourself for others."

Slaughter glanced down.

"You'll write that?"

"Yes," I said. "Did I describe things accurately?"

"Yeah, except for the part about the pain," he said. "I didn't feel any. I knew the little Spic had shot me in the jaw, but I just felt numb, like a dentist had injected the lower part of my face with Novocain. Shock, I guess. Then, after it was over, as I was sitting on the steps, things just melted away, like in a dream. It was when I woke up, under guard in the hospital, that it started to hurt like hell. I went through three surgeries to put my face back together. Kind of a waste, considering they're just going to off me."

"What was worth sacrificing yourself for?" I asked.

"Like you said, the cause. And revenge."

"I think it had to be more than that," I said cautiously.

"What do you mean?"

"The cause would have continued," I said. "You didn't kill Snyder before he had a chance to talk to the grand jury just to save the other gang members. I think there was somebody else, somebody you considered more important than all the rest of you. You guys managed to rob at least twenty-two banks in seven Midwestern states, and an armored car in Ohio. Your take was over a million dollars."

"Hell," Slaughter said, "it was closer to three million. The armored-car job was a million by itself."

"Most of it was never recovered."

"We were trying to finance a revolution," Slaughter said. "That gets expensive in a hurry. Also, we never hurt anybody."

"Until you killed Snyder and Brown."

Slaughter shrugged.

"And I don't think the bank robbery gang was ever completely broken," I said. "There have been other robberies all across the country during the past decade that are remarkably similar to the jobs you pulled. In and out in three minutes. Pipe bombs left behind to distract police. Robbers shouting phrases in gibberish that is meant to sound like Arabic."

"Lot of copycats out there, I guess."

"But there was only one Commander Carlos."

Slaughter shrugged.

"I've been in the joint for the past ten years. He's dead, for all I know. And if I did know, I wouldn't tell you."

The Nikon clicked again. Elaine had moved closer, and was standing over me, shading the lens with the edge of her hand, trying to get a shot through the glass that wasn't marred by the reflection.

"It's time," Slaughter said.

My head was killing me and the interview had stalled, so I nodded.

"She's not a photographer, is she?" Slaughter asked.

I shook my head.

"What, then? Another reporter? A secretary?"

"Nope," I said. "She's a stonecutter. She makes headstones."

"No shit?" Slaughter said.

"I shit you not," I said. "Behave yourself. No *Midnight Express* stuff, okay?"

"Yeah, I saw that movie," Slaughter said. "Irene Miracle. Man, I never thought I'd be on this side of the bars. Turn that thing off, okay?"

I hesitated, then stopped the tape recorder. I stood, took the camera and bag from Elaine, and let her take the chair. She smiled, but still looked worried as she picked up the handset.

Elaine spent the next twenty minutes listening while Slaughter talked. To pass the time I took a few photographs. Sometimes she would answer a question with yes or no, or reply to a comment with a thank-you. The more he talked, the less worried she seemed. Once I heard her tell him that I wasn't her boyfriend. She began to smile. Finally he asked her a question, and she thought for a long time before nodding.

Then the conversation was over. Slaughter pressed his palm against the glass in good-bye, and Elaine cautiously touched the glass. His hand was twice the size of hers.

She stood and I gave her the camera back. I sat down and picked up the phone.

"This story you're writing," Slaughter said. "It will run after I'm dead?"

"Nope," I said. "It's for tomorrow morning's paper."

"Kind of like my obit? Except in advance?"

"Something like that," I said. "But more of a news story. And you won't like parts of it."

"I'd like to see a copy of it anyway," he said quietly.

"I'll make sure you get one."

Slaughter nodded.

"I guess that's about it, huh?"

"Unless you want to tell me about Commander Carlos."

"Then that's about it," he said. "Funny, but I'll be dead tomorrow. You know, if I were on the other side of this glass, you'd be in a world of trouble. It wouldn't be safe, because you'd be the enemy. A traitor to your race."

"You don't think I'm the enemy now?"

Slaughter shrugged.

"The war's over for me," he said. "The revolution is up

to the next generation. After Friday my body will lie beneath my favorite white oak at Covenant compound, awaiting the resurrection."

"According to some folks, you won't have long to wait."

"What's that mean?" Slaughter asked.

"Abraham Smith says you will rise again after three days, a sword in your hand, to signal the final conflict between good and evil."

Slaughter thought for a moment.

"I'd rather have the Wesson."

Two

Elaine was quiet on the long walk out of the prison. We were escorted again by Bo, the PR flack, who tried to make small talk, but failed.

We were nearly to the gate that had the NO HOSTAGES sign on the other side before he turned and said to Elaine, "We need to talk."

She nodded.

"Talk about what?" I asked.

"Arrangements," Bo said. "Mrs. Schaeffer needs to be briefed, and there's paperwork to be signed. Do you know how to get to the Walls? It's in downtown Huntsville, about forty miles from here."

"What are you talking about?" I asked.

"Slaughter asked me to witness the execution," Elaine said.

"Then your guys were listening in," I told Bo.

"Randall Slaughter told his jailer that Mrs. Schaeffer had agreed to be one of his witnesses. He gets five, but so far he's chosen only one, a spiritual adviser."

"Abraham Smith," I said.

"Smith's son," Bo said. He then took the handheld radio from his belt and said a few words. There was a buzz, and the gate swung open.

"Okay. Let's get the paperwork started," Bo said. "You'll need to be at the Walls by five P.M on Friday. And no camera."

Elaine nodded.

"You'll have to crash at a motel for a couple of days," I said. "And we'll also have to rent you a car."

I looked at my watch.

"We can grab something to eat at that little restaurant we saw on the way in," I said. "Then we'll have to get moving."

"You're pissed," Elaine said.

"No, just concerned," I said. "Witnessing Slaughter's execution wasn't part of the story. Why did you agree?"

She paused at the door and glanced one last time beyond the chain-link tunnel to where the same two inmates were still kneading the dirt in the flower garden.

"He said he wanted to die looking at something beautiful," she said. "And he said he couldn't imagine anything more beautiful than me."

Three

I parked the aging *Traveler* van in the only shade I could find in the parking lot of Florida's Kitchen. None of the newsroom cars were running when we left, so I had to borrow the circulation van, complete with about three thousand copies of last Sunday's edition sloshing around in the back.

The restaurant was small and crowded, and we chose a table by the door. I barely glanced at the menu. When the waitress came, she asked us if we had been to death row.

"You have that media look," she said sweetly. "Who were you interviewing?"

"Randall Duane Slaughter," Elaine said.

"I'll take a cheeseburger," I said. "Coffee. Cream. And could I have some milk instead of that powdered stuff?"

"Sure," the waitress said. Then to Elaine: "His time's about up, isn't it?"

"Friday," Elaine said.

The waitress nodded. "Good Lord, it's hard to keep track of all of them these days. I have a brother at the Walls, but I lose track."

"Is he an inmate or a guard?"

"A guard, thank God. What to eat?"

"I'm not really hungry," Elaine said. "How about some wheat toast and a cup of hot tea?"

"You got it," the waitress said.

"Sure that's all you want?" I asked. "You should be starving."

"No, that's fine," she said.

The waitress left.

"What's wrong with you?" Elaine asked.

"What do you mean?"

"You haven't acted like yourself in weeks," she said.

"Not sleeping well," I said, wishing the waitress would hurry with the coffee. "It's made me cranky."

"You act like you don't even like your job anymore," Elaine said. "How many first-place investigative awards have you won in your career? A dozen? Now you act detached, like you're just going through the motions. Doesn't any of this bother you? Don't you care anymore?"

"It's just a job," I said.

"Well, it's not my job," she said.

"You said you thought it might be fun."

"Well, it was an education," Elaine said.

"So what did you and Slaughter talk about? Sex?"

"That was part of it," she said. "He said I reminded him of a girlfriend he used to have. He didn't say anything too raw. Just talked about how much he liked to make love to her, and how sorry he was that he had lost touch with her, and how unfair it was that he'd never get to touch another woman."

"That would be a sobering thought," I said.

"There was something else," Elaine said carefully.

"Was he abusive?"

"No," Elaine said. "Even though I knew he did a terrible thing, I found myself sort of liking him."

"He's a good-looking guy. Muscular."

"He mentioned a date," Elaine said.

"Go on."

"November ninth," Elaine said. "He said that something spectacular was going to happen that day, but he wouldn't say what. Does the date mean anything to you?"

"No," I said. "Generally these right-wing nuts are obsessed with a couple of consecutive dates. April nineteenth, anniversary of Waco and the Oklahoma City bombing. April twentieth, Hitler's birthday and the Columbine shooting. Nothing rings a bell regarding November."

"He also said he was going to give me a copy of his final statement," Elaine said.

"Oh? That could be newsworthy."

"He said it was private."

"Or not," I said.

"I know this guy is a neo-Nazi and did some terrible things," Elaine said. "He just seems like an ordinary guy in a shitty situation. And his name. What do you think he was destined to grow up to be with a name like Slaughter? But you know, if I met him on the street, I'd never know he was a killer. Andy, I have a hard time hating him."

"You don't have to hate him," I said. "But it disturbs me that you sort of like him."

Four

I met Elaine Schaeffer one Sunday morning in April at Oakland Fraternal Cemetery, near the northeastern corner of the massive National Cemetery off Confederate Boulevard, two miles southeast of the Capitol Building. Oakland is one of Little Rock's oldest cemeteries, and from the time it was acquired by the city until well into the twentieth century, it was called Oakland Hebrew Cemetery.

Sometime before dawn on April 25—Confederate Memorial Day in Arkansas—vandals scaled the cemetery fence and spray-painted bloodred swastikas on some of the stones in the older, Jewish section. They also took a sledge to the 1997 Jewish War Memorial, gouging fist-sized chunks from the base of the monument.

It was, of course, being categorized as a hate crime. Tension had been increasing in Little Rock since the city had denied a permit for a skinhead metal rally at Riverfront Park.

My editor, Sheryl, had called me at home that morning and asked me to run out to the cemetery on my way to the *Traveler* office to check out the damage.

I was asleep when the phone began ringing. I was dreaming about my dead father. We had replaced the clutch in some piece-of-shit hot rod that I had owned when I was a kid. I was underneath the car trying to get the splines lined up so I could bolt the transmission back to the engine, and I kept missing. I was cradling the four-speed transmission on my chest and trying to shove it up into place with both hands, but it was heavy and my arms were shaking and it was getting hard to breathe. My dad was alternately chiding me for burning the clutch out and trying to help by giving advice, and meanwhile the car was groaning and shifting around on the floor jack. I knew I had to get the transmission stabbed and bolted up and get the hell out from under there, but I was afraid I didn't have the strength to do it.

Dirt was falling into my face, and I couldn't wipe it away because my hands were filled with the transmission. Sweat was running into my eyes, and it stung. The back of my head was digging a little crater in the ground, and I could feel leaves and gravel in my hair. I turned my head, blinking and trying to clear my vision, and suddenly on the ground beside my father I could see the most beautiful red Craftsman toolbox. He carefully opened the lid and slid out one of the drawers.

"Why don't you use the right tool?" Dad asked. "Do you always have to do things the hard way?"

Then I became conscious of the ringing phone and sat up in bed, drenched in sweat, surprised that I wasn't trapped beneath a car, and a little sad as well that my father wasn't there. When Sheryl asked me to check out the cemetery, I asked her if it had been anything more than vandalism. When she said no, I told her it was a job for the beat reporter and hung up.

She called back.

Well, what if it wasn't just vandalism? She had a feeling it might be connected to the skinhead thing. She knew I had been working for months on the series about the mentally ill being held in jail for months without due process, but couldn't I just take a couple of hours this morning and check it out?

"It's Sunday," I said and hung up again.

The phone rang again.

"Don't you give up?"

"Here's the deal," she said. "Guess the color of my underwear and you can sleep in. Not only that, but when you finally roll into the office tomorrow, I'll take you to lunch at the Faded Rose."

"You're abusing your power."

"No, I'm charming."

"Are you going to pay me for the fifteen hours of overtime I put in last week? I have no life."

"Guess," she urged.

"Oh, hell," I said. "Black. I'll go with basic black."

"Sorry, but thanks for playing," Sheryl said. "Call me when you know something. And don't forget your tie tomorrow. The Young Man is really cracking down."

"I don't own any."

Half an hour later I was walking among the stones at Oakland, in jeans and tennis shoes, a blue dress shirt, and a pair of sunglasses. A pleasant morning—light breeze, green grass, blue skies. It was still too early for my allergies to kick in, so I was fairly comfortable being outside, which I avoided as often as was practical. The morning had a feeling of newness to it, like those I remembered when I was a kid. I don't know why. Perhaps it was the smell of the cut grass, or the aroma of the earth, or simply because the cemetery was quieter than the rest of the city.

Far across the cemetery at the hundred-year-old, gazebolike Confederate Monument, a ceremony was being held. Reenactors in gray uniforms were lined up, and a couple of them were holding rebel battle flags. Somebody in a suit and tie was up at the rostrum, delivering some kind of speech, but the gathering was far enough away that I couldn't hear the words distinctly, just a whispering sound on the wind. The vandalism was easy to find, because the damaged monuments were marked with yellow police tape. The cops had long gone, however. The swastikas were scrawled across monuments with the names Cohen, Epstein, Goldberg, Katzenberg, Mendehl, Rosenthal, Weiss.

But the most damage had been done to the eight-year-old Jewish War Memorial, a four-foot-diameter granite sphere at the top of a hill at the end of the road that led into the cemetery from the Jewish gate.

The monument was covered in neo-Nazi graffiti. It also had fist-sized chunks of stone missing from the sphere and base, and on the pedestal below the sphere was a Star of David and a simple inscription that had originally read: DEDICATED TO THE MEMORY OF ALL JEWISH WAR VETERANS. The Jewish star had been badly damaged, and the inscription was nearly indecipherable.

A woman in her thirties was inside the police tape, working at the base of the monument. She was wearing a pair of rubber gloves and dipping a sponge into a plastic bucket that, from the smell of it, contained some type of paint remover. She also had a toolbox beside her, filled with trowels, some plaster, a few chisels, and some things I didn't recognize. The toolbox was red. Her brown hair was tied back with a blue bandanna, and she was wearing a sleeveless denim top.

Not far from her was an old man dressed in a business suit and tie, hands in front, holding tightly to a blue cap that said JWV POST 436. The old man's dark hair had receded to the middle of his skull, his mustache was salt-and-pepper, and his pale blue eyes were filled with memories.

"Desert Storm," the man said.

"I beg your pardon?"

"My son," he said. "Daniel was killed in Desert Storm."

"I'm sorry," I said.

"Danny died when his helicopter went down during the last day of the ground war," the man said. "They were on a rescue mission. That was thirteen years ago this February. What kind of people would do this to a monument honoring him?"

"Sir, I don't know."

The woman paused and sat back on her heels.

"It's all right, Mr. Walberg," she said. "The paint's coming off, and I'll get the rest of it repaired just as quickly as possible."

She turned back to her work.

"He was twenty-three," the old man said. "Can you imagine? Just a little older than I was when I joined the Army Air Corps in 1943. We had him late, you know. Danny was an only child, and we were always so protective of him. Now this?"

"Were you in Europe or Asia?" I asked. I had pulled the notebook from my back pocket.

"Europe," he said.

"Pilot?" I asked.

"An officer? Not me. Not like Danny," he said. "I was so proud of him. Why are you taking notes?"

"Do you mind? Reporter. What was your job in the service?"

"I was just a ball turret gunner in a B17."

"A dangerous place to be," I said.

"Not as dangerous as Buchenwald, I think," Walberg said, and shrugged. "Not as dangerous as Bergen-Belsen, or Dora, or Auschwitz. How many of them survived? And who are these people that paint these hateful things on this monument and spread their lies about the Shoah?"

"The Shoah?" I asked.

"The Holocaust," the woman said over her shoulder.

"These new Nazis, these skinheads, how can they claim the Shoah is a lie?" Walberg asked. "What kind of mental gymnastics does it take to so completely deny the truth? How can they argue over the figures? What human being can imagine such numbers? Can you envision six million dead?"

"No," I said.

"Five million? Or four?" he asked.

I shook my head.

"Three million?" he said. "Can you imagine three million human faces at once? Could you remember their names, their birthdays, the dreams they held in their hearts? Of course not. No individual can. These are numbers known only to God."

He closed his eyes. "These things are known only to a parent," Walberg said.

The woman stripped off her gloves, placed them on the side of the bucket, and ducked under the police tape. She placed a hand on Walberg's arm.

"Don't you have enough?" she asked.

She had a soft Arkansas accent that was a ringer for Natalie Canerday's in *Sling Blade.*

"No," Walberg said. "Let him write the truth."

She looked uncertain.

"I'm Andy Kelsey." I said. "Sorry, I should have introduced myself first. I'd give you a business card, but I don't believe in them. Maybe you've seen my byline in the *Traveler*."

"No," the woman said.

I asked for Walberg's first name, his age, and his address.

"Daniel," he said. "Senior. I'm eighty-one."

He gave an address not far from the cemetery.

"Are you sure skinheads did this?" I asked the woman. "Maybe it was kids. Did anybody see them; were any messages left other than the vandalism?"

"Why ask me?"

"Don't you work here?"

"Of course not."

"Sorry," I said. "Too early in the morning for me."

"It's ten o'clock."

"Yeah, hard to believe, huh?" I asked.

"You know what's weird? The original design for this memorial wasn't a sphere, which represents the globe, but a fractured Star of David, to represent the Holocaust. That's what the vandals produced, unintentionally."

"When was it dedicated? I can't make out the inscription."

"Well, the monument says November eleventh, but because of a conflict with a veterans' event at the state capitol, the date was moved up a couple of days. So the answer is November ninth."

I scribbled that down.

"Look, I don't mean to be rude, but I need to know who you are."

"Just a friend of Mr. Walberg's," she said. "He and my husband went to synagogue together. I own Schaeffer Stone at Conway, and Mr. Walberg asked me to clean up this monument as quickly as I could. I won't be able to replace the gouges today, but at least I can get the filth off of it."

"What does ZOG mean?" I asked.

"I have no idea."

"So you make gravestones?"

"Make them, clean them, repair them," she said. She had the gloves on again, and she wiped her brow with her forearm. The movement accentuated her cleavage, and I could not help but stare. She saw me staring, but did not look away. "Conservation is a big part of my business, although I enjoy cutting stone the most. You know, the inscriptions. But my husband was better at it."

"Was?"

"Car accident," she said. "Two years ago."

"Sorry."

"So am I," she said. "He's buried over there."

"Was his grave—"

"Nope, they didn't touch it. Not an obviously Jewish name, I guess. But this monument must have been hard to miss."

"You like what you do?"

"I don't dislike it," she said. "It's meaningful. People are comforted by my job well done. There's a predictability to it, a finality, and a timeless quality. But still . . ."

"You wish you could do something else?"

"Don't you?"

"Always thought I was an author."

"Don't all reporters?"

"I was proved wrong," I said, then changed the subject. "Are you going to be here for an hour or so?"

"At least," she said, glancing at the damage. "Why?"

"If you don't mind, I'm going to call the desk and schedule a photo," I said, and my cell was already in my hand. "What you're doing is pretty visual. And I'd like to know more about how you're going to repair the gouges."

She frowned.

"Something wrong?" I asked.

"I'd rather not be in a photo with this," she said, motioning to the graffiti. "I just want to clean it off as quickly as possible. Frankly, I don't want to see photos of any of this in the paper. It's just ugly."

"Okay, Mrs. Schaeffer," I said. "We'll let the photographers take potluck."

Sheryl's panties of an undetermined color would be in a big knot if she could have heard me say that.

"Elaine," the woman said. "You can call me Elaine."

She reached into the pocket of her denim top and produced a business card.

"I'm not sure why you don't believe in these, but here's one of mine," she said. "Give me a call if you'd really like to know about stonecutting sometime."

"Great," I said. "I hope it's before I personally need your services."

She said it wasn't funny.

I told her it wasn't a joke—in my job I tend to collect death threats. That evening I called Schaeffer Stone and was invited to leave a voice message. I said I wasn't all that interested in stone but that I'd like to know more about her and what she would rather be doing.

Five

When the woman in the knit cap and knee-length black leather coat walked through the front door of the Independence branch of the Liberty Bank of Missouri, few people took notice. It was Tuesday, September 7, at 2:05 P.M., according to the time stamp on the security video, but it felt like Monday to security guard Walter Tyndall Jr.—the day before had been Labor Day and the bank had been closed.

As usual after a bank holiday, there had been a steady stream of customers—and the amount of cash being counted for business deposits from the three-day weekend exceeded anything that could be expected on an ordinary Tuesday.

Because it was cold and rainy out, it wasn't unusual for customers to be bundled up. But if Tyndall, the security guard, thought it unusual that the woman in the black coat was also wearing sunglasses on such a dismal day, his reaction didn't show it. He nodded politely to the woman and then looked away, his hands clasped in front of him. Tyndall, twenty-three, had been on the job for a little more than two weeks, and as with all other private security guards in Missouri, state law required no training and no background check for his employment, for which he was paid $7.35 an hour.

When Tyndall glanced back at the woman, she had unslung a Bushmaster M4 carbine from beneath her jacket and was pointing the ten-inch fluted barrel at his chest. The .223-caliber automatic resembled its older cousin, the Colt M16, but had a shorter barrel and a collapsible stock, and was designed for commando use. It was also the perfect size for the average adult woman.

Keeping the Bushmaster trained on him, with its pistol grip clutched in her right hand, she used her left to reach down and remove his .38 Special from its open holster. As she dropped the gun into a nearby trash basket, Tyndall noticed she was wearing latex surgical gloves.

"Get down on the floor," she said.

Tyndall was too terrified to move.

Behind her, two men had entered the bank. They were also dressed in black, had gym bags slung across their backs, wore surgical gloves, and both were carrying Heckler & Koch MP5 submachine guns with retracted butt stocks. Beneath the receiver of each gun was a pair of banana clips, taped together, each holding thirty rounds of .40-caliber S&W. The ammunition was the same required by the Glocks in the tactical holsters strapped to their thighs.

The bigger man was wearing a ski mask, while the smaller man was wearing a black SS officer's cap, aviator sunglasses, and a black bandanna tied over the lower half of his face. He also carried the submachine gun in his left hand. At five feet, nine inches, according to the height marker on the door frame behind him, he was the smaller of the two. The other man was a few inches over six feet.

As the door closed, the woman glanced at her left wrist to check her watch.

"Get him down now," the left-handed man said calmly.

"Cheese and rice," the woman muttered. "Get down or I'll have to kill you."

Tyndall dropped facedown to the tile floor.

"Hands behind your head. Lace your fingers."

Tyndall did as he was told.

The woman knelt beside him.

"Relax and enjoy," she said.

From this position she was out of sight of anyone peering in from the street, but had a good view of the entrance and the parking lot beyond.

While the woman was having the exchange with the security guard, the men had rushed the counter. There were only three customers in the bank at that time, a thirty-four-year-old mother holding the hand of her four-year-old son, and an eighty-one-year-old retired insurance salesman.

"Get down," the large man told the customers. "Get the fuck down *now.*"

The mother put the child beneath her, and the old man dropped to his knees and then, with some difficulty, to the floor.

"Twelve seconds," the woman called.

The bank had not been remodeled in years, and there was no barrier between the tellers and the lobby except for the chest-high counter and the broad teller windows.

Larsen, the left-handed robber, lithely squeezed through one of the windows and threw the gym bag at the nearest teller, a thin woman with blazing red hair who had worked at the bank for twenty-three years.

"Fill it," he said. "No dye packs, no consecutive serial numbers, no silent alarms. Do you understand?"

"Yes," the woman said.

"I know you have bill traps," he said. "Stay away from them. If the police show up outside, I'll assume that someone has taken that special bill from beneath the trap in her drawer. Do you know what will happen if I see police outside?"

Larsen waited.

"Tell them, Otto."

"We will fucking kill you all," the big man shouted.

"You two," Larsen said. "Understand?"

The other tellers, both younger women, nodded. The dark-haired one in front was holding her hands palms-up, while the blonde behind her had clapped her hands to her face.

"Tell me," the man said. "I want to hear you say it."

They mumbled.

"Louder."

"Yes, we understand," the dark-haired one said. "You'll kill all of us."

"Start filling."

She did.

"Place our surprise, Otto."

The larger man took a brightly colored package out of his gym bag and placed it gingerly on the floor, a few yards in front of the customers. The little boy struggled to see the box, which was wrapped in gift paper featuring alphabets, blackboards, worms, and apples. A bright red ribbon was tied around a card that said, *Back to School!*

"Look, Mama!" the boy cried.

The mother shushed him and covered his eyes.

The shorter man tossed the empty bag up into the nearest window. Then he went to the offices in the rear of the bank and led the manager and the loan officer, both men in their forties, out to take their places on the floor with the customers.

"If we think anything at all is wrong, we're going to reduce your customer base by three," the left-handed man said calmly. "If we see any police officers, you're all going to die."

A stain spread beneath the loan officer, and the cutting odor of ammonia permeated the lobby.

"Damn," the big man said. "One of 'em peed."

"Sorry," the loan officer said lamely.

"What's in the package?" This from the dark-haired teller.

"Don't ask," the large man called.

"Twenty-five seconds," the woman in the black coat called.

"You, in back," the man called to the blonde. "Stop that."

Hands still clutched to her face, she cried harder.

"Shelley, for Christ's sake," the dark-haired teller said. "They'll be out of here as soon as they get what they want."

"Smart girl. Not a hero, are you?"

"Not me," the girl said, and grinned.

"Then you'll live."

She closed the drawer.

"Are you done?"

"Unless you want the dye packs and shit."

"Good girl," the man said. "Do Shelley's drawer. Now."

She moved down and started to repeat the procedure.

"Shelley," the commander said. "Go in back and scoop up whatever cash you can grab easily from the counting tables from the weekend deposits. Don't go near the vault. Agreed?"

"Yes," she said.

The man tossed her another gym bag.

"Go," he said. "Be back in thirty seconds or I'll kill your friends. Otto, make sure she behaves herself."

"Jawohl, Herr Kommandant."

Terrified, Shelley hurried toward the back.

"What's your name?" the dark-haired teller asked the left-handed man.

"You may call me Commander Carlos," he said. "My associates are Otto Skorzeny and Eva Braun." He pronounced the last name *Brown*.

The old man on the floor, who had been listening intently, struggled to his elbows with some difficulty, then pushed his glasses back up on the bridge of his nose.

"Sons of bitches," he said. "You're using the code names of Hitler's mistress and his favorite commando? I was with Patton when we drove the Nazis all the way across France. This is what I fought for? To be robbed by pretend Nazis?"

The left-handed man came back through the window and knelt beside the old man. The man put his head down, sure that he was going to be shot.

"Look up."

The old man did.

"Third Army?" The left-handed man pushed the SS cap back.

"Yes," he said. "Wounded twice."

"I'm sorry for the inconvenience," he said quietly. "Please accept our apologies. We are not going to rob your person. The institution's losses will be covered by the FDIC. Now, if you'll excuse me, time is short."

He jumped back up on the teller's window.

"Sir, one last thing," he said, crouching in the window. "I assure you that I am not a pretend soldier. My comrades died in my arms, as I'm sure yours did. And you will discover that we are members of a very real organization."

The dark-haired teller smiled, even though the left-handed man was again pointing the MP5 in her general direction.

"What is so amusing, love?"

"This is like a movie."

"If only we could afford the willing suspension of disbelief," he said. "What is your name, if I may inquire?"

"Diana."

"Married?"

Diana smiled. She held up her left hand and wiggled her fingers. A diamond-studded wedding band glittered in the fluorescent lights.

"Happily?"

"Forty-five seconds," the woman called. "This isn't the dating game, Commander. Give it up."

"But she has such a nice . . . face," he said.

"Sorry," Diana said with a shrug and a smile.

"Stop that," the older teller said.

"I'm cooperating," Diana said. "Try it."

The older woman finished stuffing the first bag and resentfully held it out. The commander grabbed it and threw it over the counter.

"Shit," the woman in black said. "Customers. A man and woman."

"Everybody who's already down, stay down," the left-handed man said as he brought the barrel of his H&K up and placed his back against the counter. "Tellers, act natural. Quiet now."

The couple was in their early thirties, both dressed in blue jeans, and they were holding hands. The man had a Carhartt jacket over his shirt and a green John Deere baseball cap. The girl was wearing a windbreaker, and she was black. They were talking and did not see the customers and others on the floor until after they had pushed through the door and were halfway to the tellers.

"What the fuck?" the young man said.

"Hey, asswipe," the woman in black said over the sights of her Bushmaster. "Put your hands slowly in the air and look over your left shoulder."

He did.

"You too, mud puppet," the woman said. "You two are just fuck buddies, right? You're just giving it to her for some variety? You're not married or anything."

"We're married," the woman said over her shoulder. "We've got kids."

"Dammit," the woman in the black coat said.

"We don't have time for this, Eva," the left-handed man said. "I must apologize for her manners. She gets rather excitable, and often she is uncontrollable. Otto, get these folks down with the others."

"This is just fucking great," the woman said as she paced in front of the hostages, the barrel of the Bushmaster swinging in time, just inches from their faces. "It would be a kindness to kill them," she ranted.

Skorzeny escorted Shelley to the teller's area with her bag. The left-handed man took her bag, and then when he took the gym bag from Diana, he kissed the back of her hand.

"Another time, my dear," he said.

Diana smiled.

"Perhaps, Commander," she said.

"We have a problem," Skorzeny called.

He pushed the gym bag through one of the windows and scooted after it, only to find Eva standing over the mixed couple with the barrel of the Bushmaster pressed against the base of the man's skull. His wife was beneath him.

"I can do them both right here," she said.

"Not your job," the man said, knocking the gun barrel away. "There is no sisterhood. Men only."

"Like bank robbery?"

"Stand down; that's an order."

She hesitated a moment, her finger literally twitching on the trigger of the Bushmaster; then she raised the rifle to look at the watch on her wrist.

"One minute twenty," she said.

The left-handed man threw her one of the gym bags.

"Out," he said. "Get the wheels."

The larger man snatched up the other gym bag, and

within a few steps it began trailing a foul odor and greasy red and black smoke.

As Skorzeny dropped the bag, flames began licking around the handles.

"It's on fire," Skorzeny said.

"Leave it," the commander said. "Cover my back."

"I told you, no dye packs," the left-hander coldly told the older teller. "Now I don't know whether to kill all of you or not. None of you move for ten minutes and you might survive this. Any type of motion at all will set off the bomb in that package. Got it?"

"Got it," Diana said, crouched on the floor, her chin on her knees. "I want to live."

"Of course, my dear," the commander said.

A cranberry-red Ford Explorer screeched up near the front door of the bank, the woman in black driving. The two men backed out of the bank. The left-handed leader took the front passenger's seat, and he told the bigger man to get in the back seat and lie down. Then the Explorer wheeled away, in a direction not visible from within the bank, with a whispered screech of tires.

A handheld police scanner on the console crackled with traffic about a silent alarm at the Liberty Bank. In the background there was the whine of sirens.

As the Explorer left the parking lot, the woman removed her hat and glasses, revealing dyed black hair and blue eyes. The man beside her also removed his SS officer's cap, sunglasses, and bandanna, and he smoothed his short blond hair with his palm.

His eyes were the same shade as the woman's.

"Time?" he asked.

"One minute twenty-three."

"Much too long," the commander said, although he still appeared relaxed. "We really have to stick to under sixty seconds."

"We need a driver," the woman said.

"Of course," the commander said. "I'm working on it."

A police car zipped past them, headed for the bank. Its lights were flashing, but it was close enough now that it had killed the siren.

"But so far, luck is with us," he said. "By the way, that was a fine job of acting on the edge back there."

"I wasn't acting," she said.

"As long as you don't actually cross that edge."

The stolen red Explorer pulled into the vast parking lot of a strip mall, pulled around to one side, and parked next to a Chevrolet cargo van that looked very much like a fleet vehicle.

"Gloves on? Good."

They exited the Explorer, their coats covering their weapons, and they threw it all into the side door of the Explorer. While the woman took the gym bag, the left-handed man glanced quickly over the interior of the Explorer. Satisfied that nothing had been left unintentionally, he took a package from the van and placed it on the front seat. It was a prepackaged back-to-school kit from the local Target store, with pencils, pens, rulers, and notebook paper.

Then the left-handed man climbed into the side door and took a seat next to the dark-haired woman.

"All right, Otto," he said, leaning forward to talk to the big man in the front seat. "Let's exit the parking lot carefully and head south, shall we?"

Back at the branch bank, the six employees and five customers remained quite still until the little boy suddenly broke free of his mother's grasp. With her screaming for him to stop, he ran to the present and shook it. By the time she reached him, he had ripped the wrapping from the box, opening one end.

Apples rolled out.

That afternoon, after being debriefed by the local police and the FBI, Walter Tyndall Jr. resigned his job with the firm that provided security for the Liberty branch. A week later he found a job as a stocker at a neighborhood Wal-Mart.

Six

"I was simply seduced by your résumé," Sheryl Scott had said the year before, prior to introducing me to the managing editor. She was my age or a little older. I'd never asked. But it was common knowledge at the newspaper that she had been *Playboy*'s Playmate of the Month for November of 1983.

"I remember hearing about your book," she said. "It won some kind of award, didn't it?"

"Did you read it?"

"Honestly, no," she said. "What was it about?"

"Hiroshima and Nagasaki."

She apparently didn't have much to say about the topic, so she smiled and tapped my résumé. "Oh, you are so qualified," she said.

"Overqualified," Red Perkins said, growing tired of Sheryl's gushing. His white dress shirt was rumpled, his tie was askew, and his slacks were so worn that I could see the bottom corner of his brown leather billfold peeking from the fabric of his pants pocket. His fingertips were tracing the outline of the pack of Marlboros in his shirt pocket.

"So why in hell do you want to come back to the grind of a daily newspaper?" he asked.

Because nobody, including you, read my fucking book.

"Because you need me," I said. It was the only true thing I could think of that wouldn't sound desperate.

Red looked unconvinced.

"Got anything newer?" Red asked as he flipped through my clips. "This is good enough, as far as it goes—the story about the serial killer didn't stink—but how do we know you've still got it? All of this stuff is four or five years old."

"It took me three years to write my book," I said. "It's not like I've been on vacation."

"This is a young man's game," he said. "We have deadlines that are a little more often than every few years."

This guy was definitely beginning to get to me.

"Funny," I said. "When I applied for my first newspaper job twenty years ago, somebody just like you told me that what I lacked was experience. Now I'm forty, I've written several hundred major magazine stories and newspaper pieces, been across Asia as a foreign correspondent, ducked bombs and bullets, wrote a book that was a finalist for the National Book Award, and you're telling me I'm too old."

Red had taken one of those cigarettes out of the pack and was idly rolling it around his fingers. "No offense," he said, which meant, of course, that offense was intended in spades, "but we run a newspaper here. We don't have time to waste trying to be literary. Myself, I don't read fiction, because it's irrelevant. We need to tell our readers today something they didn't know yesterday."

"The book was nonfiction," I said. "It wasn't a novel."

Well, I'd blown this shot. I could feel my cheeks getting hot, but I kept my voice friendly and my smile tight.

"Okay," I said. "I do have literary pretensions. But even if I am over the hill, you still need me because there's nobody on the staff with the guts or the talent to do the stories that need to be done."

Red eyed me for a moment, then stuck the unlit cigarette in the corner of his mouth. "It's easy to be an armchair quarterback," he said. "How do you know we aren't doing the stories we should be?"

"Because I've read your paper every day this week."

"I'm still listening," Red said.

"Let me have a shot at telling those stories that nobody else has the time or the inclination for," I said. "No offense, but your newspaper is dying. To survive you're going to have to offer readers something they can't get anywhere else. They get the news in the first five minutes of any local broadcast, complete with ten-second sound bites and staged photo ops. You can't compete with the immediacy of television just by using shorter stories, label headlines, and bigger pictures. You also can't compete with the type of blanket coverage that the *Democrat*, with its deep pockets, offers."

"So, genius, how do we compete?"

"You don't," I said. "You forge your own niche by giving readers something they can't get at any paper in town or on their nightly newscast: in-depth, long-form reporting about significant regional issues."

"What do you mean by long-form?"

"Ten to twenty times longer than any story you've previously published," I said. "Near book length, in other words. Serialized nonfiction pieces that rely on immersion reporting and borrow—"

"No fucking way."

"Andy," Sheryl asked sweetly, "tell me what you mean by immersion reporting."

"It's the best term I can come up with for the type of reporting I do best," I said. "Remember New Journalism? Tom Wolfe? *The Kandy-Kolored Tangerine-Flake Streamline Baby?* Joan Didion's *Salvador?* Hunter Thompson? How about Roy Stryker? Well, I do something similar, but in addition to the long essay I add investigative reporting techniques that require a lot of shoe leather and copying fees."

"Fear and Loathing in Arkansas?" Red asked. "What about objectivity?

"Objectivity is a myth," I said. "It is humanly impossible. All individuals, including reporters, have a point of view that is implied, if not explicit, in every story. Instead of objectivity, we ought to be talking about fairness."

"Give me a concrete example."

"In how many crime stories do you ask the defendant for a statement?" I asked. "Only murders or high-profile cases involving politicians or celebrities, I'll bet, and even then only because their PR flacks are beating at the door. Ever ask some schmuck accused of making meth or who lost his house under the drug forfeiture laws for a comment?"

"Most are guilty," Red said. "Most of them keep their mouths shut on the advice of their attorneys."

"But not all," I said. "And that's not the point. The point is that everybody has a story, and some of them are damned interesting. It's something that I learned a long time ago, when I got my first job on the police beat at a small newspaper in Kansas: if your stories aren't good enough, you're not asking the right questions."

"You mentioned somebody named Stryker. Who's that?"

I was liking him more, because at least he was honest enough to admit he didn't know everything.

"Roy Stryker was the head of the photographic division of the Farm Security Administration, the federal make-work program during the Depression," I said.

"Before he sent his people into the field, he made sure he understood the stories they were about to cover. The problem with reportage today is that we have developed a culture in which we don't think for ourselves. We take the words of politicians and celebrities and lawyers and fashion stories out of these assertions."

"What's the alternative?"

"Think for ourselves," I said. "Check things out, dig for data, and bring critical analytical skills to the task at hand. Perhaps we can't do this for every story, but we do it for the important few. The trick is knowing which stories are important enough to invest the time and resources."

Red had his lighter out of his pocket now. It was a cheap butane lighter, and he was turning it over and over in his hand.

"I like his take on things," Sheryl said.

"You just like him because you think he's cute."

"I do not," she said. "I mean, he is cute, but . . . he has a point, you know. None of this stuff is new. We've just kind of forgotten in the struggle to keep the newspaper afloat."

Red actually lit the lighter, then extinguished it.

"You know what our biggest problem in the newsroom is?" Sheryl asked. "Lazy reporting."

"Let's take a walk," Red said. "I've got to light this cigarette or I'm going to kill somebody. Sheryl, stay."

"What am I, a dog?"

She came anyway.

We threaded our way through a labyrinth of corridors and seemingly hidden stairwells until we found an outside door and stepped onto the newspaper loading dock. It was a chilly morning and none of us had coats. Sheryl folded her arms while Red lit the cigarette and sucked smoke into his lungs.

"You smoke?"

I knew I was hired when he offered me the pack.

Seven

The day after I wrapped the story on the mentally ill, I took a weekday off and found myself standing on the steps of Schaeffer Stone at Conway, rattling the locked front door.

Conway is a college town about forty minutes north of Little Rock on Interstate 40, but it had taken me an additional thirty minutes to find the monument company, which was hidden on a quiet corner in a semiresidential area near Hendrix College. The business was closed for lunch.

With not much else to do, I walked around the place. The building was small, and appeared to contain an office portion in front, with a larger work area in back. A well-kept Victorian house was attached to the business.

All across the front lot were different types and sizes of monuments, from very modest narrow stones with just enough room for a name and a couple of dates, to massive polished stones with bases that must have weighed a ton or more. Interspersed between the monuments were whimsical carvings of animals: there was a frog here, a rabbit there, a rattlesnake, and a lion.

In the back were piles of raw stone, an A-frame-and-chain hoist, and a propane-powered forklift. An air hose snaked beneath the closed overhead door at the rear of the building.

Then I found a shady spot beneath a tree, sat on one of the monuments, and waited. At about one-thirty a battered 1982 Chevy pickup pulled around the corner and parked in back. A moment later, Elaine Schaeffer walked around the corner of the building, keys jingling in her hand.

"I thought you might call first," she said.

"I'm more the spontaneous type," I said. "I was going to ask you to lunch, but I figure you've already eaten."

"Lunch," she said. "But there's always dinner. You in town for a while?"

"I am now."

"Good," she said as she opened the door. "Let's talk."

I stepped inside.

"I read your book," she said.

"No shit? Where'd you find it?"

"You don't write like that," she said. "Why do you have to talk like that?"

"You don't like it?"

"Not really."

"Okay," I said. "I won't, at least not with you."

"Thank you," she said.

"Now tell me where you found the book."

"Ordered it from a used bookseller on the Internet," she said, and picked up the ex-library copy from the corner of her industrial-gray metal desk. "Five dollars and twenty-three cents, with postage."

"Retail was twenty-three bucks," I said.

She tapped the spine against her chin.

"I liked it," she said. "I had to use a dictionary to look up some of the words, but I liked it. It also depressed me."

"Guess I'm just not meant for romantic comedies."

"Didn't it depress you to write it?"

"I was depressed already," I said.

The book still had the original dust jacket, which I had been so proud of at the time: black, with the title in bold white letters at the top, over a negative image of the mushroom cloud. Now it just looked tired.

"You don't look depressed," she said, flipped the book over to look at the author photo on the back. "You just look young. And you dressed better back then. Why don't you wear a tie anymore?"

"I threw them all away."

"Why?"

"Hard to explain," I said. "What library?"

I took the book and flipped it open to the front papers. There was still a little manila jacket attached for the library card, and a rubber stamp that said: PROPERTY OF THE CORYDON PUBLIC LIBRARY. On the opposite page, in big red letters, was DISCARD. It was done in a childish scrawl that reminded me of the swastikas defacing the monuments. I knew the comparison was unfair, but it was what crossed my mind. I didn't share.

"Iowa," I said.

"Why would they get rid of it?"

"Make room for new books," I said.

"What's wrong with the old ones?"

"You're asking the wrong person," I said, handing the book back to her.

"It doesn't seem right," she said. "Libraries are like cemeteries. Would you discard the previous occupants just to make way for the new? There should be room for everybody."

"You have an unusual way of thinking about things," I said.

"I want to make a monument for them," she said.

"Hiroshima has plenty of monuments," I said. "The town is fairly crawling with them. But it's a nice thought."

"Not a monument, really, but a sculpture," she said. Her head was down as she said this, and her bangs hid her eyes. I waited. Her teeth bit her lower lip; then she continued.

"A mother and child," she said.

"Like a Madonna and child?"

"No," she said. "Not religious. Realistic. A real mother sheltering her real child. From life. But I don't know any Japanese families."

She looked up. "What do you think?"

"I think we could find someone to model."

"You think I could do it?"

"I like your rabbits," I said.

She laughed.

"Those are just garden objects, stuff I made from left-over pieces of stone. Whimsy, really. What I really want to do are figures."

She went to the metal file cabinet in the corner, squatted down, and pulled open the bottom drawer. She withdrew a paper tube wrapped with a rubber band.

"Take a look at this," she said.

She unrolled the paper and spread it on the desk, using a coffee cup and a stapler and some other things to hold the paper down. The sheet was covered with pencil sketches of figures, all nude, in pairs or threes, young and old, in various life scenes—conception, death, breast-feeding, embraces, anger, fighting, grief, caresses.

"You like them?

"Even beats the rabbits."

"My favorite sculptor is Gustav Vigeland," she said. "He did wonderful work. When I was a teenager, I went to Europe and quite by accident found myself at a park in Oslo looking at his work. It changed my life. Sounds trite, doesn't it? But this one piece just blew me away—a monolith, nearly fifty feet high, carved from a solid block of stone, covered by a hundred and twenty-one interconnected bodies."

She smiled.

"Sorry," she said, rolling up the sheet. "Corny, huh? Thanks for indulging me."

"I wasn't indulging you," I said. "You're talented."

She tossed the sheet back into the file cabinet and nudged the drawer shut with her foot. Then she brushed her hands together, as if she were done with such foolishness.

"I'm not talented," she said. "But I am determined."

"Start sculpting," I said.

"Not yet. Too scared," she said. "Have to make a living and all of that. And I'm afraid of losing myself in the work. Once I started doing that, how could I ever think about anything else?"

"Not afraid of failing?"

"I wouldn't fail," she said, and I believed her.

She was quiet for a moment, then reached out and put a finger beneath my chin. She brought my eyes up to meet hers.

"You're not having any fun, are you?"

I asked her what she meant.

"What do you think?" She locked the door of the shop and turned the OPEN sign around. "I mean in life. You're not having any fun, are you? Oh, you have this cocky attitude, but you're really not enjoying your life. You know, I'm not having much fun either. Look at me and tell me what you see."

I wasn't sure what to say.

"What do you see?" she insisted.

"Well, I see a very attractive woman in her middle thirties who is successfully running a business she inherited from her husband, who is very conscientious about her work, and who has dreams of being a real sculptor."

She moved closer to me.

"Makes me sound like Pinocchio," she said.

"I thought you just got back from lunch," I said. "Why are you closing again?"

"I'm flesh and blood," she said. "Try again."

She laced her fingers behind her head and stretched both ways, her hair bunched in her hands. The back of her neck was exposed, and it was an extraordinarily beautiful patch of skin.

"What do you want me to say?"

"You're the writer."

"I see a lovely widow," I said.

She was close enough now to touch.

I held my hands rigidly by my sides.

"I see a very lonely woman."

She unhooked the straps of her overalls and let the bib fall.

"Aren't you going to pull the shades?"

"It's daylight," she said. "Nobody can see in here."

Without bothering to unbutton it, she pulled off her flannel shirt and threw it on the desk. No bra. Then she reached down and took my hands in hers. Her palms were rough, as you would expect of someone who worked with stone, and her fingers were amazingly strong. She brought my hands to her lips, kissed each of them, and then placed my palms on her nipples.

I couldn't speak.

The overalls, which had been riding on her waist, fell to her ankles. She kicked them away. She was wearing a pair of pale blue panties.

"Is this some kind of test?" I asked.

"No test," she said. "Just some fun. You do remember fun?"

"Vaguely."

"What's wrong?"

"Nothing. It's just that—"

"You don't mind wearing a condom, do you?"

"No," I said. "I don't mind."

"Then what is it?"

"Nothing," I said.

"Is it because I'm Jewish?"

"Of course not," I said.

"Thank God," she said. "Don't believe anything you've heard. Isn't this what you had in mind when you came up here?"

"No," I said. "All right, I'm lying. Yes, it is exactly. But I just thought we'd have an opportunity to talk first."

"Oh, we'll talk," she said. "You know how badly I've missed talking to somebody who gives a shit about something besides the Razorbacks?"

"What, you don't like the Razorbacks?"

"But I also like music and art and literature and all of the other things that make life worth living," she said. "And this is one of the really big things. God forgive me, but I miss it. I want to feel a man inside me, and then I want that well-fucked feeling, and then we'll talk. I read your book and you just seemed so damned smart; don't blow it now, okay?"

"Don't you want to go into the house? The bedroom, maybe?"

"God, no," she said. "Not yet. Too many memories, you know? But out here, I've made this mine now. Just mine. Now, are you going to keep making excuses or are you going to kiss me?"

I did.

She pinned me against the desk.

She stopped as suddenly as she had begun.

I tried to catch my breath.

"You do know something about art, right?" she asked.

"A little. Um, like, Rodin?"

"Christ," she said.

"You use that?"

"Shut up; this is important," she said, disentangling

herself. She ran a hand through her very mussed hair. "Tell me what you know."

"You've got to be kidding," I said, gasping, still on my back.

"You're right, that's stupid," she said, blowing the hair away from her eyes. "Let me ask some questions."

"You said it wasn't a test."

"Okay, I lied," she said. "Well, I didn't lie, exactly; I just assumed you'd know something about art."

"This is important right now?"

"Trust me, it's important," she said.

"You mean—"

"I can't get off otherwise."

"Right," I said. "Why didn't you say so up front? 'I'll take sexual dysfunction for five hundred, Alex.' "

"It's not abnormal," she said. "I just . . . it's just . . . I prefer 'unusual.' "

I sat up. I was about to tell her to forget it when I looked over at her. She was sitting cross-legged on the end of the desk, naked, her chin in her hands. If I said she had great breasts, I would be understating the case.

"Fire away."

"Okay," she said, her blue eyes flashing. "If I had a painting of Elvis, Marilyn Monroe, James Dean, and Bogart in a diner late at night it wouldn't be called . . ."

"*Boulevard of Broken Dreams*," I said. "No, wait. You asked what it would *not* be called. It wouldn't be called *Nighthawks*, which is the famous Edward Hopper original. I don't know who painted the other one, but it's the knockoff you see everywhere in posters."

"Edvard Munch?"

"*The Scream*. Can we drop posters?"

"Good point," she said. "You passed art appreciation in college. Let's see, something harder."

"I've got something hard—"

"Shush," she said.

"Come on," I pleaded.

"Got it," she said. "Name a postmodernist."

"Art or literature?"

"Pay attention. We're still on art."

"Picasso."

"Surrealism."

"Chagall."

"Oh, my God." She gasped.

"Aren't we done yet?"

She broke away. "Falling Waters."

"Architecture, no fair."

"Fair," she said. "Architecture is art."

"Frank Lloyd Wright."

"Who's known for mobiles?"

"Calder."

"First name?"

"Come on," I said. "I passed, right?"

"You passed, you passed. Just one more question."

"No."

I pulled her to me.

"Please?"

"No."

"You can do anything you want," she said, breathing hard. She was flushed and her skin glistened with a fine layer of sweat. She was athletic, the muscles in her arms and legs were well toned, and when she breathed her stomach muscles rippled.

"Anything," she said, and kissed me. "As long as it's nonviolent, of course. Just answer one last question."

"Really?"

"Promise."

"All right," I said.

She cleared her throat.

"Name an influential twentieth-century sculptor."

"Picasso."

"Doesn't count," she said. "Better known for his paintings, and you've already used him. Name somebody else."

"I told you I didn't know anything about stone sculpting."

"Try, Andy."

"All right," I said. "Let me think."

"Remember, twentieth century."

"Still alive?"

"Not necessarily," she said.

"Oh, crap," I said. "You told me who your inspiration was. What was his name? Give me a minute."

"Clock's running," she said.

"Gustav . . ."

"Sure?"

"Augustus . . . No, that's wrong. Wait. I've got one: Christo. Bulgarian, I think. Gigantic outdoor pieces, covering miles, lots of color. That counts as sculpture, right?"

Her eyes shone.

"Not the best answer," she said as she pulled me on top of her. "That would have been Gustav Vigeland. But the judges say we have a winner."

I won't try to describe the sex.

If I take a clinical approach, it would be pornography. If I describe the emotions, it would be a romance novel.

Eight

Most stories are twice as hard and only half as good as you think they're going to be. But once in a while a story just shines. Maybe it's luck, or maybe it's a gift. But that one story can make all of those late nights and seemingly endless paper trails worth it.

"Hinterland" was one of those stories.

It began that April morning in Oakland Cemetery and, over the next few weeks, I spent most of my waking hours on it. It was the kind of story I had described when I had first interviewed at the *Traveler* a year earlier. We didn't think of it as the "Hinterland" story at first, of course. What began that April slowly grew to become a story about hate groups in the Ozarks: skinheads, neo-Nazis, the patriot Christian movement, the Ku Klux Klan. I began filling box after box with research material.

I was familiar with some of this stuff already from reading I had done as a kid, after having been briefly fascinated with a Hal Lindsey book called *The Late Great Planet Earth* (in which Lindsey claimed the Second Coming was imminent, a theme that has been popular ever since the First Coming). The rest of it I had encountered in my research since that morning in front of the Jewish War Memorial.

If this were a novel, this is the place—since I'm a lazy writer—where I'd have some bullshit scene where I kind of offhandedly explain this stuff to somebody who is puzzled by it. Otherwise, I'd have to carefully work it into the story, which is damned hard. But since this isn't a novel, I don't have the luxury of making shit up. I didn't really have a conversation with anybody that began, "You know, Frank, Christian Identity has its roots in a curious Victorian belief. . . ." So you're about to get what writers call an information dump. My editor will probably strike it, but in case he doesn't, go ahead and take a glance, if you care about context.

If not, just skip the next couple of pages. There's a bedroom scene at the end of the chapter.

Christian Identity is a direct spiritual descendant of British Israelism, a belief crystallized when John Wilson argued in 1840 that the similarity between English and Hebrew institutions and language was no mere coincidence. The idea took a firm hold on the Victorian imagination—and the royal families of England and Scotland were given "Hebrew" bloodlines—and it encouraged beliefs including that the Stone of Scone, on which Scottish royalty was traditionally crowned, was originally the base for the Ark of the Covenant.

Wilson believed that Christ's return was imminent.

In America, the belief found a willing audience in the followers of William Miller, who declared that Christ would return on October 22, 1844—followed by the destruction of the world by fire. Miller's reasoning was based on an interpretation of the passage of days in the book of Daniel (which, along with Revelation, still provides most of the grist for would-be prophets today). When Christ failed to appear at the appointed hour, it was called the Second Great Disappointment. The first disappointment had been in 1843, the date Miller first predicted the world would end, and then revised. Even after two such spectacular failures, many Millerites refused to abandon their belief, and formed the Seventh-Day Adventists.

The next big date in millennial prophecy, of course, was 1900. Although many writers attribute the modern Pentecostal movement to California's Azusa Street Revival in 1906, there is good evidence for placing its birth more than five years earlier, in the Bethel Bible School at Topeka, Kansas.

Shortly after midnight on January 1, 1901—after spending the last night of 1900 in a watch-night prayer vigil—a young woman named Agnes Ozman begged holiness preacher Charles Fox Parham to pray for her to be filled with the Holy Spirit and speak in another tongue as proof. After all, four times in the book of Acts, when people were filled with the spirit, they spoke in an unknown tongue. And Parham himself had visited others, such as Alexander Dowie and Frank Standford, whose students had spoken in tongues.

Agnes began uttering something that Parham took as Mandarin Chinese, and the other students reported seeing a halo behind her head and an unearthly glow from her face. Soon Parham and the other students were speaking in tongues as well, and the preacher believed it was to allow the uneducated to convert the Chinese in their own language. It was a sign, he believed, of a second Pentecost, an outpouring of the spirit before the Rapture, when Christ's church was to be taken bodily into heaven.

The original Pentecost, fifty days after Christ's resurrection, was marked by the descent of the Holy Ghost upon the twelve remaining Apostles. Judas Iscariot, the thirteenth disciple, had already hanged himself by this time.

In a day or two, news of the amazing things happening at Bethel Bible School was carried in the Kansas City and St. Louis newspapers, which reported that Agnes not only spoke in "Chinese" for three days, but claimed to be able to write it, as well. The newspapers were skeptical, however, and the linguists they consulted said the symbols Agnes produced were just scribbling.

Later, a one-eyed black man named William Seymour would hear Parham preach (some say from a hallway of a segregated church) in Houston, Texas. In 1906, Seymour would be called to Los Angeles to preach at the Asuza Street Mission.

Parham was dismayed by the unseemly mixing of blacks and whites at the Azusa mission, and was skeptical of their outpouring of faith, which he called "wildfire." Parham would establish his "world headquarters" for his Apostolic Faith Movement in Baxter Springs, Kansas, but his congregation would never enjoy the success of the California upstarts.

Much of the problem may have been rumors that circulated about Parham's personal life. In 1907, he was accused of sodomy in San Antonio, Texas, with an "angel-voiced" young man named J. J. Jourdan. While the charges were later dropped, the damage had been done, and a statement carried in the newspapers, attributed to Parham, amounted to a confession: He had shared a bed with Jourdan, and did not remember what might have happened in his sleep.

Parham died January 29, 1929. He had collapsed in the pulpit in Houston several days before, but made it home to Baxter Springs before expiring. No physician was consulted, because Parham did not much believe in "doctoring," feeling that all healing came from the Holy Spirit. The cause of death was listed as "exhaustion."

Not many people were ever converted to Christianity by an evangelist speaking in tongues in the convert's native language, either in Chinese or any other human language. Officials for the Apostolic Faith Church that Parham founded, and which not only survives but operates a two-year Bible college in Baxter Springs, still regard tongues as a sign of the "latter rain," but are less certain than Parham was of its earthly purpose.

At about the time of Parham's death, Anglo-Israelism got a shot in the arm when Howard B. Rand became the national commissioner of the Anglo-Saxon Federation of America.

Rand's major contribution was a renewed anti-Semitism.

Battered by the Depression, many Americans found comfort in the fantasy that the Old Testament was really written about their forebears. The covenants God made with the Israelites continued in full force and effect for white Americans, who were truly the Chosen.

By 1933, Herbert W. Armstrong—a former American Adventist, one of the groups that could trace its ancestry back to the Millerites—had established the Eugene, Oregon congregation that would eventually become the Worldwide Church of God. Through his weekly radio program, Armstrong would introduce millions of Americans to the concept of British Israelism. Armstrong predicted that the "Great Tribulation" would begin around 1972, culminating in Christ's return in 1978.

In 1995, after Armstrong's death, the Worldwide Church of God dropped British-Israelism and apologized for having taught "erroneous doctrines."

The belief continued, however, privately and in small (or not so small) churches. The movement became the glue that held various factions of the far right together, from those who were horrified by Ruby Ridge and Waco to the Oklahoma City bombers to alleged Olympic Park bomber Eric Rudolph. Not all who subscribe to this doctrine, of course, are violent nut jobs. I know a number of otherwise normal people with odd beliefs.

Sheryl, for example, believes that Jim Morrison faked his own death and now lives in Amsterdam, where he occasionally calls into the Art Bell radio show.

But Christian Identity is an ideological lightning rod.

In its most aggressive form, Christian Identity teaches that Jews and other non-whites are "mud people" without human souls because they are the offspring of a sexual dalliance between Eve and Satan in the Garden of Eden. Also, most of these groups preach that a cataclysmic battle between good (the Anglos) and evil (everybody else) is imminent, and that biblical prophecy is in full swing, and that a New World Order led by the Beast is just around the corner.

Okay, if you've skipped down, start here.

One night after Elaine and I had a particularly athletic round of sex in my studio apartment, she was lying in the crook of my arm. I loved the way she smelled. Well, I loved the way most women smelled. With Elaine, it was always like she had just gotten out of the bath and shampooed her hair, no matter how hard she had worked. Even the film of sweat on her body smelled good; it was the smell of life, of not being alone, of having somebody to talk to. I was content. Soon I was staring into the darkness and idly thinking about my research.

"Hey, where'd you go?" she asked.

"Do you believe in hell?"

"Why?"

"I just want to know."

"Do you?" she asked.

"I don't know," I said. "But I'm inclined to think that heaven and hell are really here on earth."

"No afterlife?"

"Yes, in some way," I said, "although I don't think in terms of rewards and punishments. Instead I see it as an endless cycle of rebirth, or perhaps energy that takes different forms. You know, like light being both wave and particle. We're both body and spirit, and according to Einstein's famous equation, we can convert between the two, but never be demolished."

"Sounds very Buddhist," she said. "Or New Age."

"I always thought of it as Gnostic."

"Don't know enough about that," she said.

"Jesus said we must be reborn," I said. "Funny that the fundamentalists don't interpret *that* literally."

"I don't believe in reincarnation," Elaine said. "When you're dead, you're dead. That's it. Back to dust. That's the traditional Jewish view. The world of the dead is an inanimate, unfeeling, unconscious place."

"And heaven?" I asked.

"No choirs of angels," she said. "Comfort and discomfort are simply measured in proximity to God. The desire is to be closer. Punishment is separation. Similar in some small way to the pain we experience, I imagine, when we lose somebody we love."

"A husband?" I asked.

"Of course," she said. "Or a child."

"Or a parent."

Nine

There was indeed a bird in the fireplace, just as the seven-year-old had screeched in terror when she saw the black, unblinking seed of an eye peering out.

I had knelt on the hearth for a better look.

The bird rapped at the sooty panes with its shiny beak, flapped its wings in rage, and became more tangled in the links of the fire curtain. A bird in the house inspired dread, something from the soup of collective consciousness that murmured, *Harbinger of death, messenger of despair.*

"It'll have to wait until we get back," I said.

"The poor thing is probably scared to death," Liz said, rounding the corner into the living room with her hands behind her neck in an attempt to fasten the collar of her dress. "Can't you let it out?"

"No." One of the cats serpentined around my ankles to get a better look at the prospective prey. "The damn thing's covered with soot, and I can't afford to get these clothes dirty. Besides, the cats would have an early—and very messy—dinner."

"Can't you use a glove to carry it outside?"

"I'm not going to try to hold the bird in one hand and fight those fuckers off with the other," I said, using my favorite name for them. I said it again as I knocked the orange female out of the way with the side of my shoe. "Fuckers."

"Watch your mouth. Amy will hear you."

But the girl had surrendered responsibility for the bird to me and was now planted in front of the television, watching cable. *As if she doesn't already hear the word twenty times a day,* I thought. Still, I felt guilty for saying it in front of her—and for not changing the channel.

"The bird will have to wait until later, Liz, unless you want to do it yourself."

"You know I'm no good at those things," she said, and frowned. "Come on; we're going to be late. You know you told your mother you'd see her tonight."

The hospital room was dark and the only sound was the old woman's ragged breathing. *Old?* I thought to myself. *My God, how can I think of her that way? She's only fifty-nine. But look at her. The tired gray hair, the craters around her eyes, the lined mouth. But that's not age. That's pain.*

I sat in a chair at her bedside, watching, and thought of the young mother with cosmetically red lips and dark hair and a bulky brown coat who had walked with me through a carpet of leaves on the way to Washington Elementary School.

I closed my eyes and thought of the house where I grew up, the only place I knew until I married too young. I thought of the holidays there, and how my father would come sweeping in through the doorway on Christmas Eve, home from work at last, his arms filled with presents bought at the last minute. The old man worked at Sears Roebuck, and everything from my underwear to the tires on the Torino had come from there; employees received a 10 percent discount. How sick I had grown of the Ted Williams emblem on every bat and ball glove I had ever owned.

I thought of my brother in a dark green ROTC uniform, his hair shaved close to his head so that his ears stuck out even more, and of nights at the kitchen table that smelled of brass polish. I remembered the night Danny got his commission, and how he had flipped a silver dollar to the first cadet who had saluted him on the way out of the state university auditorium.

I remembered the time Danny had taken me duck hunting, how we had waded chest-deep through freezing water carrying Ted Williams shotguns, and how frightened I had become when pellets from hunters shooting before dawn came raining down in the water around us. Most of the birdshot bounced off the brim of my hat and clothes, but a few stung my exposed wrists. I wondered then what it must be like to have someone shooting a machine gun at you, to take aim, and for the first time I was afraid for Danny. And, selfishly, I wondered how long the war would last.

I was thirteen when Danny was sent to Vietnam. Our mother hung a star in the window, and Dad listened to the news at the kitchen table every morning on a big plug-in radio. I sometimes slept on the hardwood floor of the bedroom, because my brother was often sleeping in mud. I knew myself to be a terrible coward, but in my prayers I told God to take me instead of Danny, if He had to have one of us.

I opened my eyes.

It was all a long time ago, and more than years had intervened. I looked at the calendar on the wall over the hospital bed, with the smiling Jesus and the year in bold black letters, and the fullness of the numbers seemed to mock him.

Liz came in, her heels tapping smartly on the tile.

"How is she?"

"Asleep. The nurses said she had a rough day."

"Are you ready?"

Liz worked at the hospital, in public relations. It was very convenient. She often checked on my mother during the day. I believed my mother had never liked Liz, and although she was softening toward her now, it was really too late.

"I'll be right there," I said.

I took my mother's hand and told her I had to go. She roused slightly, and looked at me through eyes dulled by painkillers. "Danny?" she asked. Her hand fluttered a bit, like a wounded bird, then found one of my fingers and squeezed.

The Christmas party was in one of the hospital's basement meeting rooms, and I breathed a prayer of thanks when I saw there was an open bar. I threw back a couple of Jack-and-Cokes and carried one back to the table, along with a plastic cup of wine for Liz. I seldom drank at home, but lately I found myself using it more and more to get through the day. I hated holidays, especially Christmas, especially this Christmas.

I made meaningless conversation with the others at the table, the people whom Liz worked with, until the meal was served. I had just begun to cut into the tired-looking roast beef when someone placed a hand on my shoulder.

"You're needed upstairs."

Liz started to get up too, but I stopped her.

"Sit and eat your dinner," I said. "I'll let you know if it's anything major."

Her eyes were wide with fear and her breath was coming in tortured gasps as the technicians worked around her.

Something was wrong; she was having some type of seizure, but they didn't know why. I moved to the side of the bed. She held out her hand, wide, grasping. I tried to look reassuring, managed a smile, said, "Everything will be okay," in an even voice. Isn't that what you're supposed to say? Her breathing became shallower and more irregular, her eyes were beginning to narrow, blood was caked on her cracked lips. Her hand slipped back on the pillow.

"Why?" she asked, fighting for the words. "Why am I on TV?"

I turned to look.

There, in the dark convex screen of the television that hung from the ceiling, was mirrored the scene around the hospital bed: I saw myself holding her hand, the technicians, and now the doctor, and my mother with her head tilted back and her mouth agape. Although the television was switched off, the reflection on the tube made it seem as if the event were being broadcast.

My God, I thought, *she is watching herself die.*

By the time I turned back to her, the eyes had already clouded.

"Let's get her downstairs," the doctor said, and they lifted her onto a gurney that I hadn't noticed had been wheeled in. I placed her hand at her side and let go.

She wasn't dead, a nurse told me, but she was in very serious trouble. A lung had collapsed and they had taken her to surgery in an attempt to reinflate it. They also suspected cerebral damage of some kind, because her pupils were not reacting equally or normally.

I sat down, picked up the phone, and had the operator ring the meeting room. As I waited, I looked at the little Christmas tree Amy had set up, and the presents beneath it.

"It's bad," I told Liz.

* * *

Just three weeks had passed since she had called me at newspaper and asked for an ambulance because her back hurt. I knew she had been drinking again because she was slurring her words. I pressed her for details. She said she had hurt her back mowing the lawn that summer and it never got better. She had quit her job at the battery plant a year before, claiming that she was just too tired to work anymore. Not only had she lost her paycheck, but she had lost her medical coverage.

"Can't it wait until morning?" I asked. "I'm in the middle of a story—"

She sobbed and hung up.

I called back, said I'd drive down and talk to her that night. If she really needed an ambulance, I'd get her one. I said it as if I were talking to a child. Then I called Liz at work, apologized, and asked her to pick up Amy and feed her dinner. I'd be home as soon as possible.

My mother lived an hour away and I played the car stereo loud all the way down. Neil Young.

I found her sitting at the kitchen table in her nightgown, a can of Coors in front of her. I sat down, took one of the cigarettes from her pack on the table, and lit it. I didn't smoke at home with Liz.

"What's the problem?" I asked, and knew I sounded smug.

"You know what's the matter," she said. "My back hurts. I told you."

"Well, if you really insist on going to the emergency room, I can take you in my car. But you don't look like you need an ambulance. Frankly, I don't know what an emergency-room visit can do for you that a visit to the doctor couldn't do better in the morning. The ER is for car wrecks and broken bones and people who are deathly sick."

She began to cry. Tears ran down her cheeks as she looked at me; then she reached out for my hand. "Oh,

Andy," she said, and pulled my hand toward her right breast. "It's here."

She parted the nightgown and pulled back the right lapel. The cancer had broken through the skin, a sunken red crater with purple edges. I had to turn my head to fight back a rising column of bile. I put down the cigarette and gripped the table with both hands. At that instant I hated her, hated the way she had shown me. How could I ever again look at any woman's breast without thinking of this moment?

"Why?" I asked. "Why didn't you ask for help sooner?"

She shrugged. She clenched her teeth and rocked forward, sobs shaking her frame. Later we would learn that the cancer was so advanced that it had spread throughout her body via the lymph system, had destroyed some of the vertebrae in her spine, and had been steadily working on her mind. It was the work of years, the doctors would say, and declared it incredible that she could have stood so much pain for so long.

As I waited for her to gather some of her things—we would go right away; she needed immediate attention and something for the pain—I looked around. There was a decade of grime on the walls around the light switches, and the same crap in the shelves that had been there when my father left when I was sixteen. Mice scurried along the baseboards. While she packed I went to my old room and looked at the typewriter that still sat on the bureau. I tried one of the keys but discovered that nothing happened. I peered inside and found an old mouse nest cradled in the keys, complete with tiny mouse skeletons. The items in the bedroom were just the same as when I was sixteen, down to the shelf with the plastic model of the helicopter gunship with the 1st Air Cavalry emblem on the nose. Danny's outfit, of course.

It wasn't a house, I told myself. It was a tomb.

I disposed of the mouse nest without telling her.

* * *

"The results of the CAT scan indicate massive trauma in the left hemisphere of the brain," the surgeon said. He was a short and squat man, with dandruff and bad pores. "There's nothing functioning there. It's simply hamburger."

"Hamburger?" I asked, startled by the inappropriateness of the word.

"Um," the doctor said, ignoring my shock, "there's nothing we can do to repair it."

I looked down at my mother. A tube was in her mouth, and the respirator was alternately filling and deflating her lungs. Her eyes were open, although one pupil was bigger than the other. I disliked the surgeon for his insensitivity, yet I hadn't the strength to object.

"What caused it?" I asked.

"Who knows?" the doctor said. "It was a stroke, and it could have been brought on by the cancer or the stress of the chemotherapy or the radiation. But one thing is certain: there is no higher mental activity there."

"I thought she squeezed my hand," Liz said, crying. "I'm sure she did."

"It's a common reflex," the doctor said. "It doesn't mean much. Basically, she is in a vegetative state."

"So we must decide if we want to disconnect the respirator," I said.

"Yes."

"How long will she last after that?"

"Not long. Fifteen minutes, perhaps. The part of her brain that controls respiration was severely damaged."

"I don't see any point in prolonging things," I said.

The doctor nodded and walked away. A nun approached and asked about my mother's religion. The nun was in her late fifties or early sixties, overweight, with gray hair and glasses, and she spoke English with a heavy German accent.

"My mother did not have a religion," I said, and as I answered I wondered idly if the nun had ever had sex, if she had ever had a man's cock in her mouth, and for a moment I could see a thick, blue-veined member sliding between her lips. I rubbed my forehead, ashamed of the spontaneous imagery. What the hell had caused that?

I was afraid I was going crazy.

"Wait, that's not quite right," I called after the nun. "I mean, she wanted to be Catholic. She never quite made it, never felt comfortable enough to go through with it. When I was a kid, she would drive around to all the Catholic churches in the towns nearby. We'd sit in the back. Told people she was shopping around."

"Do you believe it was her intention to become a Catholic?"

"I think so."

"She told you that recently?"

"Yes," I lied. "I'm sure of it." My mother hadn't discussed religion in years.

"And she wasn't baptized in any other religion?"

"No," I said, but I really wasn't sure.

"I will call the priest right away," the nun said. "This is very important."

I stood at the bedside while the old priest mumbled the words and poured the water on her forehead just above her open, unblinking eyes. The old nun put a hand on my shoulder and said I should be relieved because my mother would be with God forever.

"I'd like to believe that," I said. The room seemed to spin, and I closed my eyes against it. "This is what she wanted all of her life, but now that she has it she's not even aware of it. A loving God would not have denied comfort so long to someone who wanted it so desperately. Would He?"

It took four and a half hours for her breathing to stop after they unhooked the respirator, and by the time the funeral-home had carted the body away it was nearly dawn. I had her watch and rings and partials in an envelope in my coat pocket. Alone, I walked down the corridor to the elevator. I was already thinking of how to pay the medical bills, because Liz and I had guaranteed the hospital payment before they would admit her. Was the house still in my father's name? I had no idea. I imagined going room by room through the house, boxing things up, and the world started again to spin.

I was so numb by the time I reached home that I didn't even bother to go upstairs to wake Liz and tell her that my mother had finally died. Instead I fell onto the couch, still in my clothes, and tried to sleep. But I couldn't. There was no grief, no sadness, only a chilling emptiness. Someday I hoped I could remember the love of the young mother who had walked with me on the first day of school. But not now. Not soon.

One of the cats hissed and jumped fiercely against the fireplace glass, and I remembered the bird. I got up, walked unsteadily to the hearth, and brushed the cats away. I was sorry for treating them roughly earlier.

I parted the fireplace doors a crack and reached with my bare hand. Grasping the bird, I was seized for a moment with anger, and considered crushing it to death, but did not. The bird drove its beak into the web of flesh between my thumb and first finger, but I did not let go. Blood began to trickle down my wrist. With my other hand I untangled the bird's claws from the fire chain. It was incredible the bird had survived so long.

I removed the bird from the fireplace and blew some of the soot and ashes away. The bird had stopped pecking now, shook its head, and blinked several times, trying to comprehend the gusts of air.

It was a sparrow, I decided.

I walked outside and stood at the edge of the porch,

holding the bird up. I could feel its heart thumping against my palm. Blood ran in a stream down my arm and dripped from my elbow to the ground.

"Who would mark your fall?" I asked.

I opened my hand and the bird shot into the cobalt sky.

Ten

The *Arkansas Traveler* building is an Art Deco monster at the corner of Third and State in downtown Little Rock, and after pushing through the revolving door into the cathedral-like lobby, I paused for a moment to wipe the sweat from my glasses with the tail of my shirt. Vision restored, I was confronted by bare-breasted Truth in Italian marble staring down at me from atop the grand staircase.

"Still silent, huh?"

I was beat from the drive back from Texas in the aging *Traveler* circulation van, and the climb to the newsroom on the second floor seemed longer than usual. Along the stairway were framed front pages that went all the way back to the Civil War. I liked the July 21, 1969, edition the best—MAN WALKS ON MOON. The most recent additions, and my least favorites, were 168 DEAD IN OKC BLAST; U.S. ATTACKED: THOUSANDS DIE IN TOWERS' COLLAPSE; and INVASION OF IRAQ BEGINS.

Unlike the advertising offices downstairs, which had been redone in ultramodern chrome and glass and had lots of leafy plants and abstract wall art, the newsroom resembled a warehouse that hadn't been remodeled since the 1970s. The carpet felt greasy beneath my shoes, a long bank of fluorescent lights gave everything a green pallor, and clusters of gray desks choked the room. On top of each desk was an IBM clone that was probably obsolete when the *Trav* had bought them. The walls and columns were painted an industrial shade of green.

Only about half of the desks were occupied, and most of those thirty or so staffers were on the phone or typing furiously. Some were doing both. At least a dozen other telephones were ringing and blinking.

The room also still stank of cigarette smoke, although smoking had been banned at the paper for five years. Also, there was just a hint of chemical smell from the composing room. In the past all newsrooms had smelled strongly of chemicals, mostly from fixer fumes that wafted from the darkrooms, but now all papers used digital cameras.

Electrons are cheaper than silver-based film.

The editorial offices lining the far side looked just as bad as the rest of the newsroom. The walls were covered in that faux-wood paneling that was so popular forty years ago. I walked across the newsroom to the city editor's office, opened the door, and flopped down in Sheryl's favorite recliner. She was on the phone, and she shot me a hateful glance when she saw my collar was open.

"Let me call you back," she said, and hung up.

"Hey," I said.

Sheryl had been at the *Traveler* for twenty years, working her way up from the obituary desk, and even though she had been an editor for ten of those years, I don't think she ever identified with management.

"Where's your tie?" she whined.

"I lost it."

"Jesus Christ, Kelsey," Sheryl said. "You know the policy. They're serious about this, and I'm supposed to be your supervisor. Don't make me write you up."

"You're going to put this on my permanent record?" I asked. "After I won first place in investigative reporting from the AP last month for the series on the serial killer and the missing girls? Do you think a tie would make me a better reporter, a more capable writer, a better human being?"

"Nothing would make you a better human being." She sighed.

"Come on," I said. "You know you love me."

"I tolerate you," she said. "You know what Charlie Daniels said about you this morning?"

This Charlie Daniels, not to be confused with the country rocker, was the Arkansas secretary of state. The South is fond of electing officials who share names with celebrities or Confederate heroes. Every election year, Jefferson Davis and Robert E. Lee are alive and well on ballots from Alabama to Oklahoma.

"Daniels told the statehouse reporter that you were the last of your kind, and that he couldn't wait for you to die," Sheryl said. "Every time you walk into his office, Daniels said, it's like dealing with a character out of Hecht and MacArthur who's been sucked into a time warp, stumbled through the Watergate break-in, and then lands hungover in his office to ask stupid questions about things that happened in the distant past."

"Daniels couldn't have said that. He's not clever enough."

"He thought it was unfair that you mentioned the DWI he got back in 1990 while driving a state car, in your story on his current travel expenses."

"Whenever I piss a politician off," I said, "I feel I've done my job. And speaking of my job, you still owe me lunch at the Faded Rose," I said. "You promised back in April. It's now October."

"I've been busy."

"No, you're cheap," I said. "The whole newspaper is cheap."

"You'd rather be rich than famous? Then you shoulda been a trial lawyer. But, of course, you wouldn't sleep at night."

"I don't sleep anyway."

"Well, it's called belt tightening," she said. "Things have been rough the last few months."

"I don't see the Young Man doing much belt tightening," I said. "That brand-new Jaguar XKR he's driving is worth about eighty grand. And it's registered to the paper."

"Really?"

"I checked at the DMV."

Sheryl blinked.

"We can't even get the newsroom cars repaired."

"Surprised?" I asked, then stole from Fitzgerald and Hemingway in back-to-back sentences: "The rich are different from you and me, Sheryl. They have more money."

"Look, Andy, the rumor mill says the *Traveler* is on the block, and if a buyer can't be found, we'll simply fold. Little Rock might become a one-newspaper town."

"Little Rock already is a one-newspaper town," I said. "What's our circulation? Sixty thousand on Sunday?"

"Fifty, maybe."

"The *Democrat-Gazette* throws six times as many."

"Management is looking for any way to cut expenses," she said. "That means higher-paid staffers like you."

"Why can't it mean overpaid editors?"

Hell, I thought. It was a miracle the *Traveler* had lasted this long, since the *Democrat* (owned by the Gannett chain) had gobbled up the old *Arkansas Gazette* in 1991. The *Traveler* was the last major family-run newspaper in Arkansas, but the *Democrat* had been steadily beating the hell out of us. I figured it was just a matter of time before we too were sucked up.

"Just a word of advice," Sheryl said. "I'd keep a low profile."

I tried my best to look incredulous.

"I forgot, we're talking about Andy Kelsey here," Sheryl said. "Okay, hotshot, tell me what you have from Death Row so I can put it on the budget. Did Slaughter have anything newsworthy to say?"

"Something will happen November ninth."

"What?"

"Another Oklahoma City, the Second Coming, his high school algebra teacher's birthday, who knows?" I said. "He just gave the date. I'll check with my sources and see if it means anything to them. He also said he wasn't sorry for killing Snyder or the deputy, that he wasn't afraid to die, and that the racist revolution was up to the next generation."

"Nothing about Commander Carlos?"

"Not a word," I said. "Claimed he didn't know what had happened to Carlos, but he was lying. Of course, he would."

Sheryl nodded.

"I need the Slaughter story in an hour," she said. "Thirty inches, no more."

"You know I can't keep my grocery list to thirty inches."

"Forty, tops," she said. "I mean it. That's the news hole we have."

I pulled myself out of the chair.

"Kelsey, don't let the Young Man see you today."

"I'll go upstairs."

I swung my black Domke reporter's satchel over my shoulder.

"After that, I'm outta here," I said. "I'm beat, no kidding."

"Have a hot date with Elaine tonight?"

"Oh, Elaine," I said. "I forgot. Slaughter asked her to stay for the execution, so she won't be back for a couple of days. We probably shouldn't ask her to file a story, because she's not there as a public witness, but as Slaughter's guest."

"Elaine's watching him die? No, don't tell me." She put her hands to her face, then peeked through her fingers. "Did she get anything usable?"

I held up a Compact Flash card.

"Vacation pictures."

She snatched the card out of my hand.

"Try to reach Abraham Smith."

"I've called every other day for the past two weeks and asked to talk to Smith," I said. "I leave messages. I've asked for interviews. There's never a response."

"Call again," Sheryl said. "Now go."

Although I had a desk in the newsroom, early on I had appropriated an office in the photo department upstairs, adjacent to one of the old darkrooms, in a room where they used to store the negatives. A month before I came, management threw all the negatives in the basement, then tore the pipes out of the walls to reclaim the silver that had collected in them from decades of photo processing. I covered the gashes in the wall with poster board, discovered the phone on the old desk still worked, and talked one of the technology guys into hooking up a computer terminal. As a joke, Sheryl had scrawled a sign that said, INVESTIGATIVE OFFICE, ALLAN ANDREW KELSEY, BY APPT ONLY, and hung it on the door.

I waved hello to the photo staff as I walked through, then fished the keys out of my jeans pocket and was about to unlock the door to the storage room when the Young Man himself, J. Winslow Westervelt, turned the corner into the photo department.

Westervelt was nearing sixty, but he had always been called the Young Man. His father, Winston Westervelt, had been the publisher of the paper until he died of a heart attack in the seventies. For more than thirty years his mother, Beryl Westervelt, had been the publisher—and, from the very beginning, her husband's early death, combined with her initials, had inspired a nickname: the Black Widow.

As usual, the Young Man was nattily dressed in a respectable blue suit and a red power tie, and he reeked of cheap cologne and Gold Bond powder. When he saw me he stopped dead in his tracks. He took in my jeans, my cowboy boots, the black canvas bag over my left shoulder, and the dress shirt with the open collar.

"Maintenance?" he asked.

"Andy Kelsey," I said, opening the door and swinging it open. "I'm the investigative projects writer. We've met three or four times, sir."

"Um, sorry," he said.

"Don't apologize," I said. "You have four hundred employees working for you. Why should you remember me?"

"Because you sell papers," Westervelt said.

"Glad you noticed."

"You also accumulate more research and travel expenses than any other reporter," he said. "I think we'd make more money if I fired you."

"Ah, but wasn't it nice picking up my awards at the Arkansas Press Association and Associated Press meetings this spring?" I asked. "Think you could invite me along to pick up my own awards next year?"

"Well, the meetings are really for the publishers," he said, then coughed. "But perhaps we could work something out. Do you play golf?"

"Golf is a good walk spoiled."

Not original—Mark Twain.

"It's a great way to network."

"I'll remember that, sir."

"Andy, did you get the memo on the dress code?"

"Yeah, I think I did," I said.

"Then perhaps you could start wearing dress slacks and a tie," Westervelt said. "You know, you are really the first ambassador for the *Trav* that much of our public meets. Clothes make the first impression, you know."

"Can't judge a book by its cover," I said. "My dad used to say that more money was stolen by people in suits with briefcases than was ever taken by people with guns. Speaking of which, there's a rumor going around that the *Trav* is for sale again, and will close soon if a buyer can't be found. Any truth to that?"

"You're direct, aren't you?"

"Kind of why I'm a reporter," I said. "Would you care to step into the office, rather than chatting out here in the hall?"

"Isn't this a storage room?"

"Not at the moment," I said. I pointed to the sign.

"Thanks, but some other time," Westervelt said, and looked at his watch. "I'm already late for an appointment. Do yourself a favor, Kelsey, and buy some decent clothes."

"I like Hawaiian shirts," I said.

"Funny," he said. "You probably don't think I have a sense of humor, but I do. My family says I'm hilarious. But it's hard to be funny when you're the captain of a ship of this size."

"What about the rumor, sir?"

"Don't believe everything you hear."

"Gotcha," I said.

"Wear a tie," Westervelt said. "I wouldn't hesitate to make an example of you. We must put our best foot forward, you know."

"For the prospective buyers?"

He smiled but wagged his finger.

"For our readers," he said. "I like you, Kelsey. You're smart, but you don't know everything. One of these days you're going to become so immersed in a story that you can't get out."

He continued walking.

"I like your car," I called, then looked at my watch.

I had forty minutes in which to file the story.

It actually took me forty-five minutes, because I had to call the number for Covenant compound, and I forgot in which notebook I had scribbled the number. When I finally found it, I knew it would be a short drill:

"Hi, this is Andy Kelsey from the—"

"We know who you are, Mr. Kelsey," a calm male voice said.

"Is this Mr. Smith?"

"Reverend Smith is not available at the moment."

"Is there a number where he could be reached? I'm working on a story about Randall Duane Slaughter, and it's important that I reach Mr. Smith for comment."

"I'm sure Reverend Smith has no comment."

"Are you sure? Because I interviewed Slaughter—"

"You talked to him?" There was a flutter in the voice, a signal that the pulse had quickened a bit, perhaps accompanied by a bit of anxiety.

"Well, yes."

"On death row?"

"That would be the place."

A pause.

"Was Reverend Smith mentioned?"

I thought I had him.

"See, that's what I'd like to talk about," I said.

"Could you submit a list of questions?"

"Sorry, I'm on deadline," I said. "I need to talk to him within the next thirty minutes or so. I've called several times before, with no luck. Are you sure Mr. Smith got my messages?"

"I'm sure," the voice said.

"Let me leave my number."

"We have your number."

"When can I expect—"

He hung up.

"—to go fuck myself?"

After I shipped the story over to Sheryl's queue for editing, I refilled my cup of coffee from the pot in the photo department and walked down the stairs.

There was a man in a suit sitting outside Sheryl's office.

"Allan Andrew Kelsey?" he asked.

"Yeah?" I asked.

This guy had bad news written all over him, from his dandruff-coated shoulders to the tips of his scuffed wingtips. He pulled a narrow court paper from his jacket pocket and handed it to me.

"You've been served," he said, and walked off.

"Oh, fuck," I said.

"I'm sorry," Sheryl said. "He's been here for thirty minutes, but I didn't—"

"You didn't tell me? You let me finish the story?"

"Well, it would just be bad for everybody if I let him interrupt you," she said defensively. "Nobody else could write the story. Besides, it's just a subpoena. Which story is it over?"

"It's not about a story," I said. "I'm being divorced."

"That's a relief," she said, leaning against me. "I thought we were being sued for libel."

"Thanks a lot," I said.

"I didn't even know you were married," she said.

"I didn't know you had to be informed."

"It would have been nice," she said. "I mean, what if something happened to you? Got sick on the job, or had a car wreck?"

"An ambulance is a thought."

"Smart-ass," she said. Then her mood changed. "Oh, shit. Does Elaine know?"

Eleven

I was in the office before eight. I went to the mailroom, found the big postal tub that contained the day's editorial mail, and hauled it upstairs.

If you think you get a lot of junk at home, you ought to check out what a newspaper office gets in a day—envelopes, packages, mailing tubes, newsletters from congressmen with public money to burn, reader complaints about the comics and the TV listings, "news" releases from advertising agencies trying to sell everything from fishing plugs to edible panties, letters to the editor, hate mail to the reporters, and an occasional missive from a nutcake in Oregon who thinks he's Jesus Christ. Two or three hundred pieces of mail in all, and I ended up dumping it all on the floor to sift through.

When Red came in, I tossed God's letter at him.

"For an uneasy minute, Kelsey, I had a feeling I had been replaced," he said, and sat down behind his desk. "But then I saw it was only you."

"You're right. They wouldn't want to waste my considerable talents. Is this all of the mail?"

"Yes. You look like hell. Been up all night?"

"Yeah. Couldn't sleep. Might have something to do with my personal life."

"What the hell are you looking for, anyway?"

"A letter from a dead man."

"I'd like to see the stamp on that one," Red said.

"It's not here." I started scooping it back into the box.

"What were you expecting?

"Something from Slaughter," I said. "Kind of thought he might try to send me a message before the state of Texas sent him to his last reward."

"A dying declaration?"

"Something like that."

"What made you think that?"

"Just a feeling," I said. "The look in his eyes when I mentioned Commander Carlos and the bank heists. I thought he wanted to talk, but I could be wrong."

"We need to talk about Commander Carlos," Red said.

"What does God have to say this week?" I asked, trying to distract him.

Red opened the envelope with his thumbnail.

"Well, He says he's doing better now that they adjusted His Son Eugene's medications, and that he's sorry he got angry and destroyed that airliner in Japan. But he says it's tough being Him, you know?"

I walked over and sat on the edge of the nearest desk. The insides of my eyelids felt like relief maps of the ocean floor. I surrendered to gravity, easing my back down on the cool green surface of the desk.

"For God's sake, get up."

It was the city reporter. He had covered the Little Rock Board of Directors for years.

"This is a business. Would you try to act accordingly? Your conduct reflects badly on us all. You're a disgrace to the profession. If you had gone to a reputable school of journalism, perhaps you'd have a grasp of this."

I leaned on an elbow and cocked a bloodshot eye toward him and his bow tie.

"Absolutely," I said. "Then I could be just like you."

"My sources respect me."

"The city manager jerks you off every day," I said. "Whenever you take a piss, it's in the mayor's handwriting. Have a nice day."

Red motioned for me to follow him to his office.

"Sit down," he said as he closed the door.

I sat and put my boots up on his desk.

"Charming," Red said. "Look, I've been talking to Sheryl about the project you're working on. It seems to me we're spending an awful lot of money chasing something that might not pan out."

"That describes most investigations," I said.

"But we haven't heard much out of the militia movements since nine-eleven," he said. "Most of them have either dropped out of sight or disbanded."

"This really isn't about the militia," I said. "It's about something else."

"The bank robbers."

"Well, yes. I think Commander Carlos is still out there."

"Do you have any proof?" he asked. "Anything we can print?"

"Not yet."

Red shook his head.

"I thought Sheryl and I were free to choose our own projects," I said. "It sounds like you want us to shut this one down."

"It's money," he said. "The newsroom budget is shot."

"Newsroom budgets are always shot," I said.

"I'm not sure I can justify it."

"Okay," I said. "Who wrote the three stories that drew the biggest Sunday numbers and the highest number of hits on the *Traveler*'s Web site during the past twelve months?"

"I know," Red said. "But they were expensive. I don't know if they were worth it, even in terms of the circulation spikes. You're a champagne reporter on a newspaper that has a beer budget."

"That's good," I said. "When did you think of that one?"

"On the drive in this morning, as I was trying to decide how to explain this to you," he said.

"Well, it's better than the one you used in the staff meeting last week, that the newsroom reminds you of a joke about Communist Russia: we pretend to work while management pretends to pay us. But not much better."

"Go get some sleep," he said.

I withdrew my boots.

"How long do I have on the Hinterland story?"

"Take a week and wrap it up."

"Wow," I said. "Make room on the wall for the Pulitzer. I assume I still have a travel budget?"

"No travel budget."

"Okay," I said. "Can I continue to borrow the circulation van?"

"They're bitching. They want it back."

"I need to go to Tulsa. I'll pay for the gas."

"I can't let you do that," Red said.

"Then just let me borrow the van for another week," I said. "Look, Red, I don't even have a car that runs. Maybe you haven't noticed, but I'm broke. Everybody who works in the newsroom is. But this story is important, and I'll pay my own expenses to see it through."

As I stumbled down the stairs, I passed Hoyt Madison, the farm editor. He pushed the straw cowboy hat back on his head and told me he'd heard the news about me getting served.

"That sucks," he said. "Why don't you come out to the farm tonight? Some of the old-timers are coming out. Sheryl's coming, and some of the photo staff. Maybe it would take your mind off things."

Twelve

I went back to my apartment in north Little Rock but still could not sleep. So I sat down at the crummy little kitchen table with my checkbook and the pile of bills for the month.

The situation was dismal.

If I paid the rent, there wouldn't be enough money to pay my cell phone bill, not to mention the credit cards. The ten-year-old Plymouth in the driveway had a bad transmission, and getting that repaired was out of the question. So I wrote out checks for the cell and the gasoline company cards, because I needed those to finish the Hinterland story, and hoped the *Traveler* would cut me one of the expense checks it owed me before I was evicted.

Thirteen

When I got back to work, Red was waiting on me.

"We're wanted up on fifth," he said, and I felt my stomach drop. The fifth floor meant trouble. The publisher never called anybody up there to give them a pat on the back.

The Black Widow's office was cavernous and dark, with overstuffed chairs littering the deep pile carpet. The Young Man was submerged in one of the chairs, a pudgy fist gripping a glass of scotch. McCarthy, the paper's general counsel, was fidgeting with a briefcase on his lap. The Widow herself sat behind the big mahogany desk, her hands folded over a copy of the morning paper.

"Sit down, Mr. Kelsey," she said, indicating a chair.

"Thanks. Nice digs."

"It was my husband's office," she said evenly. "The bookshelves are the same as the day he went home for the last time; the dictionary is open to the same page. *Tendril* to *testimony*. And it will stay that way. Tradition, Mr. Kelsey, is something I'm sure you can understand, even though you don't seem to subscribe to it yourself."

"Well, new traditions have to begin somewhere."

"Indeed."

"I understand the paper is on the block."

The Young Man stood and started to say something, but the Widow held out her hand. Red nervously took a pack of cigarettes from his shirt pocket, but replaced them when he realized there were no ashtrays in the room.

"Do you know what the real tradition of this newspaper is?" she asked, and continued before I could answer. "It is an anchor for four hundred employees who have built their lives here in Little Rock. It is their livelihood and their families' security. I am keenly interested in preserving that tradition."

She paused for effect.

"We are a relatively small newspaper in the scheme of things. We have no chain or massive corporate assets on which to fall back. Given the unpredictable and nowadays adversarial nature of judges and juries, a libel verdict could mean an end to the tradition."

She nodded to McCarthy.

"I received a call this morning from an attorney in Eureka Springs who said he represented Abraham Smith and a religious organization called Covenant Ministries," he said.

"Great. I've been trying to reach them."

"Apparently," McCarthy said. "They are concerned that you will attempt to link their church to this murderer who's about to be executed in Texas."

"They are linked," I said.

"Perhaps," McCarthy said. "But their attorney, one Charles LeMaine—"

"Charlemagne?" I asked, laughing.

"—said they were prepared to file a libel suit if the name of the church is even mentioned in the same story as Slaughter. And I've got to tell you, libel suits are expensive to defend."

"Truth is an absolute defense," I said.

"Truth does not come cheaply," McCarthy said. "At least, not provable truth."

"So I've already been told," I said. "Mrs. Westervelt, are you telling me to kill this story?"

"I'm uncomfortable with it," she said. "How many other churches do we treat in this manner? Is it our policy to target unpopular beliefs for public scorn?"

"I'm not interested in them because they hold unusual beliefs," I said. "I'm interested because these beliefs have encouraged racism and murder."

Beryl Westervelt placed her elbows on the desk, made a tent of her fingers, and pressed her forefingers against her chin.

"I understand," she said. "Mr. McCarthy, please contact this Charles LeMaine, or whatever his name is, and invite Abraham Smith to contact our Allan Andrew Kelsey for comment. If they have any other questions, please inform them we don't include outsiders in our editorial decisions."

McCarthy nodded.

I couldn't tell if Red was relieved or even more anxious.

"Mr. Kelsey," the Black Widow said. "Do be accurate."

Fourteen

Sheryl held a chilled glass of sangria against her forehead and closed her eyes. Even though the sun had set and every window was open, Hoyt's farmhouse was still warm.

I was sitting on the floor, part of a circle of a dozen people waiting for Hoyt to light a joint. One of those people was an unexpected guest: Nicole Westervelt, the Black Widow's twenty-three-year-old granddaughter.

Hoyt brushed his hair away from his face and flicked the brim of his cowboy hat with his finger. "You won't share this with your granny, will you?" he asked Nicole.

"What do you think?" she said. Her eyes looked as if her party had started much earlier.

"Far out," Hoyt said.

"Don't say that," Sheryl said. "It makes you sound like a dinosaur."

"I am, baby," he said. "Hell, this is probably the last time the old *Trav* newsroom staff will ever get high together."

Hoyt took a joint from the cigar box on his lap and

placed it in the corner of his mouth. With a flourish, he lit it with a kitchen match and puffed rhythmically to get it started. On the last puff he sucked the smoke into his lungs and pursed his lips shut, then passed the joint to his left.

Ross Randolph, the paper's chief photographer, was sitting to my right with a Nikon slung around his neck. He pulled on the joint and then handed it to me. I took it carefully between my fingernails and passed it on. As I did so, my eyes met Nicole Westervelt's through the smoke.

"How many times do you suppose we've printed stories about people getting busted for pot?" she asked. Her eyes were swollen. "I mean, aren't you being a little hypocritical?"

"No," I said. "I would be a hypocrite if I said I had never tried pot, or if I condemned people who smoke. I've never done that in print. Besides, when's the last pot story we had? Oh, yeah, that couple who lost their farm for growing medical marijuana for the wife's cancer."

She frowned.

"You don't approve?"

"You go into so much detail," she said. "It's like reading a novel. That story you did on the nursing-home fire, for instance. Was the color of the dead woman's slipper important?"

"It was important. You remembered it, didn't you?"

"Yes."

A seed popped and burned a hole in Hoyt's jeans.

"Shit," he said, brushing it away.

"You're wasted," I told him. "Ross, take a picture so I can show him tomorrow just how wasted he was."

Hoyt held his hat in front of his face as Ross fired.

"That's a classic," I said.

Hoyt offered me the joint.

"No, thanks," I said. "I wouldn't want to be a hypocrite. I think I'll just have a drink instead. Hoyt, you have any whiskey?"

"No!" a half dozen voices chorused.

"Why can't he have a drink?" Nicole asked.

Hoyt laughed.

"Kelsey does odd things when he drinks," he said in a chipmunk voice. He was still holding the joint by two fingers in my direction.

I took it.

I turned back to Nicole.

"My turn to ask probing questions," I said. "How does it feel?"

"How does what feel?"

"To be heir to the Black Widow throne."

Sheryl punched me hard on the shoulder.

"No, it's okay," Nicole told her. "The question doesn't bother me. I know I was born with a silver spoon in my mouth, but I worked hard in school. I graduated at the top of my class at MU. They don't give that away."

"Not even if your family donated a couple of million?"

"No," she said, and despite her claim that such questions didn't bother her, her eyes said differently.

"But you didn't answer my original question," I pressed. "I asked how it felt."

She bit her upper lip.

"Most people do that the other way around," I said, taking an enormous hit and then passing the joint to Sheryl.

"I really don't want to be a publisher," she said. "I mean, if I could choose my own course, I'd be a photojournalist. I am a photojournalist. I know the money's horrible and the hours are lousy, but I don't care. I love W. Eugene Smith and Margaret Bourke-White. I want to fly in airplanes and hang off buildings. I want to do social-responsibility pieces that will make people cry for other people."

"You should go to Hiroshima," I said.

"I'd like to."

"Kelsey did," Sheryl said. "He was a photojournalist when he went to Japan; then he came back as an investigative reporter. Gave up the camera. He also stopped wearing ties for some reason, and it's about to get him fired."

"You were a shooter?" Nicole asked.

"Everybody has a past," I said. "Right, Sheryl?"

"Maybe if we get her really loaded she'll show us her tits again," Hoyt said.

"Shut up," Sheryl said, smoke hissing from her mouth.

"Again?" Nicole asked.

"Sheryl began her publishing career in *Playboy*," Hoyt said. He thought this was hilarious, but he was stoned.

"It was a long time ago," I said.

"It wasn't *that* long ago," Sheryl said.

Nicole looked dubious.

"I'd be a shooter if I had a choice," Nicole said. "But I don't."

"Why not?" I asked.

"My family is counting on me. After I intern in all the newspaper's departments, then I'll assume a role as general manager and become publisher when my grandmother dies. But I'm going to enjoy working with Ross while it lasts. I wish it were longer than six weeks."

"Do what you want," I said. "Get a job someplace else. The paper can survive without you."

"You don't understand," she said.

I stood up.

"You aren't going home, are you?" Hoyt asked.

"Heading for Tulsa tomorrow. I really should try to get some sleep," I said. "Nicole, nice to meet you. Good luck with your career. I wish I could tell you to follow your heart, but it hasn't done me a hell of a lot of good. Been working for twenty years, I have no retirement, and I can't even make my rent this month."

I walked out the door, but I could hear Nicole say through the open window, "God, what an ass."

"He doesn't mean it," Sheryl told her. "He's just had a rough week. Besides, you are going to inherit the fucking newspaper, right?"

Book Two:
Hinterland

Is it a small thing that thou hast brought us up out of a land that floweth with milk and honey, to kill us in the wilderness, except thou make thyself altogether a prince over us?

—Numbers 16:13

Fifteen

The Golden Driller is seventy-six feet from the top of his hard hat to the presumably metal soles of his feet, and he stands with arms akimbo in front of the Tulsa Expo Center. Inside, what is billed as the world's largest gun show takes place every fall, and there are a couple of things you notice right away after you buy your eight-dollar ticket: there's a big state trooper to check any weapons you might have with you for trade to make sure they're unloaded, and there's an equally big sign that says no cameras are allowed.

The expo center is a man-made cave filled with vendors who are selling every kind of legal gun and ammunition available, from a boy's first single-shot .22 to fully automatic assault rifles, such as the ubiquitous AK-47. The automatic weapons are for display only, since they can be owned only by federally licensed class III dealers. They are not for sale to the general public . . . unlike, say, the brass knuckles and the throwing knives.

There is also quite a bit of material that appeals to the hard-core gun show enthusiasts, the culture that was embraced by Timothy McVeigh and Terry Nichols in the months leading to the Oklahoma City bombing.

The show seemed to offer something for all budgets.

For eight thousand, you could buy a Swiss military surplus two-and-a-half ton truck. If you only had a couple of hundred, you could go home with a five-gallon coffeepot that had been converted into a doomsday "water purification system." For even less scratch, there were field surgical kits, military meals ready to eat, telescopic sights, and breakaway holsters in "ballistic nylon." I'm not exactly sure what ballistic nylon is, but there seems to be quite a bit of it.

There was also tons of war memorabilia, including Nazi banners pulled down by American GIs in towns from Omaha Beach to Berlin. The flags fascinated me in a morbid sort of way. When I was a kid, I remember a carnival came to my hometown and they had what they claimed was Bonnie and Clyde's death car, a khaki-colored 1934 V-8 Ford riddled with bullet holes. I had the same feeling about those Nazi flags. They repelled me, although I could not help but touch the heavy fabric, just like I wanted to put my fingers in those bullet holes in the doors of that Ford sedan. Some of those red flags with the bold black swastikas in the white circles were only a couple of hundred dollars, and I found myself actually contemplating buying one—but my sense of history was outweighed by the thought of the Holocaust, and also of all the soldiers on both sides who died because of what the flag stood for. I also remember that Timothy McVeigh had walked the aisles of this very show not so long before.

"I'll make you a deal on that," a man who appeared to be a World War II veteran behind the table offered.

"No, thanks," I said, wondering what the Nazi flags meant to him, and walked on.

One out of every dozen tables or so had a collection of books, and they were titles you would be unlikely to find at your local Barnes & Noble.

Five bucks, for example, would get something called *The Anarchist's Handbook* that told you how to make pipe bombs, nitroglycerin, and napalm in your kitchen sink. The book listed no author or publisher, and a disclaimer warned that the information was "for study purposes only." There was a directory, however, of where you could purchase the chemicals needed for most of the forty formulas in the book; three of the addresses—with telephone numbers—were in Tulsa.

Another anonymous booklet, *Homebrew Dynamite,* gave schematics for rigging detonators and trip wires. But the handbook that I found the most entertaining was appropriately titled *Boom,* and it took the prize for the best first sentence: *The explosion for which I was arrested was definitely impressive.* The book, the author claimed, was simply meant for hobbyists with a fondness for high explosives.

There were also plenty of copies of *Hit Man,* an infamous Paladin Press how-to book (written by a housewife with no prior experience but apparently lots of time to watch TV crime dramas for "research") that sparked a lawsuit when somebody actually consulted it before committing three murders. The publisher eventually settled out of court and agreed to drop the book from their catalog, though there are still plenty of copies available—including some full-text "public domain" versions on the Internet. The case sent shock waves through the media, and the Society of Professional Journalists filed a brief in support of Paladin, claiming rightly that it was a freedom-of-speech issue. After all, the book really was a work of fiction. What if somebody decided to murder his wife after watching Jack Lemmon in the 1965 classic *How to Murder Your Wife*? But the lawsuit was settled after the 1999 Columbine shooting and the mood of the country was swinging toward fear. It is ironic, however, that almost nobody would have heard of *Hit Man* if not for the lawsuit.

Other popular books were *Vigilantes of Christendom: The Story of Phineas Priesthood,* by Richard Kelly Hoskins, and the red-jacketed *Turner Diaries.*

The *Diaries* was written by William Pierce, under the pseudonym of Andrew MacDonald, and has become a field manual of sorts for the extreme right. Pierce was the leader of a white-power group called the National Alliance. The book describes a brutal race war and the violent overthrow of the federal government by white supremacists. It describes how a fictional terrorist group blows up FBI headquarters.

McVeigh had the book in his possession when he was arrested.

The book also influenced a 1980s terrorist group called the Order, which murdered Jewish talk-show host Alan Berg, robbed banks and armored cars, and printed counterfeit money. Bob Mathews, leader of the Order (also known as the *Bruder Schweigen,* for "Silent Brotherhood") sought to overthrow the "Zionist Occupation Government" after tax protester Gordon Kahl was shot by the FBI in Arkansas in 1983. Kahl himself was a Christian Identity believer who had killed two federal marshals after attempting to set up a shadow government in North Dakota. Mathews was also killed, burning to death in a cabin on Whidbey Island in Washington State after a standoff with federal authorities.

I picked up copies of all of them.

Even if I disagreed with most of it, I thought I needed to read the books for background, especially the Hoskins and Pierce novels. The other stuff, especially the anonymous bomb-making manuals, was just so out-there that I couldn't resist. Just wait till I showed the other kids back at the newspaper.

A large woman eating a Hershey bar added up the bill in her head, took my forty bucks and change, then pushed the books across the table at me.

"Could I have a . . ."

I had started to ask for a receipt, because I was desperately short on money and was counting on being reimbursed from the *Trav,* but I stopped in midsentence when I saw the suspicious look in her eye. I'm sure she thought I was some kind of federal agent, because who else would ask for a paper trail?

". . . sack?" I asked.

I had wimped out, feeling like a thirteen-year-old kid trying to buy a *Hustler* at the corner pharmacy. It wasn't that I thought this stuff was illegal; I was just afraid she might ask my name and address for the receipt. For a moment I had a clear black-and-white mental image of torch-bearing villagers chasing Frankenstein's monster.

"Sorry," she said. "We had some grocery bags earlier, but now we're all out. Big morning so far."

"No problem," I said.

"Where you from?"

"Kansas," I said.

"Where at in Kansas?"

"Baxter Springs."

"Nice town," she said. "Don't forget the rally."

"What rally?"

"Patriot rally," she said. "Eleven o'clock."

I asked her where, and she pointed to a curtain along one side of the expo center.

"Does it cost anything?"

"Donation, if you want," she said.

I thanked her. It was only a quarter of ten, so I had over an hour to kill. That's just one of the things that drives me nuts about reporting—you're always on somebody else's time schedule. You're either waiting for a meeting to start, or waiting for somebody to call you back, or waiting to interview somebody when they can spare you the time. Or, if you're doing an investigation, you're waiting for somebody to respond to your open-records request, or waiting for just the right break in a story. If there hadn't been so much weird stuff to see at the show, I probably would have blown off the rally.

But I didn't.

If I had, I wouldn't be writing this story, but I'm sure my life would have been a hell of a lot easier.

At about five till, I wandered over to the curtain and peered inside. A podium with a large black Bible on it faced a hundred or so folding chairs, and an American flag hung in the background. There was a blond body-builder type at the door, and when he saw the books beneath my arm, he gave me a slap on the back.

The blow nearly drove me to my knees.

"Sorry," he said, and awkwardly held out his left hand for me to shake. His right hand was bandaged.

I shook his hand.

"Good man," he said.

A dozen or so widely scattered chairs were already taken, in that curious American phenomenon that demands the maximum personal space around the individual. I took a seat in the back row. People began shifting uncomfortably as others began to fill in the gaps between chairs.

The audience was predominantly white males in jeans and baseball caps, with a few bored-looking wives mixed in. Some folks had brought their purchases with them, and the audience bristled with shotguns and deer rifles. A majority of the audience seemed to be younger guys, which I thought unusual; it had been my experience that it was difficult to force males under twenty-five to attend any kind of lecture that didn't involve a grade.

By five minutes after, all of the hundred chairs were occupied, with more people standing in back. The bodyguard stepped to the podium, motioned for everyone to stand, then turned to face the flag and led the audience in the Pledge of Allegiance. Then he turned, nodded for us to sit, and gripped the edges of the podium.

"Thanks for loving America enough to attend this weekend's Patriot Rally," he said. "How many of you are here for the first time?" About half of all the pairs of hands went up. "Good. That means you're in for a peak spiritual experience. And I'm not paid to say that, because I'm just a volunteer here this weekend."

The audience started to applaud.

"No, please," the bodybuilder said. "Save your applause for a real American hero. And that's about all the introduction for Major Curtis 'Stonewall' Carson."

The applause resumed.

The bodybuilder stepped aside and a rather stocky man in a khaki uniform stepped up to the podium. His hair was prematurely white, although he had the slow-moving manner of somebody who suffers more than his share of aches and pains. His uniform was rather curious, because it did not seem to belong to any particular branch of the service, but was adorned with medals and ribbons, and he wore a Special Operations black beret. I recognized some of them, including the Vietnam service ribbon, the Purple Heart, and the Combat Infantryman Badge.

I had never heard of Carson before, but the audience not only seemed to know who he was, but loved him. When the adulation finally stopped, he asked: "Isn't this is a great country? Right here, right now, we are exercising one of those fundamental freedoms guaranteed us by those wise old white guys so long ago in the Bill of Rights. Those of you who have been tuning in to my Christian Patriot Net on 3.925 megahertz know exactly what I'm talking about. And if you don't, you'd better get your hands on a shortwave receiver capable of tuning seventy-five-meter single sideband and start listening, to counter the garbage aimed at you day in and day out by commercial radio, television, and the newspapers."

Okay, he had my attention.

"Whether you know it or not, we are engaged in a war for the soul of this nation," Carson said. "I know we live in an age where white people are discouraged from being proud of who we are, but let me tell you that I am proud of being an Anglo-Saxon, and proud of being a Christian. It is time to stand up and be counted. How many of you young men out there are having trouble finding a job? Have you ever thought it might be because of the color of your skin, or because of what you believe?"

Now he had their attention.

"You're being persecuted for a heritage you might not even know about," Carson said. "Did you know that Anglo Saxons and other white people of good European stock are descendants of the Israelites, the chosen people of the Old Testament?" He thumped the Bible on the podium. "The promises made in this book are for you. The blood of Adam runs in your veins. We are the descendants of the ten lost tribes of Israel."

I rested my chin on my hands.

Carson went into a rather superficial gloss of the contemporary movement that has become known as Christian Identity, and he concentrated on theories about which parts of Europe account for the lost tribes—the Danish for the Dan, for example—while leaving out the historical context.

Then, after about thirty minutes, Carson was really warmed up. He was preaching Christianity and patriotism, along with some pitches for friends who were selling some bargain shotguns at the show, and the audience loved it. I liked Carson, in many ways, and even though his religious ideas were nuts, what he had to say about freedom of speech and personal liberty was just about what I was taught in high school civics class. Also, this guy had obviously fought in Vietnam, and you had to respect that. He wasn't some armchair warrior urging other people to go out and do his fighting for him; he was somebody who, no matter how you felt about that war, had gone out and fought for people like me (even though I was about eight years old at the time). Every family should own at least one twelve-gauge riot shotgun for home defense, he said, and ought to also consider obtaining a .50-caliber rifle such as the Barrett or the Maadi Griffin, because the rounds they fire were the only ones capable of penetrating the body armor in use by federal agents.

He could have slapped me and I wouldn't have been more alert.

"Firepower is the only thing that governments respect," Carson said. "When you take the lawful right to that firepower away from the people, then there is nothing to stop governments from stripping the people of every last right. They've already taken the guns away from our friends up in Canada. Guess who's next?"

Then he whipped out a blue United Nations flag from his pocket, and the bodybuilder-bodyguard handed him one of those $200 twelve-gauge Mossbergs that Carson had been hawking. He tied the flag onto end of the shotgun.

"You know what this is," Carson said. "It's the flag of the New World Order—the Antichrist. The time is coming when each and every one of you is going to have to make a choice. Will you bow your neck and accept the mark of the beast? Or will you fight?"

Carson doused the flag with lighter fluid, then held up a disposable butane lighter in his fist. I was leaning forward in my seat.

"If you don't fight, you know what you'll become?"

He lit the flag.

The synthetic material burned with a bright orange flame, and dripped sizzling malodorous goop onto the floor.

"You'll turn into this stinking residue," Carson said. "And that's not just my opinion; that's Revelation. 'If any may worship the beast and his image, and receive his mark in his forehead, or in his hand . . . he shall be tormented with fire and brimstone. The smoke of their torment ascendeth up forever and ever.' "

Amen.

Sixteen

When I was seven years old, the place where my friends and I loved to play was the one place our parents had forbidden us to go. It was a ramshackle wreck of a building on the top of a hill on East Avenue, overlooking a slow-moving and rust-colored stream. The old building stood like a sentinel at the western end of a wild two-by-three-block strip of brush and brambles that, for a kid, was a world unto itself. The other end of this wilderness was marked by an old streetcar bridge, just a block down the hill from Washington Elementary School.

The way home from school curved down brick-paved Washington Avenue to a point adjacent to the old streetcar bridge. There was another, bigger streetcar bridge a few blocks to the east, a huge reinforced-concrete structure that walked across wide and deep Spring River in several spans, but we didn't visit that bridge unless we were fishing with our older brothers, who stood ready to snatch us from disaster literally by the seat of our pants should we lean too far over the unguarded edge. The bridge went on for half a mile or so beyond the river, across a wooded island, and finally ended in a dynamited section that plunged into a brush-choked slough.

The bridges were part of the electric interurban trolley that had linked most of the towns across the old tristate mining district with Joplin, Missouri, four or five decades earlier. It was all gone by World War II, however, and what remained were these white skeletal bridges over the area's creeks and rivers.

It was an easy matter to slip under the guardrails that lined Washington Avenue, slide down the grade, and clamber to the top of the little streetcar bridge that was on my path home. The bridge didn't lead anywhere, so eventually we would get bored spitting or throwing rocks in the water below, and we would climb down into the creek itself and follow it west. I say *we* because this was not a place you would explore on your own, but only in the company of one or two of your bravest and best friends.

Because the banks were covered with thorns and vines and poison ivy, it was easiest (and most satisfying) to make your way down the middle of the stream. This was an activity we engaged in even during the dead of winter, and since the water was only up to our thighs at the deepest point, we had no fear of walking out onto the ice, and we thrilled to hear the popping sound as the ice spiderwebbed beneath our sneakers. Sometimes we fell through, laughing at first and then shivering for the rest of the walk home.

Although called "Alkali Creek" in the vernacular (so named, I suppose, because it resembled some of the salt-encrusted creaks in the West), the little creek had actually been ruined years before by the acid runoff from the many lead and zinc mines in the area. It was truly horrible-looking water, ranging in color from yellow to brown. Its surface was thick with scum, and after high water the brush on either side would be stained with an ugly high-water mark. People would also dump their trash from the bridges into the creek, and it would float down and land in the brush, or pool below a small concrete low-water dam. It was sad, because before the World War I mining boom, the stream had been known for its purity and its "healing powers." In fact, the good water in the creek and a nearby spring had been the settlement's primary draw when Baxter Springs was founded on the old Military Road in the 1850s, and the reason Fort Blair was located there during the Civil War. Human occupation along the stream, however, went back much farther; the migratory Osage had a village here before Lewis and Clark, and a trail named for their principal chief, Black Dog, led from the stream to the buffalo hunting grounds hundreds of miles to the west in the Salt Plains of what is now Oklahoma. That, at least, is the historic record, but the banks of the little stream were probably occupied for several thousand years before that, as evidenced by the flint tools found around Baxter Springs, especially along the creeks and the banks of the Spring River. Most of these objects we called arrowheads, even though the larger ones were undoubtedly spear points, and the smaller ones dart points flung by an atlatl, a type of prehistoric throwing stick.

After following the creek for the full three blocks—and finding a flint point, if we were lucky—we would emerge at the bottom of the hillside, with the crumbling yellow-walled structure above us. The foundation was rock, and once you scrambled up that you could enter the building proper. It was crumbling, filthy, and littered with fallen laths prickling with rusty nails. There were also dead bats in various states of decay covering the mud-packed floor. It was a miracle that none of us got trapped in the building, contracted lockjaw from the nails or rabies from the bats, or simply fell to our deaths in the basement below. (When we were teenagers, and while I was on a family vacation, some of these same friends climbed up into an old mine derrick that promptly collapsed, resulting in broken limbs and assorted other injuries. I was sorely disappointed when I returned from vacation and discovered I had missed the adventure.) We were aware of the danger that awaited in the rambling structure on the hillside that we called the "old yellow hotel," but that just added to our excitement. Sometimes we found odd things in the building—bookcases with crumbling tomes, pictures warped in their frames, calendars that bore dates unimaginable for those who had not yet seen their tenth birthdays. Personally, I had a habit of dragging some of this stuff home, most of which stank with mold and God knows what else.

The scariest moment of my childhood came when my best friend, a weird and moody kid named Richard Dahlgren, dared me to climb to the top floor. I did, with my heart in my throat, and had made it half-way across the floor when a rotten board gave way. I was trapped, my foot wedged, unable to free myself no matter how hard I struggled.

Richard couldn't free me either.

Eventually, he ran for home, and came back with my big brother. Danny carefully lifted me out, made sure there were no punctures or broken bones, then cuffed my ears hard so hard my ears rang.

Looking back, I'm not sure that the forbidden was the only attraction for us. There was something else on that hillside, something magnetic, and it may have been felt for generations. Who knows? Can you trust memories from childhood? The old yellow hotel wasn't even a hotel at all. Like most names for childhood things, it was a misnomer.

The building had been erected nearly a hundred years earlier as a brewery, to service the booming cattle trade. An entrepreneur named Ed Zellekin had located his brewery there to make use of some caves in the hillside for storage (there was no air conditioning in the 1870s). But the cattle trade dwindled and then died as the railhead moved progressively west, and by the time Kansas went dry in 1880, the brewery had failed on its own. The building sat unused for most of the years until 1909, when it was given to Charles Fox Parham, who converted it into a seventeen-room mansion and proclaimed it world headquarters for the Apostolic Faith Movement.

Parham, of course, was the Topeka preacher who had ushered in 1901 by watching Agnes Ozman speak in tongues.

After Parham died in 1929, the family continued to live in the mansion, and in 1937 the Bethel Bible School was founded (or rather, reorganized) at the old Parham home. In 1946, the Bible school was moved to East Tenth Street in Baxter Springs, a few blocks away. The school is still there, under the name of the Apostolic Faith Bible College.

Of Charles Fox Parham's four children who survived to adulthood, one—Phillip—stayed on in Baxter and became a grocer and avid treasure hunter. Phil died in 1963, the year before I was born, but I vividly remembering seeing his treasure-hunting legacy along East Avenue and the hillside below his father's mansion: holes dug with a backhoe and left uncovered years later.

What was Phil looking for?

My childhood memories of adult gossip are that he was searching for the Ten Commandments. That was a pretty powerful metaphor for a kid: somebody literally looking for God's law, finding nothing, and leaving unfilled holes in his wake. Why would he be searching in Kansas? Who knows?

From Parham's crumbling mansion and the hillside with the unfilled holes, you could follow the creek beneath Route 66 and to the stump of the old hanging oak a couple of blocks away.

From the hanging tree, if I turned to the north, the street would lead me, after a couple of doglegs, to the modest white four-room house at the edge of town that my family called home. The field beyond the house was where the guerrilla Chieftain William Clarke Quantrill met James G. Blunt in October 1863, killed nearly a hundred of his men, routed the rest, and seized Blunt's ambulance, papers, and sword. Quantrill was on his way to winter in Texas after shocking the nation by killing one hundred fifty men and boys in Lawrence and burning the city to the ground. General Blunt, who was Kansas's highest-ranking Union officer, never recovered his reputation after the Baxter attack, but he did arm his personal guards with Henry repeating rifles in case he ever encountered Quantrill again.

He didn't.

If I turned to the south from the hanging tree, I would find Johnston Public Library in a few blocks. The library was a good-sized brick building and had been intended as the county courthouse, but had never been used for that purpose. Some folks from the town of Columbus had the same idea, and after they refused to release the county records, Columbus became the official county seat.

The library had a wonderful iron-barred jail on the bottom floor that the librarian would let you visit if you promised to behave yourself. In the attic, the library also had a full auditorium, with seats and a stage. In between were a couple of floors jammed with books, and the library became my favorite place to visit, at least until I discovered girls.

You could also approach the library from the other direction, from Washington Elementary School, following the downtown street grid, and if you went just a few blocks out of your way, you would find yourself at Annie & Goldie's restaurant, a joint where you sat on stools and the hamburgers fried in front of you were only fifteen cents. For four bits, you could have a hamburger, a bag of potato chips, and a bottle of grape soda. And, if you were like me, your favorite time was Saturdays in the fall, when you could wear your green rain slicker with the notebook and pen in one of the big pockets, because you were a writer and knew you'd need it for notes when you reached the library. The feeling of leaving Annie & Goldie's with a full stomach, the notebook in my pocket, the slicker's hood up against the mist, and the quiet whispering sound of my tennis shoes on the wet leaves as I walked across the library lawn is probably the best memory I have.

That pretty much described the edges of my world before the age of ten, at least the places that were within walking distance—Washington Elementary School to the south, home to the north at the edge of town, Spring River the eastern boundary, and the Johnston Public Library staking out the southwest.

The library was my favorite place, or at least the place where I felt most comfortable. It beat the hell out of school, where teachers alternately labeled me as learning disabled, difficult, or gifted—depending on whether I felt like playing the game or not. I seemed to polarize teachers. They either asserted that I was "nothing special" and spent their days attempting to prove I had plagiarized my poetry assignments and made up the scientific theories I talked about in class (continental drift comes immediately to mind), or they were convinced that I had some kind of strange talent, but seemed clueless about how to deal with it. The only teacher who came close was a striking blond ex-newswoman who arrived at my junior high school years later in a white Corvette to—and only God knows why—teach English.

When she read the class the first verse of John Prine's "Paradise," I finished it. After that, she encouraged me to write, shared articles on current topics from *Playboy*, and described what it was like to crawl through a barbed-wire fence in Poland to be one of the first journalists to visit the Auschwitz death camp after the war.

I had a hopeless case of puppy love, which I eventually outgrew, but what stayed with me was the way she taught me to look at the world, and how important it was to write about what you found.

A couple of years ago, I returned to the hillside on East Avenue to see just how accurate my childhood memories were. The Parham home was demolished in the 1980s, the caves and other holes in the hillside were filled, and a historical society was erected on top of the hill. The hillside had been cleared, and around the museum was assorted heavy machinery from the mining past. There was also the Frisco railway caboose, an 1870s log cabin relocated from the nearby community of Lowell, and a tank that looked like it might be from the Vietnam era. On the other side of the stream, and on the opposite corner from the museum, was a modest recreation of Fort Blair.

The biggest thing inside the museum was a Civil War field piece that I think used to be placed in front of the city police department. If I'm right, it says MACON 1863 on the barrel. I don't know how many times I stuck my hand down the muzzle when I was a kid.

Self-consciously, I asked the museum curators about the hillside, my memories about the building that sat there, and the treasure-hunting activities of Phil Parham. So, they said, they had not heard that Phil was looking for the Ten Commandments. Seems he told most people he was looking for some kind of Civil War treasure, although he was never specific about what it was he sought. He also had a machine he used in his search, which they assumed to be a kind of military-surplus metal detector.

Then I asked about the caves beneath the brewery.

All filled in, they said, as a matter of public safety. But, they added, strangely enough there were some reports from the Parham children that the cave contained prehistoric carvings—petroglyphs. There were no photographs of the artwork, they said, although a few years ago the surviving Parham daughter had returned and they had made an audiocassette tape of an interview in which she talked in detail about the carvings.

They could not find the tape during my visit, however. They promised to search for it and inform me if they found it, but so far I've heard no news.

Pauline Parham died during the last week of 2003, and was buried in the family plot at Baxter Cemetery, not far from her father's grave. The funeral ceremony, according to the officials at the Bible school, lasted three hours and was one of the biggest local events in recent memory. When I visited she had been buried less than a week, and her grave was still mounded with dirt and an elaborate display of quickly fading flowers.

I had a strange feeling walking around the family plot, noting the names and the dates. There was Phillip, 1902 to 1963, with the Masonic square and compass between the dates. There was Claude W., 1897 to 1941, "Minister." These people had once lived in the house with the dead bats and the tetanus traps. What would they have thought of my childhood obsession with it? Would Phil tell me what he was looking for when he dug all those holes?

What would Charles Fox Parham have thought?

Better, if he could talk, what would he say? Would he defend himself against charges of homosexuality? Would he explain his relationship with twenty-two-year-old J. J. Jourdan of the angelic voice, and what had happened in Texas in 1907? Would he explain what he meant when he said, "I never committed this crime intentionally. What I might have done in my sleep I cannot say, but it was never intended on my part"?

There was no answer but the wind.

Behind, in the far corner of the cemetery, the American flag snapped and popped atop the flagpole at the entrance to National Cemetery No. 2, where the dead from the Quantrill raid were reburied in 1870, after being disinterred from a site not far from the hillside. The four corners of the site were marked by massive black cannon, and in the center was a pedestal-like monument, a date, 1863, and, far on top, a statue of a Union solider, leaning on his rifle and gazing beneath his kepi at the horizon.

Charles Fox Parham's monument is a full-sized pulpit, and it declares Parham as the founder of the Apostolic Faith Movement. It credits his wife, Sarah, as being cofounder. There are photos of both on the sides of the monument, in small oval vignettes, and an open book on top of the pulpit cites a Bible verse.

I had to stand on my toes to read it:

John 15:13.

It is a red-letter verse in my copy of the King James Version.

GREATER LOVE HATH NO MAN THAN THIS, THAT A MAN LAY DOWN HIS LIFE FOR HIS FRIENDS.

Seventeen

The sun was spiking through the trees by the time I reached Highway 187 on the west side of Beaver Lake, and the resulting picket-fence effect made it difficult to read the numbers on the rural mailboxes.

The narrow blacktop wound around a mountain that, according to my map, was appropriately named Rolloff. I had slowed the van enough that I was afraid somebody would rear-end me. There was no shoulder, and it was impossible to juggle the map and consult my notes at the same time, so I pulled over at the first wide spot.

I found myself at the entrance to a gravel path that led into a dark wood. A log chain was stretched across a pair of wooden fence posts. The posts were splashed with ubiquitous "keep out" purple, but this paint was fresh, not sun-faded to a lipstick pink, as I had seen most everywhere else. Then I noticed the white mailbox with the stick-on letters: 784. It was the box number I had been looking for.

It didn't look very dramatic.

I wasn't sure what to expect, but it wasn't this. Armed sentries, snarling dogs, big KEEP OUT signs with grinning skulls, the witch's soldiers and her flying monkeys from *The Wizard of Oz*. Certainly not a quiet path barred by a rusty chain.

I shut off the van.

A whippoorwill called in the background.

It was that time of evening when everything was absolutely still, the light was dying, and there was already a chill in the air. The creaking of the driver's door as I stepped out was thunder, and my footsteps on the gravel sounded like the stamping of wineglasses.

I walked to the chain.

"Hello?" I called. "Anybody here?"

My voice was hollow.

"Is this Camp Covenant?"

No answer, of course.

My eyes had adjusted a bit to the gloom, and at the end of the path I thought I could make out a rooftop, and perhaps the top of some kind of antenna. Or it could have been the tip of a flagpole.

I shivered.

It was the kind of involuntary core-shaking shudder that, when I was a kid, would have made me claim somebody had just walked over my grave.

My cell phone rang.

"Andy, what's wrong?" Elaine asked. "Why are you whispering?"

"I'm at the entrance to the compound."

I walked back to the van.

"Talk to anybody?"

"No," I said, climbing into the passenger's seat. "I can't raise anybody, but I'm pretty sure I'm being watched. Probably just my imagination."

"They've done studies," Elaine said. "People can tell."

"Thanks, that makes me feel better."

I started the van.

"At least you're feeling something," Elaine said. "That's more than Randall Duane Slaughter I is doing right now. He's dead."

I glanced at my watch. It was 6:45.

"Who else was there?"

"For Duane? His mother. Man, was she a wreck. And a preacher. Some guy named Smith."

"Old or young?"

"Youngish," she said. "Thirty, maybe. Kind of a jerk."

"The son," I said. "You okay?"

"Sure," Elaine said. "I'm fine."

"Absolutely sure?"

"Of course I'm sure. I would know, right?"

"Maybe," I said, glancing over my shoulder and then pulling onto the highway. "Was it traumatic?"

"No," she said. "Slaughter was calm, stoic even. He stretched out on the table, they stuck him with the needles, the warden gave the signal, and after a couple of shudders and a death rattle, he was gone."

"Did he make a last statement?"

"Yes," she said. "A statement affirming his belief in his God and his race. It ended with a selection from the Hundred and nineteenth Psalm."

"Really?" I said. "Anything familiar?"

"It didn't register with me, not like the Twenty-third Psalm would," she said. "It was brief."

"Read it," I said.

"Really?" she asked.

"I just want to hear it."

"'I will never forget your precepts, for by them you have preserved my life. My soul faints with longing for your salvation, but I have put my hope in your word. Then I would not be put to shame—'"

"That's odd," I said. "I expected something more dramatic. Do you have a copy of it?"

"Yes," she said.

"Save it for me," I said.

"Listen, I should go. I'm on a payphone in the prison."

"Elaine, there's something we need to talk about."

"Can it wait? I'd really like to get out of here."

Eighteen

The light was good. The sun blazed low in the sky, and its rays washed in through the large windows along the south wall of the nursing home's recreation room. The old man with liver-spotted hands and yellowed teeth sat stiffly in a straight-backed wooden chair across the table from me.

I brought the Nikon F3 to my eye and took a spot-reading from the old man's face. It was good, f-8 at 1/125th. I asked Masami to inquire how old he was.

"And as to your age?" she asked politely in Japanese.

The old man turned toward the sound of her voice, then blinked. "He hasn't thought about it in years," Masami murmured, adding in translation. "'Let us see. This is the seventy-fourth year of the emperor's reign, no? Then I am ninety-six. It is that simple.'"

"Is he sure?" I asked. "That would make him the oldest *hibakusha* of them all."

Masami requested his date of birth, then checked the math on a pad of foolscap perched on her knees.

"He is still reckoning time from Hirohito's reign, but I believe he is correct," Masami said.

"My God, he was already in his forties at the time." I paused and looked disapprovingly at the expanse of tabletop between us. "Help me move this out of the way. I need to get closer to this gentleman."

Masami helped me move the table to one side of the room. The old man sat as motionless as before.

I cradled the familiar weight of the Nikon F3 on my palm and focused on cataract-clouded eyes hidden by thick glasses. The old man was puzzled by the sound of the motor drive. I stopped, removed a business card from my jacket pocket, and presented it. One side of the card had my name and press affiliation in English, the other in Japanese. The old man held it without looking at either side.

"I don't think he can see to read it," Masami said.

"Please tell him."

She did.

A look of disbelief crossed the old man's face.

" 'You are an American?' " Masami translated.

"Yes."

" 'Why should I speak of this to an American, when I have told no one for more than half a century? I am *hibakusha,* of those who received the bomb—those who have been considered unclean, unfit to marry, unfit to employ. Why should I speak of this to an American, when it was America that sent the bomb? Now the whole world has the bomb, and it is my hope that Americans will also know what it is to be *hibakusha.*' "

"I am sorry," Masami said, her cheeks flushed. "Most do not harbor grudges such as this. Perhaps we should move on to our next appointment."

"No, it's all right," I said.

I sat for a moment with my chin in my hands, looking at the old man. The old man looked at the floor to avoid my gaze. Then I reached inside my camera bag and withdrew a stack of proofs, knelt down before the old man, and began placing the photographs on the floor where the old man's stare was fixed. The black-and-white photographs were of Japanese children. I had taken the photographs the day before, at an elementary school, and had processed and printed them in the makeshift darkroom set up in the bathroom of my tiny hotel room.

"Tell him I ask not for myself, but on behalf of these children," I said. "Tell him I ask for those who cannot ask for themselves."

Masami translated.

The old man looked at the face of each child, then glanced away to the window, where across the river the sun was about to set. He removed his glasses and wiped the tears away from his leathery cheeks. I pressed the record button of the miniature cassette recorder clipped to the strap of my camera bag as the old man began to speak.

Masami translated:

" 'On the morning of that day, some of the children were sent with crowbars to clear fire lanes through the city. The older children, those in high school, were making rifles in the factories, but the junior high school students—such as my thirteen-year-old son, Kenji—were sent with these crowbars into the city to make the streets wider.

" 'The city had been extraordinarily lucky so far to escape the firebombings that had devastated Tokyo and other cities, but here the occasional B-29—"*B-San! B-San!* the children would sing"—caused no alarm. Incendiary bombing required flocks of the birds, and before that day a solitary aircraft held no terror for Hiroshima. But it is wise to be prepared, so these children, as I say, were given this crowbar work.

" 'The morning of that day, Kenji had asked to borrow a pair of my heavy work pants to wear while clearing the streets. In the smallness of my heart I said no. Kenji merely nodded his acceptance and set off to his work.'" The old man paused. "'It was the last time I was to see my boy alive.'"

"What did you experience that morning?" I asked.

It was beyond imagination.

"Please," I said. "*Dojo.*"

"'It was a few minutes after eight o'clock, and I was still at home, preparing for my work in the shipyard. There was a blinding flash from the center of the city. Our home was three kilometers away from where the bomb struck, but the terrific wind that followed blew down our house and the heat set the trees and telephone poles on fire. Our neighbors who were out-of-doors were horribly burned and their clothes blown from their bodies. They walked pitifully with their hands in front of them, the flesh hanging in strips from their arms. They were driven insane by the pain and the horror, and they sought out water of any kind to cool their wounds. The dead or dying floated in every water tank and swimming pool, and the rivers were choked with blackened corpses. Those who were close to the center of the city, near the Aoia Bridge, were luckier, because they were turned to dust, leaving only their shadows on the ground.

"'After doing what I could for my wife, who had been hurt in the collapse of our house, I walked toward the city to find Kenji. I have never seen such destruction. Streetcars were packed with dead bodies, and corpses littered the streets. I had never seen people with such wounds. I asked myself, "Are these people from Hiroshima? Do we have such people here?"

"'I saw some children from Kenji's school, and they were in pitiful shape. I asked what had become of my son, and they said they did not know. Later a girl told me she had seen Kenji, burned and naked, shivering at the river's edge.'"

The old man paused.

"'It has been many years now. Those of Kenji's class who survived are old men now, but they are few; many who weren't killed by the firestorm were mortally sickened by the black rain that came. I myself am ancient, and I do not understand why I have been allowed to live so miserably long, unless it is for the smallness of my heart. I have not told this story before, except over and over to myself. And always I ask myself how Kenji felt, dying alone and naked, with his body lost and his soul never to join his ancestors.'"

The old man stopped, and his chin sank to his chest as he stared at the photographs on the floor. Masami, who had very carefully kept her emotions in check during the translation, now hid her face in her hands.

I had not taken a single photograph during the old man's story. I looked at the sterile environment of the nursing home's recreation room and laid the camera aside.

"Ask him," I said, "to come to the river with us tomorrow evening. Tell him it is important for the photograph to be made near the spot where Kenji died."

Masami asked. The old man refused.

We left the nursing home and Masami hailed a taxi. It was a relief to be inside a vehicle, insulated at last, to be whisked down Hiroshima's broad streets by an emotionless man wearing white gloves. We had interviewed sixteen people in twelve hours. We were spent from the day's work, from examining in detail the suffering of those who had lived through the atomic bombing. During the translations, the phrase *it was beyond imagination* kept recurring, and I asked Masami if it was a literal translation of what the *hibakusha* told her, or whether it was her own kind of shorthand.

Masami was insulted.

"Sorry," I said. "I didn't ask the question very well.

The phrase seemed significant, and I wanted to be sure it was exactly what was meant. The imagination does recoil when confronted with what happened here. You've done an outstanding job today of establishing rapport with the subjects, and if my photographs are successful it will be because of you."

"Please forgive me," Masami said. "I too am tired."

I thumbed through the magazines in the vinyl pouch hanging from the back of the seat. I loved the design and use of color—especially neons—in the magazines, and the quality of the photo reproduction. There were the photo weeklies, *Friday* and *Focus*, and a few illustrated magazines—what Americans would regard as comic books, except these magazines explicitly depicted complex sexual story lines, with rape and bondage the predominant themes.

"I don't get it," I said, flipping through the pages. "The Japanese are so Victorian about sexual issues, I'd be afraid to ask a girl here for an evening out. Yet there's this kind of material in the taxis. The phone booths are plastered with advertisements for prostitutes, and the nudity on public television would shock the average American."

"You have never been to Nippon before?"

"No."

"You are experiencing culture shock," Masami said. "There is a logic to the things you point out, although I can understand why it must be confusing to you. There is a very strict dating code here, and that is why the women seem so unapproachable. But there also exists . . . Let me see; what is the term? A 'double standard' when it comes to the sexual freedom of men. Mistresses are not uncommon, and women are treated like possessions, an attitude that is encouraged by the social code. The nudity you speak of on our television is not what we consider obscene, but genital nudity is strictly forbidden. Am I making some sense of this?"

I nodded. "How come you're so open about all this?" I asked. "I've talked to half a dozen people about the same thing, but I've gotten no straight answers. Everyone was polite, but evasive. When I asked the reporter from the *Chugoko Shimbun* about all this, he just smiled and said the police remove the posters from the phone booths at least once a month, thank you for asking. I really feel like a stupid gaijin. Tell me, do you think I smell like hamburger?"

"No," Masami said, and laughed. "Some Americans maybe, but not you. To me you smell like film and fixer and pipe tobacco."

"I've been trying to quit. I'm addicted to this particular blend you can get only in the States. It smells like peaches."

Masami laughed. "Does it taste like peaches?"

"No," I said. "When I was in Tibet, I nearly went crazy because I ran out for two weeks and there was no way to get more in, except by sherpa."

"You have been to Tibet?"

"Yes, to the northern plateau for a story on what the Chinese have done to the nomadic tribes. My God, some of them still use matchlock rifles. I made some good images, but my interest went beyond photography. I was looking for something. Spirituality, I guess."

"Did you find it?"

"I don't know."

"That is a strange answer."

"I've looked in a lot of places, and I find something in each place, but the picture is incomplete. There's still so much left to investigate. Hell, I still have the peyote hunt to do."

"Peyote hunt?"

"Magic mushrooms."

"Ah," she said. "I myself have been searching. Last year I stayed for a month in a monastery in Sri Lanka studying Tantric Buddhism. . . ."

The cab wheeled into the driveway of the hotel, and

Masami fell silent. I shouldered my camera bag, got out of the cab, and fumbled for the correct combination of multicolored bills.

"I will see you in the morning, six o'clock?" Masami asked.

"Actually," I said as I counted out sixteen thousand yen in an assortment of bills and coins, "I was hoping you'd have dinner with me."

Masami hesitated.

"I'm sorry if I have made you uncomfortable."

"No, it's not that," she said.

"Look, in a week I'll be on the other side of the world and we might never see each other again. I'm attracted to you, in spirit as well as in flesh, and if you feel the same way it would be a shame to waste this opportunity. If you don't feel the same way, then forgive me for presuming too much."

At four o'clock in the morning, I sat in a chair beside the bed, smoking and watching Masami sleep. She lay nude on top of the sheets on her side, black hair spilling on the pillow around her. The room was lit by the glow of the lamp on the desk, and when the pipe was cold I laid it aside and picked up the Nikon.

Standing on the chair over Masami, I braced myself against the wall, focused carefully, and pressed the shutter gently for a 1/15th-second exposure.

She stirred and looked up.

"Isn't it real," she asked sleepily, "unless you make a photograph of it?"

"It's real," I said, climbing down from the chair. "It's just that you are so beautiful and the morning is so perfect."

Masami sat up and rubbed her eyes. "Maybe not so perfect after all," she said. "Would you be so kind as to hand me an orange juice?"

I withdrew a bottle from the well-stocked refrigerator

under the desk, opened it, and handed it to her. Masami drank, then pressed the cool bottle to her forehead.

"What do you mean, not so perfect?" I asked.

"It was something I tried to tell you last night, when I hesitated in the cab."

"You're married," I said.

"Yes," she said, closing her eyes. "How did you know?"

"Married women have a certain . . . style," I said. "I am very jealous. Who is he?"

"A photographer, like yourself," Masami said. "I seem to have a weakness for photographers. He works for the *Asahi Shimbun* in Tokyo, and he is very good. His specialty is sports. He does not write as you do, however."

"I understand," I said.

"You are not angry?"

"Of course not."

"But you told me you were married."

"Why should it matter?"

"It is different for women."

"The double standard."

"Yes."

"We have it in America as well," I said.

"I was afraid."

"Don't be," I said. "It does nothing to spoil the perfectness of the moment. We have each other, here and now. Tomorrow? Who knows about tomorrow. It is impossible to guess beyond the moment. So why should I let anything spoil our here and now?"

Masami placed her head on my shoulder. "I am not afraid of spoiling us," she said. "We do not have time to spoil us. I am afraid of spoiling my marriage. I am a bad girl, no?"

"You are a very good girl, and the things you have experienced in your life amaze me. We have been on the same drive for truth."

"Yes," Masami said. "I suppose in any other generation I would have been confined to the house, to raising children and servicing my husband in whichever manner pleased him. But I was fortunate enough to have come of age during a time when the yen was strong against the American dollar, when secretaries flew to New York for weekend shopping trips, and when girls like me could afford overseas educations and adventures of the soul. To be liberated and work as an interpreter and meet fascinating men like you . . . Tell me, aren't you ever afraid?"

"Afraid of what? I asked, laughing.

"The world," she said.

"No," I said. "But then, I've never had to dodge bullets. I was beaten up once, by a cop, while I was covering an antigay demonstration. But I haven't done anything compared to what the shooters went through in Vietnam."

"Soldiers?"

"Well, yes. And these kinds of shooters," I said, and mimicked holding a camera to my eye.

She nodded.

"Will you tell your husband about me?" I asked.

"Of course," she said. "Someday, when I am very gray . . ."

Masami went back to sleep, but I could not, so I sat in the darkness and smoked. I watched from the window while the sky lightened in the east. The hotel wasn't far from the center of the city, where the bomb had detonated fifty years before. Now there was a park there, and in the center of the park was a tomblike memorial in which they placed the names of those who had died, or at least the names of those who had died and were still remembered by others. Some families had perished completely, with no one left to remember.

I picked up the Nikon, and my jacket and tie, and left Masami a note that I couldn't sleep and had gone to the park to make some photographs. Outside, the brick sidewalk was wet with dew. The smell of the rivers, and of the sea, and of the markets where meat and fish were cooked over open fires hung close to the ground. It stirred something in the pool of collective memory—it was the same smell one found in Japan or Tibet or the Yucatan, the smell that characterized civilization.

It was getting hot, and was already twenty-six degrees Celsius. The forecast was for the temperature to hit thirty-eight degrees, or about a hundred degrees Fahrenheit, before noon. Sweat began to form on my forehead as I walked down the broad streets, where traffic was still sparse, and I quickly made my way to the park. Later there would be a hundred thousand people sitting in the August sun to watch the prime minister lay a wreath on the memorial cenotaph beneath the dome-shaped canopy in observance of the anniversary. Now everything was dark and lonely, and the platforms for the politicians blended into the darkness.

I walked to a stone bench a few yards away from the cenotaph and sat down. I took out my pipe, filled it, and fired the bowl with a butane lighter. It was dead calm, and the smoke circled me like a wraith.

The morning was not so much different than it had been fifty years ago, I thought. Clear and hot. People preparing for work or stoking cooking fires to prepare the day's ration of rice. Bicycles beginning to fill the streets. But then the streets were narrow, crowded on either side by wooden homes and neighborhood shops. The streets today were ridiculously large and well paved and very American, a legacy of the ultimate instrument of urban renewal.

Before August of 1945, Hiroshima had been extraordinarily lucky. In fact, there was even a rumor circulating that Harry Truman had a distant relative living in Hiroshima, and that had saved the city. But the truth was that Hiroshima, a city of 350,000 situated on seven rivers—literally, the name means "broad island"—just wasn't militarily significant enough to bother with. That changed, however, when it came to select targets for the work product of the Manhattan Project. The military looked for cities that had not yet been damaged, so they could accurately access the damage caused by this new type of bomb. In that sense, Hiroshima was perfect—and so became the broad island in the history of civilization.

At seventeen seconds after 8:15 A.M. on August 6, 1945, a four-and-a-half-ton bomb nicknamed "Little Boy" in honor of FDR was dropped into the center of the city. The AP was the T-shaped Aoia Bridge, and the *Enola Gay* bombardier's aim had been perfect.

The bomb had been one of two working prototypes that had been built by the top-secret Manhattan Project, and each bomb was of a slightly different type. The Hiroshima bomb was a gun-type uranium device, which worked by sending a chunk of uranium down the barrel of a gun to smash into another chunk, which created the critical mass necessary for the explosion. The bomb that would be used against Nagasaki was a more sophisticated plutonium bomb that used a carefully designed layer of explosives, which were cut into sections that resembled a soccer ball, to implode a plutonium core to achieve fission. Although the bombs took different approaches, both were designed to achieve the splitting of atoms and release the vast amounts of energy promised by Einstein's famous $E = MC^2$ equation—the transubstantiation of matter into energy.

The Manhattan Project had cost more than two billion wartime dollars—more money, it is believed, than had been spent on the whole of scientific endeavor since the beginning of time. At twelve kilotons, the equivalent of twelve thousand tons of TNT, the uranium bomb was small compared to today's weapons, which have multiple warheads of several megatons each.

Modern thermonuclear weapons use fusion, in which a fission bomb is used as a primary device that sets off a chain reaction in a secondary, which uses a plutonium rod to fuse deuterium and tritium, an isotope of hydrogen gas, to make helium—and one very hot explosion. It is the same process that fuels our sun, which is busy turning hydrogen into helium and other products, such as sunlight.

The Hiroshima bomb exploded eighteen hundred feet above where I now sat. All of those who turned to look at the brilliant flash were blinded, most of them felt their internal organs being ruptured and cooked, and others who were nearer to ground zero were simply vaporized. Even those who entered the city as much as four days after the blast died. The radiation killed them slowly, and nobody knew what the sickness was. The American military quickly claimed that reports of a mysterious disease lingering after the bombing was a Japanese attempt to provoke sympathy.

In all, nearly 140,000 people died in Hiroshima between August and the end of 1945. Casualties in Nagasaki weren't as severe—only seventy thousand—but the strike on Nagasaki had been as flawed as Hiroshima's had been technically perfect. The second bomb had originally been scheduled to be dropped on Kokura, but bad weather caused Nagasaki to be selected as an alternate target. Smoke from nearby forest fires had obscured the aerial view of Nagasaki on August ninth, and the bomb missed its aim point—the Mitsubishi naval yards—and landed instead beyond a hill, in the largest Catholic community in all of Japan. Ground zero was an elementary school. The hill shielded Nagasaki (and the shipyards), but the Catholic community was obliterated.

Something flitting from tree to tree in the mist brought me out of my ruminations. The amorphous figure emerged from the palms and advanced across the flagstones toward the ground zero memorial. Other figures were also moving through the trees, and for a moment I was confused. *What the hell?* I asked myself. *Ghosts?*

As the figure approached the cenotaph, it became clear that it was an old woman in a long white robe. White was the Buddhist color for mourning. She knelt and bowed, then lit a stick of incense and placed it upright in a sand-filled pot in front of the memorial. Then others came one at a time, bowing and praying and leaving burning incense in memory of their dead.

By the time the sun was above the trees, the mourners, like the mist, had vanished.

I avoided the ceremony, having little tolerance for either crowds or politicians, and instead Masami and I walked slowly through the A-Bomb Museum. I looked at the full-scale mock-up of the bomb, saw the five photographs taken that day—including one of a group of burned and ragged survivors huddled on a bridge—and stared through glass at a charred school uniform that had been taken from the body of a child.

We signed our names in the visitor's log. On the opposite page, we noticed the signature of a corporal who had visited from the U.S. airbase at Iwakuni, not far from Hiroshima. *We would do it again if we had to,* the soldier had remarked. *My country right or wrong.* In reply, I wrote, *H. G. Wells said that human history has become a race between education and catastrophe.*

Later we sat on the steps outside.

"I don't know what the point of this is," I confessed. "I can't get a grip on this story; I don't know what it is that should be told through my photographs. How can one possibly convey what happened here fifty years ago?"

Masami held my hand.

"You know the Nobel Peace Prize?"

"Of course," she said.

"You know what inventor Alfred Nobel's other contribution to humanity was?" I asked. "Dynamite. The Nobel family was in the business of inventing underwater mines, torpedoes, and other weapons."

"Ironic," she said.

"I'm sorry," I said. "This story is really getting to me. Whole families wiped out. I guess I'm feeling guilty."

"For being an American?" Masami asked. "Don't be. Look at what my country did to China, to Malaysia, to the Philippines—millions dead. Look what we did to Korea. My God, we shipped their women here to be prostitutes. And you know how the Japanese military treated prisoners of war."

"A Japanese apologist?"

"Of course," she said. "My grandfather was an officer in Manchuria. I have no illusions about what he did. But look how far we've come in two generations. In one generation, in fact. My father is a businessman, which afforded me a university education. All due to having lost the war and adopting a U.S.-framed democratic constitution and a free economy."

"Pax Americana," I offered. "We're all really at the mercy of our circumstances, aren't we? If things had turned out a little differently, perhaps you would be visiting California and I would be translating as you interviewed bomb survivors in, say, Oakland."

"The Man in the High Castle," she said, referring to the Philip K. Dick novel.

"Something like that."

"It's the book they should have made into a movie first," she said. *Blade Runner* had come out a few years before.

"I'm tired," I said. "All the photographs I have taken in my career, and all the misery they depict. I don't know anymore if it actually does raise the collective conscious or if it simply celebrates violence. I'm too close to judge. And I figured this assignment would be a nice break, out of the desert and away from the jungle. Sleep in nice hotels and talk to polite, unarmed people. Instead I've gotten a glimpse of what the end of the world looks like. Those photographs inside the museum, the five that were taken that day—I can't imagine what it must have been like for that photographer."

"Why don't you ask him?" Masami suggested.

"He's still alive?"

"Of course," she said. "Soda-*san* lives here in Hiroshima."

"He didn't die from the radiation poisoning?"

"No. Not everyone did, you know. They don't know why, but Soda-*san* didn't even get sick. He's seventy-five years of age, but is still in quite good shape."

"All of this has made me realize how incredibly precious and unpredictable life really is, and how fragile relationships are," I said.

"Life and freedom are rare gifts," she said, "but so are death and responsibility. What counts is what we make of them. You should not despair, Allan Andrew Kelsey. You count for more than you know."

We walked together from the outskirts of the city, from where Yoshiro Soda still made his home, toward the center of the city. Soda was a small man, barely coming up to my chin, but he was animated and quite pleased that an American photographer had come to ask him about that day. Masami, sandwiched between us, kept up a running translation.

Soda wore a 1960s Nikon F around his neck, but then, he said, he had carried a 6×6 Mamiya and two rolls of film—enough for twenty-four exposures. But he could bring himself to make only the five photographs. The first two were taken on the street outside his house, which had been blown down by the blast. They showed little more than a smoldering pile of rubble. Being employed as a photographer for the *Chugoko Shimbun* newspaper, he naturally started walking toward the center of the city, where the big, black, mushroom-shaped cloud had risen. Halfway there he took a photograph of a policeman with a bandage around his head. He showed them the spot where the photograph was taken.

The farther he went, Soda said, the more his mind recoiled at what had taken place. Never had he seen such destruction; never had he seen so many corpses. There were bodies floating in the river; there were bodies on the sidewalk; there were bodies packed into the trolley cars. It was beyond the imagination, Soda said. He finally stopped at the last bridge before entering the heart of the city.

"This is the bridge?" I asked after we had walked for nearly thirty minutes. It was hot and we all were sweating. The bridge we were approaching looked very old, and no longer carried traffic. There was a construction fence around it, and a large orange sign.

"Yes," Masami said. "This is it. The sign says that the bridge is being demolished to make room for a new bridge. It is a good thing you came when you did. This will not be here another month."

The gate on the construction fence was locked, but there was slack in the chain and Soda easily squeezed through. I managed to get through with only a rip in my jeans.

As I held the chain, Masami folded her arms and ducked demurely through.

"Is this safe?" she asked.

"We'll be careful," I promised.

"Photographers." She sighed.

Masami walked with us to the center of the bridge. I was shooting photographs as Soda described what he saw that day, while Masami translated.

There was an odd line of thought running through my

head as I stood on the bridge. *What is the nature of light? Is it wave or particle? Why does it appear to change according to the method used to observe it?*

With a sweep of his hand, Soda described the scene that confronted him that day. There was a group of junior high school students standing huddled on the bridge. They had been helping clear fire lanes through the city, and they all had been severely burned. They held their arms stiffly in front of them, their smoldering flesh hanging in strips, and they were crying for relief. A policeman was standing in the middle of the group, crying, pouring cooking oil—the only thing he could find—over their burns.

Soda then heard the most pitiful moans of all, and he looked over the rail, and on the riverbank beneath the bridge was . . .

Masami paused briefly, although Soda continued.

"What is it?" I asked. "What did he see?"

"A naked and severely burned child, obviously near death," she said. "He could not tell if it was a boy or girl. Soda brought the camera up to his eye and was suddenly ashamed at having even thought of making a photograph."

"What are the odds?" I asked.

"There were hundreds of dying children in this area," Masami answered.

Soda had stopped talking and was watching our faces with concern. He asked Masami if anything was wrong.

She apologized and urged him to continue.

"'I should have climbed down the riverbank and stayed with the child while it died, but I was too frightened. Death was all around. So I left someone's child to die alone, and from that moment I have carried the weight of it. With tears brimming in my eyes and nineteen unexposed frames of film remaining in my camera, I walked back home in shame.'"

We were at the far end of the bridge, and I was using a

200mm lens to come in close on Soda's face. Soda was weeping. In the background, where the policeman had poured cooking oil over the burns fifty years ago, there was a pachinko parlor, which is a type of pinball arcade. The facade of the building was dominated by a billboard-sized painting of the Statue of Liberty.

I had my photograph, and I offered Soda one of the few Japanese phrases I knew: *"Domo arrigato." Thank you very much.* As we walked back across the bridge, I stopped and looked over the railing at the riverbank below.

Nothing but mud and stones there.

I slung my Nikon over my shoulder, then hooked a forefinger behind the knot of my necktie. I tugged until it came free.

I weighed the tie in my hand. It was blue-and-silver striped.

"What's wrong?" Masami asked. "Too hot?"

"No," I said. "Tell me, what did all of the men that caused this have in common?"

"You mean the bomb?" she asked.

"The wars, the bombs, the atrocities," I said. "Every goddamned thing. What have all military officers and politicians and the scientists and the captains of industry on all sides worn since at least Victorian times?"

"Neckties," she said.

I flung the tie off the bridge.

It fluttered down, twisting in the breeze, and landed limply in the water.

Nineteen

I picked up Highway 62 and headed east toward Eureka Springs. I was unlucky enough to get stuck behind a motorhome with Nebraska plates whose driver seemed to be stricken with a deadly fear of plunging down a mountainside, so I saw mostly brake lights for the next twenty minutes.

It was full dark when I reached town.

I pulled into the first motel I liked, an old tourist court tucked into a curve along East 62. The old motel reminded me of my childhood vacations. As I slid my credit card across the counter, I thought about how much things had changed. My father had never used a credit card on those vacations; now you couldn't even check into a motel without one. I was given the keys to cabin number six, just behind the office.

The cabin was chilly. There was an old-fashioned gas heater in the bathroom, and since I was planning on taking a bath before I crashed, I lit it. There was an avocado dial phone on the desk, and it took me what seemed like several months to place a call on my phone card.

"Hello," Elaine's voice said. "Sorry, you've got my machine. Leave a message."

I didn't. I knew she would be on the road until long after midnight, but I just wanted to hear her voice.

To keep from being left alone with my thoughts, I turned on the television. I found CNN and turned the volume down to a murmur. Still, news that the terror alert had been elevated to orange seeped through.

After taking my shower, I felt somewhat better.

Some blond gal on CNN was still talking about the elevated alert, and what the Department of Homeland Security was recommending that Americans should do:

"Exercise caution when traveling, pay attention to travel advisories," she said. "Review your family emergency plan and make sure all family members know what to do. Be patient. Expect some delays, baggage searches and restrictions at public buildings. Check on neighbors or others who might need assistance in an emergency."

She wasn't finished yet.

"Review stored disaster supplies and replace items that are outdated," she said. "Be alert to suspicious activity and report it to proper authorities. Develop a family emergency plan, share it with family and friends, and practice the plan. Also, Homeland Security Director Tom Ridge is again advising that every American family should have several rolls of duct tape and plastic sheets on hand to create a family 'safe room.'"

She said Ridge had again shrugged off criticism, and maintained that duct tape was a perfectly rational defense. Cut to a shot of Ridge at a podium:

"Obviously, I think there's been some political belittling of duct tape," he said. "But the Centers for Disease Control and other professionals will tell you that duct tape and a secure room and a couple of gallons of water to tide you over for a day or two is precisely what you might have to do in the event something occurs. And I don't worry so much about the negative commentary from elected officials, because I think most Americans get it."

"Most Americans are scared shitless," I muttered. "And based on what? What in hell is a 'credible' but non-specific threat? A bad case of the jitters? A disturbance in the force? Voodoo intelligence? Or does the administration just want to scare the hell out of everybody so badly that they won't dare vote against an incumbent?"

I flipped through the channels and found a rerun of 1964's *Zulu* on AMC. Nigel Green was telling Jack Hawkins, the hysterical preacher locked in the camp jail, to be a good fellow and to not frighten the chaps.

Twenty

I woke up before dawn and couldn't get back to sleep—not something I was used to. So I got up, kick-started the heater in the bathroom, showered, and shaved. I dressed in clean jeans, a fresh dress shirt, my dark jacket, and the usual cowboy boots. I called the desk to ask where the nearest restaurant was, but there was no answer. Guess it was still too early.

So I walked up to the side of the highway, looked around, and discovered a Best Western with a restaurant across the street. There was not much traffic yet, so I strolled across the highway.

It was downright cold that morning, and I was glad to reach the motel restaurant, where I was led to a table, declined the usual Ozark breakfast buffet, but ordered some toast and coffee.

I took out my notebook and started to write Elaine a letter. I must have made six starts, and then crossed them all out. What could I say? I slid the notebook aside and ate my eggs. Then I asked for a local phone book.

I jotted down the phone numbers and addresses for the local newspaper and the Carroll County Sheriff's Department. I was surprised that the county seat was in Berryville, a few miles to the east, because I thought Eureka Springs had a courthouse downtown. Since I despise people who talk on cell phones in restaurants, I waited until I had paid and stepped into the restaurant lobby before taking out my cell phone.

I dialed the number.

"Hi, this is Andy Kelsey from the Little Rock *Traveler*," I said. "Could I speak to the sheriff, please?"

"Sheriff isn't in," the dispatcher said.

"Can you tell me when to expect him?"

"Don't know," she said.

"It's important that I talk to him."

"All I can do is take your number," she said.

I gave her the cell number and she disconnected.

"Great," I said. Then I caught the eye of the cashier. "Excuse me, could you tell me if the local newspaper is a morning or afternoon paper?"

"Which newspaper?" he asked. "There's a couple."

I named the one I had the number for.

"Afternoon."

I consulted my notebook, then dialed the paper. I asked the receptionist for the news department, and after the phone rang a dozen or so times somebody answered.

"Barbara Bell."

"Hi, Barbara. This is Andy Kelsey, and I'm an investigative writer for the *Traveler.* I'm doing a story in connection to the Covenant compound, and I was hoping you could spare twenty minutes to share some background with me."

"I don't know what I could tell you," she said. She sounded very young. "I don't think we've ever done a story on them. They are out of town and we just carry a lot of, you know, municipal news and photos."

"I just want a local perspective," I said. "Whenever I'm doing an out-of-town story, I always pay a visit to the local newspaper."

"Sure, I'd be happy to talk to you," she said. "How about tomorrow afternoon?"

"Sorry, but I'm only in town for the day," I said.

"Gosh, I've got a pretty heavy day," she said.

"How about lunch?"

"I have a Rotary Club meeting. Or maybe it's Kiwanis. Lord, I forget. Before that, I have to cover a press conference in Basin Park for a local artist who's been charged for growing marijuana to treat his multiple sclerosis. It's turned into kind of a big deal."

"This afternoon?"

"I have an early deadline," she said. "But, you know, I might have a few minutes before the thing at Basin Park. I could meet you there, say, nine forty?"

"Great," I said. "That's the park downtown, right? See you there. I'm wearing jeans, a dark jacket, and cowboy boots."

The traffic was heavier now, so I darted back across the street. It was not yet eight o'clock, so I packed and threw my stuff into the van, then went back into the cabin. I sat at the little desk, steeled myself, got out my calling card, and dialed Elaine's number. Some conversations you just don't want to have on a cell.

"Schaeffer Stone."

"Glad you made it back safe."

"Andy," she said. "Where are you?"

"Still in Eureka Springs."

"When are you coming back?"

"Tonight," I said. "I've got a few stops to make today. I'm trying to get a line on the Covenant compound. Should be back by eight o'clock, if you're up for a late dinner."

"Sure," she said. "I got kind of a strange order today. I'll tell you about it when you get here."

"Elaine, I've got something to tell you," I said. I supposed I should have waited until dinner, but I just wanted to get it over with. "My wife filed for divorce."

Silence, except for the usual bad long-distance connection sounds. Static, and very far off in the background, another conversation bleeding through.

"Say that again," she said finally.

"My wife filed for divorce," I said.

"That's what I thought you said," she said. "So you're married?"

"Technically," I said.

"Is that like my husband is technically dead?" she asked. "Or, perhaps, like being technically blind or technically guilty?"

"Okay," I said. "I should have said 'legally.' Yeah, I'm legally married. We don't live together anymore, but—"

"Still man and wife."

"Yes."

"Anything else you'd like to tell me?" she asked. "Any felonies in your background? Better yet, any violent crimes you haven't been convicted of? Serial killings?"

"No," I said.

"And I'm supposed to believe you?" she asked. "And what about all of this shit about searching for the truth in your career? I thought all reporters had was their credibility. What kind of credibility do you suppose you have with me, Andy?"

"Not much," I conceded.

"Children?" she asked. "Are there children?"

"Yes."

"Oh, Andy," Elaine said. "How many?"

"One. A girl. Amy. She lives with her mother in Overland Park."

"How old is she?"

"Thirteen."

"How long have you been married?"

"Fourteen years."

"You sonuvabitch," she said. "You know my religion takes a rather dim view of this sort of thing, don't you?"

"I didn't think you were religious."

"Oh, shut up," she said. "She filed against you? Do you want this?"

"It's complicated," I said.

"I'm sure it is."

"She filed it here, because Arkansas is a fault divorce state and there are advantages, for her."

"What are the grounds?"

"Adultery," I said.

Another one of those grueling long-distance pauses.

"So," she said. "I can expect to be called as the other woman in your divorce trial. Some lawyer is going to put me on the stand and ask me whether I slept with a married man. My answer is going to make me look like a fool and make you look worse."

I didn't answer.

"You don't know what this does to me," she said. "How could you not mention that you were married and had a child?"

"It started as fun, remember?" I said defensively. "That's what you said. Then, when things got serious, I didn't know how to tell you. I didn't think about it that much, really. And we haven't known each other that long."

"Six months," she said. "Not long in geological time, is it?"

"Calm down," I said. "We can talk over dinner."

"No, I don't think so."

"What do you mean?"

"I don't want to see you, Andy."

"For how long?"

"About the middle of the next ice age."

Twenty-one

It didn't sink it at first, of course. Because I'm a guy, I slammed the receiver down, even though I knew it was my fault. Anger is always good to keep you from thinking about the implications of your actions, and after I slammed down the phone I was seeing red and hearing rivers rushing in my ears.

An hour later I was still mad, but had calmed enough to check out of the motel, head downtown, and find a place in one of the five-dollar stalls to ditch the *Trav* van. I walked over to Basin Park, where not much was happening yet. I dropped a few dollar bills in the open instrument cases of a half a dozen buskers working the park, then crossed over and walked up the east side of Spring Street. I was feeling some pressure, and my goal was a tobacco shop I knew was up by the post office. Perhaps I would buy some roll-your-own cigarettes, or some cigars, or perhaps a pipe and some tobacco. Anything you could light and inhale. I hadn't smoked in years, but this morning in Eureka Springs the urge had come back strong.

The street was already busy, and I found myself turning my shoulders sideways to pass the tourists who were standing flat-footed on the stone sidewalks to gawk at the merchandise in the shops. There must have been some kind of biker event in town that weekend, because there were a couple dozen nice Harleys thumping their way up the street, frustrated by the same motor home with Nebraska plates that had given me so much trouble the day before. If he continued the way he was going, he would soon reach a turn that he wouldn't be able to maneuver the trailer around.

The stone sidewalks had been hosed off in preparation for the day's business, and they felt clean beneath the soles of my cowboy boots. Also the washing probably contributed some feel-good negative ions. As I passed an art place called Satori Arts, a blonde sitting on a stool just inside the door called out to me.

"December," she said.

I stopped.

"Say again?"

"I'm right, aren't I?"

"About what?"

"Your birthday."

I walked into the shop. It was one of those upscale galleries that sold jewelry, paintings, and sculpture.

"Tell me I'm right," she said.

"You're right," I'm said.

"Really?"

"No," I said.

"Damn," she said.

This woman on the stool was older than me by more than ten years—in other words, she might have been fifty—but she had wonderful tan skin and a terrific golden mane of unkempt hair. She was also dressed in layers of linen, which gave her a kind of angelic appearance, and her smile was seraphic.

"I'm close, though," she said, her eyes narrowing. "I know you're a Sagittarius. So you were born in November."

"Okay, you guessed it," I said. "But you had two swings. That brings the chances down to what, one in six? Not bad odds for guessing."

"I didn't guess," she said. "I knew."

"Another street magician?"

I turned to walk out.

"I'm not a magician," she said. "I'm an astrologer. I knew you were a Sagittarius when you walked past. It's written all over your face. And you're carrying your burden on your shoulders. Man, what are you dealing with?"

"Nothing I can't handle."

"Keep that up and you'll destroy yourself," she said.

"I thought you needed a bunch of information to do a reading," I said. "You know, exact place and time of birth. The year?"

"I do," she said. "Where were you born?"

"Baxter Springs. It's in Kansas."

"What time?"

"Four thirty in the morning," I said.

"Year?"

I hesitated.

"Come on, don't be one of those guys who is sensitive about how old they are," she said. "You're just a kid compared to me. Besides, age is a state of mind, an illusion."

"Maya?"

"Exactly."

"Nineteen sixty-four."

"Good year," she said.

"You don't know my birthday," I said.

"November 30."

Had I told her that? I couldn't remember.

"Is this going to cost me something?"

"Yep," she said. "Thirty bucks. Can you handle that?"

I shook my head and began to walk out.

She was off her stool, had crossed the room, and had placed her hand on my arm. "You don't know how badly you need me right now."

I looked at her. Her green eyes sparkled. Her skin smelled like vanilla.

"For thirty bucks, I'd better get laid."

"Sorry, I can't help you with that," she said. "Don't you masturbate? That should help."

"Sorry," I said. "This is way too personal."

"You brought it up. Lunch? How about the Basin Block Café, right down the street? Can't miss it. Say, eleven?"

"Can you make it eleven thirty?"

"See you then," she said, and hugged me.

I walked on, not sure of what had just happened.

I found the tobacco store, inhaled the aroma for a while, and decided I liked the smell better than I liked smoking. I ended up buying a five-dollar plastic bag of peach-scented tobacco and slipping it into my jacket pocket.

I walked back to Basin Park and chose a bench in the sun to wait for Barbara Bell. It was warmer now. I still had a lot of time to take in the buskers and distribute a few more dollars in the instrument cases.

A van from KARK Channel 4 in Little Rock rolled past on Spring Street, obviously looking for a place to park. A few minutes later a crisp-looking young reporter in a tie and a bored cameraman with a tripod slung over his shoulder appeared. While I was watching them, Barbara Bell had come up behind me.

"Andy Kelsey?" she said.

I stood.

We shook hands; then she sat on the bench next to me. She was a large woman, but not fat—just very muscular and large-boned. She was not quite as young as she had sounded on the phone, but almost.

"What would you like to talk about, Mr. Kelsey?"

"As I said, I'm doing a story in connection with the Covenant compound on Beaver Lake. Whatever you could tell me in terms of background would be very helpful."

I took out my notebook and uncapped my pen.

"A story in connection with the camp?" she asked, and smiled nervously. "Does that mean a story about the camp, or a story you just don't want to tell me about?"

"I'm an investigative reporter," I said. "I'm doing a story that the folks at the Covenant compound won't like very much, and part of it has to do with the execution of Randall Duane Slaughter and a group of bank robbers who called themselves the Aryan Republican Army."

"ARA," she said. "Thought those guys were out of business."

"I'm not so sure," I said.

"What can I help you with?"

I opened my notebook. "Some nuts-and-bolts stuff, first," I said. "I called the sheriff's office, and they were not exactly what you would call helpful. What's the sheriff's story?"

"Orval Clark? He hates everybody," she said. "He lost the Republican primary, so he's a lame duck until the new sheriff takes office in January. He's also a real sonuvabitch, if you'll pardon me."

"You're excused," I said.

"Clark is a throwback to the bad old days of law enforcement," she said. "I hate dealing with him, but I'm thankful he spends most of his time in Berryville."

"There's not a courthouse here?" I said. "I thought the building down by the city offices was the courthouse for the western district of Carroll County, or something like that."

"The county shares the building with the city," she said. "The only reason there is a county office here is because of all the marriage licenses they sell. The only place that sells more licenses, they say, is Las Vegas. But if you want to visit the sheriff or conduct any other county business, you have to go to the county seat at Berryville."

"Got it," I said. "Ever any trouble at the Covenant compound?"

"Not that I'm aware of," she said. "The Covenanters keep to themselves. They pay in cash. They generally avoid the city proper because it has become just too liberal for them. You probably know that Eureka Springs has become the New Age capital of Arkansas. Lots of artists, psychics, intuitives, bikers, UFO enthusiasts. A big gay population in recent years. It's driving the *Passion Play* crowd nuts."

The Great Passion Play, on the eastern edge of town, was once the city's largest tourist draw and is still advertised as America's number-one–attended outdoor drama.

"How's attendance?"

"Down, I understand," Barbara said. "But it still draws probably five hundred people a night during the summer. That's not bad for a town of two thousand residents. But the feeling is that more families are coming for the shopping and the arts now than for the play."

She paused.

"Know much about the play?"

"No, never been."

"Ever hear of Gerald L. K. Smith? He was a famous preacher and racist who moved to Eureka Springs in 1964 to make a fresh start. He kept publishing his anti-Semitic newspaper, *The Flag and the Cross*, in California, but wouldn't allow it to be distributed in his new hometown. Within two years he had dedicated the Christ of the Ozarks statue on Magnetic Mountain. It was designed by one of the Mount Rushmore sculptors and intended as the centerpiece for a religious theme park."

"The *Passion Play* is the result."

"Yep," she said. "Smith had planned for a full-size recreation of Jerusalem during biblical times, but all that was built was one wall, which you can see for yourself if you ever decide to visit the play."

"I'll take your word for it," I said.

"Eureka Springs was a tourist trap long before Smith came to town," she said. "It started during the Civil War, when a doctor located a hospital in a cave here and later sold the water as a healing remedy. By the 1890s, people were coming here to take the water. The outlaw Bill Doolin was arrested in that ice-cream parlor across the street, but of course back then it was a bathhouse. But tourism as we know it really came out of Smith's vision in the mid-1960s."

"How could such a rabid antiracist get the town behind him?"

"Whatever else he may have been, Smith was charismatic," Barbara said. "Mencken called him the best orator he had ever heard, bar none. And I'm not sure everybody in town really understood who he was, no more than folks do now. Ask the families who hand over their hard-earned cash for tickets to the *Passion Play* who Gerald L. K. Smith was, and I think you'd get blank stares."

"It's not the kind of stuff they print on those paper place mats for you to read while you're waiting on your ham and beans," I said.

"Exactly," she said. "But it's not really a secret, either. The townspeople know. They just don't talk much about it. After all, Smith died in 1976. Nobody here is preaching anti-Semitism now."

"What about the Covenanters?"

"They don't advertise it," she said. "Like I said, they keep to themselves. Of course, there are all sorts of rumors about the compound."

"Like what?"

"Underground bunkers," she said. "Caches of arms and ammunition. Nazi flags. People getting roughed up when they get too near the boundary. Stuff like that. But I've never seen evidence that any of it was true."

"Ever meet Abraham Smith?"

"Wouldn't know him if I did," she said. "Look, what you have to remember is that most of this stuff you're talking about, this hate stuff, as the big papers like to call it, is in the past. Remember the CSA?"

"The Covenant, the Sword, and the Arm of the Lord," I said. "I don't remember them, but I've read about them. Had a compound on Bull Shoals Lake. Run by a guy named James Ellison, who chose the spot because it was so remote he figured it would be spared during the end times—and because there was no appreciable black population. In the 1980s they planned to blow up the Federal Building in Oklahoma City. The feds finally busted them in 1985."

Another television crew had arrived, and now there were a couple of video cameras set up a few yards from us, near the base of the statue of the World War I soldier that dominated the park. One of the reporters was holding up a notebook for a white balance; then the camera lens swung our way.

"Ellison was a lunatic," she said. "Part of what finally brought them down was when they started wife swapping, because it created dissension. All religious nuts get around to that sooner or later. But that was twenty years ago."

"Yeah, but do you remember on what day the raid started? April nineteenth."

"So?"

"The same day Oklahoma City was bombed, ten years later," I asked. "My point is that this stuff never seems to go away; it just goes underground for a while. And there are three areas in the country that seem to be particularly good breeding grounds for this stuff: the Pacific Northwest, the Tennessee–North Carolina border, and the Ozarks."

A man in a wheelchair had arrived, and some of his friends were passing out press releases. Others were carrying hand-lettered signs that called for an end to what they called the new prohibition.

"I'd better go to work," Barbara said.

"Thanks," I said, standing with her. "I appreciate your time."

"I hope you don't think we're all rubes here," she said. "A lot of us know the truth. But I have my hands full just covering the shenanigans at city hall, you know?"

"No sweat," I said. "And I'd never describe you like that."

She smiled.

"Do me a favor," she said. "Don't describe me at all."

"If I do," I said, "I'll be scrupulously honest."

She looked unsure.

Then she asked, "Whatever happened to Ellison, anyway?"

I capped my pen.

"He spent some time in jail," I said. "When he was released, he went to Elohim City, a Christian Identity compound in eastern Oklahoma. That's the place that Timothy McVeigh called before the Oklahoma City bombing."

Twenty-two

The astrologer was late.

When she finally arrived, I was halfway through my cheeseburger.

"Didn't think you were coming," I said.

"We got busy," she said. "Had to sell some art."

She knew the waitress, so she grabbed her sleeve and ordered some type of vegetarian wrap sandwich and hot tea.

"I don't even know your name," I said.

"Summer," she said, holding out her hand.

"Real name?"

"Everybody asks me that," she said. "Summer Schwartz. Nobody would make that up. And who are you?"

I told her.

"That your real name?" she asked.

"Most people call me Andy."

"Okay, Andy. What are you doing in Eureka Springs?"

"You're the astrologer," I said.

She laughed. "I'm not a psychic," she said. "I don't read minds. And you aren't the usual type I deal with."

"Who's the usual type?"

"Tourists," she said. "Those I sell the art and jewelry to. Then there are the bored housewives desperately seeking meaning in their life, or the sincere and artistic men who are desperately seeking meaning in their life, or the idealistic young people—"

"—who are desperately seeking meaning," I said. "Do you give it to them?"

"Sometimes I help them find it," she said.

"For thirty bucks."

"You don't think I should make a living?"

"Everybody should make a living," I said. "But I get uncomfortable when people promise more than they can deliver. Do you promise more than you can deliver?"

"What I promise is an opportunity for insight," she said. "And I think I deliver."

"Ever watch Penn and Teller?"

"No," she said.

"Know what I do for a living?"

"No."

I told her.

"I'm not surprised," she said. She pulled a paper from her bag and spread it on the table. "Take a look at your chart. You are predisposed to any profession in which investigation, analysis, research, and solving mysteries is important. Sagittarians make great spies, and they tend to be very verbal."

The chart had twelve segments and a number of tangents drawn across it showing, I supposed, the arrangement of the planets at the hour of my birth.

"You had a very difficult Saturn return seven years ago," she said. "Everybody has this, every twenty-eight to thirty years, when Saturn returns to the natal position, and it can last three years or so."

"Everybody's life is tough around thirty."

"Not like yours," she said. "It was hellish. Did you learn the lesson you were supposed to?"

"Didn't know I was being tested."

"Oh, not good," she said, tapping the chart. "This unfinished business will come back to haunt you, if it hasn't already." She glanced up at my face. "Oh, sorry. Struck a nerve?"

"Not particularly," I said.

"Right," she said. "Also, truth is particularly important to you, although your Sagittarius nature can often allow you to descend into secrecy."

"That's contradictory."

"Typical for your sign," she said. "This is an area you need to watch, particularly in the next few weeks. Is there anything in particular you're working on that could lead you into ambiguous territory?"

"No," I said. "I'm always straightforward about what I do. When people aren't going to like a story, I tell them. If they don't like it, they can—"

"That's your adversarial nature," she said.

"I prefer to think of it as assertive."

"Sagittarius men," she said, and shook her head.

"What sign are you?"

"Pisces," she said. "You know, like Jesus."

"Jesus was a Capricorn," I said.

"No, he wasn't really born in December," she said. "He was born under Pisces, which was appropriate because He ushered in the Age of Pisces—"

"It's a song," I said. "Kristofferson. You know, we hate what we don't understand?"

"Don't know it," she said.

Her food arrived.

"I always wanted to write," she said.

"Write what?"

"A book about the vampires we meet every day," she said, then took a vicious bite of her wrap.

"Emotional vampires," I said.

"No," she said. "Real vampires."

"A fantasy novel, then."

"No, a nonfiction book," she insisted. "The planet's been teeming with them for thousands of years, from ancient Egypt right up until today. I can't believe how many I've met since I moved here. This place is just a vortex for them. It must be the magnetic energy."

"Then you must believe in David Icke's theory that history has been controlled by a group of reptiles in human form from a higher dimension. That the reptile leaders included the British royal family and Boxcar Willie, and that they have a secret underground base beneath Lampe, Missouri, where they abuse human sex slaves?"

"Christ," she said. "That's just silly."

Twenty-three

On my way to Berryville, I tried to check in with Sheryl at the newsroom, but got her voice mail instead. Since she never checks her voice mail, I didn't leave a message. Then I dialed Elaine's number, but ended the call before her phone had a chance to ring. She had sounded pretty sure that she never wanted to talk to me again, at least not for the next ten or twelve thousand years.

I parked on the west side of the public square in Berryville, in front of the 1880 courthouse, expecting to find the county offices. Instead, I found the Heritage Center Museum, operated by the county historical society, and it occurred to me that it wouldn't be a bad place to ask some questions.

Admission was only two bucks, and the museum had rooms devoted to different turn-of-the-last-century themes—a pioneer school, a barbershop, a moonshine still, an undertaking parlor. I learned that Berryville had been burned by both sides during the Civil War. It didn't take long to take all of this in, and when I was finished I asked the old guy who had taken my money and handed me my ticket if the society had any information about the Covenant compound.

And when I say this guy was old, it wasn't a judgment call. This guy had to be ninety, but his eyes were sharp and his white hair was neatly combed. His clothes were immaculate. He hooked a thumb beneath his suspenders, looked me over, and asked, "Got connections to the Covenanters?"

"I'm a reporter from Little Rock. I was actually looking for the county offices to do some land-title research on the area when I found the museum. Thought there might be a county history or something that mentions them."

"Nope," he said. "They're a little new for us. They've only been here since the thirties."

Yeah, that would only be seventy years.

"Nineteen thirty-six, as I understand it," I said.

"Don't know much about it," he said. "But Jericho Ridge was a tourist camp for years before they came."

"Jericho Ridge?"

"On the south side of Rolloff Mountain," he said. "Most of it is underwater now."

"Why is it underwater?"

The old man snorted. "You aren't from around here," he said. "The army corps of engineers didn't start building Beaver Dam until 1960. Flooded the entire White River Valley above it, and whole towns were submerged. Jericho was one of 'em, and the ridge was named for the town—or the other way around. Nobody remembers now."

"How big was the town?"

"Big enough for a post office, a dirt main street, and a few dozen houses," he said. "Lots of places on the lake are named for places that are just memories now: Coppermine, Rocky Branch, Lost Bridge. On the other side of the lake is the pyramid that Coin Harvey built."

"A pyramid?"

"Never heard of Coin Harvey?" he asked in disbelief. "He made his fortune in silver mining, wrote rags-to-riches books for boys, and ran for president on the Liberty Party in 1932. Lost to FDR, of course. Became disillusioned and believed that civilization was on the brink of destruction, so he built a pyramid at his resort and stuffed it with artifacts from human civilization."

"Like what?"

"A car, a sewing machine, books."

"The pyramid is still there?"

"Underwater," he said. "Or at least most of it is, except for when the water is really low. Then you can see most of the amphitheater as well."

"What happened to Harvey?"

"Died in 'thirty-six, which is about the same year the federal government started planning to dam the White River," he said. "Officially it was for flood relief, because there was a devastating flood in 1927. But others believed it was a pet New Deal project to submerge Harvey's pyramid—and erase his memory. Looks like it worked, if fools like you don't know about him."

"Pardon me?"

"Folks. *Folks* like you."

Right.

"Why did Coin think it was the end of the world?"

He shrugged. "I met Coin," he said. "I was just a kid, but he seemed like a rational man to me. Smart. But depressed, like many of us. Things were pretty bleak during the Depression; the Japanese were bleeding Asia dry; the Spanish Civil War began."

"Did the Covenanters believe it was the end as well?"

"Don't know," he said. "They bought their land cheap,

partly because of the flood and partly because you couldn't grow anything on it. Just rocks, you know. Then, when the government built the dam, they refused to be relocated. Moved their church and their cemetery to higher ground, and ended up with lakefront property. Worth a fortune now."

"Did the Covenanters admire the Nazis?"

"Beats the hell out of me," he said. "But it wouldn't have been surprising, or all that unusual, at least not before the war. Not many of us knew what Hitler was really up to. A lot of folks admired what was going on in Germany."

"How's that?"

"The Nazis made things look orderly, progressive, prosperous. They were first-class bastards, but most of us didn't figure that out until later. In the thirties there was an outspoken pro-Nazi movement, especially among preachers. Anti-Semitism was common. We just didn't think deeply about it, just like we didn't think about separate drinking fountains for whites and coloreds. It was a fact of life."

"Did *you* think about it much?" I asked.

"Not until April 1945," he said. "Buchenwald. I was just a nineteen-year-old corporal trying to survive. After that I was an old man, and have been ever since."

"I've seen the pictures," I said.

"Doesn't come close."

"I imagine not."

He brightened. "Speaking of pictures, I think we have an old photograph of Jericho Ridge. Wait here."

He went in the next room, and I could hear him rummaging for a bit. Then he returned with a manila envelope and spilled the contents onto the counter. There were a couple dozen black-and-white photographs that were becoming sepia-toned with age.

"Here it is," he said.

He plucked a photo from the group.

Written in ink in one corner was a year: 1928.

A group of smiling men and women in summer whites were standing in front of a wooden sign that said CAMP JERICHO, and the ridge behind them looked formidable. Just visible was a rock wall and a keyhole-shaped entrance into the cliff.

"Is this a cave or a mine?"

"Cave," he said. "Had some curious carvings back inside it."

"Petroglyphs?"

"Human figures, turtles, birds, reptiles," he said. "Obviously prehistoric, although some people thought they were the secret to some kind of treasure."

"Were they?"

"Not that I know of," he said. "I guess they thought they were left by the conquistadors. Others thought they may have been older than the Spanish."

"Prehistoric."

"Older than that," he said.

"What could be older than that?"

"I don't know," he said. "There were just a lot of crazy theories floating around. You know how people are. A lot of people visited the cave. It was deep and had passages that went far back into the bluff, but the entrance was wide and had a level floor. They held dances and so forth there. The Ku Klux Klan even used it for a while in the twenties."

"Great," I said.

"Every community had the Klan back then," he said. "It was like a fraternal organization. They put their hoods on and marched in parades on the Fourth of July and so forth."

"Like Rotary, but with cross burnings and lynchings?"

"You have a very peculiar sense of humor."

"Racism is always funny."

He ignored me. "See the top of this bluff in the

background? The knobby point with the cedars? That's all you can see now. When you're standing on top of it, you're looking down into the water of Whisper Cove."

Twenty-four

The county offices were in the new courthouse, a few blocks past the square and adjacent to the public library, which provided a convenient place to park. I started at the register of deeds and asked to see a property map of Rollover Mountain.

I spent thirty minutes with the map and jotted down the parcel number of every piece of property in the vicinity of those pink fence posts I had visited the night before. Then I asked to see the current tax records for the list.

"Why do you want them?" the clerk asked, taking a pair of reading glasses from his shirt pocket and slipping them over his nose. He was a middle-aged man in a blue western shirt and a bolo tie in the shape of an arrowhead.

I told him I was a reporter for the *Traveler* and that I was making the request under the state's Freedom of Information Act.

"I don't know about this," he said. "Jan, under the post–September eleventh laws, are we supposed to be giving out this information?"

Jan was an older woman in a bulky sweater with a grinning jack-o-lantern on the front and a black cat on the back. Apparently you had to be an eccentric dresser to work there.

"I'm not sure," Jan said in a whine. "Should we be giving out names and addresses and the amounts they paid in taxes? That seems awfully personal."

"You've already shown me the parcel map," I said. "Some things have been restricted under the FOIA, but not this. I'm not asking for a sectional of Beaver Dam or the schematics of the nuclear power plants at Russellville. How can you close tax assessment records? Do you think I'm going to track these people down and terrorize them?"

It was the wrong thing to say.

Jan picked up the phone and dialed the sheriff's department quicker than you could say, *Open records violation,* and in thirty seconds I was in handcuffs and sitting in a plastic chair in the booking room of the sheriff's department downstairs. I didn't think the deputy would actually take me in after she'd seen my driver's license and press card, but I had been wrong.

It wasn't the first time.

"How do I know that card is real?" she said.

All she had to do was check with the newspaper, but she obviously found the idea of dragging me to the sheriff's department more appealing.

"Could I speak to Sheriff Clark?" I asked her.

She walked off.

An hour later they still hadn't booked me, but I wished they would because my wrists were getting swollen. Eventually a man in a brown suit, a narrow brown tie, and cowboy boots walked up to me and asked dismissively, "You the reporter fellow causing the trouble?"

"I'm the reporter," I said, "but all I did was ask for some public records. Didn't think that was causing trouble."

"Jan said you had a mouth on you," he said.

Clark was in his mid-sixties, and when he put his hands on his hips it brushed his jacket back enough that I could see the butt of a stainless five-shot Charter Arms Bulldog on his hip. They are truly nasty guns, and were among the most powerful snub-nosed revolvers made.

"Come on into the office," he said, and led me down the hall.

"Aren't you going to uncuff me?"

"Patience," he said.

I stepped into his office and he shut the door. On the far wall was an Arkansas flag, with the diamond-shaped stars and bars of the Confederacy. His desk was a big wooden affair with the usual law enforcement appointments: speed loaders, equipment catalogs, a few loose hollow-point rounds in .44 Special. But the thing that caught my attention was a mason jar with a pair of what looked like shriveled plums floating in it.

"Are those what I think they are?" I asked.

"Testicles," Clark said.

"Human?"

"Of course they're human," he said. "We had a case a couple of years ago where a twenty-eight-year-old male and known sex offender was accused of raping a grandmother. A week before the trial somebody broke into this dirtbag's mobile home and cut his nuts off with some pianer wire. Unfortunately, the suspect was acquitted."

"Not guilty?"

"Legally."

"What about whoever castrated him?"

"Never caught 'em," Clark said. "Personally, I think they deserve medals. They did what the courts should have. I keep the nuts in my custody because they are evidence in an ongoing investigation."

"Charming," I said.

"You are a smart-ass," Clark said. "And because you're here as a person of interest in a possible terrorist case, I'd start cooperating, if I was you."

"What do you want to know?"

"Did you threaten to terrorize county residents by finding their addresses at the assessor's office?"

"Of course not," I said.

"But you did use the word *terrorism.*"

"I asked the clerk if he thought I could use the information to terrorize somebody," I said. "There's a difference. Also, I believe those are open records."

"What did you want 'em for?"

"I was researching a story," I said.

"About the Covenanters?" Clark asked. "Aw, don't look so damned surprised. You're not the first reporter to stop at the courthouse and start nosing around maps of Rolloff Mountain. What the hell else would you be looking for?"

"Ever have any trouble with them? Take any reports?"

"Son, you're not in a position to be asking questions just now," Clark said. "Besides, I make it a policy never to release records from this department, period. You want to sue me? Go ahead."

This guy was not only a sadist; he was smart.

"I don't know about the assessor's policy, but it seems to me they are doing a good job protecting the security of county residents. Can't find fault with that. As far as those property records being open, I just don't know. It would take a goddamned egg-sucking lawyer to answer those questions."

"Fine," I said. "That's something for you to take up with the newspaper's attorney."

"Who do you think you are?" Clark asked, putting his boots up on the desk and lighting a Lucky Strike. "Why do you think you can come in here and start asking questions about people who have lived here for longer than you've been running your nut?"

The smoke rolled from his nostrils.

"Maybe because it's my constitutional right?"

He sprang forward like a rattlesnake, knocked the mason jar to the edge of the desk, and pointed the Lucky Strike in my face. The jar teetered for a moment, then fell.

I caught it in my manacled hands.

"I'm sick of hearing about fucking constitutional rights," Clark said. I could feel the heat from the tip of the cigarette, and the smoke burned my eyes. "I've been hearing that shit for forty years and look at the shape we're in. Hell, this county used to be a decent place to live, and now it's just a goddamned Sodom and Gomorrah. I'll bet you're one of those faggots. You sure as hell look like it to me."

I nudged the jar back up on the desk.

"Yeah," I said quietly, moving away from the cigarette. "I'm a faggot. What're you going to do about it?"

Okay, it was the wrong thing to say, but I couldn't help myself. I wasn't going to give this sadist the satisfaction of hearing me protest that I really liked chicks.

The Bulldog came out of the holster.

"Then I should just splatter your brains all over that wall," he said. The stubby barrel wavered in front of my face. He hadn't thumbed the hammer back, but that didn't matter; the gun was double-action and his finger was on the trigger.

"You're going to murder me?"

"It wouldn't be murder," he said.

"What about the law?"

"I answer to a higher law."

So he was crazy in addition to be his other obvious personal problems. I figured I was going to die right there, handcuffs on, and he would claim I had made an escape attempt or went for his gun or some other bullshit story that wouldn't hold up, but I would be just as dead.

I remained quiet.

Right move.

He suddenly turned the gun to the ceiling, then returned the gun to its holster.

I started to ask him if he had called the paper, but my voice was too dry to speak. I swallowed a couple of times, then managed to speak.

"Did you call?"

"I found out who you are," Clark said. "And you can forget about writing a story about this. Nobody would believe you, anyway."

"Writing a story about what?" I asked. "Don't know what you're talking about."

Clark smiled.

"I'm going to give you some friendly advice," he said. He walked around the desk, produced a key from his jacket pocket, and removed the handcuffs.

I resisted the urge to rub my wrists.

"Get the hell out of my county and don't ever come back. If you do, I'll catch you on some lonely country lane at night and put one of these slugs on my desk into the back of your head. And your murder will remain unsolved for as long as anybody who ever knew you is still alive, because I know how to do it and get away with it."

He held out a manila envelope containing my billfold, my watch, the notebook, and everything else I had had in my pockets when they brought me in.

Everything, that is, except the little bag of peach tobacco. I supposed they kept that on suspicion of narcotics, and I had no doubt it would come back positive if I insisted they either test it or give it back.

"Understand?" Clark asked.

"Perfectly," I said.

"Good," he said. "Now get the hell out of here."

Twenty-five

As I walked to the van, which was still parked in front of the courthouse, my legs were shaking. The envelope was under my arm, and I had to fish the keys out of it in order to unlock the door.

I climbed in, then took the cell phone out and dialed the *Traveler* newsroom. Sheryl answered on the second ring.

"Andy," she said. "We have to talk."

"No kidding," I said.

"What's wrong?"

"Had kind of a run-in with the sheriff," I said.

"Yeah, I know," she said. "Got a call from the sheriff wanting to know who you were. But we've got a bigger problem. Not we, exactly, but you."

"What do you mean?"

"The Young Man saw you on television at noon."

"What are you talking about?"

"He said he saw you sitting on some park bench taking notes during a story about some guy who was protesting his arrest on medical marijuana," she said. "I told him I didn't think so, because you weren't assigned any kind of story like that."

"Oh," I said. "I was there. I was interviewing a woman in the park for background on this Covenanters story, and there just happened to be a press conference there. So?"

"So you weren't wearing a tie."

"Of course not."

"Can't you just tell me it wasn't you?" Sheryl asked. "Listen to me, Kelsey. Just tell me it wasn't you on that park bench, that it was just somebody who looked like you. Okay?"

"No, it was me."

"You're not listening," she said. "Tell me it wasn't you."

"But it was me," I said. "Why should I lie?"

Sheryl sighed.

"Dammit, Kelsey," she said. "Think."

I did.

"Sheryl, I'm not going to lie."

"Okay, then," she said. "Kelsey, you're fired. Those are my instructions. You have been warned several times about violating company policy. I'm sorry, but the Young Man has me backed into a corner—"

I ended the call.

There was nothing but the sound of my own heart beating for a few moments.

Then I called Elaine's number.

She was home.

"Elaine? I really need somebody right now."

"Kelsey, I understand," she said. "Why don't you go fuck your wife?"

Then she hung up.

Twenty-six

It is a strange feeling to wake up and not know where you are, and stranger still not to know precisely *who* you are. For a moment I thought I was in a nightmare, or experiencing some weird form of sleep amnesia, or perhaps suffering a stroke.

I felt so bad that I thought I must be in the hospital following some kind of car wreck, but when my eyes focused enough to take in my surroundings, I noticed that instead of a hospital bed I was in a wooden bunk. On the ceiling above somebody had placed a weird bumper sticker: There was the famous NASA picture of Earth from space, and beside it, IMAGINE WHIRLED PEAS.

My head felt like somebody had been using it for punching practice—which turned out not to be such an inaccurate impression—I was so dehydrated that my throat felt like it was on fire, and I had that old aching feeling that I knew was associated with alcohol. So I had been drinking. I could vaguely remember driving back to Eureka Springs and pulling the *Traveler* van into the first bar I encountered the night before, But I did not know exactly what had happened.

I reached for my billfold and found it was gone. My car keys were missing as well, as was my cell phone. My jacket was gone, my blue dress shirt was ripped and stained with blood from my nose and mouth, and my blue jeans were in pretty sorry shape but seemed largely intact. I guess it shouldn't have been a surprise that my favorite cowboy boots were also missing.

Of course, I had a pretty good handle on my name in a few minutes, and the details of most of my past life, with the exception of the last twenty-four hours or so.

Looking around the room, I noted that it looked spartan but clean, sort of like a Boy Scout camp hut, and the quilt that covered me was one of the old-fashioned kind that had likely taken thousands of hours to complete.

What kind of place was this?

"Where the hell am I?" I asked myself.

"So you're awake," a girl's voice said. "I would appreciate your watching your language, however. You're at Camp Covenant. You know about it?"

"I've heard of it," I managed. On the interior, my mind was racing. *The Covenant compound? I'm in a world of shit and have to get out of here.* I tried to sit up, but the pain in my ribs was too great.

"I'll bet *that* hurt," she said, watching my face.

I drew my left wrist to my face, but my watch was gone as well. That hurt. My soon-to-be ex had given me that watch, and I had been wearing it when a cop had beaten me up while I was on assignment in 1983 covering an anti-AIDS demonstration in Joplin, Missouri.

"What time is it?"

"About four P.M.," she said. "You've been sleeping all day. We didn't find a watch, if that's what you're looking for. Figured you might have had one because of that white band on your wrist. You were pretty roughed-up. Were you robbed?"

"Apparently," I said. "Could I get a handful of Tylenol?"

"Sorry, we don't believe in the pharmaceutical scam here," she said. "We used to be allowed homeopathic remedies, but we rely solely on the power of God to cure us now."

"Then could you *hurry* Him up?"

"Don't let Father hear you say anything like that."

The girl smoothed the dress over her knees, then clasped her hands together, closed her eyes, and began to pray fervently. "Oh, Lord, please hear my supplication to ease the suffering of this wandering sinner, who thoroughly regrets his wicked ways and honestly seeks the true path. . . ."

"Hold up," I said, touching her elbow. "Please don't do that. Get off your knees. I may be a sinner, but I'm not sure I regret it all that much. Also, I don't deserve your attention."

She smiled and stood up.

"How badly hurt am I?"

"You've had a beating, that's for sure," she said. "But no broken bones, no internal injuries. You'll survive."

"You should be a nurse."

"Can't work outside the home," she said. "Father says it is God's will for women to stay close to the hearth and to tend the children."

"What's your name?"

"Rachel."

"Rachel, I'm very grateful," I said. "Can you tell me where they found me?"

"In the middle of Highway 187 at about two forty-five in the morning, down on your hands and knees," she said. "At least, that's what they tell me. You would have been killed if one of those logging trucks had come around the curve with you crawling out there."

"Who found me?"

"A couple from North Carolina," she said. "They arrived late, toting the little Airstream trailer, and they said your eyes shone red like those of a deer in the glare of the headlights."

"Funny," I said. "I have blue eyes."

"Yeah, but the reflection is from the retinas," Rachel said. She sat down on the bed next to me, felt my head, and then took a bowl of water, soap, and a clean white towel into her lap. "Let's get you cleaned up."

She was an attractive young woman of perhaps twenty in a plain blue dress with tawny brown hair braided down her back. Her eyes seemed to be a shade of green, and it complemented her tan skin perfectly. She had a bowl of warm soapy water and a clean white towel that she set in my lap.

"This is a good week for you," she said. "We're just finishing up the Feast of the Tabernacles and preparing for the Last Great Day. This is the most joyful celebration on our calendar, and one in which we celebrate our abundance, and our tradition requires Father Smith to extend hospitality to strangers in need."

"Are you related to Abraham Smith?"

"I'm Rachel, his granddaughter. Also his favorite."

"Peculiar the way you say that."

"It's just the truth. Everybody knows it."

"How many other grandchildren are there?"

"Just one, Leah."

"So your father is . . ."

"Joseph Smith, of course," she said.

"But you called Abraham Smith your father. . . ."

"Everybody calls him that," she said. "I call my own father simply Dad."

"Heavily biblical," I said.

"That's right," she said brightly. "How do you know my grandfather?"

"Who doesn't know your grandfather around here?" I asked.

"You're absolutely right. Rachel and Leah were the patriarch Abraham's daughters-in-law, not granddaughters," she said pensively. "But I suppose there are certain similarities. Our family specializes in biblical synchronicities and legerdemain."

"Those are some pretty big words," I said.

"Sorry," she said. "They denote meaningful synchronicities—"

"—and sleight of hand, I know. The former comes from Jung."

"Cool," she said. "So you've had some education?"

"I know things."

"Do you know your name right now?"

I did, but I wasn't about to give her the full version.

"Yes," I said. "Allan Andrew."

"Allan Andrews," she said, feeling how the name sounded in her mouth, and I did not correct her. She pulled a clipboard from alongside her and grasped a freshly sharpened pencil. "Can you sit up and we can have a little chat? My grandfather will want to know certain things."

Head spinning, I slung my dirty socks out of the bunk onto the floor and sat up.

"Shoot."

"Home address?"

"Don't have one anymore."

"Last known?"

"You mean the last place I called home?"

"Yes," she said.

"Little Rock."

"Any relations left there?"

"Unfortunately, no."

"I'm sorry," she said. "What were you doing in the woods to get all banged-up?"

"I can only guess that it had to do with drinking," I said. "It appears that I don't tolerate alcohol well, but this is the first time I've actually blacked out and can't remember a thing."

"What do you do for a living?"

"I'm unemployed," I said. "I just lost my last job. . . ."

"Alcohol?"

"That came after."

"What sort of things can you do as far as trades or a profession?"

I thought for a moment.

"I can fix cars," I said. "Not light work, either. Heavy work. Clutches, water pumps, fuel pumps, hydraulics, suspension, carburetors and fuel injection, even overhauls with the right tools. About the only thing I can't work on is automatic transmissions."

"There's a great garage here, but we haven't had anybody who knew what they were doing in a long time," Rachel said. "Father will be glad to hear this. How'd you learn how to do this stuff?"

"My dad ran a service station for years along Route 66," I said.

"Thought you said you were from Kansas."

"Sixty-six cuts across the very southeastern corner, going from Missouri to Oklahoma."

"Ah," she said. "Family business. No ring on your finger, so you must not be married."

There was no ring on her finger, either.

"Any religious upbringing?"

"Not really," I said. "At fourteen, I was saved at a church revival, but it didn't seem to stick."

"Ah, but you're a born-again Christian," she said. "That's good. Denomination?"

"Southern Baptist."

"Good start," she said.

"Rachel, what's all this for?" I asked.

"You're a stranger in need who appeared literally at

our front gate during the festival where we celebrate the bounty of the Lord and anticipate His coming," she said. "Father has an obligation to offer you our hospitality. In return, you're expected to contribute something to the camp while you're getting back on your feet. It helps to know what people have done in the past, or what they like to do."

"Fine," I said. "I wouldn't mind."

"Father will want to meet you soon, but I'll stall him until I can find you some presentable clothes. Looks like you are around five-nine, a hundred and seventy pounds?"

"I'm five-ten," I said.

"Shoe size?"

"Nine and a half."

"Okay," she said. "I'll see what I can do. This is one of the visitor's cabins. These were left over from the days when this was a tourist camp way back when, but we use them for the feast days now. You can consider this bunk yours for a while."

"Do I have to stay here?"

"Of course not," she said. "Walk around when you feel like it. This mountain and valley are really quite beautiful. But I wouldn't get too close to the perimeter fences, okay?"

"Perimeter fences?"

"They're easy to spot, since they are marked with orange caution tape."

I smiled and waved as Rachel left, then flung myself back down on the bunk. What in God's name had I gotten myself into? I still didn't understand how I got into the Covenant compound, but it sounded like one of those boneheaded things that sometimes happen—I was so drunk that I was robbed and left in the middle of the highway to be ground to goo beneath the wheels of a log truck.

I had a flash of memory of ordering a Jack and Coke and placing a hundred-dollar bill on the bar. "Make it a double."

"No problem," the bartendress had said.

The place seemed strongly country-and-western. It had a dozen motorcycles out front, a couple of pool tables, a jukebox, and a Confederate battle flag on the wall.

"You look like you need this," she said as she placed the drink in front of me.

"That obvious?"

"Afraid so, cowboy," she said.

I took a sip of the drink and decided I'd better stir it first. But after owning four of them in a row, I had gotten over the habit of stirring them first, and then a thirty-something redneck with a red beard and a shaved head approached the bar, asked for a longneck Bud and tapped his dollar bills on the bar as he waited. When the bartender leaned over the cooler to retrieve the beer, he nudged my elbow and shot me a conspiratorial grin.

I just smiled.

"Finger lickin' good," he said.

"I heard that, Deacon," she said, her back still to us. Later, when the bar closed, I remembered being so drunk that Deacon offered to give me a ride to a motel. First I insisted on going to the van and throwing the keys in the front seat, because I wanted nothing more to do with the newspaper. Then I got into his pickup truck, and that was the last I remembered.

Rachel came back in about twenty minutes carrying a bundle of things. There was a black King James Bible on top of clean jeans, a blue-and-black flannel shirt, and a pair of hiking boots. Also some boxer shorts and athletic socks, a clean but well-worn towel, and a plastic bag with a cheap toothbrush, soap, and a comb. She placed them at the foot of the bed.

"When you're ready," she said.

"Thank you, Rachel."

"Borrowed them from my uncle," she said. "He's about your size. Well, he's not really my uncle, but we all call him that. Uncle Karl. He's gone now, but I'm sure he wouldn't mind."

"What am I supposed to do with this?" I asked, weighing the Bible in my hand.

"Read it," she said.

"I tried, when I was a kid," I said. "Started out well enough, what with God creating heaven and earth, and that bloody business with Cain and Abel, but then there were all those *begats*. I skipped over that part only to discover that things got even bloodier, what with the killing of newborns, and incest, and men taking multiple wives *and* sleeping with their wives' handmaidens."

"You're very wicked."

"Not as wicked as the stuff in this book," I said. "It's really very filthy. Of course, those were the parts that interested me the most. Lot's daughters getting him drunk and then taking advantage of the old fool was priceless. If it were a novel, it would be banned in every high school library in the country."

"Those were different times."

"The thing that finally killed it for me was that it urges slaves to obey their masters," I said. "This was a few days after I was saved at that church revival, and it just destroyed me. How could I believe in a book like that?"

"That thing about slaves obeying their masters is a homily."

"I thought Abraham Smith says that every word in the Bible is literally, fundamentally true," I said. "You can't pick and choose. He certainly doesn't say it's a homily when the Bible talks about the role of women, does he?"

Her eyes flashed. "You must be feeling better," she said finally.

"No, I still feel like I was run over by a logging truck," I said. "It's actually quite painful for me to argue these points. But it would be dishonest if I told you different. But, as you request, I'll read it again. Who knows? I might have another conversion."

"I can't talk to you anymore," she said.

"I didn't mean to offend you," I said.

"Sure you did. You just called into question everything my family believes. If I didn't know better, I would think that you were sent by Satan to challenge my faith."

"You're too smart for that," I said. "Your vocabulary shows that you have read far more than gospel, and I knew you had doubts. What was it you said about your family? Synchronicity and legerdemain? Those aren't words you pick up in Sunday school."

She looked down at the rough wooden floor.

"I don't know what to believe," she said. "It's easiest just to go along. Anyway, I brought you these," she said. She clasped my hand, turned it palm up, and dropped a half dozen generic acetaminophen capsules in it.

"Thanks," I said. Now I was feeling guilty.

"Don't tell anyone."

"What happened to the rule about letting God do the healing?"

"I keep a bottle of these under my bed," she said. "I get headaches that I just can't pray away. I'm sure it's because I'm weak, because I doubt. Since you're unrepentant, I suppose I'm doing you no harm, either."

Twenty-seven

I woke before dawn the next morning and ventured outside to the concrete-block shower house. There was a bare yellow bug light inside the building, so I didn't have much trouble finding my way in. The water was unheated, but as shocking as it was, I felt better after I had cleaned up and put on the new clothes. The jeans were a little tight, but the shirt felt comfortable enough. I rubbed my hand across my cheeks and felt the stubble, but the things Rachel had brought me the day before had not included a razor or shaving cream.

My plan was to limp out of there as quickly as I could and thumb a ride back to Eureka Springs. Problem was, I didn't even know where in the compound I was—and, as bad as I still felt, my curiosity was killing me about what the rest of the camp looked like and what was going on.

But it was still too dark to venture far beyond the cabin, so instead I got the Bible from inside and held it across my knees as I sat on the wooden steps. The electrified perimeter fence that Rachel had mentioned was just a few yards behind the visitor's cabin, and there was a path that led through the woods in the opposite direction. It was very quiet at first, but as it got a little lighter in the east the woods began to rustle with life. A doe and a couple of fawns passed by a few yards away on the other side of the fence, being very stealthy, but a couple of ground squirrels that couldn't have weighed a couple of pounds each bounded over the fallen leaves, sounding like elephants.

Then a couple of men came up the path to the shower house.

They wore running shorts and T-shirts, and had clean clothes beneath their arms and towels slung across their shoulders.

"Hello, brother," one of them said as they approached.

I returned the greeting.

Time to go, I told myself after they entered the shower house. Should I follow the perimeter fence or the path that certainly led down into the camp? The fence might go for a mile or more before I found a place to cross, and even then I might not be near a road. No, better to follow the path, walk through the camp, and find my way to those pink fence posts along Highway 187.

As I limped down the path, I was surprised to find that I was thinking of Rachel and regretting not having an opportunity to tell her good-bye.

Twenty-eight

The path wound around a half dozen or so cabins like the one I had just left, then took a decidedly downward slope. There was little wind yet, so I could clearly make out the sound of waves lapping against rocks, and I knew I was headed in the general direction of the lake.

After a hundred yards or so the woods opened and I found myself in a clearing with neatly cut grass and a path laid out in river gravel. The clearing was covered with tents, motor homes, and campers. Most were still asleep, but there was movement here and there among the campers.

Beyond was a cluster of buildings that reminded me of an elementary school, perhaps because of the pair of yellow Bluebird buses parked to one side. Toward the back of the campus was a trim white church building with a steeple in front. It was an unusual church, however, because joined to the back of the building, and butting up against a low bluff, was a tall reinforced-concrete structure that looked like nothing so much as a castle keep.

The tower rose three stories into the morning sky, had a few arrow slits for windows, and was painted a light yellow color that I suppose was meant to be taken as golden. On top of the tower were some antennae and, above them all, a flagstaff. While I watched, a couple of flags were being raised, accompanied by trumpet music from some industrial-looking loudspeakers. The first was a large American flag, and beneath it was a somewhat smaller flag obviously based on the familiar Confederate battle flag, only the colors were scrambled.

The background was blue, the crossed bars were white and outlined in black, and the bars had twelve stars. There was a cross in gold in the center of the flag, and in the center of the cross was a five-pointed star about twice as large as the others, bringing the total number of stars to thirteen. At the top of the flag, against the blue field, was a word in the same golden color as the cross: MANASSEH.

The flag was odd, because I had never seen obvious religious symbolism incorporated into any kind of Confederate standard. Because of "Manasseh," I guessed the stars did not represent the thirteen confederate states, but instead the twelve tribes of Israel and the "thirteenth tribe." In Genesis, after Joseph returns from Egypt, after serving as Pharaoh's dream analyst, and presents his sons Ephraim and Manasseh to his elderly father, Jacob, the patriarch adopts his grandsons as his own—adding a thirteenth tribe to the twelve he has already sired. In addition, Jacob also bestows the birthrights of wealth and dominance to the grandsons, including the fathering of "a great company of nations" to Ephraim and a single "great nation" to Manasseh.

Since the 1800s, it has been a matter of faith among some Christians to identify Ephraim as the ancestor of Great Britain and Manasseh as the forebear of the United States. This, of course, offers a rationale for Anglos to believe they are descendants of Abraham and therefore entitled by birth to the Old Testament covenants.

But I always thought the most interesting part of the story was that *Manasseh* means "to forget"—and that Ephraim's mother, Asenath, was the daughter of a ranking Egyptian priest. Wouldn't this make Anglos of equal Israelite *and* Arabic racial and spiritual descent?

Talk about being your own worst enemy.

As the flags were hoisted to the top of the staff, amid the trumpet blasts, those moving about the camp stopped what they were doing, turned to face the tower, and placed their right hands over their hearts, just as I had done in grade school. But instead of reciting the Pledge of Allegiance, the Lord's Prayer came over the loudspeakers, and everyone joined in.

"Our Father . . ." a few dozen voices began.

The prayer was the long version, from the Sermon on the Mount, and it was obviously the call for the camp to begin the day, because more voices quickly joined in, people emerging from tents and campers and cabins. Instead of finding myself in a relatively deserted camp, I suddenly found myself surrounded by perhaps two hundred people, all with their hands on their chests, gazing at the yellow keep. So I turned and placed my hand on my sternum as well, and recited along. What could it hurt?

By the time the prayer reached its conclusion, there were a couple of hundred voices united. "Forever and ever. Amen," rolled across the camp.

I glanced at my wrist to find out what time the camp opened for business, but of course I had forgotten that my watch and just about everything else I had on me had been stolen by the sonuvabitch I had met at the bar.

Then there was the beginning of an announcement, interrupted by earsplitting feedback screech from the loudspeakers on the tower. It echoed from the surrounding hills until somebody turned the gain down.

"Good morning, brothers and sisters," a male voice boomed. "This is Brother Joseph, and I'm here to remind you that Father Abraham will be addressing the camp in twenty minutes in Covenant Temple. Father has an important message for us this morning, and it is vital that you attend. Also, in other business, we want to remind parents that children are permitted in the beach area only under supervision, and only during times between youth classes. Also, all adolescent and adult females must wear *one-piece* bathing attire. . . . That is all."

I looked longingly down the path that almost certainly led to the highway, and then back to the tower. Abraham Smith was going to speak? What might he say in the comfort of a willing audience? And what were my chances of sneaking out unnoticed if I stayed in the camp for another half hour or so to find out? Then I spotted a white oak on the hillside just beyond the tower, and beneath the tree was a fresh grave, mounded with dirt and covered with fresh flowers.

Randall Duane Slaughter.

"Good morning, brother," a young man said in passing.

"Morning," I said.

He was a couple of steps along when I noticed he was wearing a watch.

"Do you have the time?" I asked.

"Certainly," he said, turning back to me. "It's six thirty-seven. Hard to believe so many sleepyheads are just rolling out of the sack, isn't it?"

"My dad always claimed the day was wasted if you weren't up by six," I said.

"Say, I don't believe we've met." He held out a bony hand. "Franklin Werner," he said. He had a weird vibe to him, as if he didn't quite live in the real world. He was in his late twenties, his hair was a bird's nest, and although he was dressed rather conservatively in a wrinkled white shirt and dark slacks, the cuffs of the slacks ended far above his ankles, displaying a pair of electric-green socks.

"Nice socks," I said.

"Yeah, I bought two gross of them at discount store for ten bucks," he said. "That's two hundred and eighty-eight pairs. Enough to last me for the rest of my life. I only have to wash them once a year, and I never have to worry about finding the right pair when I reach into the underwear drawer in the morning—they're all the same."

"But what about the color?"

"They're all gray to me," he said. "I'm color-blind."

"Right," I said. "Then that is clever."

"And you are?"

Crap, crap, crap.

I admired his socks while trying to think of a convincing alias, and finally settled for telling the truth—or at least most of it.

"Allan Andrew," I said.

"Pleased to meet you," he said. "Andrew. That's Scottish, isn't it? I'm one of the volunteer engineers at the shortwave station in the basement of Kingdom Tower."

"I'm mostly English and Irish. So that's what those antennae are for."

"Some of them, yes," he said. "But the Kingdom Hour broadcast is relayed via repeater to the tower on the top of Rolloff Mountain, where we have a fifty-thousand-kilowatt transmitter that provides coverage on sixty meters for most of North America."

"I have no idea what you just said."

"Not into technology?" Werner asked.

"Not unless it has nuts and bolts," I said.

"I guess you could say I'm nuts about volts," he said, laughing so hard at his own joke that he leaned forward and slapped his thigh. "What do you do?" he asked finally. "You look like you've been wrestling alligators."

"Had an accident a couple of days ago," I said. Then I sighed. "No, that's not true. It's embarrassing, but I was beaten and robbed on the highway outside. The folks here were kind enough to give me a place to get my feet back under me."

"Good Lord," Werner said. "Are you all right?"

"Just bruised," I said.

Werner took a worn leather wallet from his back pocket, opened it, and removed a crumpled twenty-dollar bill.

"It isn't much, but you might need this."

"That's very kind of you, but I can't."

"Take it," he said. "You'd be doing me a favor. I might be among strangers someday, in the same situation, and I would hope that the same kindness would be extended to me."

I took the bill.

"Thanks," I said. "How about your address so I can pay you back?"

"Forget it," he said. "Just pass it on someday, when you are in a position to."

"All right," I said, smoothing the bill and putting it into my jeans pocket. "Thank you, I will. Say, are the broadcasts archived? On tape?"

"We have them all on compact disc," he said. "If you're interested, come by and you can check some out, along with a personal CD player. We use MP3, so we can get forty of Father Abraham's messages on a single CD. Exciting, isn't it?"

"Incredible," I said honestly.

"Say, are you interested in electronics?"

"Not really," I said. "Built a little Heathkit radio when I was a teenager. It was a lot of fun; then I discovered cars and girls."

"They usually go together," Werner said.

"Are you a ham?" I asked.

"I used to be. Then I let all my licenses, including my

commercial license, expire years ago, when the FCC went to the online registration system," Werner said. "I didn't mind filling out the forms and mailing them to Gettysburg, Pennsylvania, but I couldn't stand the idea of being in any kind of federal database. It's just another kind of Social Security number. There will come a time when it will be just as dangerous to own shortwave equipment as it will be to own a gun, and I don't want to help the jackbooted thugs find me."

"Right," I said.

I considered asking him how he managed to operate the transmitter without a federal license, but thought better of it. After all, the FCC was too busy handling the thousands of complaints about Janet Jackson's exposed nipple to give a damn about an illegal operator who probably had never had a single complaint filed against him.

"Stop by the station and I'll give you a tour," he said. "It's in the basement of Kingdom Tower. Of course, broadcasting is just a small part of what we do now. A lot of the ministry is on tape or streaming audio over the Internet."

Twenty-nine

I hung out at the edge of the woods until it was nearly time; then as the church filled up I drifted over and slipped into the back. Everybody I met smiled at me, probably because of the Bible I was clutching. I tried to remember the last time I had been in church, and, ruling out the times I had gone to churches on stories, realized it must have been ten years. My wife had dragged me to a midnight Mass at Christmas, or perhaps it was an Easter service, and I had had a suffocating feeling because I couldn't push out of my mind the sins that had been committed in the name of Catholicism, from the Inquisition on. I also thought about the Catholics in Nagasaki who assumed that ground zero for the "Fat Man" plutonium bomb had been their church and elementary school because they had somehow displeased God.

I had some of that same sick feeling inside the Covenant Temple, but was also fascinated. The interior was similar to most other Protestant churches I'd seen, including rows of arched stained-glass windows, and the pulpit and choir section and so forth in the back. An American flag stood in the left corner of the church, and the Manasseh flag on the right. Behind it all was the bluff on which the tower was built, and a spring trickled down the rocks into a pool in a man-made grotto at the base. I stared at this for perhaps a minute or so before I spotted a reinforced steel door on the right side, and some heavy buttressed I-beams that obviously provided support for the Kingdom Tower above.

After everybody got seated, and before the big double oak doors were shut, I had about thirty seconds in which I could have gotten up and walked out. The sick feeling and the fascination struggled inside me, and I almost did walk out, and then told myself that this was part of my job, that I would never have another chance to hear Smith address his flock.

It wasn't until after the doors shut that I realized I didn't have a job anymore. I no longer worked for a newspaper. I hadn't written a single negative word about these people—and probably would never have the opportunity—so what did I have to worry about? I had betrayed no one, so there would be no successors of Randall Duane Slaughter on my trail. I was not on assignment, and the only legitimate reason I could think of for being there was because I didn't have anyplace else to go.

After I took the path down to the highway, then what?

Assuming I managed to stay out of the way of testicle-collecting Sheriff Clark and his minions and hitched a ride into Eureka Springs, was I to call Sheryl at the *Traveler* collect from a pay phone to beg for my job back? Call Elaine and ask her to come get me and let me live with her because I couldn't afford a place of my own? Even if she consented, I'd have to sleep in the monument shop because of her thing about not being intimate in the house. Should I call my wife? She had filed for divorce, so her intentions were clear. My parents were gone and my brother, Danny, had been missing in action and presumed dead for more than thirty years.

To hell with all of it, I thought.

Then Abraham Smith and his family took the stage behind the pulpit.

Smith looked older, of course, than the pictures of him I had seen in the news stories at the *Traveler* morgue, and I guessed that he was in his mid-seventies now. While he had had a full head of hair in most of those photos, he was now completely bald on top, with a fringe of white hair on the back and sides that reminded me of a tonsured monk. Although he also had a beard in those grainy old photos, he was clean-shaven here, and he wore a black suit with a white shirt and a gray tie.

He did have one thing that was prominent in nearly every old photo I had pored over: a walking stick made from the branch of an almond tree.

His only son, Joseph, helped him up onto the stage, but other than having some trouble with his left knee, the old man seemed agile enough. The granddaughters, Rachel and Leah, also stepped up onto the stage, and with studied reserve took a couple of chairs at the back. They were both wearing very conservative blue dresses, but the matching clothing could not hide the fact that Rachel was the most attractive. Leah was heavier, with olive skin and dark hair.

They were the only women left in the family.

Their grandmother, Abraham's wife, had died of pneumonia in the early seventies after lingering for weeks, despite (or rather, I should say, because of) an around-the-clock prayer vigil instead of conventional medical treatment. Their mother, Sarah, had met a more direct end: she had been struck by a bolt of lightning out of a clear sky while walking across the compound lawn in 1989. If anybody pondered the irony of this, it was never reported.

Rachel spotted me sitting in the back and gave a small wave.

I waved back.

What I wanted most at that moment was to fuck Rachel silly.

Typical male stress reaction, healthy response to a good brain and a nice rack, feeling sorry for myself over being divorced and being dumped, or simply a suicidal flaw in my character.

Take your pick.

As Abraham Smith walked to the pulpit, silence descended on the already subdued church. Although Joseph was ready to catch him if he fell, the old man made it all the way by himself, then handed the staff to his son and gripped the edges of the pulpit with liver-spotted hands to steady himself.

The old man paused just long enough to be dramatic.

"When Moses was in the wilderness," he said with surprising vigor, "and the Israelites were grumbling that there was no water to drink, God spoke to Moses and told him to strike a rock with his staff. Now this was the same staff that Moses had used to turn the Nile to blood and bring down the other plagues upon Egypt, so that Pharaoh would let his people go. And in the desert, when Moses struck this rock with the staff, the Lord brought forth a gushing spring of freshwater for the people to drink. . . . And while this was indeed a miracle, it is not the most amazing part of the event."

The old man looked out over the congregation, and I'm sure that everyone felt he was peering deeply into their souls. I must admit that I felt a little uncomfortable beneath that gaze, even though I knew it was theater.

"The most amazing thing was that for the next forty years, this rock followed the Israelites through the wilderness, and they never again lacked for fresh water. Of course, you also know that while in the wilderness, the Lord rained down bread on the Israelites every morning, through His manifestation known as the Ancient of Days. What miracles!"

He motioned to the rock bluff behind him. "Look. Does it remind you of anything?"

The congregation murmured in appreciation.

"I don't know how God made that water-producing rock to follow the Israelites for forty years, or how He caused the bread to appear every morning, and I don't suppose it is in God's plan that I will ever know in my lifetime," he said. "But I do know that when the valley was flooded, we moved our church to higher ground and consecrated it on this bluff to remind us of God's promise. That was forty years ago this fall. And like the Israelites of old, I believe that our time in the wilderness is about to come to an end. But just as Moses heard then, I hear a lot of grumbling."

Everybody seemed to sit a little straighter.

"There were those among us who believed that Brother Slaughter would return from the grave after three days, as one of the two warrior prophets that signal the coming of the Lord. Yet this is the morning of the fourth day and he is not among us. This is not a reason to abandon your faith. God's plan is infallible, but His timing is known to no man. But I can assure you that the timing is close, very close. We are living in the last days, and those who cannot see that are blind. Jesus said these things will come to pass."

He held up his hand and began ticking items off on his fingers.

"False prophets. How many of you have seen the Reverend Sun Myung Moon on television marrying thousands at once and not felt a bit unsettled, or passed the New Age section in a bookstore and not felt the chill of wickedness? Jesus said many will be deceived by teachers of false Christianity. Every night on the news we are assaulted by those who would have women in the clergy, or advocating religious sanctions for homosexual marriage."

His pronunciation of *homosexual* was filled with venom.

"There will be wars and rumors of war," he said, his voice rising. "In less than one hundred years we have lived through two world wars. We are currently fighting a holy war on two fronts, in Afghanistan and Iraq, that was prompted by a horrendous attack on the financial capital of the free world that cost thousands of American lives. I don't know about you, but the images of those towers collapsing caused me to reach for my Bible."

Applause.

"The United States and the former Soviet Union have more than thirty thousand nuclear warheads, and a new member to the nuclear club is likely to be communist North Korea. India and Pakistan already have nuclear capability. India and Pakistan? How could this happen?"

Shaking heads and moans.

"There will be famines and plagues and earthquakes. You all know what has been going on in Africa. Earthquakes are happening with a frequency that is confounding scientists, and do I even have to mention AIDS?"

There was scattered clapping and "Amens." Several had their arms raised, palms out, as if they could receive Smith's message through their hands.

"The Mark of the Beast: the Bible says there will come a time when we cannot buy or sell without it. Well, how many of you have attempted to find employment, apply for a credit card or bank loan, or even tried to cash a check without being required to give that federal identification number? Not asked, mind you, but required to give it."

Everybody's hand went up.

"How many of you have refused to surrender your children to the beast? How many have refused to register them for Social Insecurity?"

About half of the hands remained up.

"And if these things are not enough, consider this: the nation state that calls itself Israel was established in 1948 in Palestine, and we move ever closer to the rebuilding of the temple. When that happens, watch out, because the time of our Lord has come."

Smith lowered his voice.

"Now, I don't know when we will take the Dome of the Rock back and start building the third temple," he said. "I don't know when the last trumpet will sound, and the sun will be darkened, and the moon will not give its light, and the stars will fall from the sky, and the powers of heaven will be shaken. Then we will be called to meet our Savior in the air. But I do know this: there are those among you who will live to see this and never taste of earthly death."

Smith turned and motioned for his staff. His son came forward and presented it to him, and Smith hoisted it slowly over his head with one hand, and then pointed it over the congregation, moving slowly from right to left.

"Do not abandon the faith of your fathers," he said. "Our time in the wilderness is nearly done. Keep your covenant with God. And part of that covenant is tithing. The water that keeps this ministry alive is cash."

Smith was a terrific speaker, but I was disappointed that his "vital message" was about something as pedestrian as money. I was expecting something more militant. In comparison to Major "Stonewall" Carson's urging his audience to fight the New World Order to the death, Smith's message was bland indeed. But that may have been the difference between a soldier and a preacher.

Deacons appeared and began passing wicker baskets down the aisle. Rachel was watching me as the nearest basket came my way, and for a moment I thought about throwing the twenty Werner had given me and taking ten or fifteen dollars in return. The folks here had been pleasant enough, they had taken me in after I'd been beaten up and left for dead in the middle of the road, and one of them had even given me money. Then I thought, *To hell with it.* I couldn't spare even a couple of dollars. Besides, would they have treated me the same had I been something other than white, or if they had thought I was gay? Either way, whether I contributed or not, there would be no escaping my own hypocrisy. To stand on principal was to be an ingrate; to be grateful was to help a cause I despised.

When the basket finally came to me, it was filled with cash—several hundred bucks, mostly in tens and twenties, and no checks. I just shrugged and passed it along.

Rachel smiled.

Thirty

At about the same time Abraham Smith was dunning his flock for money, the woman known as Eva Braun was counting down the seconds in the lobby of the First National Bank of Corydon, Iowa.

The bank had been experimenting with extended hours for its customers, and the main bank was now opening an hour and a half earlier, at seven A.M.

The bank was small, there was no security guard, and perhaps because few patrons knew about the new hours, or perhaps because they knew but didn't care, there were no customers in the bank. A couple of tellers were filling gym bags with money, and the bank's employees were facedown on the floor in front of Eva. Karl Larsen was behind the teller cage, saying gently but firmly that the tellers would be killed if he found any dye packs, consecutive serial numbers, or silent alarms. Eva was keeping her finger on the trigger guard of her Bushmaster and was barking orders for the employees on the floor to keep their heads down.

"Thirty seconds," Eva said.

"Get on the floor," Larsen told the tellers as he threw the gym bags over the counter. Then he squeezed through one of the teller windows, went to a brown paper bag he had left by the front door, and removed a fruit basket. Among the apples and orange and pears were half a dozen red tubes, all tied to a common fuse.

"I'd like all of you to remain where you are for ten minutes," Larsen said as he placed the basket on the top of a courtesy table with blank deposit slips, pens, and calendars in the middle of the lobby. "If you don't, if we hear a single siren, we will explode this package by remote control, and I can promise that none of you will survive the blast."

The palm-sized GRS radio on Larsen's belt crackled.

"Incoming, incoming," Skorzeny's voice crackled. "One man, about forty. Business suit."

Larsen took the radio from his belt.

"Can we beat him to the door?"

At that moment the man's hand gripped the front door. As he reached out, his jacket swung open a bit, and both Larsen and Eva saw a glimpse of a badge and the butt of a handgun.

Eva looked at Larsen.

"Get down," Larsen said quickly. "Lie flat. Hide your gun."

She did, covering the Bushmaster with her coat, and Larsen stood over her with his H&K.

The man stopped in his tracks a few feet inside the bank when he saw the employees on the floor. He had short-cropped hair, was wearing a dark suit and a red tie, and in his right hand he was clutching a pay envelope from the City of Corydon. His name was Richard Caruthers, he was a detective with the city police, and this morning he was unlucky enough to have entered the First National Bank to open an old-fashioned savings account. He intended to place a hundred dollars every month in the account and, when he retired in twenty-seven years, planned to have $118,319 with which to purchase a sailboat.

He'd worked out the math that morning on his calculator.

"Good morning," Larsen said, holding his assault rifle at the ready. "Officer, you'll be good enough take your service weapon from your belt very slowly with two fingers and place it on the floor, please."

"Shit," Caruthers said, withdrawing the weapon as instructed. It was a Browning 9mm, and he knelt as he gently placed it on the floor. "Two of my buddies are right behind me."

"Doubtful," Larsen said. "Do as you are told, or you will be shot. Place your hands behind your head, stand slowly, and take your place with the others."

Caruthers looked over his shoulder.

"Another car," Skorzeny said over the radio.

"See?" Caruthers asked.

"What kind of car and how many occupants?" Larsen asked calmly.

"Piece-of-shit minivan," Skorzeny said. "One occupant. Female."

"Politely tell her the bank is closed, and be firm if you must," Larsen said. Then he turned to Caruthers. "Nice try, officer." He motioned with the barrel of the gun. "Now get over there."

Holding his hands behind his neck, Caruthers walked over and knelt next to Eva. He unlaced his fingers and used his hands to lower himself to the floor.

"Bring the car," Larsen spoke into the radio. Then he turned and glanced over the counter to make sure the tellers were still down, and when he did Caruthers brought his right leg up and reached down his pant leg to find the backup revolver in the ankle holster.

"Looking for something?" Eva asked, smiling behind her sunglasses.

The barrel of her rifle was pressed against Caruthers's

neck. She had rolled onto her left side, propping her head up on her left hand, and was holding the Bushmaster casually in her right, with the safety off and her finger on the trigger.

"Good job," Larsen said as he walked over and relieved Caruthers of the snub-nosed .38. "This is truly a nasty little gun. Not very accurate, I imagine. We saved your life today, you know, because you wouldn't have stood a chance."

A five-year-old Grand Am came to a screeching stop in front of the door.

"I do wish he wouldn't do that," Larsen said.

As Eva shouldered one of the gym bags, Larsen took a disposable butane lighter from his pocket and lit the fuse sticking out of the fruit basket.

The fuse burned brightly.

Larsen snatched up the second gym bag, and then both he and Eva raced for the Grand Am.

"We desperately need another man," Larsen said.

"Why not another woman?" Eva asked.

"Behave yourself," Larsen said as they piled into the Pontiac. "You have enough testosterone for all of us. Pull away, Otto. No squealing tires, mind you."

Inside the bank, Caruthers sprang for the basket, but before he could reach it something whizzed over his head. As he ducked, a full barrage of Saturn missiles followed, bouncing off the walls and ceiling and exploding on the floor. Then a pair of smoke bombs ignited and spewed green and yellow plumes into the lobby.

Caruthers decided to place his sailboat money elsewhere.

Thirty-one

Rachel grasped my arm and pulled me over to meet her grandfather, and I was relieved when he didn't offer to shake my hand. As a matter of fact, I did not see him shaking hands with anyone, or touching people on the shoulder or the arm, or any of the other things that one expects a preacher to do after a service. He was very careful, in fact, to avoid making skin contact with anyone, including members of his own family.

"Do you drink?" Smith asked.

"With disastrous results."

"You'll not do it here," he said. "Drugs?"

"No."

"That's something, at least. You like women?"

"As opposed to what? Puppies?"

I got a look worthy of Clint Eastwood.

"Are you mocking me, son?"

"Well, yes," I said. "I like to have sex with women, also with disastrous results. Not immediately, of course, but eventually. I end up feeling trapped and the women come to hate me for reasons that probably have something to do with my complicated relationship with my mother. Nothing incestuous there, but she committed slow suicide in a way I don't care to discuss. Now, if you want to know what kind of women turn me on—height, weight, body type, hair color—and what acts in particular get me off, I'd be happy to share that with you."

"Are these unnatural acts?" the old man asked without so much as batting an eye. Rachel had her face in her hands, and I couldn't tell if she was laughing or trembling with fear.

"No," I said.

The old man grunted.

"You've got quite a hard-on for God, don't you?" he asked. "You think you're the only one who has suffered, the only one who has been down and out, the only one who has had a difficult relationship with a parent?"

"I'm not sure I believe in God," I said.

"Oh, you believe," Smith said. "You wouldn't be so damned angry if you didn't. That's all right, son. You're not the first to wrestle with God. Jacob wrestled with Him all night in the wilderness, and we know how that one turned out."

"Didn't Jacob think he was fighting his brother, Esau?"

"At first, yes," the old man said. "But at daybreak he discovered it was really the Lord, and Jacob looked upon His face and lived. At least you have some backbone, which is more than I can say for my own seed."

The son was standing close enough to hear this, and although his cheeks burned with shame, he said nothing.

"What's your name?"

"Call me Allan."

"Rachel tells me you know something about cars," he said. "In the shop behind the canteen there's an old Ford pickup that nobody can get to run. If you can fix it, you can stay on here as our mechanic. No pay, room and board only."

He turned, then paused.

"Remember this," he said. "You can wrestle with your faith while you're here, but don't wrestle with me. You pollute my granddaughter and I'll castrate you myself."

Thirty-two

The truck was a faded yellow 1971 F-150 with rust stains, a flat tire, a dead battery, and a 360 engine that had not run in so long that the pistons were stuck in the bores. On both doors, in very faded stencil lettering, was LAMAR MUNICPAL AIRPORT.

With the transmission in neutral, I tried to turn the engine by hand, but it wouldn't budge, even with a two-foot cheater bar on the crankshaft damper.

It was going to be a long job.

The shop was a mess. It had two bays, and the dust-covered truck took up one of them. Concrete floor. No air-conditioning, but it did have electricity. Tools were scattered everywhere, beneath boxes and trash, so I didn't even know what I had to work with. After a few minutes of looking, I found a spark plug wrench and a can of oil on the old wooden bench. I cracked the insulators on half of the plugs, but once I had them all out I poured a cup or so of oil into each cylinder to cut the rust around the rings. Then, with nothing else to do but wait a few hours, I started to clean the shop.

I was tired after a couple of hours, but I kept at it, and I rested every so often when my bruises got to hurting too much. It was a strange sensation to be working without a watch. The only way I knew what time it was, was by the steady sweep of the shadows beneath the open bays. I was aware of some noise from the camp, kids yelling and playing, people talking, and the sound of footsteps on the path outside, but people left me to my work. Back in Little Rock, if somebody had offered me a job working on cars, I would have refused. In fact, I probably would have been insulted. But here there was no pressure. I wasn't working for a paycheck. Besides, my father ran a service station once and worked on his own cars for years. If the truck had been anything newer than about 1980, I probably would have been lost, because that was about the time I stopped working on hot rods. But I knew cars from that era, and I especially knew Fords, so I was fairly confident that with just a little luck I could make Old Yeller bark again. What she was mostly suffering from, I thought, was neglect. I found working on these cars from my childhood therapeutic in the same way that people liked to mow their grass on weekends, or edge their lawns, or whatever. It was work that required a fair amount of elbow grease and a minimum of cerebral cortex. It wasn't that you weren't thinking about what you were doing; it was simply that you were on a kind of autopilot that ran itself, or that you approached a state of flow where things seemed effortless. When I first began writing longer newspaper pieces I had experienced this to some extent, but my enjoyment depended on how soon the story was needed, how much hell the subject of the story would raise, and how staunchly I would have to defend my reporting. It had been years since I had experienced the flow, and I was amazed that I was feeling it simply from cleaning a shop in preparation to work on an old truck.

I must have found a hundred sockets: regular and deep well, in quarter, three-eighths, and half-inch drive, metric, and SAE. I cleaned the dirt and grease from them, then placed them according to size in the toolbox drawers. There were also dozens of screwdrivers, box and open-end wrenches, pliers, hammers, ratchet drivers, and just about everything else you could think of. Some of the tools had a patina of rust, but all of it was serviceable, and it was apparent from the brands and styles represented that the collection was the haphazard product of thirty or forty years.

By the time I had the shop cleared of trash, the floor swept, and the tools returned to their proper places over the workbench or in their boxes, it was growing dark outside—and I was happy. I was pleased at the work I had done that day, and anxious to start again in the morning.

But I was also exhausted. I was hungry and could smell the food from the kitchen. But all I wanted at the moment was to shower. After that all I could do was crash naked into the bunk under the WHIRLED PEAS bumper sticker.

I slept better that night than I had in years.

I woke at first light, but kept my eyes closed, just thinking about how good it was to lie in the bunk and feel all parts of my body. Usually my body seemed detached from me, something I had to slog out of the sack and then take to the shower. But this was different. I still had aches and pains, but the stretching helped. I was on my back, my arms behind my head, my legs splayed over the bunk, and as I arched my back my erection waved to the ceiling.

"Impressive," Rachel said.

"Sorry," I said, quickly turning over. I reached for the blanket on the floor.

"Don't be," she said. "I look at naked men."

"How long have you been there?" I asked.

"Long enough," she said, climbing up onto my back. "Say, would you like to know the kinds of men I would perform natural acts with?" Then she lowered her lips to my ear. "And there are some unnatural acts I would consider with you as well."

"I'm not all that impressive," I said. "Just average."

"Oh, you're a bit above average in length and girth, I'd say," Rachel said, and she tried to reach beneath me.

I grasped her hand.

"What're you trying to do? Get my nuts cut off?"

She sat up and flipped her hair over her right shoulder.

"I don't think anything Granddad could say would scare you away from fucking me," she said.

"I'm afraid of the old goat," I said. "What is it with castration with folks in this neck of the woods? Is there a season for it? A bag limit, so to speak?"

I sat up, snatched the blanket from the floor, and laid it over my lap.

"You still have a tent," Rachel laughed. "Oh, how you *do* flatter me."

"I'm inspired."

"You were inspired before you knew I was watching."

"Yes, but I was thinking about you."

Rachel laughed. "Want to get some breakfast?"

"There's only one thing I'd like better," I said.

She put her arms around me and placed the crown of her head against mine. The top of her blouse was unbuttoned enough that I had a good view of her breasts.

"Later," she said.

"Fair is fair. I want to see all of you."

"Later," she said.

She kissed me. Her tongue flicked inside my mouth. I broke away and placed my head between her breasts. She smelled like vanilla.

"How old are you?" I mumbled.

"Does it matter?"

I lifted my head.

"Of course it matters," I said.

"I'm twenty-three," she said.

"Did you come here just to tease me?"

"No," she said. "At least, not intentionally. Did you wash your clothes last night? No, I didn't think so. I brought you some clean things, and then I saw you lying there, and you looked so good."

"Do you know how old I am?" I asked.

"It's normal for an older man to be attracted to a younger woman, isn't it?" she said. "And the other way around."

"Only if the man has money," I said. "Or perhaps if he represents everything her family hates."

She walked slowly to the door, then turned.

"Do you?" she asked.

"Perhaps."

"My grandfather doesn't think so," she said.

"He doesn't know me."

She smiled.

"I suggest you dress and, um, somehow get rid of *that* before breakfast."

Thirty-three

After the initial cold snap the first night I had arrived in Eureka Springs, which frosted the trees with red and gold, things had warmed up and we were enjoying a terrific Indian summer.

The days passed in a way that I had not known before, or perhaps had forgotten. I woke at dawn, showered, and ate breakfast with Rachel in the canteen, and then went to the shop and worked on the old yellow Ford truck. Getting the engine unfrozen was just the first step, although I was relieved to discover there seemed to be no fatal flaws inside the block—no dropped rods, holes in the tops of the pistons, or holes punched through the cylinder walls into the water jackets. The battery in the truck was quite dead and was incapable of being resurrected by a trickle charger, but I "borrowed" another battery from an old Chrysler parked outside the shop that would hold a decent charge. Once the battery was hooked up, I was able to clip a couple of leads to the ignition solenoid and turn the motor over with the starter. Of course, with the spark plugs removed, it would not start—but the motor spun easily and the motor oil pumped through the lubrication system.

Then, when I did a compression test on the engine, I discovered several burned valves. That meant I had to disassemble the engine down to the short block, which required removal of the intake and exhaust manifolds, valve trains, and heads. That took most of a day, and it was heavy work, because the cast iron intake manifold alone weighed seventy-five or eighty pounds—not an easy burden to wrestle by hand, and I ended up literally climbing into the engine bay to get a better handle on it. There was much more to it than this, however, but it will give you some idea of the tedium required in diagnosing and fixing a major engine problem.

But it didn't seem like tedium to me at the time. It felt more like therapy.

I would often work through lunch, and when I did Rachel would bring me a sandwich from the canteen. More than once I noticed her sister, Leah, watching disapprovingly as I ate my sandwich and drank from a bottle of cold water while Rachel and I chatted under the shade of a tree outside the shop.

I noticed that I was feeling much better. I could work longer hours without tiring, and I was growing stronger. I knew I was losing weight because I wasn't sitting at a desk most of the day, surviving on junk food between assignments, and going home too mentally exhausted to use the weight bench I had bought six months before. Well, I had been using it, in a way. It was a great place to hang clothes from.

After about a week of this routine, Rachel came to my cabin after I was fast asleep and woke me by touching me on the arm.

"What time is it?" I asked.

"A little after midnight," she said. "Thought you might want to go for a walk with me. It's a beautiful night. Interested?"

I hurriedly dressed; then we slipped past the shower house and the other cabins and skirted the perimeter fence down toward the lakeshore. Rachel obviously knew where she was going, so I let her take the lead. We walked across the wide and deserted swimming beach, and then picked our way up the rocks to the top of Jericho Ridge.

We were seventy-five or a hundred feet above the camp at the top of the ridge, and we had a great view of the lake stretching to the west, and the lights of the tiny community of Monte Ne on the other side. Just to the southwest was a cove surrounded by rocky bluffs and heavy woods, and I could make out the dim yellow lights of a covered dock, a pontoon boat, and a couple of fishing boats in the slips.

"Whisper Cove," I said.

"How did you know?"

"I know things," I said. "Where does the path from the dock lead?"

"My house," Rachel said. "It's hidden by the trees and separated from the rest of the camp by a wooden bridge over Whisper Creek."

She pointed to the lake.

"Do you know what's out there, underwater?"

"Coin Harvey's pyramid and amphitheater on the other side," I said. "In the middle, near the river channel, is the old town of Jericho and the remainder of what once was the rest of the camp."

"You've been talking to some of my family," she said.

"Nope," I said. "I saw some old photographs of this area some time ago. The Ku— I mean, the cave and so forth, and the places where the lake flooded. The entrance to the cave is underwater, right beneath us."

"Yep," she said. "That's where the Ku Klux Klan cave is. That's what they called it before we came, wasn't it? It's all right. It flooded before I was born. Old Abraham renamed it the Cave of the Martyrs. He had a vision that the cave was host to the spirits of John the Baptist, Saint

Paul, the other apostles . . . and Adam. Says he talks to them down there. Crazy, huh?"

"No crazier than Joseph Smith proclaiming that Adam and Eve lived in Missouri," I said. "Or that Independence will be ground zero for Christ's return. Ever *been* to Independence?"

She laughed. "How come the only good Christian is a dead Christian?" she asked.

"Also applies to outlaws, kings, and other mythological figures," I said. "And they're not really dead—from King Arthur to Jesse James to Elvis, they're just waiting for the right time to come back. Anything of the cave left above water?"

"Not here," she said. "But there's a passage that goes from here all the way to the base of Kingdom Tower. That's why Abraham built it there. It's just beneath the bluff where the fake water runs down."

"It's not a real spring?"

"Used to be, but it ran dry about ten years ago. So grandfather installed an electric pump beneath the floor to keep it flowing. Not quite as impressive, huh?"

"It's showbiz," I said.

"No kidding."

"Is your grandfather a racist?"

"Duh," she said. "What would you call somebody who used to write pamphlets about the dangers posed by the communists, the niggers, and the kikes?"

"He doesn't preach that anymore?"

"He was pretty militant in the eighties. I remember some of it—banners proclaiming white power, radio programs denouncing the Jewish media conspiracy, rallies with neo-Nazis and that damned metal music of theirs. Seminars on home defense and combat shooting. He was really disappointed when the Cold War ended."

"There's still China."

"Doesn't work people up like the Soviets did," she said. "After the CSA compound got busted, he cleaned up his act. Stopped preaching the outrageous stuff, distanced himself from the more violent organizations. Of course, there was a rise in interest generated by Waco and Ruby Ridge and the Oklahoma City bombing, and things peaked during the ridiculous Y2K scare. But that ended with a whimper instead of a bang, and then we had nine-eleven just a year later. That pretty much dried things up."

"You mean attendance?"

"I mean money," Rachel said. "This whole place runs on cash."

"I saw a lot of money in the collection plates," I said, "but that couldn't account for more than a few tens of thousands of dollars each year. That wouldn't even provide for the upkeep on this place."

I could see Rachel smile in the starlight. "You're very curious, aren't you?"

"Always have been," I said.

"Look," she said. "What old Abraham takes in during services is just pocket change. Most of the money comes in through the mail."

"From where?"

"Donations from people who listen to the shortwave broadcasts or get the tapes or the pamphlets or the Bible study. We get money from all over the world—the Netherlands, England, Scotland, Australia. We report very little of it, of course. How's the IRS going to track checks written on South African accounts?"

"South Africa?"

"We used to get a lot of money from South Africa. We even had a lot of South African families move here after the end of apartheid, but none of them stayed long."

"Why not?"

"Guess it wasn't what they expected," she said. "They tend to be a fairly independent lot, and to be a part of the camp you need to be fairly . . . well, dependent on somebody else to do your thinking for you."

"I can see that," I said. "But you know, I've kind of enjoyed not having to think for myself. Strange, but I never thought I would."

"That's what we call the honeymoon period," she said. "It ends for most people, except for the very sick or the elderly. The closer you are to shuffling off this mortal coil, the more you are willing to accept that somebody—anybody—has the key to everlasting life. With you, I can't imagine it lasting much longer. I think your life sucked so badly that you were desperate for a change. You're just on vacation."

"Could be," I said. "So how much does the Covenant compound take in every year?"

"Old Abraham prefers Covenant Camp," she said. "*Compound* suggests an armed camp. Have you seen any guns?"

"Not yet," I said.

She smiled.

"How much?"

"Like I said, it started drying up after Y2K and nine-eleven," she said. "Before then we might get a million or two a year. Now we're lucky to get a couple hundred thousand. But that's not counting the old folks who die and leave us everything in their wills, which can be pretty lucrative. That adds a few bucks to the old pot."

"Sounds like a lot for a rural ministry most folks have never heard of," I said. "How do you know all this?"

"Abraham doesn't trust my father," she said. "Seems he was taking some off the top for gambling and prostitutes. So he entrusted the books to my mother. After she was killed, he gave me the job of keeping the books."

"I can see why everyone considers you his favorite."

"Pathetic, isn't it?" she asked. "He knows I like to think for myself, and still trusts me. God knows, he loves backbone."

"He knows you won't steal."

"No, I won't steal," she said. "But he also knows that to really think for myself, to lead my own life, I'm going to have to turn my back on all of that money. He's promised me the ministry, you know. He says America is ready for another Aimee Semple McPherson."

"The one who faked her kidnapping and ran off with her male secretary?"

"Wouldn't be a bad life, would it?" she asked. "It's just acting. I could put in fifteen years or so, make a fortune, and then throw it away for a sex scandal while I was still young enough to enjoy it. The sad thing is that I don't think I can give up the money. Old Abraham certainly knows his favorite granddaughter."

"Is Abraham Smith acting?" I asked.

"That's what bothers me," Rachel said. "He's spouted this shit for so long, I actually think he believes. But you know what is bothering him most right now? He can't find the money Randy Slaughter hid."

"The bank loot."

"Sure," Rachel said. "Oh, Gramps never planned or participated in any of the jobs himself, but he certainly shared some of the proceeds. Only after a while, Slaughter got tired of spreading the wealth among people who didn't actually take the risks, so he started setting some aside for himself."

"And that secret died with him."

"Maybe," Rachel said. "Old Abraham kind of expected Slaughter to let us know, in the form of his last statement or something—you know, some kind of clue. These guys love that cloak-and-dagger shit. But all Randy did was give a few verses from Psalms, all mixed up."

I grunted noncommittally.

"Hey, let's go swimming."

She took my hand and led me down the ridge to the deserted beach. She kicked off her shoes and, standing barefoot in the sand, peeled her blouse over her head.

Then she unbuttoned her shorts, let them fall, and kicked them off.

She was wearing only panties.

There was enough starlight that I could make out her slim legs, her rounded hips, her flat stomach. Her breasts were small, like a teenager's, but with large nipples.

"Aren't you afraid we'll get caught?"

Rachel laughed.

"What would they do?" she asked. "Go tell old Abraham that his favorite granddaughter was skinny-dipping with the new mechanic on the beach? Believe me, nobody has the guts for that. If anything, my worthless father would give me a lecture and that would be the end of it."

"I hope you're right," I said, stripping off my shirt and my jeans, "because I am kind of fond of my testicles."

"So am I," she said. Then we ran for the lake.

She swam out about thirty yards, with me in pursuit. Then she stopped, stretched out, and floated on top of the water.

"The water's chilly, but warmer than I thought."

"It will be for another week or so," she said. "Can you float? Try this. Look up into the sky."

I did. It was a cloudless night, and the Milky Way was a glowing, star-filled band across the sky. As we floated, our bodies lightly touched.

"How many billions of years do you suppose we are staring into?" I asked.

"My grandfather would claim six thousand years. Nine forty-five A.M. On a Tuesday."

She laughed and found my hand, turning herself toward me. We came upright and treaded water together, holding hands.

"How deep is it here?" I asked.

"Let's find out," she said.

Before I could reply, she put her arms around me and kissed me hard on the mouth. She exhaled as she continued to kiss me, and she squeezed me hard so that I would exhale too. As we began to sink her body felt wonderfully warm against mine, and the deeper we went, the colder the water was and the warmer she felt. We kept kissing and sinking until our bare feet finally touched the rock bottom.

Thirty-four

Werner, the electronics nut, brought me back the gaskets and spark plugs and valves I needed from an auto-supply store in Eureka Springs. Rachel had given me a few bucks to pay for the stuff, so I didn't have to spend the crumpled twenty I still had in my jeans pocket. Werner asked me if I wanted to ride with him into town in his 1968 Volkswagen Microbus, but I declined. If we ran into anybody in Eureka Springs I had talked to before finding myself at the Covenant compound, it would have been difficult to explain. Also, the floor of the Microbus was rusted out on both sides, and I didn't want to watch the highway whizzing by underneath. So I just made a very detailed list of the things I needed and gave it to him, along with the money.

"Very precise," Werner said, approving of my list. I had also included the truck's vehicle identification number so that in case the parts store had any questions, they could look it up on their database.

"You know what's wrong with it?" Rachel asked.

I was sitting on a top of a five-gallon plastic bucket next to the flat driver's-side front wheel, spinning the lug nuts off with a four-way wrench.

"There was a lot wrong with it," I said. "But I think I've diagnosed most of it. Engine seized, burned valves, broken vacuum hoses. The distributor is loose as a goose, the points were burned up, but I think I can set the new ones to where it will run. There was actually quite a set of tools beneath all the trash in here. Even a hand-cranked valve grinder. It won't be a fancy job, but it will work. What does old Abraham want with this truck, anyway? It couldn't be worth more than four or five hundred bucks."

"Who knows?" Rachel said. "Maybe it has sentimental value." She paused. "No, there's not a sentimental bone in his body."

I got the tire off, moved it to one side, then rolled the replacement over. Luckily I had found a spare with decent tread beneath the bed of the truck, and although it was flat, it held air after I filled it from the shop's air compressor.

"You're going to have some company in your cabin tonight," Rachel said.

"Yeah, I counted on that," I said.

"That's not company, that's sex," she said. "But I do like talking to you."

"I like talking to you too," I said. I picked up the spare, shoved my foot beneath it to keep it at the right height, then cocked it a little to line it up with studs and shoved it home. "But you infuriate the hell out of me sometimes."

"I like the stuff we talk about."

"Rachel," I said, as I started to thread one of the nuts on a lug, "you need to get out of here. You're too smart for this. Ever think about going to college?"

"I'm a woman, remember? My job is to have babies."

"I thought your job was to take over the ministry, make a fortune, and then embark on a series of sex scandals until you're too old to enjoy it."

She laughed.

"You can do whatever you want," I said. "You're Abraham's favorite granddaughter. If you told him you wanted to go to college, he'd send you in a heartbeat."

"Yeah, but he'd send me to some *Bible* college in a place like Tennessee or North Carolina or Nebraska," she said. "Can't say I find that very attractive."

I stopped, wiped my hands with a shop cloth, and took her hand.

"Rachel," I said, "listen to me, because this is important. You have to get out of here. If you don't, you're going to self-destruct. You're well on your way to that with me."

"Christ," she said. "You're in love with me, aren't you?"

"No," I said.

"Bullshit," she said. "You've fallen in love. What, you think you're going to rescue me? Steal me away from my tribe and take me to a new land where my eyes will be opened? How biblical."

"Suit yourself," I said.

"You can't think I love you," she said.

"Right now I don't think you love anybody," I said. "You're too busy hiding behind those walls of uncultivated intelligence, sarcasm, and anger. You're a spoiled brat, and your grandfather wants you to follow in his footsteps because he knows you're exactly like him. You're just a couple of steps away from being so embittered that you embrace hate as a lifestyle. Doesn't it mean anything that you're too smart for that?"

"Nothing means anything," she said.

A single tear rolled down her cheek.

I turned back to the truck.

"You don't have to leave with me," I said. "But you have to leave. Get the hell out of here. Go to college, get a job, have a life. If you stay here you'll become something ugly."

"You stupid fuck," she said. "How am I going to get a job or enroll in college? I don't have a birth certificate or a Social Security number or a driver's license. I don't even exist. That's what old Abraham has always told us: outside these walls, *we don't officially exist*."

I kept my attention on threading the rest of the lug nuts.

"Plenty of colleges have dropped using Social Security numbers as student identification," I said. "Missouri has, I know. The state line is what, fifteen miles away from here? There are only a few hundred colleges across Missouri. As for a birth certificate and driver's license, there are ways to get those. You don't want to be Rachel Smith so your family can't find you? Hell, I can tell you five different ways fugitives reinvent themselves. The most common is to search graveyards until you find somebody born about the same time you were, do a little research, and become them in another part of the country—and use *their* Social Security number."

I knew she was listening, because I didn't hear any footsteps walking away. She coughed, and I thought she was going to say something, but then a black Jeep Rubicon pulled into the driveway in front of the shop.

"Here's your company," Rachel said.

Then she walked out.

A man in a black T-shirt jumped out of the Jeep and watched Rachel walk away. His blue eyes seemed amused. He lit a cigarette and took a long draw, then leaned against the fender of the truck.

"I've seen that walk before, my friend," he said. "I suggest flowers and chocolates. If you're guilty, I suggest you maintain your innocence and claim it was all just a misunderstanding. If you're innocent, then I suggest you issue a blanket apology for everything you have ever thought or done."

"Who are you?" I asked.

"Karl Larsen," he said, offering his hand. We shook, even though my hands were again greasy. "I understand we're going to be cabin mates for a few days. How's it coming with the truck?"

"We'll know tomorrow," I said.

"Outstanding," he said. "It'll be running then?"

"With some luck."

"And without luck?"

"Hard to say," I said, and shrugged. "I think the motor will be okay, but the truck hasn't moved an inch yet. The clutch or the tranny could be bad; the brakes might be shot. Anything. It's been sitting for a long time."

"I see," the man said, then took a long drag of his cigarette and exhaled through his nose. "Well, do your best."

"I will," I said, tightening the last of the lug nuts. "If you don't mind my asking, why are you interested in this old truck?" I asked. I was lowering the floor jack that held up the front of the truck. "Abraham didn't tell me why he wanted it fixed."

"Oh, that's a simple one," he said. He smiled before he flicked the cigarette through the shop door. "It was my father's."

Thirty-five

The cabin had been crowded, what with Larsen and his huge friend Skorzeny in the other bunks. There was also a very strange dark-haired woman, who introduced herself as Eva, who came by and spoke with Larsen in low tones outside for a few minutes, then left. Larsen was friendly enough, and made pleasant conversation without giving any specifics about himself.

Skorzeny was very quiet, and both he and the girl seemed anxious.

I turned in early, but Larsen and Skorzeny stayed up late, talking softly and occasionally laughing. Their body language had suggested that although they were very close, there was no question but that Larsen was the leader.

They were still asleep when I woke, showered and dressed, and went down to the shop. I knew it was time to go, but I would finish the truck first. I had spent too much time working on that damned truck to walk away without hearing it run.

Then I would just walk out.

I had gotten most everything done before quitting the day before, and there remained only a few hours to bolt the heads and manifolds back on, hook up all of the tubes and plug wires, and then check everything one last time. I had already drained the gas tank and put in a couple of fresh gallons. Then I filled the radiator with a mixture of half water and half antifreeze, connected the battery cables, splashed a little gas into the throat of the carburetor to prime it, and slid behind the wheel.

The key was already in the ignition.

I depressed the clutch, pushed the accelerator to the floor to open the butterfly valve, and turned the key. The starter spun for only a second or two before the engine hit, raced for a moment with a clatter, then died. I paused, made sure nothing was smoking or on fire, then turned the key again while I pumped the accelerator pedal.

The engine started.

The valves clattered for a moment, then quieted. As the engine warmed, some oil that had been smeared from my hands onto the exhaust manifolds began to smoke. I took my foot off the accelerator and the engine settled to an idle, with just a trace of smoke coming from the exhaust. That would stop when the rings seated again.

I put the column shift into reverse, looked behind me, and backed the truck out of the shop. Then I drove it in a circle in the parking lot. The steering, the transmission, and the brakes all seemed operational.

I parked the truck back inside the shop and killed the motor. Then I slammed the door, leaving the keys in the ignition, and turned to walk out of the shop.

Karl Larsen was standing in the door.

"Congratulations, old man," he said. "Seems you did it."

"How's that?"

"I saw you circle the parking lot."

"It's still a little rough," I said.

"Sounded fine to me," he said.

He wore a black leather jacket against the morning chill. He walked a little closer and offered me a cigarette.

"Thanks, but I quit," I said.

"Good for you," he said, lighting the cigarette himself. "Nasty habit, really. I should quit as well, but I'm afraid I don't have the fortitude for that. Say, where were you headed just now? You seemed to be doing so with some deliberation."

I knew I was in trouble by the way he was looking at me.

"The motor still doesn't sound right to me," I lied. "I thought I heard a rod knocking, which might put a piston through the side of the block."

"Really?" he asked.

"I was heading to find Werner to take me into town for the bearings," I said. "To make sure it's okay, I'll have to drop the cross member and the oil pan and replace the bearings."

"Sounds like quite a job," he said.

"I'm afraid it is."

"Um," Larsen said. He unzipped his jacket, revealing the butt of the biggest automatic pistol I had ever seen. Except for the black grips, it had a gold frame.

"I think you're lying," he said. "I think you did quite a good job on the truck, and now you're intending to walk out of here and leave the lives of all of us."

I ran a hand through my hair. I needed a cut.

"I don't get it," I said. "Why would you threaten me over a thirty-year-old truck unless you're a sadist? But you're not a sadist, are you? This is over something else. Why don't you want me leaving here alive?"

"Old Abraham said you were smart."

"I have no idea who you are," I said.

"I told you," he said. "I never lie about my name. It's too important to me. It was my father's name, you see."

I sighed. He unholstered the pistol, holding it in his left hand, and crossed his arms. The barrel nuzzled against his right shoulder.

"Do you know what this is?"

"A phallic substitute?"

"It's a Desert Eagle in fifty-caliber Action Express," he said. "It is one of the most powerful handguns in the world. There is one round in the chamber and seven in the magazine. It fires a three-hundred-grain bullet at fourteen hundred feet per second, which, if you know anything about firearms, you know is comparable to a big-game rifle."

"So you're going to kill me?"

"I think I might," Larsen said.

Strange, but I wasn't scared. I was outraged. I thought Abraham had sent him to blow my nuts off with that big gun of his, and I would much rather he simply shot me dead.

"Are you trying to scare me because I've been fucking Rachel?"

"I beg your pardon?"

"You heard me," I said. "She claims she's not in love with me, so I can't call it making love, can I? You want to kill me, then go ahead. But just promise me that you'll tell Rachel yourself what happened, okay? Enjoy your fucking truck."

I walked out of the shop.

"Andrew," he called.

I kept walking.

"Stop."

I made it to the path.

I heard footsteps running after me.

Crap, I thought. *He's going to shoot me in the back. How far will it blow me forward?* I wondered. *Will I end up with pine needles in my mouth and my guts in the dirt?*

"I was just trying to protect Rachel," he said. Larsen was beside me. "But perhaps I think you need to be protected from Rachel."

"You have a funny way of expressing concern," I said. "What do you use if you really like somebody, a rocket launcher?"

"That's good," he said. "The capacity to maintain a sense of humor in a stressful situation is a very good sign of character."

I stopped and shoved my finger into his chest.

"Look," I said. "I have no character. I have no money, I have no job, I have no family. For a couple of weeks I had someplace to stay here, and many people were very kind to me, and Rachel was probably too kind. I don't regret a damn thing I did with Rachel, except that I failed to convince her to get the hell out of here. She doesn't belong here, and if you're as smart as you seem, you damned well know it."

In an instant he had grasped my hand, turned my wrist over, and was now threatening to crack my elbow over his other arm, which was locked onto my shoulder.

"Hurts, doesn't it?"

"Fuck you," I said.

He increased the pressure and my knees buckled.

"Don't touch me again," he said, then released me.

I fell to my knees.

"You're right, of course," he said. "Rachel doesn't belong here. I've always been close to old Abraham, and I've always considered Rachel a niece."

"That's why she calls you Uncle Karl." I was cradling my elbow against my side.

"You'll be fine," he said. "It was just hyperextended for a moment. Nothing broken."

"Thanks for the advice," I said. "I'll remember it the next time you try to break my other arm."

"Sorry, old man."

"Why the hell do you talk like that?" I asked. "It's British, but mixed with other things. I can't place it. What is it?"

"My father was American, but my mother was from Birmingham," he said. "I grew up in a great many places, including Vietnam and South Africa."

"That explains it," I said.

"There's nothing wrong with the truck, is there?" he asked.

"No."

Larsen paused. "I'm sorry," he said finally. "I have misjudged you and have treated you badly. Common sense says that I should kill you to protect not only Rachel but the rest of us. But I cannot. Your word to mention us to no one is good enough. You may go."

I got to my feet.

"Or you may stay."

"Why should I?"

"Because we need you," he said quietly. "Not one person in twenty would have reacted the way you did just now. Most would have groveled, begged, and attempted to make any promise in order to save their lives. You didn't. Of course, we'll have to do something about your mouth."

"And why do you need people like me?"

"Because we have an important job to do in exactly three weeks," he said.

"I don't even know what today is," I said.

"Tuesday the nineteenth," he said.

There were twelve days left in October, so three weeks would make it . . .

Why couldn't it have been any other date?

"November ninth," I said.

"Yes."

"What kind of job?"

"I cannot tell you yet," he said. "But you may accompany us on some small errands we have yet to do. It will require some traveling, some initiative, and also a degree of risk. The certainty of a prison sentence, if caught."

My breathing had become shallow and quick. I could keep walking, and never know what Randall Slaughter meant by citing November ninth as the day of judgment, or I could stay and probably get myself killed in the process of trying to find out.

"You don't have time to think this over," Larsen said.
"I've made my decision," I said.
I offered my hand.
"Commander Carlos, I presume."

Book Three: Wildfire

When I would have healed Israel, then the iniquity of Ephraim was discovered, and the wickedness of Samaria; for they commit falsehood, and the thief cometh in, and the troop of robbers spoileth without.

—Hosea 7:1

Thirty-six

The dump car was a five-year-old Crown Victoria with 150,000 miles on the odometer. The vehicle had once belonged to a sheriff's department in Kansas. Larsen had bought it through a third party for a song, but the plates were current Kentucky issue. Although it had the usual dings and scrapes of daily use, it had a strong V-8 and the requisite police speed and suspension package, but I knew it was a great car from the first time he pulled it into the shop next to the old yellow Ford pickup because the throaty rumble from the Vic's dual exhausts told the story.

The light bar, radios, and decals had been removed from the car, of course, but it still had the spotlight on the driver's windshield post, and it sported an all-black paint job. I cleaned up the body, removed what remained of the adhesive that still outlined SHERIFF'S DEPARTMENT on the fenders and the trunk, and checked the fluids and the air pressure in the tires.

"What do you think?" Larsen asked.

"It looks like an unmarked police car," I said, "and it'll do a hundred and fifty miles an hour, if that's what you need."

"Forty miles an hour should do quite well," he said. "But I think it is amusing that it does indeed look like an unmarked car. That might actually come in handy."

After he closed and locked both of the overhead shop doors, he asked me to open the trunk. He lifted a duffel bag, placed it in the trunk, and unzipped it.

The bag was filled with an assortment of guns, smoke and fragmentation grenades, gas masks, and several thousand rounds of ammunition. He picked up one of the handguns and offered it to me, butt first.

"I told you, I'll drive. No guns."

"It might be necessary," he said. "I need to know you can at least fire the damned thing if needed."

"Christ," I said, taking the Glock from him.

I opened the action, made sure the chamber was clear, and then dropped the magazine out of the bottom. The clip was empty. Then I rammed the magazine back home, released the action, and handed the gun back to him.

"I'm not a big fan of Glocks," I said. "They're like something out of *Robocop*. Also, I suppose you handed me a dry piece just to see if I'd try to put a round in you first?"

"What *are* you a fan of?"

"Shotguns," I said. "What I'm most familiar with is the kind of stuff you hunt ducks with. You know, twelve-gauge with long barrels and interchangeable chokes."

"We'll have to compromise on the barrel length," Larsen said. He picked up a short-barreled riot gun and handed it to me.

I opened the action and a green shell filled with double-aught buckshot flew out of the ejector. Larsen caught it in his hand.

"This one's wet," he said.

"I'm drunk with trust," I said as I removed the other rounds from the loading port on the bottom of the receiver. The magazine tube extended the full length of the barrel, and the rounds just seemed to keep coming.

"Seven rounds?"

"We don't hunt ducks with these," he said.

It was a Benelli M4 semiautomatic with an 18.5-inch barrel and a pistol grip.

"You can keep this one in the car," he said.

"Fine, but I'm not hurting anybody."

I tried to hand the shotgun back.

"If it comes down to your life or that of someone else," Larsen said, "you might change your mind." Instead of taking the gun, he reached into the duffel bag and withdrew a map.

"Are you familiar with Tennessee?" he asked.

"Not really," I said, slinging the shotgun over my shoulder.

"Then you need to pay close attention," he said. "In three days, on Friday, at oh seven hundred hours, I want you to be in the parking lot of the Casey Jones Village at Jackson, Tennessee. It is a very cheeky tourist attraction on Highway 40, about an hour on the other side of Memphis."

"There was really a Casey Jones?"

"Don't be an idiot," he said. "There's a big parking lot with an information gazebo in the center and shops around the perimeter. Park the Crown Victoria near the gazebo and then walk to a restaurant called the Old Country Store, where my friends and I will be having breakfast. Trying not to call too much attention to yourself, join us."

"Okay," I said.

Larsen withdrew a bundle of hundred-dollar bills from the bag. He broke the seal on the bundle with his thumb, then counted out five of the bills.

"This will get you there and then some," he said. "Do a little planning, because I will expect the car to have a full tank of gas, and you need to be rested. So spend the night someplace close, but don't—"

"—draw attention to myself, got it."

"Buy some dark clothes along the way," he said. "Jeans, T-shirt, jacket. And get some decent shoes. Boots, preferably."

There was a knock on one of the overhead doors.

"Hey, Allan?" Rachel called. "Are you in there?"

"Just a minute," I called.

I handed Larsen the Benelli. He placed it beside the duffel bag, then slammed the trunk lid.

"One other thing. I wouldn't speed if I were you. Not with all of that firepower in the trunk," he said, "and stolen plates to boot."

He turned the lever that unlocked the door, then swung it up.

"Uncle Karl," Rachel said. "What's going on?"

"Just talking some business with your friend," he said.

Rachel frowned. "You're not recruiting him, are you?"

"Recruiting me for what?" I asked.

"Karl knows damn well what I mean," she said as she crossed her arms. "You get him in any kind of trouble, Uncle Karl, and I will never forgive you."

"It seems he has gotten into enough trouble just left to his own devices," Larsen said, and bussed Rachel on the cheek. "Do be careful, my dear. I hope you're using protection."

Rachel's face burned.

Larsen walked out.

"Thought you were mad at me."

"I'm always mad at you," she said.

"Why?"

"I'm mad at everybody," she said. "Look, old Abraham is in a rare mood this morning."

"How's that?"

"He's been down in the cave talking to Adam and the patriarchs again," she said. "He said they called to him in the night, and they tell him the final conflict is coming."

"Armageddon?" I asked.

"The battle of the wheatfield."

"If I went down there, would they talk to me?"

"If you were as crazy as old Abraham," she said. "Or maybe he has some angle. I don't know. He also said the spirits demand a punishment tonight. Midnight, on the swimming beach."

"Who's being punished?"

Rachel bit her lip. "A woman I know," she said.

"Why?"

"Look, Allan," she said. "The camp is very different when the festivals are over and the tourists leave."

"I thought they were pilgrims."

"Christ, they're tourists. We're a tourist camp for the gullible. We take anybody as long as the money spends. We even had a little old black woman who came to Saturday services for years, listened to old Abraham's typical racist messages, and always gave a five-dollar offering. I asked her once why she came, and she told me she liked things here, that they were orderly, and that she thought my grandfather was right in preaching against interracial marriage."

"She was probably a spy for the Southern Poverty Law Center. What did this woman you know do?"

"She admitted that she had a relationship with a Mexican."

"You mean she had sex with a Hispanic?"

"Yes, but I really think he was a Mexican national. Worked for Tyson at one of their poultry processing plants. No, wait. He was Guatemalan. Worked double shifts. Quit at one plant, went to another."

"When did he have time for sex?"

"This woman met him on the weekend, and before she knew what was happening, she had fallen in love with him. She said he was a gentleman. Kind, clean . . ."

"And a hard worker."

"Problem was, this woman was married."

"That would be a problem," I said. "According to the Bible, only men are allowed to fuck their sisters-in-law, their slaves, or anybody else God tells them to. So what happened to the Guatemalan?"

"She's sworn never to see him again."

"Too bad," I said. "What's going to happen to her?"

"We'll find out tonight," Rachel said. "So what were you and Karl really talking about?"

"What does it matter?"

"It doesn't," she said.

"Right," I said. "That's why you told Larsen you'd never forgive him if something happened to me."

"Get over yourself," Rachel said.

"Say, the patriarchs didn't mention anything to Abraham about any dates coming up, did they?"

"Dates?"

"Yeah, like some dates coming up pretty quick. First week in November or so?"

"What the hell are you talking about?"

"Just something in the back of my mind," I said. "Maybe something I read."

"Didn't know you read about prophecy."

"Well, there's not much else to read in that cabin," I said. "There's the Bible you brought me, and then there's that stack of pamphlets your grandfather has published for the last thirty years. Some of them are pretty racy. I especially liked the one about Satan seducing Eve in the garden of Eden and fathering Cain. . . ."

"Racy," she said. "That's a play on words."

I smiled.

"Allan," she said, "there's something I should have told you that morning when you woke up. I just didn't know how to say it. You see, I wasn't completely honest."

"Christ," I said.

"Some reaction," she said.

She was genuinely angry. What could she possibly have to tell me? That she already had a boyfriend? I had become a pretty good judge of when people were lying in twenty years as a journalist, and when I asked her about November, I was sure she was telling the truth. She may have suspected that her uncle Karl was some kind of criminal, but I don't think she knew he was Commander Carlos. Otherwise he wouldn't have taken such care to hide the guns from her. The best thing for Rachel now would be to quit hanging around, and the sooner I made her hate my guts, the better.

"You aren't pregnant, are you?"

"No," she said.

"Well, you fucked me pretty quick. I assume I wasn't the first."

She was so shocked her jaw actually dropped.

"A sexually transmitted disease? That's usually how these conversations begin. 'I don't know how to tell you this, but . . .'"

"You are unbelievable," she said, fuming. "Yeah, that's right. I'm pregnant. I've been fucking around too, and I'm carrying a little baby and I don't know who the father is, but I need some patsy to marry me and not seem to notice if the kid is a different color than we are. Also, I have a really nasty case of genital herpes. That's not contagious, is it?"

Thirty-seven

Late that night I climbed to the top of Jericho Ridge and waited for whatever was going to happen on the swimming beach below.

The nights were getting much cooler, and I buttoned my plaid shirt up over my T-shirt. It was a beautiful night, and the Milky Way looked just like it did the night Rachel and I had kissed and descended to the bottom of the lake. I was feeling pretty rotten. Perhaps I had laid it on too thick with Rachel, but I wanted to make sure she wouldn't look back. I was determined to be in this long enough to figure out what November ninth meant, and things might get pretty ugly before I knew. What I was doing had nothing to do with journalism. I wasn't even a reporter anymore. But it had everything to do with finding out what this group of wackos was up to. What if they were planning another Oklahoma City bombing? I didn't have enough data to give the FBI or anybody else the information to stop it. If I left now, and several hundred people died, how could I live with myself? Then again, the prospect of being a getaway-car driver wasn't appealing either. But how was I going to know what they were planning if I didn't prove myself in some way that would gain their trust?

My job was not to get caught.

I knew I was making a bargain with the devil, but I didn't have a choice, at least not until I had more information. Then, after I had what I needed and went to the authorities, I would be looking over my shoulder for the rest of my life, always expecting to be killed on the steps of some courthouse just like Randall Duane Slaughter had executed his Robert Ford—the snitch—on the steps of the Bowie County Plaza in Texas.

Oh, well. I had expected to meet my death by the time I was thirty, anyway. I had beaten that by ten years. What did I have to regret?

Down on the beach I noticed a fire had been lit near the shore. The family had gathered in a semicircle, and it was obvious they weren't intending to roast marshmallows.

Before them was a woman.

She was wearing some sort of loose-fitting white robe, like the kind I'd seen people wear when they were baptized, and she was kneeling in the sand in front of Abraham Smith. She had dark straight hair and a trim figure and seemed to be in her middle thirties, and I could hear her crying. I felt sorry for her and the Guatemalan.

Abraham Smith was lecturing her, and as he spoke, her sobbing became more violent. He was apparently giving her a very stern reprimand. But then, at the edge of the firelight, I noticed that a man was furiously working a post-hole digger. Was it the woman's husband? When he had finished one hole, he moved about three yards away and started with equal vigor on another.

Meanwhile, the old man's son had dragged over three pieces of four-by-four-inch lumber. Two of them looked like they were eight or ten feet long, a standard size from the lumberyard. The third piece was half the length of the other two.

Together, the husband and Joseph roped the longer pieces together in the middle, then hauled them up and inserted the ends into the freshly dug holes. Then, while Joseph held the X-shaped frame upright, the husband placed the shorter piece behind to brace it. Joseph allowed the frame to tilt back, and when it touched the brace more rope was wrapped around all three. Finally the husband took a sledgehammer and tapped the brace firmly against the frame, then repeated the process with each leg.

They each took a coil of rope, tied the ends firmly to the woman's wrists, and threw the ends over the X-frame. They then began walking down the beach in opposite directions, and the woman was pulled back against the crossed beams.

My God, I thought. *They're going to crucify her.*

Rachel and Leah were standing next to their grandfather. Rachel had her hands to her face, but Leah didn't so much as flinch as the woman was pulled tight against the cross. Now I noticed there were many other people on the beach as well, most of them just shadows outside the circle of firelight. I don't know how many there were, but it had to be at least a couple dozen. Most seemed to be men, but I'm sure I saw some dresses as well.

If Larsen was there, I didn't see him.

The husband grasped the woman around the waist and lifted her a couple of feet while Joseph scrambled to loop the rope around the tops of the beams. As the woman's feet left the ground, the group began to murmur. It was scary as hell. I couldn't make out what they were saying at first, but then it became louder: "Whore, whore, whore . . ."

I was on my feet now.

Joseph, the shrimpy little bastard, stood in front of the woman, grasped the front of her gown, and ripped it open. Her breasts spilled out.

I desperately wanted to help the woman, but what could I do? If I rushed down there and gave an impassioned speech about those without sin casting the first stone, they were likely to tear me to pieces. I had seen crowds turn violent before, from antiabortion protestors to soccer fans, and pleas for understanding never worked.

Rachel was pleading with Abraham. He turned his face away from her, and she fell in the sand and grasped the old man's cuff. He shook her away.

Rachel screamed.

It wasn't a scream of fear, but of frustration. She grasped a handful of sand and threw it in the old man's face, then walked away. Some of the people started to pursue her, but the old man held up his hand.

Rachel disappeared into the darkness.

Well, that settled it.

This woman was hanging by her wrists from a classic Roman crux decussata—by tradition, the cross on which Saint Andrew, patron of Scotland, was executed, the same "Saint Andrew's cross" that appears on the Scottish and Confederate flags. The crux decussata was much more common than the crux immissa, the Latin cross, the traditional T on which Jesus is depicted.

If the woman were left hanging from her arms like that for any period of time, she would die. Even though she was only a couple of feet off the ground, her legs were unable to support the weight of her body, and her diaphragm was struggling with the extra weight. Eventually she would become exhausted and unable to breathe, no matter how hard she tried.

Did these morons even know what they were doing? Perhaps they thought this was simply torture and humiliation instead of murder.

As I climbed down the ridge as fast as I could, my foot slipped and I dropped, my forehead glancing against a boulder. I slid the rest of the way down, and when my feet hit the ground I barely managed to keep my legs beneath me. My forehead wasn't badly injured, but I could feel blood dripping down the right side of my face.

The chanting continued.

The woman was gasping for breath.

As I crossed the beach, I took off my plaid shirt and let it drop. I didn't want anybody to grab it, spin me around, or use it to pin me. By the time I reached the woman, I had also picked up a chunk of driftwood that was about the size of a baseball bat.

"What the hell do you think you're doing?" the husband demanded, lunging out of the shadows just as I reached the base of the cross. He had his fists clenched and was about two steps away when I swung the driftwood with both hands.

It hit him perfectly on the chin.

The driftwood snapped in two amid a crack that sounded like a home run from my Little League days. The guy spun and dropped face-forward into the sand.

The crowd was stunned. The chanting stopped, and they stood staring at me, their wide eyes glinting in the firelight.

I jumped up and grabbed the end of one of the beams, trying to work the rope free of her wrist.

"Kill him!" Leah screamed.

The mob—it was no longer a crowd—rushed forward. They grabbed my waist and I found myself with three or four men and a couple of women on top of me. Fortunately, none of them had any idea of what they were doing, so I had taken only a light shot to the jaw and a couple to the ribs before the earsplitting sound of a submachine gun on full automatic ripped across the beach.

I could feel the sand spraying over me as the crowd scrambled for cover. Karl Larsen was standing a few yards away, his H&K MP5 at the ready, pointed toward the sand and with a bit of smoke wafting from the muzzle.

Rachel was standing behind him, her hand on the back of his leather jacket. Skorzeny and Eva were there too, standing on either side and slightly behind, watching the crowd.

"What in bloody hell is going on here?" Larsen asked.

I got to my feet.

"Are you hurt?"

"No," I said, wiping the blood from my face with my forearm.

"Then be a good lad and get her down."

"Love to," I said.

Keeping his left hand on the pistol grip of the MP5, Larsen pulled a folding Gerber knife from his belt with his right hand and opened it with a flick of his wrist.

While I cut the ropes with the Gerber, Eva draped the woman with my discarded shirt. Skorzeny grasped her around the waist and gently lowered her to the ground.

"Abraham, are you daft?" Larsen asked. "You were well on your way to killing this woman. Was that your intent? Morality aside, do you know what kind of consequences that would have?"

"It was the will of God," he said.

"What bloody bullshit," Larsen said.

He slung the MP5 over his shoulder.

"Go home, all of you," he said. "Nothing happened here. If our neighbors across the lake ask, we were just setting off some fireworks as part of our rather peculiar beliefs."

The crowd began to disperse.

"Abraham, old friend, you and I will talk tomorrow," Larsen said.

"Is she badly hurt?" I asked.

Rachel was kneeling over the woman.

"No, I don't think so," she said.

"Does she have somewhere to go?" I asked. "She obviously can't go home, with a beast like that waiting for her."

"I'll find a place for her," Rachel said.

I turned to walk away.

"Thank you," Rachel said.

I stopped.

"Do you know what your sister said?" I asked. "She told the crowd to kill me. Not stop me, or hurt me, but kill me. You're wrong about taking over the ministry, baby. She'll never let you. How long, Rachel, do you think it will before you're up there on that X-shaped cross and Leah is screaming for the congregation to kill *you?*"

Thirty-eight

In the morning an orange 1982 Chevrolet pickup with a bad muffler ambled across the compound toward the grave of Randall Duane Slaughter.

The Chevy came to a stop at the base of the low hill and then, gears grinding, it began to move slowly backward. I could see Elaine Schaeffer leaning out of the driver's window, one hand resting on the door skin, the other on the steering wheel, her head turned.

I stepped back into the shadows of the shop.

Elaine got out, pulled on a pair of work gloves, and went to the back of the truck. An old A-frame hoist was mounted in the back of the truck, and she began hooking some chains onto a wooden pallet on which rested a small granite stone.

I was confused.

What was Elaine doing here?

Then it made sense to me. Slaughter had apparently asked her to make his stone, and Elaine, being Elaine, had apparently agreed.

She couldn't have known where I was.

I fought back an urge to run across the compound toward her, to tell her what had happened during the last few weeks, to tell her how much I missed her and how sorry I was.

But I couldn't.

It would have put us both in too much danger. And she had made it clear she never wanted to speak to me again.

Granting that wish was the only thing I had left in my power to give. And considering the events of the night before, I figured it was best if I just got out of there. To make Jackson by that afternoon, I had to get started.

I got into the Crown Vic, started the engine, and headed for the highway without looking back.

Thirty-nine

Larsen called it the Two Percent Club.

While we ate pancakes and bacon in a booth of a down-home restaurant at the Casey Jones Village at Jackson, Tennessee, Larsen patiently explained to me the rules of the game.

Our table was far away from the nearest customer, and Larsen asked the waitress to fill our coffees only when beckoned, saying we had an important business deal to discuss.

"Oh, I'll bet's it's *international,*" she said.

"How'd you know, love?" Laying on the accent even thicker.

She walked away beaming.

Larsen took a sip of his coffee, then began.

"There's a bank robbery in the United States every fifty-two minutes," he said. "That is according to the FBI's Uniform Crime Reporting system. It amounts to a little more than ten thousand robberies per year, although the figures tend to increase when the economy is bad. The clearance rate for bank robbery is astonishingly high, fifty-eight percent. That means the odds favor getting caught. The only higher clearance rate for a major crime is murder, at sixty-two percent."

"Bank robbery seems like a very bad career move for a professional criminal," I said.

"Yes, but that is precisely where the figures are misleading," Larsen said. "The average bank robber is *not* a professional criminal, but an amateur."

Statistically, the odds are twenty to one that the robber is male, is acting alone, he said, and commits the robbery between nine and eleven A.M. on a Friday. Presumably banks have more money on Friday because it is payday for most people. Of these lone male gunmen, Larsen said, 86 percent have never committed a prior offense—in other words, amateurs.

"The really interesting part is that most bank robbers weren't really looking for money per se," he said, "but were looking to fulfill another need, usually for drugs. Also, even though bank robberies are portrayed on TV and in the movies as always involving firearms, more often than not guns are *not* used."

Eva nodded. This was obviously chapter and verse to her.

"Only one-third to one-half of all bank robbers are packing, which explains why the incidence of violence is surprisingly low," Larsen said. "While most robbers will use the specter of violence—a threatening note passed to a teller, for example—violence is seldom a consequence."

Only two percent of robbers are willing to use violence, he said. Kidnapping or hostage taking takes place in less than two percent of cases, and murder occurs in less than one percent.

"What do you conclude from this?" Larsen asked me.

"The goal is to be in the two percent that are well armed and willing to use violence," I said, "but to avoid dropping into those categories that include murder, kidnapping, and hostage taking."

"Precisely, old boy," Larsen said. "For a professional, that two-percent line is the difference between life and death. The goal is to use overwhelming force and get away quickly. But once that first shot is fired, the survival rate drops dramatically. If a hostage is actually taken or killed, the chances of survival are nil."

As an example, Larsen cited the 1997 North Hollywood Bank robbery, in which two well-armed men in heavy body armor attempted to shoot their way out of a robbery gone bad. Although the robbers initially had the upper hand in the bank and the street because of their superior firepower (they had assault rifles versus the sidearms for the first cops on the scene), they were no match once LAPD tactical teams arrived. The suspects also had too much body armor, which prevented them from moving as swiftly as they needed. LAPD SWAT chose the right weapon, in this case highly accurate .223-caliber AR-15s. The rifle gave them the range and accuracy to take the suspects legs out from under them, even while the policemen were hidden behind cars. Once the suspects were on the ground, they were killed.

Skorzeny was paying more attention to his blueberry pancakes than to the lecture.

"Skorzeny," Larsen said sternly. "Do you have an interest in surviving?"

"Sorry," he said, wiping his mouth.

"Good, then pay attention," Larsen said. "We must control the robbery situation from the start, have a plan to get in and out as quickly as possible, and be willing to think on our feet to come up with an alternative before being forced to pull the trigger."

Skorzeny nodded. Eva's eyes were shining.

"Once that happens, it is no longer a robbery, but a battle, and we are essentially a very small squad cut off by a poorer-equipped but larger and better-organized force," Larsen said. "Our only hope is to find an egress. Once we are surrounded, the battle is over. Surrender is out of the question, and the squad will be killed in the field—and killed particularly quickly if police or civilians have suffered losses."

A few seconds of silence descended on the table.

"Karl," I said, "I understand the two-percent concept, and how important it is to go up to that line without going beyond it. But what I don't understand is why anyone will still engage in this activity when doing it correctly seems so difficult, doing it wrong is laughably easy, and the rewards seem meager."

"Ah," Karl said. "Here is the bottom line: even though most robberies net only a few thousand dollars, which is quickly recovered, we two percenters are responsible for huge losses among banks and armored-car companies."

"How much?" I asked.

"This is the best part," Eva said, a gleam in her eye.

"Last year, seventy million dollars was stolen from banks in the United States," he said. "Of that amount, only twenty percent was ever recovered."

Forty

We robbed three banks in three days.

The first was a Union Planters branch in Jackson, Tennessee, just around the corner from where we had breakfast, and things happened so fast I don't remember much.

Less than a minute after Karl Larsen and his two accomplices entered the bank, I was pulling up to the front and they were coming out carrying gym bags full of cash. They hit the floor of the Crown Vic as I pulled smoothly across the parking lot.

In ten minutes we had made an uneventful trip to the drugstore, where Larsen had stashed the other vehicles.

Larsen stayed behind a moment after Eva and Skorzeny bailed out. I cracked the driver's door and vomited blueberry pancakes onto the asphalt.

"You did well," he said. "That's a perfectly normal reaction. You'll get over it."

As I closed the door and straightened behind the wheel, he handed me a handkerchief.

"Thanks," I said.

"You'll meet us at ten hundred hours the day after tomorrow at Lake Catherine State Park at Malvern, Arkansas."

"It's a big park," I said.

"There's a visitor's center and gift shop overlooking the lake," he said. "There's a patio between the gift shop and the parking area. Can you remember that?"

"No problem," I said.

"Good," Larsen said, and opened the passenger's door.

"Oh, you might want to hide that a little better," Larsen said, indicating the Benelli riot gun on the seat beside me. He didn't know that I had unloaded it before the robbery.

"What about the car?" I asked.

"Dump it and buy another," he said.

"We can't use it again?"

"Don't be daft," he said. He handed me a bundle of hundred-dollar bills from the gym bag. "And be discreet."

Good. It would give me time to contact Sheryl at the *Traveler*, even if I had to go there in person because she never answered her goddamned phone. I had stopped at pay phones three times on my way to Jackson and tried to reach her, but the phone rang until it switched over to voice mail. After the tone, all I got was a message saying her mailbox was full. I had to talk to Sheryl, because she was the only one I trusted to call the FBI and explain the situation.

Larsen got out, gave me a little salute, and slammed the door.

I put the Crown Vic in reverse.

"Wait," Eva said.

I stepped on the brakes.

She opened the passenger's door and got in.

"You didn't think we were going to let you make the trip on your own, did you?" she asked, pulling the seat belt across and fastening it. It seemed an odd gesture, considering we had just committed an armed robbery.

As I wheeled the car toward Interstate 40, we passed three police cars, all running hot toward the Union Planters branch. None of them gave us a second look.

Eva watched them in the rearview mirror.

"Something wrong?"

"No," she said.

"Isn't Larsen worried that you're riding with me in the dump car?" I asked. "Doesn't he think that's too big a risk?"

"Nope," she said. "He knows that if we're cornered, I'd kill both of us to prevent giving the operation away." She took the Benelli and tossed it across the seat onto the back floorboards. "You hungry?"

•

Eva paid too much for a seven-year-old Buick Regal at a used-car lot at De Valls Bluff, Arkansas. She followed me to the next town, where we cleaned out and wiped down the Crown Vic and left it in the parking lot of a hospital.

We spent the night in a room with double beds at a Holiday Inn Express at Pine Bluff, and I have to admit I enjoyed sleeping in a decent room and eating delivery pizza, even if it was with somebody who had sworn to kill me should the need arise.

The only argument we had was over what kind of pizza to get. Eva wanted thick-crust and I wanted thin. Eva wanted anchovies and I can't stand them.

We ended up ordering two pizzas.

Eva snapped on the television and, as she flipped through the channels, she asked if I had a girlfriend.

"Well, there's Rachel," I said.

"She's not your girlfriend," Eva said, taking another bite of pizza. "You may be fucking her, but she is definitely nobody's girlfriend. Anybody else?"

"Yeah," I said.

"Serious?"

"Not anymore," I said.

"Oh," she said. "How's your face?"

"What?"

"Your face," she said. "You know, from the beach party the other night? That was crazy. I felt sorry for the woman, and I thought for sure you were toast."

"Me too," I said. "So what's the story with you and Skorzeny?"

"No story," she said. "We aren't an item, if that's what you mean. We met Karl and he gave us new lives."

"As Eva Braun and Otto Skorzeny."

"Why not?" she asked.

"That makes Larsen Hitler," I said. "And Eva was . . ."

"Yeah, I know. But it's different. I'm just devoted to him, that's all. Before I met him I was a mess. My life had no direction, I hated myself, and I had tried to kill myself half a dozen times."

"That explains the scars on your wrists."

"Yeah," she said, pulling up her sleeves. "Pretty gruesome, huh? Typical of a borderline personality disorder. How about that scar on the back of your right hand?"

"I was beaten up by a cop a long time ago," I said. "While his partner had me down on the ground, he cuffed me, turned my hand over, and ground his heel into my palm. Hurt like hell and took the skin right off."

"What did you do to get beat up?"

"Wrong place at the wrong time," I said. "Antigay demonstration."

"Which side were you on?" she asked carefully.

"I'm not gay," I said. "But I wasn't marching."

She nodded.

"So you're borderline?"

"Yeah," she said. "It sucks."

"Are you gay?"

"Bisexual."

"So if you're not with Karl or Skorzeny, what do you do for . . ."

"Release?" she asked with a smile. "Whatever I want."

After meeting the others at the state park, we drove to Arkadelphia, where we hit the Regions Bank and a branch of the Elkhorn Bank & Trust within ten minutes of each other. I was driving the Regal, of course, so I had no idea of what was actually happening inside at the time, but things seemed to go smoothly enough. At each bank Larsen left a grinning plastic jack-o'-lantern filled with Halloween candy and a bundle of road flares bound together with black electrical tape. Afterward we wiped down the Buick and dumped it in the parking lot of the Arkadelphia Christian Church.

Then I vomited and we all piled into a battered blue Ford Econoline van with Larsen at the wheel. We headed southwest on Interstate 30.

"Texas?" I asked.

"We don't rob banks in Texas," Eva said.

"It's hard to control the locals, everybody is armed, and the consequences are rather dire if you're caught," Larsen said. "Relax, friends. We're going on holiday."

Forty-one

"*¿Adonde vas?*"

Larsen smiled and shot a confused look at the customs officer.

"I'm sorry; I don't speak Spanish."

"Where are you going, sir?"

We had gotten the red light coming over from Del Rio and were pulled over, with a grim-faced customs official on each side of the Econoline.

"Villa Acuña," Larsen said.

"Ciudad Acuña," the official corrected him. "It hasn't been called a village in some years. How long will you be staying?"

"Just the day."

"Sightseeing?"

"Yes."

"Returning tonight?"

"Yes."

"You are a long way from home, Mr. Pierce," the officer said, looking at the fake Montana driver's license on the clipboard in front of him. Equally fraudulent were the registration and insurance papers to match the license. "Do you have someplace to stay?"

"I'm spending the week with my sister and her family in Del Rio."

Eva was in the passenger's seat, and she removed her sunglasses, placed them on top of her head, and flashed a winning smile.

"Hi, I'm Peggy."

"Buenos tardes," he said. "And the two gentlemen?"

"Her husband and his friend," Larsen said.

The officer looked past Larsen to where Skorzeny and I were sitting. I waved.

"Ah," he said. "Do you mind if we take a look inside?"

"Not at all," Larsen said.

Eva turned to me. "Would you mind, Al?"

I slid open the side cargo door and sunlight flooded in. The officer on Eva's side stood with his hands on his belt and looked us over from behind a pair of aviator sunglasses.

"Do you have any electronics?"

"No," Larsen said.

"Any guns or explosives?"

"None."

An hour ago there had been enough hardware and ammunition to start World War III and enough money to keep it going for a day or two. Now it was divided among storage lockers in Del Rio.

The guy behind the sunglasses shrugged.

"Bueno," the officer said, and handed the license and other papers back to Larsen. "Have a good time and be careful, please. Tell me, please, your speech. *¿Inglés?"*

"Oh," Larsen said. "British, yes. Emigrated to America years ago but could never quite lose the accent. Cheerio."

I slammed the door shut and we pulled away.

"Why did you call me Al?"

"Al and Peggy Bundy," Eva said.

Forty-two

It was late afternoon by the time we pulled the van into Boy's Town, in the desert just outside of Acuña. We were following a taxi that had picked up a couple of college students downtown. The road was so badly plagued by potholes that top speed was about thirty miles per hour, unless you were looking for an excuse for some dental work. The terrain also became remarkably rugged the farther we went, and by the time we rolled through the entrance to the fenced compound it seemed like a moonscape.

There were guards with automatic rifles walking the perimeter.

"Jesus Christ," I said.

"Don't worry," Larsen said. "They pay them to make sure nothing happens to the nice American tourists. As long as you have money, you can get whatever you want here—drugs, women, young boys. Mexican politicians are always saying they've cleaned it up, that they've put Boy's Town out of business, but they never do for long. Business is too good."

There were half a dozen buildings in the compound, most of which had signs that claimed them to be bars or dance halls. The taxi pulled up to the entrance of the largest building, a green affair with flashing lights, and deposited the college students.

Larsen parked the van in the middle of the lot.

"Say good-bye to the Econoline," he said. "We're leaving it here for the vultures. We'll take a taxi back and just walk across the bridge to Del Rio."

Larsen walked past the entrance to the green building.

"Do you know where you're going?"

"Trust me, love," he said.

We followed Larsen to a structure that was faded to the same shade as the landscape, and he held the door open for us. There was no sign, as there had been on the other buildings. Eva and Skorzeny walked inside, but I hesitated.

"What's wrong?" Larsen asked. "Don't you trust me?"

"If I were you and was thinking about getting rid of somebody," I said, "I might bring them to someplace like this. It's a perfect spot for a murder—not only is it remote and beyond the jurisdiction of the United States, but it has its own law enforcement, which I'm sure is the best money can buy."

"I'm hurt," Larsen said. "If I wanted to get rid of you, you would already be dead."

I stepped inside.

The door closed behind us.

It was as dark as a tomb inside. All I could see were some forty-watt bulbs over an old-fashioned bar to the side, a few more dim lights over a stage, and some white Christmas lights that serpentined around the metal columns spaced around the room. Another string of lights traced the outline, in right angles, of some stairs on the far side.

I bumped into a table.

"Careful," Larsen said, taking his sunglasses off and propping them on top of his head. "It appears we have the place to ourselves, or nearly so."

Slow-dancing in front of the stage was a biker couple. They were both wearing jeans and leather. She had her arms wrapped around his neck, and he had his hands beneath her halter top, which was untied in back. There was no music.

"I wonder how many donkeys that stage has seen," Eva said.

We grabbed one of the tables near the back wall and crowded to one side of it, where we could all keep an eye on the biker couple. He was busy removing the halter, and she didn't seem to mind.

A waiter materialized and asked what we wanted to drink.

The others ordered Dos Equis and I asked for bottled water.

"Come on," Larsen said. "Live a bit. We're celebrating, and you can't toast with a bloody bottle of Aquafina."

"All right," I said. "Bring me a Tecate along with that water."

The bikers had switched positions. She was now dancing with her back to him, his hands were locked beneath her breasts, and from the way the Christmas lights glinted in her eyes, I knew she was making sure we were looking.

The waiter brought the tray, placed the drinks on the table, and lit Larsen's cigarette as soon as he had pulled it from the pack. When Larsen gave him a hundred-dollar bill and told him to keep the change, the man gave a stiff little bow and asked if we required anything else.

"Not at the moment."

Larsen held his beer aloft.

"A toast," he said. "May we all live to a hundred years—and have an extra year to repent. Cheers."

We clinked bottles and drank.

"Health," Skorzeny said.

We clinked and drank again.

I held up my bottle.

"'My boat is on the shore and my bark is on the sea,'" I said. "'But before I go . . . here's a double health to thee!'"

"Bloody hell," Larsen murmured. "Byron."

"One does not have to be English to read it," I said.

"And a wit to boot."

"I am lightly armed," I said, "but I try to use what I have to my advantage."

"Eva?" Larsen asked. "Your turn."

"I'll drink to the man in the boat," she said.

We all laughed raucously.

The waiter brought another round of drinks, including another bottle of water for me, even though I had not yet opened the first. "On the house," he said quietly. I noticed that he left an additional drink at the table, something in a short glass that looked like a mixed drink.

"Did you order this?" Eva said, examining the drink. She sniffed it, then returned it to the table. "Doesn't seem to have any alcohol in it."

"It doesn't," Larsen said. "Probably Coca-Cola."

"Who's it for?" Skorzeny asked.

"Her," Larsen said, and nodded toward a teenage Mexican girl standing beside Eva.

"Hello," the girl said with a heavy accent. "Would you like company?"

She said her name was Maria, and she was extraordinarily beautiful. She was wearing a tight turquoise blouse and a long black skirt with a slit up the thigh. Her earrings were tiny carved skeletons.

"Don't be rude," Larsen said.

Eva offered her a chair.

"Gracias," Maria said.

"Yaqui?" Larsen asked.

She nodded.

"It is a cottage industry," Larsen explained. "Families from the interior send their daughters to work here for a few years. It is not considered improper. These girls often provide the only financial security their families will ever know."

Maria sipped her drink.

"You are on vacation?" she asked.

"Indeed," Larsen said.

Maria rested her hand on my leg.

"I like your earrings," I said.

She flipped her head, and the little skeletons danced.

"They are for the Day of the Dead," she said.

"Is it November second already?"

"Not yet," she said. "It's Sunday. You call it, *cómo se dice*, All Hallow's Eve."

"Halloween," I said.

An old man walked up to the table. He carried a wooden tray slung around his neck, and on the tray was a car battery. Cables ran from the battery terminals to a couple of handgrips.

"Five dollars," the old man said.

Larsen shook his head.

The old man shrugged and walked toward the biker couple.

"What was that about?" I asked.

"Foolishness," Larsen said. "Grab the handles and see how long you can hold on. Or, if you're too drunk to stand, you can shock yourself back to consciousness."

A couple minutes later, an old man with the Polaroid appeared. We squeezed to one side of the table, with Maria wedged between Eva and me. Eva had been knocking back her beer, and, although she was quiet, I could tell from her eyes that she was quite drunk. Larsen paid the old man, then placed the photo on the table while the image began to trace itself like a ghost in the emulsion.

"Is anyone lonely?" Maria asked.

"From time to time," Larsen said. "Tell me, if we were lonely, what would we do about it?"

"We would go upstairs," Maria said.

"I see. And what would we do up there?"

"Whatever we like," Maria said.

"And how much would that cost?"

"It depends on what you like," Maria said. "What most people like starts at sixty dollars for one half-hour."

Larsen picked up the Polaroid. The image was nearly formed.

"Nice," he said. He slid it across the table. "What about eighty dollars?"

"Pardon?" Maria asked, not understanding.

"You're right; I'm being cheap. Let's say a hundred dollars. Would that be all right?"

"Well, yes . . ."

"You're right. If a hundred is good, two hundred is better. And using that logic, we might as well make it five hundred. Would that be acceptable?"

Maria looked at the floor. "I do not know what you want," she said quietly.

"You are the most beautiful girl here?" Larsen asked.

"Please," Maria said.

"You know the answer," Larsen said. "Be honest. It is all right. What is the phrase? *¿La mujer más linda aquí?*"

"Yes," Maria said. The she added quickly, "And my sister."

"Do you like Eva?"

Understanding blossomed on Maria's face.

"Ah, you like to watch?"

"No," Larsen said.

Maria shrugged.

"I am not so sure," she said. "It is usually . . ."

Larsen nodded.

"Eva, would you mind if Otto lent a hand?"

She murmured that it would be all right.

Skorzeny began to protest.

"Please," Larsen said as he placed money in Otto's hand. "Don't tell me you don't share this fantasy with ninety-eight percent of the male population. Go on. Have fun; you've earned it."

Maria took Eva's hand and they both stood. Eva smiled, thanked Larsen, and then put her arms around Maria and kissed her passionately. Then Maria led her away, with Skorzeny trailing behind.

The biker couple watched the trio walk up the stairs.

Larsen smiled.

"What about you?" he asked me. "What would make you less lonely?"

"Sorry, but you can't buy it here."

"Still in love," Larsen said. "A hopeless bloody romantic, is that it? Thank God I don't share that handicap. Shortly I intend to find Maria's sister and determine for myself whether she was telling the truth."

He finished his second beer. The waiter brought yet another round. Now I had three unopened bottles of water. I pushed the Tecate aside and opened one of them.

Perhaps thinking about Elaine had cleared my head, or perhaps I knew I'd never get another chance alone with Larsen, but I decided to press my luck.

"Are you going to tell me what you're planning, or do I have to continue wondering when I'm going to get a bullet in the back of my head?"

Larsen smiled.

"Have you ever heard of an infernal place called Mount Weather?"

Forty-three

Mount Weather, Larsen explained, is the secret underground base that is the headquarters for the shadow government that runs the United States.

It is located forty-six miles northwest of Washington, D.C., sunk into a granite mountain near the town of Bluemont, Virginia, near the West Virginia border. It is officially called the Western Virginia Office of Controlled Conflict Operations, and it is a massive underground facility maintained by the Federal Emergency Management Agency.

Owned by the federal government since 1903, it started life as an artillery range and a weather station. But in 1936, the U.S. Bureau of Mines started excavations that resulted in the massive underground complex we now have today.

So secret that most members of Congress don't even know it exists, Mount Weather was originally constructed during the dark early days of the Cold War, and is an underground city with everything necessary to carry on the executive functions of government: a Pentagon and a White House, down to a duplicate version of the Oval Office.

Mount Weather has streets and sidewalks, apartment complexes, hospitals, bowling alleys, and its own freshwater pond. It stores enough food and supplies to last the entire community a month without ever seeing daylight. Mount Weather had color television before the rest of the country even dreamed of it, so that real-time televised war meetings could take place in living color.

For forty years it has also been the repository of known pieces of information on every American: their Social Security numbers, their birth dates, their employment, education, and health histories, their spending habits, their sexual proclivities, even samples of their DNA.

It is the headquarters for a group of a hundred other underground relocation centers that would, in the event of a national catastrophe, be the new homes of those deemed most capable to survive a national catastrophe. It is also the center of a system of concentration camps that are being covertly built across America, to hold those who are not lucky enough to get into any of the one hundred elite centers. It is presumed that in time, we will simply die out.

Mount Weather stands ready, on the word of the president, to assume the duties of governing the United States. It was the "secure location," Larsen said, that Vice President Dick Cheney was whisked to in the days following the September 11 attacks.

It will collaborate with the United Nations, Larsen said, to declare martial law, which in turn will usher in the New World Order.

For that reason, Larsen said, it must be destroyed.

"What, with a fuel-oil-and-fertilizer bomb?"

"Amateur stuff," Larsen said. "Effective, but works only on above-ground targets."

"So what do you propose?"

"Ah," Larsen said. "I'll show you when we get back home."

"Good," I said. "So I guess you're waiting until you find out who wins the election before actually carrying out the plan?"

"It doesn't matter who wins the election—America will still be ruled by the Zionist Occupation Government."

"ZOG," I said.

"Right."

"Then why November ninth?"

Larsen laughed.

"It's the anniversary of Kristallnacht," Larsen said. "'The night of broken glass.' That's the night in 1938 when the Nazis finally started in earnest to drive the Jewish cancer out of Germany."

Kristallnacht was an extended race riot, with Nazi gangs roaming German streets, breaking the windows of Jewish homes and business, and burning 101 synagogues. Seventy-five thousand Jews were arrested and sent to concentration camps, and ninety-one died of beatings.

The excuse for the frenzy was when seventeen-year-old Herschel Grynszpan decided to assassinate the German ambassador to France because his family had been forced out of their home and business in Hanover by German police. At the embassy in Paris on November 7 Grynszpan failed to find the ambassador, however, but settled for shooting the third secretary, Ernst vom Rath.

Rath died two days later, on November 9.

It was just what Goebbels, Hitler's chief of propaganda, was waiting for. He launched a radio offensive that claimed Grynszpan's attack was part of an international conspiracy against the Third Reich. The result was not only the violence of Kristallnacht, but a pogrom that took whatever rights were left to German Jews.

I failed to understand why Larsen would believe

Americans would find this date significant, much less be inspired to begin a race war then.

Larsen, however, was adamant.

I asked him why, as an Englishman, he would even care. After all, hadn't the Nazis tried to destroy England? Hadn't he ever heard of the blitz?

"My grandmother was a member of the Irish Republican Army," he said. "She was secretly hoping the Nazis would win, because it would mean a free Ireland. She was a Nazi collaborator, so I come by the Totenkopf honestly. By the way, the skull-and-crossbones device was used by the English Black Brunswickers long before the SS adopted it. But you don't hear much about that, or the English occupation of Ireland, here in the States."

"We know a little," I said. "What about your parents?"

"My mother was English, of course, and my father was an American CIA officer. We lived all over the world, and eventually he was stationed in Vietnam. He worked with the Montagnard tribesmen in the central highlands, and when Saigon fell in 1975, the Americans left all of those magnificent 'yard bastards to fend for themselves. There were two million in 1975. Now the communists have killed all of them but three hundred and fifty thousand. Not only because they were our allies, but because they are predominantly Christian."

"And you?" I asked. "What's your story? You hardly seem a good candidate for a rac—" I almost said *racist*. "Race warrior."

"I had some trouble when I was a kid," he said. "After the war were living near CIA headquarters at Langley, Virginia, and I fell in with the wrong crowd. I stole a police car and got caught. I ended up spending a couple of nights in a District of Columbia jail."

He paused.

"And?"

"The second night I was beaten by a half dozen black gang members, forced down on the floor, and was gang raped," he said. "While I was in jail my father died of a heart attack. It made things incredibly . . . painful. I've hated the black bastards ever since."

"So your life of crime began early."

"Not really," he said. "A few years after that I enlisted in the army. Desert Storm. I saw what we did to the Iraqi people the first time. Now I can't believe we're doing it again, only this time it's worse."

"You were in the American army?"

"Nope," he said. "I held dual citizenship, so it was no problem to enlist in the British army. I was a commando."

"Rank?" I said.

"Just a corporal," he said.

Then he turned nostalgic.

"My father had this Zippo lighter that he carried during operations with the Montagnards, and I carried it with me on every mission. Unfortunately, I lost it recently."

Forty-four

Larsen had planned well, because once we crossed the border into Del Rio, we walked a short distance to a fenced parking lot, where we retrieved his black Rubicon.

After we visited the two storage sheds, there was little room in the Jeep besides the four of us, so we ended up tying some of the gym bags on the top and fenders. Eva particularly thought this was hilarious, and begged Larsen to allow her to drive. He consented, and she immediately hopped into the driver's seat. She donned a pair of headphones, put a Dresden CD into her personal player, and turned the volume up so loud that Skorzeny and I, sitting in the backseat, could hear it even when we were on the highway.

At every gas station and restaurant we stopped at on the way back, I tried to find a pay phone to place a 911 call, but I was never alone for long enough. Besides, what would I say when they asked what kind of bomb was going to be used to destroy Mount Weather, and where could I be reached for more information?

We pulled through the pink fence posts and into the Covenant compound at about nine the next morning, and Eva parked the Jeep in front of the shop, where the yellow 1972 Ford truck waited.

"Come with me," Larsen said.

As I followed him to the church beneath Kingdom Tower, I could hear the children singing in the school beside the canteen. It was Tuesday morning, November 2—Election Day in the United States and, interestingly enough, also the Day of the Dead in Mexico.

"The lake is low," Larsen said, looking out over the water. "You can see where the high-water mark was just a few days ago."

The church door was unlocked, and Larsen swung it open for me.

"How did you know the event would take place November ninth?" he asked suddenly. "I only remember saying something important would happen during the first week or so in November."

"Eva mentioned the date during the trip from Tennessee to Arkansas," I said calmly as I stepped through the door. "But she said nothing about the target."

"She couldn't," Larsen said, closing the door behind us. "She doesn't know yet."

The church was empty.

We walked down the aisles, past the pulpit, and Larsen took out a key and unlocked the metal door on the side of the miracle spring bluff.

After I passed through, he locked the door behind us.

The place was built like a bunker. No, strike that. The place *was* a bunker.

We went down one flight of stairs, paused on the landing, and Larsen unlocked another steel door. While he did, I peered down the stairs. I couldn't tell how far they went down.

Larsen let me in; then I waited in the darkness while

Larsen turned the lock on that door. Then he found the light switch, and I found myself standing at the bank of a concrete room, perhaps twenty feet by forty, that itself was a small church. There were folding chairs in rows, and an aisle that led to a big wooden pulpit. Behind the pulpit was a red Nazi banner, with a white circle and a black swastika, and it hung vertically, the way I had seen them in old newsreel footage.

"Is that the real thing?"

"It's not a battle flag," Larsen said. "But yes, it is the real thing, a party banner like the ones that hung in every municipal office in Germany and its occupied countries. Some GI probably grabbed it and stuffed it in his pack on his way through some little town on his way to the Rhine."

Larsen walked down the aisle and knelt behind the pulpit. He moved the pulpit, revealing a metal door in the concrete floor. He grasped a metal ring and swung the door up, revealing a vaultlike depression that was probably three by four feet.

Side by side were a couple of bombs with orange nose cones, a pair of yellow bands behind, and green casings. Stenciled in black on the sides of both was the designation USAF B67 and a serial number. An eagle-and-swastika design had been added in high visibility orange paint beneath each serial number.

"How powerful are these?"

"Depends on the yield you dial in via the PAL and AMACS."

"What do you mean, yield?"

"I mean kilotons," he said. "These aren't big bombs, like a megaton warhead used on a submarine or an ICBM, but they will produce a healthy explosion. Say, a fraction of a kiloton to twenty-five or thirty."

I thought I would vomit.

"Nukes?" I said.

"Beautiful, aren't they?"

"This small? I thought suitcase nukes were the small ones. You know, the ones Russia lost a few years back?"

"Sure," he said. "But they're worthless now. Tritium has a limited shelf life. Because they use uranium they are poor dirty bombs."

"Hadn't thought of that."

"But these are fresh," Larsen said. "A new kind of earth penetrator called Falling Star. So secret only a few people in the military even know about them."

"Then how did you get your hands on them?"

"Why do you think we've been robbing banks?" he asked. "You see me living in a big house? No, we've been working for a cause. These bad boys are going to make the world sit up and take notice."

"Why two?" I asked. "There's only one target."

"What if one's a dud?" he asked. "We need a backup."

"Good thinking," I said.

He lowered the door, then motioned for me to help him move the pulpit back over it. "At first I thought we were going to have to strictly go with a dirty bomb," he said. "It would work, but it might not accomplish everything we hoped for in regard to Mount Weather. After all, that granite's pretty thick, and it has a blast door comparable to the one at Cheyenne Mountain."

"So how were you going to destroy it?"

"They have to breathe, don't they?" he said. "There are air shafts dotting the facility. Get close enough to one, explode a dirty bomb, and you're going to flood the complex with so much radioactive gas that the scrubbers will never be able to handle it. Nobody will be able to live down there for a few thousand years."

"Or, depending on the wind, for a fifty-mile radius."

"Exactly," Larsen said. "But now that's our backup. Werner had developed the circuits he believes we need to mimic the PAL and AMAC systems, so we can actually use it as a thermonuclear device. That will take care of the shadow government, huh?"

"I don't know what a PAL or an AMAC is," I said.

"Safeguard to keep from firing the damn things."

"But how are you going to deliver them? Don't you need a missile or an airplane?"

"We're going to use the truck you repaired. The weapon and Werner's entire electronics package will fit right into the bed, with room to put a camper over them."

"Your father's truck."

"Nah, I lied about that," he said. "It's just another old truck."

"Werner, the nice guy who is the shortwave engineer."

"Can you believe it? He really is a genius. He figured out that the government cut some corners to reduce the size of the electronics systems, and he found a way around them. He's only got one, though, but we'll have the other as a dirty-bomb backup. Kind of like Hiroshima and Nagasaki, huh? Two different types of bombs?"

My mouth was dry.

"How many kilotons?" I asked.

"Maximum," he said. "We want to make sure we got all of those soulless fuckers."

That was it. I had everything. It was time to get out, to make some pleasant talk with Larsen, tell him how impressed I was, and then say I was dying to take a shower and skip over the perimeter fence and run like hell until I found a phone to dial the closest FBI office.

"I'm impressed," I said.

"Exciting, isn't it?" Larsen asked. "You know, Allan, I had some doubts about you early on. But after that night on the beach, during the attempted crucifixion, I knew both your head and your heart were in the right place. As they used to say, you're a credit to your race."

Yeah, I thought. *The human race.*

"Man, I'm beat," I said. "Didn't realize robbing banks was so much work. I think I'll head up to the cabin, take a shower, and find some clean clothes. May take a nap after that."

"Sounds like a plan," Larsen said as we walked up the aisle toward the door. "I may do the same."

Larsen unlocked the door, and when he swung it open Leah Smith was leaning against the wall on the opposite side of the hallway, her hands behind her back, a smile on her face.

"My grandfather is unhappy with you," she told Larsen.

"He'll get over it," Larsen said. "Soon everything will be different."

"I'll say," Leah said, and brought something from behind her back. It was a wallet.

I froze in horror as I realized it was *my* wallet.

She opened it and took out the driver's license.

"What have you got?" Larsen asked.

"Something you'll be very interested in," Leah said. "I found it in Rachel's room, hidden at the back of her unmentionables drawer. This is certainly an unmentionable, isn't it, Mr. Kelsey?"

Larsen took the license, looked at the picture and the name, then looked at me.

"You'll be interested in this as well," she said, handing him my press credentials. "Seems she's been hiding quite a lot about her boy toy from us."

Larsen took the press card and, together with the license, held them both for a long time with his left hand.

"You're that reporter," Larsen said, struggling to believe. "You're the guy who wrote the story about Slaughter, and who old Abraham complained kept calling here, and who Clark told us he rousted out of the courthouse in Berryville."

What could I say? I ran up the stairs.

"It's locked, remember?" Larsen called. "No use. That's the only way out."

I tried the door anyway.

"Sonuvabitch," I said.

I could not believe how close I was to getting away with the complete story. A matter of minutes, or perhaps even seconds. I struck the door hard enough with my right hand to bloody my knuckles, then turned to look down the stairs.

Larsen had the Eagle in his left hand.

"Are you packing?" he asked.

"No," I said.

"Come on down and let's make sure," Larsen said. "You know the drill. Hands behind your head, fingers laced."

Larsen frisked me, and when he was satisfied that I indeed had no gun on me, he struck me backhanded across the face.

I stumbled backward, but managed to keep my footing. I probed my jaw with my tongue, tasted the coppery tang of blood, and found a loose tooth.

"Do you know I don't have any dental insurance?" I asked. I know it sounds absurd, but it was the first thing that came to mind.

Leah laughed derisively.

"You know what I can't stand?" Larsen asked.

He brought the Eagle up and pointed it between my eyes.

"Traitors."

"Wait," Leah said. "You can't kill him."

"Why not?" Larsen asked. He was so angry that the front sight on the barrel was wavering.

"Because you don't know who he's told," she said.

"Dammit," Larsen said, and the barrel of the Eagle came up.

"But I have some ideas how you can find out," she said.

"How?" Larsen asked.

"Rachel," she said. "Then, if he doesn't care enough about her for that to work, there's always that kike bitch he's been fucking from Conway."

Forty-five

"Elaine's here?"

"No, but we know where she lives," Leah said. "It's as easy to kill her there as it is here. Easier, actually, because we can make it look like a robbery. Right, Karl?"

"She's right, I'm afraid," Larsen said, following me down the stairs with the gun drawn.

"Fuck her," I said. "Kill her, I don't care."

"Okay," Larsen said. "We will."

Shit, that worked well.

"Could you show me Rachel?"

"No," Leah said.

"I think it's customary," I said. "You know, you have to show the person you're blackmailing the person you're threatening to kill, so they will know they are still alive? Otherwise, you have no leverage."

"No," Leah said.

"Then I won't tell you anything," I said.

"Oh, you'll talk," Larsen said.

"Or what, you'll kill me? Kill me."

"You don't mean that," he said. "Oh, perhaps you do now, but you won't once we pull your fingernails out with pliers and slice your nipples off. Cattle prods are useful, and battery cables attached to testicles seem also to work well."

"You're bluffing," I said. "I know you, Larsen. You may be crazy, but you're not a sadist. Let me see Rachel."

Larsen paused.

"All right, but only for a moment."

"Crap," Leah said, but led the way down the hall, unlocked a door, and swung it open. Rachel was sitting in a chair, her hands tied behind her back, and a red rubber ball in her mouth. Leah took the ball out of her mouth so she could talk.

"Have they hurt you?" I asked.

"Not yet."

"What were you doing with my billfold?"

"I found it in the weeds along the highway where we found you," she said. "I thought I had hidden it well enough for the others not to find, but I was wrong. I'm sorry. I was going to give it back to you eventually."

"Why didn't you?"

"I didn't want you to leave," she said. "I also figured out you were probably here for a story, and I thought you might be my way out of here. But I was conflicted. Also, since you weren't honest with me about who you were, I was acting childish, I suppose, and pretending that I didn't know the truth."

"I understand," I said.

"What are we going to do?" Rachel asked.

"I'm going to do whatever it takes to make sure you're safe," I said. "It's that simple. So don't worry. This won't last that long. Besides, they're not going to kill old Abraham's favorite granddaughter."

"He doesn't know she's here," Leah said. "You know, accidents happen . . . like being hit by lightning while walking across the lawn, or falling down a bluff, or being hit by a car on the highway. That's pretty much in God's hands."

"Ignore her," I said. "You'll be fine."

Larsen jerked me toward the room.

"Don't worry," I called; then Larsen punched me in the stomach and I went to my knees, and that was how he pulled me across the threshold.

Rachel began to cry.

Leah slammed and locked the door.

"Got a plan?" Leah asked.

"Indeed I do," Larsen said, and he kicked me in the ribs. "Unfortunately, it's going to cost me something I didn't intend on losing yet. Be a love and leave me alone with whatever his name is for a few moments."

Leah nodded and bounded up the stairs.

Larsen lit a Marlboro. He was using a cheap book of matches he had picked up at a restaurant somewhere.

"Did I hurt you?" he asked.

"Yes." I gasped.

"Good," he said. "Now, here's the deal, as you Americans say. We are going to rob one last bank. Or rather, you and Eva are going to rob one last bank. Tomorrow, say ten o'clock?"

"Tomorrow?"

"It's Election Day. Fits with the Aryan Republican Army's modus operandi, don't you think?" he said. "Eva will be in charge."

"I'm the getaway driver?"

"No," Larsen said. "You're in the bank, helping."

"Then who's driving?"

"Oh, I will drive you over myself," Larsen said. "But then I'll drop you kids off to have your fun. I don't expect you will need anyone waiting for you outside."

"You're going to tip them off?"

"Absolutely not," he said. "But things do have a way of going wrong."

"Even if I'm killed, you don't know who I've tipped off. What's that going to accomplish?"

"You haven't told anyone," he said. "I had Charles LeMaine call your paper and inquire after you. He was told you no longer work there, and haven't for weeks. Believing this might just be a cover, he sent someone to talk to your landlady at that pitiful little apartment in north Little Rock. She also said you've been gone for weeks, skipping out on the rent and leaving her with a junk car in the driveway."

"There really is a Charles LeMaine?"

"What's odd about that?"

"Never mind," I said. "Maybe I'm working for the feds and all of this is just really good cover."

Larsen scoffed.

"From what Charles was told, the authorities hate you nearly as much as we do," Larsen said. "You do have a way of getting under people's skins, don't you? And if you had been working for the FBI, you wouldn't have participated in the robberies, even as the wheel man. Now, the feds, as you say, do have you on camera at three recent robberies. . . ."

"I never went inside."

"You don't think the entire parking lot is under video surveillance?" he asked. "And you weren't wearing much of a disguise. So it would not be too uncommon for you to be killed in a robbery. I can see the *National Enquirer* headline now: 'The over-the-hill reporter who turned to a life of crime instead of reporting it.' "

"That's more of a photo caption, I think. You know, beneath the mug shot of me in the orange prison coveralls."

Larsen shrugged.

"What makes you think I'll do this?"

"Because Rachel will be killed if you don't," Larsen said. "We will torture her, of course, to make sure she knows nothing, then kill her. Unfortunate, but we must know whether you have compromised the operation. Of course, Elaine Schaeffer is as good as dead, the victim of a rapist who will break into her home three days from tonight."

"I'll do this," I said. "But you have to promise me that you will leave Rachel and Elaine alone."

"The Jewish woman is not negotiable," Larsen said. "But I think yes, we could agree to spare Rachel death and discomfort. Frankly, I think she would do anything to remain in the security of her family, no matter how badly she thinks she wants out."

Well, that was one of two. Once I left the compound, perhaps I could find a way to warn Elaine and contact the authorities.

"Will Eva know what is happening?"

He got me to my feet, then pushed me into a bare room just like the one Rachel was in, and locked the door.

"There's a Bible in there," Larsen called through the door. "You would be wise to make use of it."

"Is there a gun inside?"

After a few hours of not being able to sleep, I cracked the Bible and leafed through it. All those books from my childhood: Genesis, Exodus . . . Revelation. I closed the book, then let it fall open to a page and read the first verse I saw.

Deuteronomy, Chapter 28:

The Lord will smite thee with madness, and blindness, and astonishment of the heart: And thou shalt grope at noonday, as the blind gropeth in darkness, and thou shalt not prosper in thy ways: and thou shalt be only oppressed and spoiled evermore, and no man shall save thee.

Forty-six

The Farmers and Drovers Bank of Springfield, Missouri, was on the corner of Gladstone and Republic, just north of Highway 60 on the south side of town. On the side of the bank was a mural depicting a cowboy, quirt in his hand, driving his horse across some mythical prairie.

Larsen pulled the Sunday school van into a parking lot near the bank, then turned to look at us in the seat behind. Eva was sitting beside me, dressed in black, and for the duration of the trip she'd had one hand on the back of my neck and the other pressing a Glock into my rib cage.

"It's time," Larsen said.

Eva pushed the gun harder against me, and I opened the door and got out of the van. She put the Glock in her pocket and followed, then got one of those ubiquitous gym bags from the back.

"Thank you, Eva," Larsen said.

She smiled as she adjusted her sunglasses and the floppy hat.

"My pleasure," she said.

Then she shut the door of the van and Larsen drove off.

"Let's go," Eva said.

"We don't have to do this," I said.

"Look at it this way," she said, adjusting the Bushmaster for a better fit beneath her long black coat. "How often do you get to make history? At least people will remember your name. What could be better?

"Not doing this at all?"

She took the Benelli from the bag and handed it to me.

I tried to hide it beneath my jacket. I didn't even check the receiver, because I knew it would be empty.

"During the jobs, I knew you'd been carrying it unloaded on the seat beside you," Eva said. "It confused me, but I didn't say anything."

"I didn't want to hurt anybody," I said.

We had walked across into the bank's parking lot.

"What if I run?"

"I'll shoot you," she said. "And then Larsen will shoot Rachel. Look, the only chance you have is to do this right. Take command, use the threat of violence, don't let things get out of control. Otherwise, people will get hurt."

"The two-percent rule."

We paused at the door to the bank.

"It looks good out here," she said.

Through the glass, I could see a few customers milling about the counter.

"Not now," I said. "There's too many people in there."

"Now," Eva said. "You first."

I took a breath, pulled the ski mask over my face, and pushed through the doors into the lobby, holding the shotgun at the ready.

"Everybody freeze!" I screamed. "This is a robbery."

It was a very nice lobby. In the middle, atop the customer-service kiosk with the usual calendars and deposit slips and such, was a large Frederic Remington bronze, or at least a copy of one, of a mustachioed cowboy on a rearing bronc.

The teller's cage was curved, with recessed lights—and, I'm sure, surveillance cameras—above. There was also a clock on the wall in the center behind the tellers, and it probably had a wide-angle video camera hidden in it.

There were four tellers behind the counter, three women and a man, and six customers. No security guard. Ten people that I could see, and that included a mother and her two small children, twin boys. All of them turned to look at me.

"I'm not kidding," I said.

"They don't know what to do," Eva suggested. "Tell them to get down."

"Good idea," I said. "Everybody down—get down on the floor."

"Not the tellers," Eva said.

"Right," I said. "Everybody except for the tellers."

The tellers got back up.

"Eva, would you rather do this?"

"No," she said.

She threw me the gym bag.

"Twenty seconds," she said.

I threw the bag over the top of the teller's cage and told them to start filling it.

"No dye packs," I said.

"No alarms," Eva said tiredly. "No consecutive serial numbers."

The twin boys were watching with keen interest while the mother was attempting to shield their eyes. The other customers were sprawled haphazardly in the bank lobby, some with their hands over their eyes, others watching covertly. A few still had checks or money and deposit tickets in their hands.

"Go supervise the tellers," Eva said. "Carlos always does."

I tried to walk around the end of the cage, where there was a little swinging door.

"Don't open it," Eva said. "There's a magnetic contact that, when it is broken when the door is opened, will trigger the silent alarm. Carlos usually either jumps over the door or squeezes through one of the teller windows. The windows look pretty easy."

"Right," I said.

I jumped up and slid through.

"Okay, that's enough money," I said.

"But you said to fill it," said the nearest teller, a middle-aged woman in a business suit.

"I've changed my mind."

"What, you don't like our bank?"

"Forty seconds," Eva called.

"Lady, I've had a rough day," I said, taking the bag from her. Then I lowered my voice: "Look, I just want to get out of here, okay?"

"No," she said, and continued to fill the bag.

"For God's sake, Margaret," the teller next to her whispered. "Do what he wants."

"He reminds me of my son-in-law," Margaret said. "Always giving orders, but never really knowing what he wants. I suppose you're going to want me to make you a ham sandwich next? Loan you money? Get my daughter pregnant again?"

"I don't need you to loan me money," I said. "I'm robbing your bank, remember? Whatever you do, don't trip the alarm in that drawer."

"I just might," she said.

"Sixty seconds," Eva called.

"God *damn* it," I screamed, leveling the Benelli at her and placing my finger on the trigger. "I don't want a ham sandwich, I don't need your money, and if your daughter is anything like you there is no chance that she will become with child by me. Do what I say because it is for your own fucking good. Or are you too stupid to understand that?"

She shook her head.

"That's enough money," I said. "Put the bag on the ground and back away."

I returned to the lobby with the gym bag.

"Impressive," Eva said. "I almost believed you were really going to shoot her."

"How can I shoot her when I've got an empty gun?"

"I beg your pardon," Eva said. "That Benelli has six rounds in the magazine and one in the chamber."

"Shit," I said. "You mean I nearly . . ."

"A little more pressure on that trigger and you would have sacrificed a mother-in-law for the cause. It is now one minute and twenty."

"Okay, we have to find a way out of here," I said.

I walked over to the customers.

"I want to see your car keys," I said. "Reach slowly into your pocket and hold them up."

The mother was frightened. She tried to speak, but couldn't. Tears rolled down her face. "Mine are in my purse."

"You others," I said. "I want to see your keys. Now. Hold them high."

Keys rattled. Change spilled from pockets and rolled across the tile floor. Slowly the other customers held their keys aloft.

I picked the nearest set.

"What do these go to?" I asked the young man.

"A Ford Escape," he said.

"Christ," I muttered, and tossed the keys back. I snatched up a set from a middle-aged guy in a business suit. "What about these?"

"Don't take my car," he pleaded.

"What is it?" I asked.

He balked.

I thumbed through the set and found an ignition key with a Mercedes logo.

"Where is it?" I asked. "What color? Come on, there aren't that many cars in the lot."

"One minute forty," Eva called.

I moved the barrel of the shotgun toward him. "Tell me, or I'll get a car from somebody else and kill you anyway."

"The silver one," he said. "The Kompressor. First row."

"What the hell kind of name is that for a car?" I asked. "Did the Nazis win?"

Somebody's cell phone began ringing. It scared the hell out of me at first. The ring tone was the theme song for *The Mickey Mouse Club.*

Why hadn't I thought of asking for a cell?

"Whose phone is that?" I demanded.

The young mother sobbed.

"It's mine," she said. "It's in my—"

"Your purse, I know," I said.

I knelt and found the phone beneath some disposable diapers in the big canvas purse. I pushed the answer button with my thumb.

"She'll call you back," I said, and hung up.

I ran over to Eva.

"One minute fifty," Eva said.

I picked up the gym bag.

"Let's go," I said, heading for the door.

She didn't move.

"What are you going to do, shoot me?" I asked. "We don't have to do this. We have a way out."

She said nothing.

"You stay if you want," I said.

"Two minutes," Eva said.

She took off her hat and sunglasses and threw them

down. Then, while still looking at me, she slowly raised the barrel of the Bushmaster up and fired a single round into the ceiling.

If you've ever been unfortunate enough to hear a gun discharged indoors, or even a firecracker, then you know how loud it was.

Half of the customers screamed.

Smoke swirled around the barrel of the gun while a bit of plaster sprinkled down from the ceiling.

"Do you want to die?" I asked.

I turned and headed for the door.

She put a long burst across the ceiling. An alarm began to ring somewhere while the sprinklers came on and created a sudden rainstorm in the lobby. The borrowed cell phone in my pocket rang again, adding the *Mickey Mouse* theme to the chaos.

I continued walking.

"I'll shoot you if I have to," she said.

"Then shoot," I said.

I put the gym bag on the floor and put the Benelli across it. Then I took the cell phone, canceled the incoming call, and dialed Elaine's number.

She answered.

"Don't hang up," I said. "You have to get out of the house now. Go someplace where nobody can find you. Somebody is trying to kill you. Do it now."

"What the hell are you talking about?"

"There's no time to explain," I said, reaching for the bank door. A pair of Springfield police cruisers were wheeling into the parking lot, lights on but with no sirens. Then Eva opened up behind me and turned the door in front of me into a shower of broken glass, while I hit the floor. She continued to fire and the slugs stitched across the hood of one of the police cars and shattered the light bar.

"Kelsey!" Elaine screamed.

"Go now," I said, and dropped the phone.

The cops had taken cover on the far sides of their cars.

I ran for the cover of the kiosk beneath the Remington bronze. Eva was already there, her back against the base. She had slapped a fresh magazine into the Bushmaster and was now taking her Discman from her pocket.

"What now?" I asked.

She snugged the headphones over her ears, turned the CD player on, and slipped it into the pocket of her leather jacket.

"We fight," she said.

The now-familiar strains of Dresden issued from the headphones.

"You'd better pick up that riot gun," Eva said. "We've gone from a bank robbery to a battle. But I prefer this to a siege. Cool, huh?"

"Not really."

She took the Glock from her belt and offered it to me.

"Take this."

"No," I said.

On the street outside I could see other police cars zipping by in both directions, undoubtedly blocking off the street. I was sure we were already surrounded.

One of the telephones behind the teller counter began ringing.

"That'll be the cops," Eva said. "Standard operating procedure. Have one of the tellers answer it."

"Margaret," I called. "Answer the damned phone."

This time she did so without protest.

"It's for you," she said.

"Can you transfer it to the phone on the table above me?"

The phone began to ring.

I reached up, found the phone, and pulled it down to the floor.

"This is the Springfield Police Department," a calm

and nearly cheerful voice said. "Do you mind telling me the situation in there?"

"This is a mistake," I said.

"I'm sure it is," the pleasant male voice said. "Is anyone hurt?"

I put the phone against my chest.

"Is everybody okay?" I shouted.

Murmurs.

"Is anybody hurt?" I asked.

"No," the Mercedes guy shouted.

"Nobody's hurt," I said into the phone.

"That's very good," the negotiator said. "How many people do you have in there?"

"A dozen people in the lobby, and perhaps a few more employees in the back," I said. "Don't shoot, because they're all coming out in about thirty seconds—"

Eva had ripped the line out of the back of the phone.

"Don't negotiate with the enemy," she said. "We'll send the people out. But they don't need to know any more than they already do. Go ahead; take care of getting everybody out."

I stood.

"Come on," I said. "Everybody slowly get up and walk outside. That's right. Margaret, get everybody out of the back, would you? Thanks."

They didn't need to be told twice.

"Can I have my keys?" the Mercedes guy asked.

"What do you think?"

"Just asking," he said, palms up.

"Buy American next time, huh?"

One of the twins waved good-bye as he stepped with his mother across the broken safety glass toward the entrance. I waved back, and the mother started to cry again.

Then I went back and sat down beside Eva.

"Come on," I said.

She lowered the headphones.

"Last chance," I said. "Let's book."

"Why didn't you go with them?" she asked.

"And leave you here?"

"You're just afraid I'd shoot you in the back."

"You wouldn't shoot me in the back."

Eva shrugged.

"I don't want you to die," I said.

"But I want to die."

"I don't," I said.

"Too late," she said. "The cops are going to make Swiss cheese out of the place in about thirty seconds. This is what Karl wanted, remember?"

She put the headphones back over her ears.

Everybody had cleared the bank by now.

Eva stood up. I reached for the edge of her coat, but she knocked my hand away with the butt of the rifle. Then she opened up and began walking toward the entrance, the .223 casings rolling and bouncing across the floor.

The interior of the bank seemed to explode.

A fusillade from perhaps two dozen guns tore into the lobby. Some were firing their service pieces, while a few others had AR-15 rifles. I tried to crawl beneath the tile floor while papers and bits of wood and glass were tossed in the air, and I could hear several of the rounds hitting Eva's body. They made a sickening piercing sound as they entered her leather jacket and came out the other side. She kept firing, however, until one of the rifle rounds hit her in the face.

I saw a softball-sized chunk of black hair and bloody skull from the back of her head skitter past me on the floor.

Then there was an ear-popping bang and a blinding light as the police lobbed flash-bang devices into the lobby, followed by several tear-gas canisters.

I crawled to my feet gasping for air, half-blind and

with my ears hurting so badly I was convinced they were bleeding. The last thing I remember was tripping and hitting the floor beside Eva's body, my hands sticky with blood, not knowing if I had been shot.

Forty-seven

"What's your name?"

It was a female voice, but not one that would be a good candidate for one of those 900 numbers advertised in the backs of men's magazines. No, this woman's voice was as cold as one could get and still be considered human.

I didn't how long I had been out, and I had the mother of all headaches. I was sitting in a wooden chair, my hands bound behind me, and the room was either completely dark or I had gone blind. There was also a peculiar taste in my mouth.

"Where am I?" I asked.

"Just answer our questions," the woman said. "What's your name?"

I told them.

"How long have you been a terrorist?"

"I'm not a terrorist," I said. "I'm a reporter, or at least I used to be."

"Your partner is dead."

"I know," I said. "I saw it. And she wasn't my partner.

She forced me into that bank at gunpoint because I was going to tell the FBI about—"

Somebody smacked me across the face with something. Not hard enough to loosen any teeth, but hard enough to sting, both physically and psychologically.

"Was anybody else hurt?" I asked.

"Answer the question," the woman said again. "How long have you been a terrorist?"

I thought for a moment.

"I'd like to speak to a lawyer."

"That's not possible," the woman said. "You are a person of interest in the war on terror and perhaps an unlawful combatant. As such, we may hold you without representation and interrogate you for however long we deem necessary. Such interrogation can last from a few hours to a year or more."

"I'm an American citizen," I said.

"That has yet to be determined," she said.

"You can't hold me without charges," I said. "The Constitution demands a speedy trial. And even if I weren't an American, even if I were an enemy soldier, the Geneva Convention prohibits this type of treatment. This is the kind of stuff you would expect from the fucking Nazis."

"This is why we kept you sedated," the woman said dryly.

"Where am I?"

"Camp Yankee Zulu," she said.

"Where's that?"

Another smack across the face.

"You can keep hitting me, or you can listen and realize I'm telling the truth," I said. "I've been trying to escape and contact the FBI about a bomb plot that is scheduled for November ninth."

I waited for the smack.

"Go on," she said.

"You know who Commander Carlos is?"

"Keep talking."

"He showed me a pair of bombs he said were nukes. He used a number for them—B67, I think. He said they were nicknamed 'Falling Star.' He intended to destroy a federal facility called Mount Weather. He believed it was the center of a conspiracy to take over the United States."

There was silence.

"How long have I been here?"

There was no reply except the closing of a door.

"Shit," I muttered.

I don't know how many hours I waited. It's hard to tell when you're tied to a chair in the dark. Eventually, of course, I had to go to the bathroom, and I called for someone to untie me. Nobody came.

I ended up pissing myself.

Finally I could hear the door open. Then I heard a light switch being flipped, and I could see a hazy glow through my blindfold. Somebody untied it from the back, and I sat blinking against the glare.

In front of me, I could make out a man in a dark suit.

"You guys don't believe in restroom breaks, huh?"

"Sorry about that, but it was necessary," he said.

I could feel somebody untie my hands. Looking over my shoulder I saw it was a woman, also in a dark suit. She was thirty or so, and very businesslike, with hair that just reached her collar. She reminded me of the ads you see for smiling young professional women running for county office. This woman, however, did not smile. She also didn't speak, so I don't know if she belonged to the voice I had heard earlier or not.

"Can I get cleaned up?" I said. "This is kind of embarrassing."

"In a bit," he said. "First you have to tell me what Commander Carlos told you about this plot."

"Who are you?"

He took out a wallet and showed me credentials that suggested he was with the Central Intelligence Agency. I don't remember his name. As I said, I had a headache, and was not exactly feeling my best. But I remember what he looked like: about fifty years old, dark hair that was graying at the temples, a deeply weathered face, and brown eyes that seemed perpetually sad.

I told him everything that Larsen had told me, from the first day we met until that day he showed me the bombs in Kingdom Tower.

"Did you see the PAL and AMACS electronics packages he referred to?"

"No," I said.

"But you did see the devices."

"Yes."

"So you saw the blue ones."

"No," I said. "They were green, with orange tips and yellow stripes. They weren't very big—maybe three or four feet long, and narrow."

"What kind of truck was it?"

I told him.

"Do you think you would know it again if you saw it?"

"Of course," I said.

"Good," the man said.

A soldier came in with a change of clothes, a towel, and a washbasin. The man nodded toward the woman in the dark clothes. She left the room, but the soldier stayed, standing near the door with his hands behind his back and his eyes direct forward.

"You're going to watch?" I asked.

"Believe me, it's not a part of the job I enjoy," he said.

I began to clean myself up.

"Do we have your cooperation?" the man asked.

"Do you believe that I'm not a terrorist or a bank robber?"

"I believe you're not a terrorist," the man said. "The

bank robbery charges will also be suspended if you fulfill our expectations."

"Suspended, but not dropped."

"That's right," the man said. "The statute of limitations, however, will expire in five years. Then you're free. Not a bad deal, if you ask me."

"Was anybody else besides Eva killed?"

"No," he said. "Some police officers suffered some minor injuries, but nothing serious. All of the hostages are okay. Speaking of the woman, do you know what her real name was?"

"I have no idea," I said.

"Can you help us out?"

"How?" I asked.

"We need to find that truck you described."

"If I can," I said. "I'd like some answers in return. How'd I get here?"

"You were taken under guard to a Springfield hospital after the fiasco at the bank, and once the Bureau was alerted, you were flown here. Sorry, but I can't tell you the exact location."

"That means it's not in the United States."

"It's in a U.S. territory," he said.

"How long have I been here?"

"Five days," he said.

"I don't remember being here that long."

"Not many do."

"So today is November ninth."

He nodded.

"What time?"

He looked at his watch.

"About nine hundred hours," he said.

"We're too late."

"That's Zulu," he said. "It's three o'clock in the morning on the East Coast. So, you see, we do have a few hours. With luck, it will be enough."

I slipped on a pair of jeans and a khaki T-shirt.

"So what's Karl Larsen's story?" I asked.

He looked at me thoughtfully.

"Come on," I said.

"I'm going to tell you," he said slowly, "but only because you're never going to see or hear from me again. Once you walk out that door, you're going to be in the hands of some other folks, and Camp Yankee Zulu will cease to exist. Also, you will never be able to prove what I tell you, because there is no documentation to back it up. As far as anybody will know, it's just a story you made up."

"Cut to the chase," I said.

"Everything Karl Larsen told you is a lie," he said. "He did not serve in the first Gulf War, his mother was not a member of the Irish Republican Army or a Nazi sympathizer, and his father did not work for the Central Intelligence Agency in Vietnam or anywhere else. He was not gang-raped in prison. Karl Larsen is not his name, and, as a matter of fact, he is not even English."

"Then what is he?"

"Somebody who very slowly but very surely went insane," he said. "It wasn't his father who was with the CIA; it was Larsen. At least, that's the name we gave him about ten years ago. It was just after the Oklahoma City bombing, and we were very concerned about domestic terrorism. It was our number one priority, in fact, for several years. So we created a life for Karl Larsen, complete with a family history and a British accent, and sent him into the Covenant compound."

"I can see why the British thing would work."

"They loved it," the man said. "Larsen did an incredible job of infiltrating these right-wing groups, including the neo-Nazis. Then, slowly, his behavior became erratic. His reports stopped coming on a regular basis. Eventually his picture showed up on a surveillance tape participating in a series of bank robberies with a racist organization called the Aryan Republican Army."

"What about Mount Weather?"

"That's a conspiracy theorist fantasy," the man said. "Do you know the first time Mount Weather was mentioned, although under a slightly different name? It was in 1962, by authors Fletcher Knebel and Charles W. Bailey II, in a novel called *Seven Days in May*. You read the book, or at least saw the movie, right?"

I nodded.

"That information is forty-two years old," he said. "Do you think we'd still be using that complex now? It's absurd. No, I suspect Larsen's real target is not Mount Weather, but either CIA headquarters at Langley, Virginia, the Pentagon, or perhaps Fort Meade in Maryland."

"The National Security Agency," I said.

"Fortunately, all targets are within forty miles of one another. We've been tracking Larsen for years, but somehow have never managed to catch him. He's just too smart. Insane, but smart."

"So these things he has—they're really nukes?"

"Yes," the man said. "They were stolen from a rail shipment in March. Frankly I don't think he has a prayer of a chance of actually detonating one, because it's not that easy to defeat the safeties. I can't imagine some backwoods electronics buff will be able to emulate the PAL and AMAC system. Even if they could, they would still need the six-digit code."

"Larsen had a lot of money," I said. "Maybe he bought them. That's something that could be stolen and not missed until it was actually used, right?"

The man said nothing.

"What made Larsen snap?" I asked as I laced up the combat boots they had given me.

"He lost his grip on reality," the man said. "Most people lead lives of quiet desperation, as the saying goes. They may wake up every day and harbor a secret desire to murder their boss, or decide that no jury would convict them if they murdered that philandering husband or nagging wife, but very few act on it. But when you're engaged in espionage and you're under deep cover, sometimes the fantasy becomes more attractive than reality. He had people willing to die for him. That's pretty heady for a mere mortal."

"Look, how do I know you're telling me the truth? Your story seems even more far-fetched than Larsen's. A ten-year-old CIA operation that went horribly wrong?"

"I would be skeptical myself," the man said. "Except for one thing."

He pulled a lighter from his pocket and handed it to me.

It was the one Larsen had described to me.

It was an old Zippo.

One side said, NHA TRANG VIETNAM, 1966–67. The other said, YEA, THOUGH I WALK THROUGH THE SHADOW OF THE VALLEY OF DEATH I SHALL FEAR NO EVIL, BECAUSE I AM THE MEANEST SONUVABITCH IN THE VALLEY.

"That's the lighter we gave him as part of his identity kit," the man said. "We found it in the railway tunnel where the Falling Star nukes were stolen."

Forty-eight

The soldier blindfolded me again, placed my hand on his belt, and led me through a maze of hallways. We emerged outside, because I could feel the wind and the sunshine on my face, and the distinct smell of the sea. The only sound I could hear, however, was the sound of a helicopter turbine.

The soldier put a hand on top of my head, made me crouch, and walked me to the door of the chopper, where I was pulled aboard.

"Make sure he keeps the blindfold on until you're out to sea."

"Absolutely," the reply came.

I was strapped into a seat, an aviation headset was placed on my skull, and I could hear the sound of turbines become a whine. Then we jumped into the air, and I could feel us make a swing to the left and then level out.

"You can take off your blindfold," I heard a crewman beside me say over the headset.

I removed it and found myself in an army assault helicopter. The interior was illuminated by red lights to preserve the pilot's night vision.

"What kind of chopper is this?" I asked.

The crewman held up the headset cable and indicated a button.

"Push to talk," he said.

I pushed the button and asked the question again.

"It's an army UH-60A Blackhawk," he said. "Crew of six, top speed one hundred and eighty four miles per hour, external payload of about four tons."

"Range?" I asked.

"Nearly fourteen hundred miles with auxiliary tanks," he said.

"Are we armed?"

"You bet," he said. "Hundred-and-five-millimeter howitzer and seven-point-six-two-millimeter machine guns."

"You're being pretty ready with this information," I said.

"It's public record," the crewman said. "And since you don't have a watch, I don't think you can calculate just how far out in the Atlantic we were. It's still dark, so you can't see any landmarks."

"So Camp Yankee Zulu remains a secret."

"Never heard of it," he said, then smiled. "I'll be your babysitter for this operation. My name is Gunnery Sergeant McMasters, but you can call me Gunny."

"I thought gunnery sergeants were marines," I said.

"Semper Fi," McMasters said. "I am a marine. But this is a mixed operation, and I was drafted because the folks with the scrambled eggs on their hats thought my specialty would be useful."

"What's your specialty?" I asked.

"That's classified," he said.

In what seemed like a few hours, the sun came up behind us and the sea and sky lightened. We made landfall over what McMasters told me was Virginia, and soon we were skimming over Chesapeake Bay. Then we made land again, and the fall landscape was beautiful.

McMasters listened on a channel I couldn't hear. Then he turned to me.

"We have a visual on what may be our target on Interstate 70 about an hour west of Baltimore," he told me. "Maryland State Police are trailing it. An early 1970s yellow Ford F-150. That's right, isn't it?"

"Nineteen seventy-one," I said. "Kind of a rust bucket. The doors says something like 'Lamar Airport,' but it is so faint you can't see it unless you're standing right next to it."

"Are you sure?"

"Yes," I said. "I worked on it long enough to know."

"Worked on it?" McMasters asked.

"I tore the engine down to the short block," I said.

"Did you ever take down the vehicle identification number?"

"Yeah, when I sent somebody to buy parts. But I don't have the VIN with me."

McMasters thought for a moment.

"Do you remember the place where they bought the parts? If it was one of the franchises, they'll have the VIN in their computers."

I told him I thought it was the Autozone store in Eureka Springs or perhaps Berryville. But I said they wouldn't be open for several hours yet.

"They will now," McMasters said. He looked at his watch, then spoke on his private channel. Twenty minutes later we were just a few miles from the spot where the Maryland troopers were trailing the yellow truck. At about the same time, McMasters wrote down a long number on the clipboard strapped to his leg.

"Autozone in Berryville," he said.

McMasters asked to be patched through to the troopers.

Below us we could see the highway. I still couldn't see a yellow truck, however.

"Have the trooper attempt to pull him over," he said. "Have them use extreme caution."

We waited.

Finally I spotted some flashing red and blue lights on a half dozen cars behind a yellow truck.

"Are you sure?" McMasters asked.

He turned to me.

"No match," he said. "It's a 1973 Ford, and the driver is an old man. In the back are several hundred pounds of soil for his greenhouse."

McMasters spoke to the pilot.

The helicopter banked and we turned to the south.

"What time is it?" I asked.

"Zero eight hundred hours," he said.

"We're running out of time," I said.

McMasters listened carefully on his headset.

"Okay, we have another target," he said. "It's on Interstate 95 approaching Washington, ten miles out. We've already had a Virginia trooper attempt to pull him over, but the driver would not yield. At this point, it is a slow-speed chase. No way to check the VIN."

The helicopter increased speed.

"What about the writing on the doors?"

He asked.

"Tell them to use binoculars," he said. "Surely there's somebody stationed ahead at a right angle." Then he turned to me. "They're looking," he said.

In less than two minutes he turned to me again.

"Does it say 'Lamar Municipal Airport'?"

"Yes," I said.

McMasters looked at his watch. Then he was talking to someone else on the channel. "Sir, we barely have time to intercept," he said. "Yes, you could scramble jets, but can we blow a hole in the highway in the middle of the morning rush into the city? That might trigger the dirty-bomb effect we are trying to avoid."

He listened intently for a moment more.

"Yes, I agree. We'll have to take that risk. Thank you, sir."

McMasters sighed, then got on another channel.

"Take the driver out now," he said. "It must be a clean kill. Then get the hell out of the area. Yes, that's right."

McMasters looked at me.

"Sniper," he said.

"Then what?" I asked. "It might be on a timer, attached to some mechanism that releases when the driver is killed, anything. What are we going to do?"

"Play it by ear," he said.

In less than ten minutes we were circling the scene, where the yellow Ford truck had rolled to the side of the road and come to a stop beside a guardrail. The truck now had an old camper shell over the bed.

The area around the truck was deserted, but there were plenty of flashing lights just a few miles down the road in each section. Also, we were in a heavily populated area somewhere in Alexandria. In every direction all I could see were stores and homes.

"That it?" McMasters asked.

"Yes," I said.

"Then hold on," he said.

The Blackhawk descended and landed in the middle of the interstate, perhaps thirty yards from where the pickup rested. McMasters unstrapped himself and ran over to the truck to inspect it. He had produced a pistol from somewhere in his flak vest and was holding it in front of him.

"Why's he doing it alone?" I asked over the intercom.

"Radiation risk," he said.

McMasters jerked open the driver's door.

Skorzeny rolled out onto the ground.

His head was a bloody mess.

Then McMasters walked to the back of the truck, pistol still in front of him, and flipped up the door to the camper shell. He peered intently in the truck bed for a moment, then slammed it down again.

McMasters keyed the radio in his vest.

"It looks operational," he said, then waved his armed for the helicopter to approach. "Let's get it out of here."

The Blackhawk lifted off, circled until the nose was pointed into the wind, and then approached the pickup and hovered over it. A crewman used a remote control to lower a large hook down to McMasters.

"Kelsey," McMasters asked over the radio. "Where the hell do I attach this thing?"

I thought for a moment.

"Come on," McMasters urged. "Best guess."

"It has to ride upright?"

"That would be helpful."

"Take the cable through the windows in the cab," I said. "Then loop it around the trailer hitch or the frame behind the bumper and then loop the hook back over the cable on top."

McMasters didn't bother to roll down the passenger's window, but simply tossed the heavy hook through it. He pulled the hook through the driver's window, slammed the door, and pulled plenty of slack through. Then he went to the back and fussed for a moment before finding a spot to thread the cable through. Then he climbed on top and hooked the cable.

"Let's go, let's go, let's go," McMasters said. He was standing on top of the camper, dimpling the top with his feet, motioning for the copter to pick him up.

We descended as one of the crewmen took up the slack in the cable. The wind was whipping us around a bit, and I was afraid the blades would decapitate McMasters. Then he was climbing aboard through the open side door, the pilot was slowly rising, and we could feel a jerk and hear the groan of metal as the cable became taut.

Then the pickup was off the ground and we were headed toward the sea.

McMasters plugged in his communications set.

"Good job, Gunny," I said.

"Save your congratulations," he said. "We're not out of the woods yet."

"What's the plan?" I asked.

"Out to sea," he said. "It looks like the damn thing is operational."

"How much time do we have?" I asked.

"Who knows?" he said. "This ain't the movies, so there's no countdown in big red letters."

"You're going to drop me off somewhere, right?" I asked.

McMasters smiled.

"Sorry," he said. "No time. We may have three hundred and fifty kilotons swinging beneath us. So I'm afraid you're in it for the long haul."

The pilot shortened the cable until the truck was just a few feet below us, to keep the pendulum effect to a minimum, and then poured on as much speed as he dared.

"Where are we going to drop it?"

"The wind is from the east," he said. "We'd better be at least a few hundred miles out to sea. At this speed, that might take us three hours."

Suddenly there was some turbulence, the helicopter dipped, and the top of the truck scraped the bottom of the helicopter. Then the cable snapped tight and nearly jerked us out of the sky. For a moment I was sideways in my seat, looking down over Maryland.

The pilot swung in a circle, gaining control of the aircraft, then continued east.

The hoist operator shortened the cable even more.

"Shit," McMasters said. "That was close."

I vomited all over my boots.

As I was wiping my mouth, I heard a roar. I lifted my head. An F-15 Eagle was passing, attempting to fly slow enough to check the helicopter for damage.

Then he hit the throttle and was gone.

"He says we're okay," McMasters said. Then he listened for a moment to his channel. "We have coordinates, a place in the Atlantic on the other side of the Hatteras Plain. An alert has been issued for all private and commercial vessels to evacuate the dump zone."

I nodded.

"Can you swim?" he asked.

"Why do you ask?"

"Here's the thing," McMasters said. "We're only going to have enough fuel to make the DZ. Then we're going to have to ditch in the ocean."

Forty-nine

A thousand feet over the drop zone, the crew released the cable at the hoist and the yellow Ford fell toward the sea. The Blackhawk shot up, suddenly free of its load, and then turned to speed away.

"If we're lucky," McMasters said, "the impact will disrupt the electronics package. That should disarm the bomb."

"Or set it off," I said.

We watched from the open side door as the truck seemed to fall forever. Then, a moment before it hit the water, McMasters swung the door shut and told me to close my eyes.

Nothing.

The crew erupted in cheers.

We were five miles away when the we saw the brilliant light reflected from the surface of the ocean. It lasted only a moment, and when we looked behind us there was the chillingly familiar mushroom cloud rising over the ocean. The interior of the cloud was seething with orange heat.

"God help us," I said.

McMasters listened intently for a moment on the commset, then turned to me.

"We've got an AWACS in the air," he said. "They say it's low-yield, maybe the size of Hiroshima. We're far enough away that we'll be okay. No radiation risks. Get ready for the shock wave."

We could see it racing across the ocean. Then it lost speed and, by the time it reached us, it felt like the turbulence we had experienced on the way out.

"Talk about lucky," McMasters said. "A few more KT and we'd be upside down in the drink."

Then the whine of the turbine began to lower in pitch.

"Time to swim," McMasters said, and began to gather up some survival gear. He threw me a flotation vest. We had already tugged on survival suits. "Don't worry; it won't be that bad. The Atlantic is cold, but it's daylight, and we'll have a coast guard chopper picking us up in a few minutes."

I struggled into the vest and then McMasters yanked a cord hanging on one side. We were losing altitude quickly, but the engine was still running.

"That's your beacon," he said. A light began flashing on the vest. "It also sends out a radio signal. With any luck we'll get the raft deployed. The pilot will try to keep us in the air for a moment and let us jump out, and then ditch the craft a little farther on. Otherwise we'll have to swim out while it sinks and not get tangled in the blades."

McMasters swung open the side door.

"Get ready," he said.

We were still three or four hundred feet above the waves.

Then the engine died, and the pilot began to autorotate the chopper. The sea rushed up to meet us, but the pilot managed to keep some forward motion.

A few seconds before the chopper hit, McMasters kicked me out of the door, and the rest of the crew members followed. When I struck the water, it felt like I had landed on a solid block of concrete, and I sank for several long seconds before my vest and survival suit brought me back to the surface.

The sea was rough and I found myself bobbing like a cork.

The Blackhawk hit the ocean about a hundred yards away, amid a terrific plume of water, and now there was a froth of bubbles around it as it sank.

McMasters and the other crew members were bobbing not far away. As we swam toward one another, somebody asked McMasters where the raft was. He shouted that he had lost it.

Then we waited, shivering, until a couple of coast guard rescue divers dropped fin-first into the water from a white-and-orange Sea Dragon helicopter.

A basket was lowered from helicopter.

"No," McMasters shouted, pushing the basket away. "Get the pilot first."

One of the rescue divers lowered his mask to his chest and placed a hand on McMasters's shoulder.

"There's no beacon and nothing to be seen from the air," the diver said. "I'm sorry, but from what we can tell, he didn't make it."

Fifty

There was still one bomb left, and it was at the Covenant compound near Eureka Springs, Arkansas. After drying me off and giving me another change of clothes, the coast guard headed for its base in Atlantic City. From there, McMasters and I were put on an FBI jet and flown directly to northwestern Arkansas. In flight, I took one of the phones built into the plane's seats and tried to call Elaine, but I got her answering machine. Then I asked one of the FBI agents to please have her business checked to see if anything was amiss. After we landed at the Springdale airport, we were taken by an Arkansas Highway Patrol helicopter to the spot on Highway 187 where the pink fence posts marked the entrance to the compound.

"You know this place?" McMasters asked.

"Unfortunately," I said.

Sheriff Clark was standing amid a gaggle of law-enforcement officers near the entrance. As I passed him, I felt like tapping him on the shoulder and asking if he remembered me. But what would be the point?

The lead FBI agent broke from the group of cops and trotted over to us.

"Kelsey?" he asked, and shook my hand. "McMasters?"

"Yes," I said.

"What's the situation?" McMasters asked.

"They've barricaded themselves in the part of the compound called Kingdom Tower, which is part of the church," he said. "The church apparently runs their own school as well, and the school was full this morning. They have perhaps fifty kids hostage in the church building."

"Are they talking?"

"The only person they'll talk to is some nut called Stonewall Carson," he said. "He apparently was a Green Beret or something in Vietnam, and is now considered a moderate force among these so-called Christian patriots. He's down there now, trying to get them to release the kids."

"Any luck?" I asked.

"Not yet."

"Is the entire Smith family in there?"

"As far as we know," he said.

"Anything else?"

"They say they have enough aircraft fuel stored in the tower to turn the whole place into a pile of molten glass," he said.

"And set off the remaining bomb in dirty mode," McMasters said. "That's why they haven't been blasted out yet. Send a couple of missiles in there and you ignite the jet fuel, if that's what they really have in there, and you accomplish what they want. If they don't have any jet fuel, we can just wait them out."

"Larsen would never stand for a siege," I said. "It's my guess they really do have the jet fuel in there. The question is how we get the kids out first."

"You know these guys?" the FBI guy asked.

"Yeah, but they consider me a traitor."

"But you were intimate with one of the daughters?" he asked.

"Word gets around," I said.

"You think you could get far enough to talk to her?"

"I can try," I said.

"Get him a Kevlar vest," McMasters said.

"No vest," I said. "They'll just see it as another sign of cowardice. Also, this blue jumpsuit I got from the coast guard won't impress them. Get me some jeans and a shirt."

The FBI man turned and picked out a couple of the deputies who were my size and ordered them to take off their jeans.

"What?" they asked.

"Fucking do it," McMasters said. "Now."

The deputies were wearing uniform shirts, however. I looked around and spotted Clark, who was wearing a blue dress shirt. He seemed to be about my size, and I pointed him out.

McMasters hustled him over.

"Take your shirt off," he said.

"The hell I will," Clark said.

"Not negotiable," the FBI agent said. "Take it off now, or face obstruction charges."

He grudgingly came out of his suit and tie and began unbuttoning the cuffs.

"Remember me?" I asked.

"Can't say I do," Clark said.

"Still got the testicles on your desk?"

"Fuck you," the sheriff said as he handed me the shirt.

"Trooper," the FBI agent called. The state trooper hustled over. "Place the sheriff in custody pending the filing of formal charges."

While the trooper removed the nasty little Bulldog from the sheriff's holster, Clark stared at me with hate in his eyes. Then another trooper jerked his hands behind his back, cuffed him, and led him away.

I had already peeled out of the jumpsuit, had the jeans on, and now was buttoning the shirt. It wasn't a bad fit, but it was a little chilly for just a dress shirt.

"Oh, by the way," the agent said. "Our agents in Little Rock checked that address in Conway you gave us. We couldn't find Elaine Schaeffer."

"Hope for the best," I said.

McMasters, the FBI agent, and I hopped in an Arkansas National Guard Humvee and were taken down to the compound. There was a mixture of law enforcement and military vehicles arranged in a semicircle around the church building, with the Kingdom Tower and the bluff in the background. Between the soldiers and SWAT teams, there were probably a hundred guns trained on the building.

Stonewall Carson was standing behind one of the Humvees, speaking through a bullhorn.

"Abraham Smith," he was saying. "You know this is not what God wants for his Chosen. Let the children go, and then we can talk this out."

There was no response.

"Are you having any luck?" the FBI agent asked.

Carson shook his head.

"Then your time is up," McMasters said, taking the bullhorn from him. "It's getting dark and we have to do something quick, or we'll be in this for the long haul."

"Let me keep trying," he said.

"Think this is a conspiracy of the New World Order?" I asked. "Aren't those your friends in there threatening to kill the children of their own congregation?"

"Well, you have to remember Abraham was asked by God to sacrifice Isaac to show his faith."

"Right," I said. "And you know, of course, that the Koran says it was Ishmael that Abraham was asked to sacrifice? All of you fundamentalists are just fucking nuts. Six hours ago I watched a mushroom cloud spread over the Atlantic, and a very good man sacrificed himself so that many thousands of others could live."

Carson started to argue, but McMasters cut him off.

"He's telling the truth," he told him. "So take a hike, huh?"

"Okay," the FBI agent said. "Your turn. Got a plan?"

"Yeah," I said.

He handed me the bullhorn, but I refused it and simply walked toward the church.

"Abraham Smith," I called. "Can you hear me?"

There was no response, so I kept walking.

"Abraham!"

I was about halfway to the church door.

"What do you want, Kelsey?" Larsen called from the top of the tower. He was dressed in his black field jacket and the SS officer's cap. "Haven't you done enough damage?"

"Skorzeny's dead," I said. "Don't you care?"

"Not really," Larsen said.

"Well, I have a deal that you might care about," I said. "You can have me in exchange for the children. That's a pretty fair trade, isn't it? One traitorous soul in exchange for the lives of fifty innocents?"

He didn't answer.

"You know how many people I sold you out to?" I asked, then laughed. "You just wouldn't believe it. I played you like a violin, Karl. But I guess you'll never know the full story."

"I should kill you from here," he called down.

"You could," I said. "But you'd never live to brag about it. Look at the firepower around you. This is a siege, Karl. Let the children go. You'll still have me for a bargaining chip. Besides, I eat less. You could keep me hostage for a month for the same amount of food and water you'd use for these kids."

No response.

"All right," he said. "Come forward."

"No," I said. "Let the children go. I'll start walking forward as soon as the first one comes through the door. By the time the last one is out, I'll be inside the church."

"I'm coming down," Larsen called.

In less than a minute the church doors swung open. Larsen stood there, the MP5 slung over his shoulder.

"No tricks," he said. "Or I'll kill every child I see."

"No tricks," I said. "Let them go."

"Go on, children," Larsen said. "Slowly, now."

Single-file, the children began to walk down the path toward me. Most of them were elementary-school age, dressed in the sharp blue jumpers and little suits of a Christian school. All of their faces were stained with tears, and many were still crying quietly.

I started walking forward.

A little girl in front began to run.

"Slow down, kiddo," I said. "Just walk. Everything is all right. Your parents are waiting for you."

Some of the Guardsmen and the SWAT team had placed their weapons down and were kneeling, waiting to sweep the children up as they reached them. By the time the last child was out, I was walking across the threshold into the church.

Larsen grabbed me by the shirt, pulled me inside, then slammed the doors behind. He pressed the muzzle of the MP5 against my throat.

"You piece of shit," he said.

He was patting me down, making sure I didn't have a gun hidden in an ankle holster or taped to the small of my back.

"I've been called worse."

"You are worse," he said.

"Is Rachel okay?"

"So far," he said. "She's downstairs."

Larsen forced me down the aisle, where Abraham Smith, his son, and Leah were sitting on the raised area around the pulpit.

"I didn't think we'd see you alive again," Leah said.

"Disappointing, isn't it?"

Larsen hit me in the kidney with the butt of his rifle. I fell with a groan to the red carpet. I hadn't been on my knees in a church since I had attended that revival meeting in 1973.

"Know what your problem is, son?" Abraham Smith asked me. "You just haven't spent enough time on your knees."

I looked up at Joseph.

"Are you going to let them get away with this?"

"God's will," he said.

I groaned and put my head down. I was in pain, and so tired that my head had this weird buzzing sound in it, but I was also buying time to think. The only person I really had to worry about was Larsen. The rest of them didn't appear to be armed.

"Get up," Larsen said.

"I can't."

He pressed the muzzle of the MP5 against my neck.

"Then you might as well die on your knees," he said.

I knew I wouldn't have a better chance. My days as a crime reporter had taught me that the closer a person with a gun is to you, the better your chances of disarming them, and your best chance is if they are holding it against the back of your neck, because it is a smaller target than your torso. Of course, before you tried this, you had to be sure you were going to die if you didn't do *something*.

I twisted and whipped my right arm as hard as I could toward the barrel, managing to knock it away just as Larsen pulled the trigger. The gun chattered, spewing bullets across the pulpit and the bluff at the back of the rock, and I grabbed the barrel as he tried to bring it back down toward me. One of the stained-glass windows shattered, and the barrel burned the hell out of my palm, but I did not let go.

At eight hundred rounds per minute, the clip emptied in a moment.

Larsen let the sling carrying the MP5 fall from his shoulder as he reached for the Desert Eagle in its holster. Meanwhile, I snatched up the machine gun and, holding it like a baseball bat, swung it as hard as I could.

The barrel connected with Larsen's chin.

He stumbled and fell backward onto the carpet. He still had a grip on the Eagle, however, and I knew I was dead. There was no way I could cover the distance between us and wrest the pistol from his hand.

He got to his feet, the Eagle in his left hand, and felt his chin. He glanced at the blood on his fingertips. Then Leah's sobbing distracted him.

Both of us glanced toward the pulpit.

Joseph was dead in his chair, having been hit by one of the stray bullets from the MP5. Leah was at his feet, her head in her hands.

"This will be a distinct pleasure," Larsen said.

He brought the barrel of the pistol down, took careful aim, and then was knocked backward, a neat hole in his temple. A fraction of a second later, I heard the report from the sharpshooter's rifle.

The open window, where the stained glass had shattered and fell, had afforded a clear shot.

Larsen was dead before he hit the floor.

I stepped on his wrist and took the Eagle from his hand.

Then I turned toward the altar. Joseph and Leah were still there, as before, but Abraham was gone. The door to the right of the bluff was open.

"Shit," I said.

I went through the door and paused at the landing, not

knowing if Abraham had gone up or down the stairs. But I knew where Rachel probably was being held.

"Rachel!" I called as I went down the stairs.

I came to one of the doors and tried the knob.

It opened on the Nazi chapel with the bomb beneath the pulpit.

"Rachel!" I called again, going to the next door.

"I'm in here," she said.

I tried the door. It was locked, of course. Behind me I heard something wet pouring down the stairs.

"Stand back," I said. "Get away from the door."

I aimed the Eagle at the knob, covered my face, and fired. I missed, putting a nice hole in the door.

"You okay?"

"Yeah," she said.

"Stay covered," I said.

I backed up, took aim, and fired three quick rounds at the knob. The last one blew it completely through the door, and I could hear it bounce inside.

"Jesus, are you trying to kill me?" Rachel asked.

I kicked open the door.

She was crouched in the corner, and one of the bullets had splattered the concrete next to her. Her cheek was bleeding.

"Good to see you, too," I said. "Come on."

I took her hand and pulled her up the stairs.

"What's that smell?" she asked.

"Jet fuel," I said. "He's going to light it."

"Oh, my God," she said.

"Is there any other way out?"

"No," she said. "That's the only way."

"You're sure?" I asked.

"The cave's downstairs," she said. "But most of that is underwater."

"I'll take water over burning every time," I said.

We started to race down the hall.

Then I stopped.

"Go on," I said.

"What the hell is wrong?"

"The bomb," I said.

"What bomb?"

"There's a nuclear bomb in the Nazi chapel," I said. "This tower is like a chimney. The jet fuel fire will get so hot that it will melt the casing and create a dirty bombing. Nobody will be able to live at Beaver Lake for maybe the next thousand years."

"Tell me you're kidding," she said.

"How much can you lift?"

"What does that have to do with anything?"

"The bomb weighs four hundred pounds," I said. "If we can get it out of the chapel and into the water, then it won't get hot enough to melt the casing. It's the only way."

"I can't lift four hundred pounds," she said.

"Two hundred. That's all you have to lift."

"Look at me," she screamed, showing me her arms. "Does it look like I can lift two hundred pounds? I'm a girl. I don't have the upper-body strength."

At that moment a door opened down the hall.

It was Werner of the green socks. He stood there, a ham sandwich in one hand and a diet Coke in the other, chewing.

"Hey, what's the shouting about?" he asked.

"Do you know what's going on here?"

"The feds are out there," he said, then took another bite of his sandwich. His nose wrinkled. "Is that gasoline?"

"Jet fuel," I said.

"It's burning now," he said. "I have a very sensitive nose."

I grabbed him by the hand and pulled him down the hall.

"Hey," he said, dropping his sandwich.

"Shut up," I said. "You're going to help us carry this other bomb down these stairs to the water. How much can you lift?"

"I don't know," he said.

In the Nazi chapel, I shoved the Eagle into my waistband, knocked the pulpit aside, braced myself, and pulled the trapdoor open. The bomb was still there.

"Okay," I said. "I'll get on the big end, and you and Rachel get on the other. On three we're going to lift it out."

Werner bent over.

"No, crouch down," I said. "Lift with your legs."

"Good advice," he said.

We grabbed the bomb and slowly managed to ease it up onto the floor.

"Oh, my God," Rachel said, gasping. "That has to be more than four hundred pounds."

"Let's go," I said.

We picked it up again and managed to walk it down the aisle and through the door. Then we put it down on the floor with a clang.

Already it was warm in the hallway.

"I can't go any farther," Werner said, wheezing.

"Me neither," Rachel said. "If that thing is four hundred pounds, then I'm a size four."

The hallway was just big enough to roll the bomb down it.

Above we could hear the sounds of a fire.

"Let's go," I said.

I reached the top of the next set of stairs and let the bomb fall down. It clanged and bounced and went all the way to the next landing.

"Is that safe?" Rachel asked.

"Got a better suggestion?"

We ran after it; then Rachel helped me roll it to the edge of the next series of steps. More banging and scraping and bouncing. We followed it down, stepped through the doorway, and found ourselves in the cave. Heat was rolling in waves down the stairs, so I shut the door behind us.

It left us in darkness. There was also a terrible stench.

"Which way?" I asked.

"I don't know," Rachel said. "My grandfather never let me down here. God, what is that smell?"

Suddenly the cave was flooded with light.

"Now I know why," Rachel said.

Randall Duane Slaughter was staring at us from a dozen yards away. He was propped in a sitting position against a boulder. His eyes were open, his bald head gleamed, and his body was swollen by putrefaction.

"That's just gross," Werner said.

"Hello, Rachel," Abraham Smith said. He was sitting in a rocker, a .38 revolver in his lap. Beyond him was a pool of water. "Welcome to the Cave of the Martyrs."

"Abraham, what have you done?"

"God's work," he said. "Now this will be our home, but only for a little while, until the Lord comes back. Your mother is here. Don't you want to say hello?"

"Oh, my God," Rachel said.

Sitting on a rock behind him was a skeleton in a tattered dress that had once been white. On the other side of Abraham was another skeleton, one that had become disarticulated. The jaw lay on the muddy ground.

"And I suppose that's Grandmother?"

"Why, yes," he said.

I glanced around the cave. The walls were covered with petroglyphs of birds, turtles, human stick figures, weird spirals. There were also handprints, lizards, and snakes.

"Oh, what's that?" Abraham said. "John the Baptist says hello."

"Abraham, you're insane," Rachel said.

"We don't have time for this," I said. "Help me get the bomb into the water."

"I think not," Abraham said, patting the revolver in his lap.

This was a problem. It was getting warmer in the

cave and before long the inferno on the other side of the door would use up what little air was left. Whether it was my imagination or not, I was struggling to breathe.

"What are you waiting for?" Rachel asked.

"What do you want me to do?" I asked. "He's got a gun."

"Oh, for Christ's sake, can't you be a hero for once?" Rachel asked. She snatched the Desert Eagle from beneath my shirt. "Cover your ears."

Holding the gun in both hands, she shot Abraham Smith in the chest. The .50-caliber slug knocked him backward, out of the rocker, and he ended with one foot in the water.

"Outrageous," Werner said, his hands still over his ears.

"Ever watch horror movies?" I asked, a little too loud. My ears were ringing like I was on the inside of a church bell. "They always come back."

She walked over, picked up the .38, and threw it in the water.

Then she put three more slugs into Smith.

The action remained open on the last shot and the clip dropped out of the butt. The Eagle was empty. She threw it aside.

Rachel's jaw quivered.

"Don't think about it now," I said.

She nodded.

"We can't roll the bomb over these rocks. We have to carry it. Werner, help us. This is the last time, I promise."

We carried the bomb to the water's edge, knocking Slaughter off his perch in the process.

"God, he stinks," Werner said.

The heat was nearly unbearable. Behind us the door was glowing red. Suddenly Rachel lost her grip, and the bomb dropped to the rock floor.

"I'm light-headed," she said.

"We're losing oxygen fast," I said. "It's the fire. Come on; we're almost there."

We picked it up once more. My back felt like it was going to break.

"Okay," I said as we neared the edge of the water. "On three, we throw it."

"Three," Rachel said quickly.

We gave it a shove.

The Falling Star made a huge splash and was gone.

"Now what?" Rachel asked.

"We follow it," I said.

"Swim out?" she asked.

"We might make it," I said. "The water's low, so maybe the whole passage isn't flooded." I was really light-headed as well. "Take a deep breath and let's go."

"I can't," Werner said.

"There's no choice," I said. "We either stay here and die or try this."

"I can't swim," Werner said.

I nodded. Even though it was justice of sorts, I felt sorry for him.

"Your device worked," I said.

"It did?" He brightened.

"One hell of bang," I said. "Big as Hiroshima."

I grabbed Rachel's hand.

"God, if you're listening," I asked, "a little help?"

Then we jumped into the water.

The pool was much deeper than I had imagined, and I had only the dimmest notion of which direction the lake was in. But the deeper we went, the colder the water got, and I figured that was a good sign. With Rachel gripping the back of my jeans, I swam as hard as I could. My lungs burned and spots floated in front of my eyes. I couldn't see a thing, but I kept going. Then my lungs began to spasm, and I fought the urge to breathe. I kept swimming until I began to choke on water, then kicked for the surface, expecting to find myself trapped in a rocky deadend.

My head broke the surface of the water in a dark passage, and I coughed, spewed water, and gulped in cool night air. I pulled Rachel up beside me. She was coughing as well, and I slapped her on the back.

Then, at the far end of the passage, I spied a sliver of night sky.

"Come on," I said, dragging her back into the water. We felt our way slowly down the passage, trying not to bump our heads on the rocks, and finally arrived at the mouth of the cave. We slipped through the opening and into the lake.

We swam around the point and climbed up onto the swimming beach. On the horizon, the flames from Kingdom Tower reached toward the Milky Way.

Fifty-one

Three days later I was sitting in front of a computer in the *Traveler* newsroom. Elaine had been found safe at the home of Mr. Walberg, the guy who had grieved for his son at Oakland Cemetery. It took little to convince Sheryl to give me my job back, and she promised I would never have to wear a tie.

I took a sip of bad coffee from the pot in the photo department. Every muscle in my body ached, despite the handfuls of Tylenol I had taken.

Then I opened a new file and slugged it "Hinterland."

Everything seemed back to normal.

In thirty minutes the lights in the newsroom blinked; then the power to all of the terminals died. My story disappeared as the screen went dark.

A collective groan went up from the newsroom.

Red came out of his office. He had a cigarette in his hand, and this time he pulled out his lighter and actually fired it up.

It was a bad sign.

"People," he said. "Listen up. I have an announcement."

"What, the *Trav* didn't pay the light bill again?" somebody from the sports department called.

Red ignored it.

"I'm sorry to have to tell you this," he said, "but the *Traveler* has been sold. The new owners have decided not to keep any of the former staffers."

"None of us?" Sheryl asked.

"Only the Westervelts," he said. "The Black Widow will continue as publisher. For the rest of us, we're out of a job. We're expected to be out . . . well, *now*."

Fifty-two

Elaine drove while we rolled across the historic one-lane bridge that crossed the White River at Beaver, six miles west of Eureka Springs. As the battered Chevy pickup left the wooden planks and hit the pavement again, she gave me a look that suggested I was crazy.

"Are you sure you know what you're looking for?"

I held the GPS unit in my lap.

"I'm sure," I said. "Slaughter's final statement was a kind of code. The hundred and nineteenth Psalm is the longest book in the Bible, so it's very useful for codes. That's why he mixed up the verses—the real meaning is in the verse numbers. Stop here."

"Okay," she said.

We were in front of the tiny Beaver post office.

"Listen," I said. "These verses are from chapter ninety-three, verses eight and sixteen: 'I will obey your decrees; do not utterly forsake me. I delight in your decrees; I will not neglect your word.' Then we have chapter thirty-six, verses thirty-six, four, and eighty-three: Turn my heart toward your statutes and not toward selfish gain. You have laid down precepts that are to be fully obeyed. Though I am like a wineskin in the smoke, I do not forget your decrees."

"And those are GPS coordinates?"

"Sure," I said. "That makes 93.816 west and 36.483 north."

"Which is where?"

"Right about there," I said, motioning toward a springhouse on the other side of the road.

She pulled the truck over and we got out.

"Why didn't you tell anybody about this?" she asked.

"I could be wrong," I said.

We walked into the springhouse. The floor was dirt, except where the spring bubbled up on the far side where it was mud.

"Stay by the door," I said.

I got down on my hands and knees and plunged my hand into the water, feeling around in the mud and gravel on the bottom.

"What are you looking for?"

"This," I said, and withdrawing a shoe box that had been wrapped in multiple layers of plastic.

"What is it?"

"Slaughter's bank loot," I said. "His share of the lost armored car heist. Or you could look at it this way: It's the start of your career as a sculptor. It's an education when my daughter, Amy, is ready to go to college. It's years of therapy for Rachel. And it's security for the family of a young helicopter pilot who was killed while ditching in the North Atlantic. Don't you think that's fair?"

"It's illegal," she said.

"There's a difference," I said.

We walked back to the Chevy. Using my pocketknife I slit the plastic. There was bundle after bundle of hundred-dollar bills. I put the package on the seat between us and covered it with my jacket.

"Let's go," I said.

Elaine started the truck.

"What about you?" she asked.

"I'll be fine," I said. "I think I'm going into a new line of work as a private detective. Except I'm going to be a *public* detective. I'll work for free, but on one condition: that no matter what happens, no matter where the investigation leads, I get to write a book about what I discover. Eureka Springs seems like a good place to set up shop, doesn't it?"

She nodded, was about to pull out onto Highway 187, then suddenly stood on the brake.

"Kelsey," she asked slowly, "who is Rachel and why does she need therapy?"